E-book ISBN: 978-1-956136-77-7

Paperback ISBN: 978-1-956136-86-9

Hardcover ISBN: 978-1-956136-89-0

PARLIAMENT HOUSE PRESS

www.parliamenthousepress.com

Cover illustration by: Aleksandra Skiba

Edited by: Malorie Nilson and Megan Hultberg

Note: This is a work of fiction. Names, Characters, Places and Events are products of the author's imagination, and are used factitiously. These are not to be construed or associated otherwise. Any resemblance to actual locations, incidents, organizations, or people (living or deceased) is entirely coincidental.

PRAISE FOR WILDBLOOD

"*Wildblood* is a grisly journey of self-discovery, but with mobsters and monsters. Vrana's story-telling encompasses character growth that will make you cry, with a lot of stray limbs flying about. The urban setting Vrana paints is the perfect blend of dark and twisted, and complemented with characters you can't help but fall in love with. *Wildblood* is a blood-thirsty, gritty urban adventure, with a main character who can step on me whenever he wants."
   – Stacey McEwan, author of *The Glacian Trilogy*

"A gritty adventure through a dark, supernatural version of Boston, complete with bad-ass and morally grey characters that keep you turning the pages."
   – C.N. Crawford, author of the *Demon Queen Trials*

"Gritty, sexy, and steeped in diverse lore, *Wildblood* is the perfect dark urban fantasy."
   – Jenny Hickman, author of *A Cursed Kiss*

"*Wildblood* is a raw, unflinching, emotional gut punch! Combining the dark strangeness of dreamscapes with real-world terrors, Vrana weaves a compelling tale of mobsters and monsters, but also of found family, bravery and, ultimately, love."
   – Katya de Becerra, critically acclaimed and Aurealis-winning author of *When Ghosts Call Us Home*

WILDBLOOD

A. J. VRANA

CONTENT FOREWORD

This book grapples with themes of post-traumatic stress disorder, bereavement, suicidal ideation, implied abuse of a minor, and kidnapping (not depicted) and contains scenes of graphic violence. However, where there is pain and injustice, there is also a journey of processing and healing from trauma. This book sends its men to therapy, allows its characters to find new families, celebrates healthy relationships, and fosters unconquerable love. For every nightmare, there is a moment of awakening; for every struggle, a salve.

For those harboring their monsters. Don't be afraid.

"I'm not Death. I'm the fucking calamity that wields it."

— KAI DONOVAN

1

KAI

NOTHING FELT BETTER than a sharp blade slicing through the larynx of an overconfident shit-talker. Well, almost nothing. Sex felt better, but only when Kai's companion wanted to fuck him as badly as the owner of that larynx wanted to end him.

Scrapping inhibitions was easy; absconding jail time was not. He wished getting away with murder were simpler, though he had the good sense not to bother. There were other ways to scratch the itch—to get drunk on triumph. He just had to follow the rules. And tonight, there'd be no blades slick with blood, only knuckles scraped raw from pummeling muscle and bone.

A puff of air glanced off Kai's cheek as he slanted his shoulder to avoid the incoming strike. The Sicilian stumbled past him, limbs flailing to slow the inevitable fall. Kai savored the taste of it—the bittersweet bite of helplessness that wafted from his attacker.

But Kai wasn't a sadist—not much, anyway—so he cut the panic short with a heel to the back of the knee. The man's leg buckled, and he crumpled like a stale cracker. The fighters that frequented the Confessional were ornaments. Like hollowed gourds with menace carved into them, they looked unnerving, but a tumble off a windowsill was enough to crack them open and leave them rotting in the sun.

The Sicilian caught himself and straightened, then whirled on Kai, throwing a wide arc of a messy hook that should've been a straight punch to the throat. Even the best-trained fighters got sloppy when they were tired.

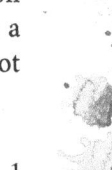

Still, Kai let the blow land, angling his jaw to lessen the impact. He had to make it look convincing. An assault on his ribs followed, and he stumbled back, wincing when he heard a crack. His senses were both a blessing and a curse; he could detect every minute change in his opponent's body—and in his own. The adrenaline masked the pain, but the tell-tale sign of a fractured bone wrenched at his animal senses.

No matter. A fracture wasn't a break.

The crowd roared as Kai's heel grazed the edge of the makeshift ring, and a dozen hands groped at his sweat-slicked skin, fingers running through his dark, disheveled hair. He regained equilibrium before the onlookers could thrust him forward, and he shrugged off the prying hands. Some nights, it felt like everyone wanted a piece of him.

He gritted his teeth and spat a coppery glob onto the floor. Connor, a hulking Irishman of a bartender, threw up his arms and wailed in protest. It would be his mess to clean. Kai ignored his friend's bellyaching—somehow louder than the clamor—and flashed his winded opponent a bloody, shit-eating grin.

The ruddy Sicilian blanched at the sight of that baleful smile—a wolfish, cutting thing that promised more than victory. It promised pain.

Raising his fists, the boxy Italian darted forward, but Kai was done playing cat and mouse. Pitching a leg back and twisting his body away from the incoming punch, Kai pivoted to his opponent's unguarded side, then drove a punishing uppercut straight into his kidney. Tendons tore against his knuckles, organs compressed, and several ribs snapped like dry pretzels. The Sicilian lurched, blood propelling from his mouth and splattering over Kai's bare shoulder.

Their eyes met, and with a balmy smile, Kai patted the man's cheek. "Put some ice on it," he said, then blithely pushed him aside. The Sicilian toppled and hit the floor with a weighty thump, rasping for breath.

A momentary hush fell over the ruck before they erupted into cheers, the foundations of the bar rattling like a hut in the middle of a hurricane.

Kai sucked in a shaky breath as the hands returned, this time with their bodies, swarming him from all sides. It was mayhem almost every night, the no-touch policy afforded to the fighters rarely enforced. People came back for more than the blood sport; they relished laying hands on the most dangerous thing in the room. Kai gave his audience a sliver to slake their thirst before the onslaught overwhelmed him, and he pushed his way through the throng. Only when he reached the bar did they stop grasping for him, and he plunked himself down on a stool in front of Connor.

"What'd you say to that poor man?" the bartender asked as he dried a pint glass, the shamrock tattoo below the inside of his elbow catching Kai's gaze. His *Southie* T-shirt was speckled with water, his shoulder-length blonde hair carelessly tied back, loose strands flying free around his stubbled jaw after a night of yelling and taking orders.

Kai yanked at the Velcro of his hand wraps, unraveling them slowly. While most fighters wore blue or beige, Kai's were a bright yellow with *CAUTION* printed over them in bold black letters. They were a gift, and no matter how stained they got, he refused to switch them out. He reached over the oak counter and nabbed one of Connor's dish towels, wiping the sweat and blood from his neck and face. "Told him to put some ice on his kidney."

"You bastard," Connor chided. "He'll be pissing blood for weeks."

Kai's lips curled into a smirk as he helped himself to a glass of water, then rinsed out his mouth. Red-tinged liquid found the drain, and he ran his tongue over his teeth, sucking away the dregs of the metallic flavor. "Yeah, well, he cracked my ribs."

"Your ribs will heal by tomorrow," Connor reminded him.

Kai chuckled darkly, then gestured toward the shelves of booze wreathed in green Christmas lights that stayed up year-round. "Get me whiskey."

His freakish speed, strength, and recovery weren't common knowledge, nor was his ability to shift into a stygian wolf that could maul an overfed albatross with an eleven-foot wingspan. He could've taken out the Sicilian before anyone blinked, but a reputation for being invincible wasn't as compelling as bouncing back from the gates of hell. That, and his employer liked it when he dragged things out. Everyone loved a spectacle, and Kai Donovan was South Boston's finest.

"Fuckin' beast, man," someone whispered from several feet away. "How many people do you think he's killed?"

If they only knew.

"Whatever," replied another. "My buddy could kick his ass."

Connor slid a tumbler of tawny liquid across the counter into Kai's awaiting hand. "Don't you dare," he warned when he caught Kai's attention drifting toward the gossip.

"Wouldn't dream of it," Kai replied dryly, then took a sip of his drink.

He loved this place too damn much to spark a bloodbath. Nestled on the ground floor of a converted nineteenth-century row house, the Confessional was home to Boston's seediest crowd, its once fawn-colored bricks grimy and stained with the decades. Rumor had it that one of the chefs had defenestrated a man back in the '80s, but the sordid gossip only added to the ambiance. The back of the bar was sectioned off by an iron gate door and wood panels that ran across the width of the room, marking the entrance to the improvised ring. Large openings like windows in the wall gave everyone in the Confessional a view of the fight, and the partition doubled as a convenient obstruction in case of a police raid. Connor fronted the area as a private event space complete with tables and seating, but every regular knew its true purpose. When the floor was cleared, patrons filed through the gate or poked their heads through the faux windows in anticipation.

"By the way..." Connor tipped his chin to the side. "She's been eyeing you all night."

Kai tracked the motion to a woman at the opposite end of the bar. Her friend grabbed her arm, egging her on upon realizing he was looking their way. Vibrant auburn hair cascaded over the woman's shoulders as she fiddled with the straw in her glass, her smoky eyes catching his across the room. She smiled, and her gaze flew to the empty seat next to her.

Kai squared his shoulders to Connor. "What do you want me to do about it?"

"She's here every time you fight. You should cut her loose—let her down easy."

Kai snorted into his glass. "It's not my problem she's ogling me every Saturday."

"And Sunday. And Tuesday. Some Thursdays too." He squinted in contemplation. "Pretty sure she's here on Fridays as well."

"If she wants a rejection, she can come here and ask me for one herself."

"Oh, you're an asshole."

"Never been good with feelings," said Kai.

"That's a lie." Connor jabbed his bare chest, then topped up the whiskey. "You're a good guy, somewhere in there."

Kai grumbled and gulped down his booze, scanning the patrons until he found who he was looking for. Sergei—a pasty Bratva middleman with a love of white dress shirts and leather suspenders. His slicked-back sunflower hair gleamed under the dim amber-lit sconces drilled through the wall. The teal Victorian wallpaper garnished with raspberry-colored floral patterns fissured around the mounts to reveal a craggy foundation. Everything in Boston was built atop an older world entombed beneath the last-laid bricks.

Connor shook his head. "That damn Ruski stands out worse than a turd in a bouquet. Russians don't belong in my bar."

"I'm Russian, you big dumb Thor."

"Thor is Scandinavian." He waved Kai off with a bear-like hand. "You're a Donovan. You're Irish."

Something between a laugh and a whimper crawled out of Kai's throat. "I've told you a thousand times—that was Alice's name."

"The snarky old bat who raised you?"

Kai nodded. "She took me in after my parents died—when I was ten. And my *parents*," he emphasized, "weren't Irish."

"Kai isn't a Russian name either," Connor pointed out.

"Not sure it's my real name." He shrugged. "But it's the only one I've got." It was also the only one he could remember. He figured it might've been a nickname. Maybe he'd been a Nikolai, but in the end, it didn't matter. Kai was as good a name as any, and it'd grown on him over the years. He clanked his tumbler down as he rose. "Got to go for a bit."

"Fine, fine, go conspire with your people," Connor groused as if Kai hadn't grown up in small-town Washington.

Kai kicked his stool under the counter. "If it's any consolation, my mom was Tatar."

Connor glanced his way and frowned. "You remember her?"

Drawing a half circle around the rim of his glass, Kai shook his head, his eyes trained on the puddle of brown liquid swirling with melted ice. "Just random fragments. Can't remember what she looked like, but I know she hated smoked fish."

"Who the hell eats smoked fish?"

Kai smirked, his dark mahogany eyes sparking with red mischief. "Russians."

"At least you drink whiskey." The bartender grinned. "May as well be Irish."

Kai barked out a laugh and spun away, weaving through the swooning bodies now populating the marred floor. He hadn't bothered changing, his naked torso and athletic frame earning him a few curious glances. Sergei certainly wasn't the tallest man in the room—a solid head shorter than Kai's imposing six feet and two inches—but he was always easy to find. He had a peculiar smell about him—a vinegary cocktail of irritation and apprehension that wormed beneath his coiffed veneer.

"You did good," Sergei said without making eye contact, the remnants of a Slavic accent sharpening his vowels. Sometimes he opened conversations with Kai in Russian, but today he'd chosen English, code switching to blend in better with Connor's crowd. His hands were shoved in his pockets as he rocked from heels to toes.

The guy hardly ever smiled. Sometimes, Kai forgot they were the same age—just barely out of their twenties. He never thought he'd make it to thirty-one, yet here he was, contending with the farce that was adulthood. "As long as you're not asking me to fix fights, I'll play."

Sergei's pale blue eyes swept over Kai's grimy body, evaluating every muscle, every groove sculpted by adversity. "I'm surprised you bleed."

The corner of Kai's mouth quirked. "Still flesh and bone." He raised a hand and curled two fingers toward himself. "Now pay up, *milyy*."

"Right, right." Sergei reached into his pocket with a mutter, ignoring the term of endearment—*darling*. Out came the wad of cash, bills counted with bank-like precision. "Your cut," he declared, slapping a portion into Kai's palm.

Sergei had never done him dirty, but Kai checked the math anyway. He was only peripheral to Bratva, a snarky, tough-as-nails punk Sergei contracted for underground fights, and he intended to keep it that way. It'd been a good investment for them both.

Kai rolled the cash into his fist and nodded. "Thanks."

"Don't mention it." The blonde mobster replaced the money with a box of Parliaments, fiddling with the lid. He halfway popped out a cigarette, then shook it back into the case. "I'll need you tomorrow night."

Fuck. Kai knew there'd be something else. Sergei was always a stoic son-of-a-bitch, but the tartness to his scent seeped out like water from a leaky faucet. "Tomorrow's my night off."

"Tough shit." Sergei's teeth clamped tight. He was clearly itching for a smoke. "It's important. The guy coming in—he's good, and I need my best."

Kai snorted at the meagre compliment. "Then you should've given me tonight off. My ribs are cracked."

Sergei fixed him with an icy stare, his lips tugging into a frown. "They'll heal."

Kai swallowed his irritation. Sergei didn't know much, but he knew that Kai wasn't ordinary, and he kept that secret like bones beneath a gravestone. One of them needed the money, and the other wouldn't have his operation squandered by accusations of cheating. Besides Connor and Sergei, no one in the business knew that Kai could take a gunshot wound to the chest and wake up the next day with little more than a few gnarly bruises and a tiny shot glass made from bullet casing. Sure, he could be killed, but it would take more than a lead nugget.

"Fine, I'll be here, but you're paying me double." Kai wasn't in a negotiating mood, and Sergei didn't even flinch at the demand.

"I need you to finish it in one round," the shorter man said. "That'll get you double."

"One round, huh?" A reverse of the usual request. The little shit in suspenders wanted people betting against Kai, ratcheting up the winnings for the underdog. He wasn't a fan, but he supposed taking a few hits evened the odds, even if by an inch. A split lip, a bruised jaw, a bloody grin. It kept the crowd hooked like writhing worms, but it always ended the same way: with Kai fucking his opponent out of the night's earnings and a working pair of kidneys.

"I want him out fast," Sergei reiterated. "He's made a name for himself, and there's a lot on the line."

Kai clicked his tongue and raised a finger. "All right. One round."

Sergei nodded, the tension bracketing his mouth finally easing. "Good."

Kai stalked back to the bar, money in hand, and hopped over the counter.

"Hey!" Connor griped as Kai invaded. "You've got to sit on the other side like everyone else."

"Relax, I'm on my way out." He shoved his hand wraps into his jacket, grabbed his change of clothes, and hugged the wall into the adjacent corridor. One of the staff yelped when he strode into the kitchen and proceeded to strip off his sweatpants.

"Christ on a cracker!" the cook yelled as she stirred a pot of stew, eyes darting between her business and his.

Kai shot her a wry smile as he zipped up his jeans and threw on a gray T-shirt. "You're welcome, Carol."

"I didn't thank you, you cocky sack of testosterone." She let the ladle clank against the rim of the pot and planted her hands on her hips, her frizzled orange curls fleeing her hair net. "There's a damn bathroom right down the hall."

"Too far. Too occupied." Kai slipped on his black leather jacket and flung his sweatpants over his shoulder, then grazed the inside of his pockets to double-check for the wraps and his wallet.

"Hey," Carol called to him as he turned to leave. He stopped and glanced over his shoulder.

She shook off the ladle, then traced a circle through the air. "Nice butt."

Kai blinked, then erupted into raucous laughter as he exited the kitchen.

"Going home?" Connor asked as Kai poured himself a final shot of whiskey and dropped a twenty by the till.

"Yep." Kai threw back his farewell drink, then slid the glass down the length of the bar where Connor caught it.

"Say hi to the girls for me."

The prospect of home warmed him more than the liquor. When had he gotten so fucking squishy? "Will do."

After a parting knock on the shoulder, Kai left Connor to his sloshed patrons and waded to the front door.

The mid-October air soothed his sticky skin, and even in the dark, he could make out the ochre and burnt red hues of autumn foliage—courtesy of his sharp sight. As the noise from the bar faded, the quiet of the midnight street enveloped him, and he settled into an easy stride. Kai absently thumbed the bills in his pocket, his thoughts drifting. Who did Sergei want beaten in a single round? Was he concerned about Kai's odds, or were his nerves fraying prematurely?

No, that couldn't be it. Sergei was cautious, not paranoid. Whoever this opponent was, he had to be something. The stakes wouldn't be twice as high otherwise.

Kai's hand dropped to his side, and he breathed in the cool air tinged with rain and sodden earth. It didn't matter. The rest of the night was his. He fished out his wallet and checked for the old keepsake that followed him wherever he went: a tattered piece of lilac birthday card marked with Alice's shaky scrawl. It was all he had left of her.

Happy Birthday, Kai Donovan.

She'd written his sixteenth birthday present right into the card. Before that moment, he hadn't been a Donovan. He didn't even remember the family name he'd been born with. After six years together, Alice finally gave him a new one: her own.

He craned his neck to admire the moon, swollen with silver light. Alice never cared for clichés, but every day of the six years he'd spent under her roof, she'd sworn by a single adage: *home is where the heart is.*

He'd always thought it was stupid; a kid couldn't choose his home. But the hardest part wasn't being born into a home he didn't choose. It was watching the pretenses fall away and the walls of the house crumble to ruin, because *home* wasn't a given.

The hardest fucking part, he'd learned, was finding his damn home.

2

MIYA

WARM BUTTERY LIGHT spilled over the scuffed walnut counter, the grains etched with lovers' words and the slow, steady caress of time. Motes of dust hung in the air, dancing under the honeyed glow. Leaning on her elbows, Miya squinted at the messily carved names as she groped for a peanut, then tossed it into the air.

A pair of three-pronged talons dug into her skin as the raven on her shoulder thrust out his beak and caught the morsel, quickly gobbling it down with a satisfied croak.

"Good catch, Gavran." Miya absently scratched his silky breast. The raven purred his approval, preening Miya's wavy dark brown tresses. She traced the copper chain around her neck, her fingers lingering on the edges of the fang-shaped labradorite pendant. Her thumb rubbed the fissure marking its smooth surface like an old scar. Angling the stone toward the light, she admired the flashes of purple, meadow green, and gold, veins of black sluicing through the vibrant hues.

The dream stone. It was her talisman from another world.

The bar had been quiet for most of the night, the last patron filtering out not long ago. Sometimes, folks came into the King of Spades for a cartomancy reading and wound up buying several drinks as they badgered Miya to make their decisions for them. Everyone wanted their future told by the Dreamwalker, but the Dreamwalker couldn't tell the future. She only showed them what they refused to face, and that was far scarier than unforeseen misfortunes.

Scared people, it seemed, liked to drink.

Dahlia Rose Baron, better known as Crowbar after scaring off a burglar with her namesake, was the new owner of the rustic establishment. A bartender by trade, she'd concocted her own specialty cocktail menu, pushing her potions on people whenever they ate up too much of Miya's time at the divination table. Miya didn't mind their probing, and the earnings weren't bad, but it was a far cry from what she needed to stay afloat.

"Man, I can't believe we got this place for so cheap." Crowbar inspected the shelves for mildew—a fixation given the age of the building. Aside from the layers of dust, an occasional piece of missing wallpaper, and a few cosmetic hiccups, the four walls they'd christened the King of Spades hadn't been difficult to flip into a grungy dive bar with felt cushions on the stools and old road signs nailed to the walls. There was even an antique brass mirror and, above them, a gothic chandelier that'd graced the ceiling since circa 1920, imbuing the bar with a proper séance vibe. "Can't believe no one wanted it, all because of a rumor."

"I always thought people would be less superstitious in a big city," Miya said as she stroked Gavran's beak. "But I guess even the most rational people get squigged out by ghosts." She hailed from Black Hollow, British Columbia, a small town cocooned in forest. Everyone there believed in the same fable, and the only difference in Boston, she'd found, was that there were many fables, and a greater diversity of people to offer their faith.

Crowbar arranged the bottles back in their proper places. "Why take a chance, right?"

Miya's muddy green eyes caught her friend's stormy gaze. Crowbar had experienced her own share of supernatural traumas. "I wouldn't take the chance."

A long sigh left the former Louisiana bartender as she ran her fingers through her pink hair, cropped short with a killer fade she managed on her own. The praying mantis tattoo with *MANEATER* stamped beneath it flashed across Crowbar's forearm as she pivoted. She was covered in ink, but the mantis had always been Miya's favorite. "After Syd died...after I found out what really happened to her—a damn demon taking Vince and—"

"I know," Miya said quietly.

It'd been two years since Crowbar learned the truth about her sister. Police had ruled Sydney's death a domestic homicide—an explanation Crowbar struggled to swallow. Syd's husband Vincent had no cause to murder his wife and take his own life, but the police preferred mundane explanations. Not many knew that angry spirits could metastasize into something malevolent, reliving traumas and inflicting them on others. Vince was driven to the unthinkable by one, and although Crowbar finally found closure, the truth had torn her open and exposed her to a new world.

"Joke's on all of us, I guess." Crowbar laughed grimly. "Didn't think this place would actually be haunted."

Miya's gaze drifted to the presence crouched in the corner by the bar. The spirit wasn't very imposing—about two feet tall with a fox's tail, shaggy slate gray fur, and cat ears perched upon a rotund head. Paws boasting opposable thumbs made the little creature remarkably dexterous, adept at causing trouble. When they'd first moved in, it threw a tantrum befitting of a toddler its size, hucking cutlery off the counter, tearing napkins into confetti, and wreaking havoc with the plumbing. The real estate agent had been desperate to get rid of the century-old, two-story edifice, stuck on the market for years with no bites. At first, Miya thought the rumors of a poltergeist were just local intrigue, but the hearsay had some merit. "It's not exactly haunted…"

Crowbar whirled around and threw her arms up. "What's that supposed to mean?"

Gavran trilled and fluttered his wings, sharp feathers scraping Miya's ear.

"*Haunting* implies something unwanted, something that doesn't belong. This thing—it's lingering, but it's not really haunting anything. It…" she trailed off, searching for the right words. "He belongs here."

Crowbar crossed her arms over her chest. "It still talks to you?"

Miya frowned, watching the small creature prattle on in Russian. "He…tries."

Their otherworldly companion went rigid. Wide glassy eyes, shimmering like emeralds, darted to the door just as the bell on the frame chimed in welcome.

"We're closed," Crowbar called, and Miya cursed under her breath for not locking up sooner.

Their visitor didn't heed her. Heavy fishing boots dragged

across the musty old floorboards, the languid, uneven gait belonging to a gangling figure in a taupe coat that kissed the floor. The stranger's face was obscured by the droopy rim of a large fishing hat.

"I'm sorry," came a man's raspy voice, his vocal cords sounding like they'd been sanded raw. Something wet warbled in his throat as he opened his mouth and said, "I seek the Dreamwalker."

"Buddy, we're closed," Crowbar repeated. "Come back tomorrow. We open at four."

The man's head rotated toward Crowbar, hitching as though his neck were a gear in need of oiling. Her breath audibly halted, and Miya rose from her stool. Gavran pumped his wings and hovered beside her, but their visitor seemed unperturbed by the corvid keeping the staff company.

"What do you want? A reading?" The hairs on the back of Miya's neck stood on end as caution gave way to alarm. She kept a low profile, and few in town knew her as the Dreamwalker. If necessary, she and Crowbar could defend themselves against a single man, but the prospect remained unwelcome. In her twenty-six years, she'd found no empowerment in lashing out from a corner. It felt sticky, tasted acrid, because she shouldn't have been shunted into a corner in the first place.

"I'm not here for that," he reassured, his voice softening as though the hand wielding the sandpaper had opted for a finer grit. "I'm here for your other services."

Miya's gaze briefly darted to their cat-like resident in the corner, his planetoid eyes still glued to the stranger. She wasn't just a fortune-telling barmaid. She frequently crossed into the dreamscape—a realm that floated in tandem with the waking world—and helped people exorcise otherworldly visitors, entities that latched on to darkness. Ridding people of their literal demons often meant confronting their figurative ones. The Dreamwalker did more than traverse the dreamscape and ignore material bounds. She bore every secret that festered in the murky gap between denial and acceptance, grief and catharsis, guilt and surrender. She lived in the liminal—in those uneasy borderlands between all that was certain in the world.

Miya's spine went rigid as she eyed the peculiar man. "What do you need?"

He moved closer, though it would be wrong to say he walked. Even as his feet slid against the floor, and she heard the *thump, thump, thump* of his boots, he appeared to float, simply gliding through air. He stopped in front of Miya, only the bar between them. A gnarled, bony hand like knotted wood withdrew from a coat pocket, wavering as it placed a folded piece of paper on the counter.

"Someone is lost. And I believe"—his gaze lifted, the rim of his hat tipping back to reveal rich cedarwood eyes and a long, sullen face hidden beneath dense snarls of silver beard—"only you can find them."

Miya swallowed thickly. She knew word got around, but the people who came to her were never like this—never so sure. They were cautious, donning skepticism like camouflage even as they wrung their hands and pried for answers to questions that often had none. This man—he was different. He really *believed*. Yet belief required the absence of knowledge, and Miya sensed she was in the presence of someone rife with knowing.

She picked up the paper, damp between her fingers, and unfolded it. A name was scrawled in shaky blue ink: *Caelan Carver*.

"Who's Caelan?" Miya asked.

"Someone dear to me. Someone beyond my reach." His voice dipped, his face lowering before he retreated to the door. He paused at the threshold, his eyes finding Crowbar's. "I'm sorry," he said slowly, "for entering uninvited."

"No worries, dude," the bartender stammered, confusion sketching her face.

The door swung open then, nearly removing the stranger's nose as a tall man in a worn leather jacket strode in. An overgrown undercut of unruly black hair eclipsed the muggy bulb by the door, the buttery light haloing a powerful frame. This one, at least, was familiar.

Miya sighed a breath of relief.

Kai.

He scanned over the stranger with a bored expression, his hands concealed in his pockets. After a cursory sniff, his nose wrinkled, and he pushed past the older man who was now on his way out.

Kai spared one last slit-eyed stare at the stranger, then

approached the bar, the chandelier light catching the red tinge in his otherwise brown eyes. Miya thought they looked like burnt clay —a thing forged in fire, warm but hardened by hellish flames.

"Woodsy," he said as he slid onto a stool and shrugged off his jacket.

Miya blinked at him. "What?"

"He smelled woodsy." Kai didn't elaborate, throwing the jacket over the counter and rolling out his shoulders. Fresh bruises bloomed along his jaw, and his teeth scraped over a scab on his bottom lip.

"Do you need ice?" Miya asked, ignoring his assessment of the stranger's scent.

Kai shifted his attention from the wall of bottles, meeting her riffling gaze. "I'm good."

"Ibuprofen, then?"

The corner of his mouth quirked up. "I'm fine, Lambchop."

The wolf and his lamb—a vestige of their time in Black Hollow and a legacy that transcended their meagre decades on earth. They'd orbited each other for lifetimes, ancient things fated to collide.

Miya acquiesced with a sluggish nod. Seeing him hurt needled her even if he never wore his pain. He loved fighting, and it was a means for income—his only means. He took the role seriously, and although Miya earned her keep, Kai ensured there was enough to tide them over for more than a month at a time. Purging people's demons paid all right, but not as well as underground fight rings.

Miya traced Caelan's name, the ink seeping from residual moisture. "The old man who was in here...what do you mean he smelled woodsy?"

Kai shrugged. "Guy smelled like sick trees in a dying forest. Kind of rancid. I don't think he's human."

"Neither do I." Miya pinched the damp paper between her fingers. It felt like a piece of the old man—a sliver of bark broken from the bole. Gaze flitting up, she leaned over the counter and breathed in. "You smell like bourbon, blood, and man tears."

Kai chuckled and lightly pinched her nose between his teeth. "Connor says hi, by the way."

Miya squeaked and pulled back, rubbing the irritation away. "I say hi back. He should come over and have a haunted sleepover with me and Crowbar. We can watch chick flicks and slashers."

"That's...a contrast." Kai reached for the dish of peanuts, and Gavran swooped down to peck at his straying fingers. He glowered at the bird, dodging the stabs that left divots in the wood. "Shit-for-brains," he grumbled, then glanced at Crowbar, tipping his chin up in greeting. "How's your domovoy?"

Crowbar offered a nervous grin. "I honestly don't notice the little guy. It's not like I can see him." She gestured to Miya. "Ask your girl. She interacts with him more than I do."

Miya rested on her elbows and poked her head over the counter, peering at their bar gremlin. "He seems content. Still trying to teach me Russian, I think, but it's been a while since he's thrown lettuce at anyone."

When they'd first checked the place out, Miya found the spirit huddled in a corner on the interior of the bar. The moment he laid eyes on her, he shrieked like a banshee and fled to a back room. After emerging from hiding, she caught him muttering in Russian and asked Kai if he knew what they were dealing with.

"An ethereal squatter," he'd said, and after a vicious glare from Miya, he explained that it was a domovoy—a spirit tied to a household, providing protection and warnings of impending hardship. Empathically tethered to family, a domovoy shared in the emotional lives of the people it resided with. This one, it seemed, had been left behind by its kin over a century ago and had grown angry from the abandonment. The further the building fell into disrepair, the stronger the domovoy's resentment.

"What do we do with it?" Miya had asked upon the discovery, to which Kai had scoffed, "Give it bread or some shit."

And so, they did, offering leftovers and bar snacks. The domovoy's mischief subsided, and he settled into his corner, eyeing people as they filtered in and out. Sometimes, he even played with Gavran and watched over Crowbar when she retreated upstairs to her apartment on the second floor. Their chef Bastien had followed Crowbar from their hometown in Louisiana, but he refused to dither at the King of Spades alone after sundown. He'd demanded they paint the ceiling haint blue to ward off ghosts—which they did—though Miya could've sworn the domovoy liked the new color.

"At least he's being less of a shit," Kai said blithely, and the domovoy shook a munchkin fist at him. Kai unzipped his jacket pocket, then yanked out a bill, pushing it toward Miya. "Want to get me a whiskey?"

"Whiskey!" Crowbar balked. "That's all you ever drink. Try one of my brews."

"All right." Kai grinned. "I'll play. What's your best poison?"

Crowbar flashed a triumphant smile, her hazel eyes shining with excitement. "The Rusalka. Absinthe rinse, Benedictine, bitters, rye whiskey, cognac, and sweet vermouth, complete with activated charcoal, green luster dust, and a lemon peel garnish."

Kai's brows shot up as Miya's jaw nearly hit her shoes. Rusalka had been the architect of Crowbar's bereavement, and Kai had suffered his own run in with the demoness.

"Dark." Kai gestured with a come-hither motion. "Hit me up."

"You don't have to pay for it." Crowbar grabbed the bottles, but Kai shook his head.

"I'll pay." He glanced at the paper in Miya's hands. "What's that?"

"A job, maybe." She showed him the name. "Missing person, apparently. I'll have Ama look into it."

Kai hummed his disapproval at the mention of the name. He rose from the stool and helped himself to Crowbar's electric razor, which she kept in a junk drawer under the bar. Ambling to the brass mirror on the adjacent wall, he tilted his head and began trimming his undercut, tufts of loose hair falling on the domovoy. "She's still lurking in Southie?"

"Sure is," said Crowbar as she finished making his drink. "My girlfriend's not just hot; she's a badass, and I'll get her to kick your knees in if you don't clean your fur up off my floor."

"Your cat-goblin will eat it," Kai droned, roughly tousling his bristly mane to dislodge any stray strands. He always kept it short on the sides and longer at the top, though it was perpetually wild and seemed to grow faster than weeds in spring.

Crowbar opened her mouth to bark back when Miya interrupted. "It's true," she said meekly. "I've seen him eat hair. And earwigs."

Crowbar pushed the Rusalka across the counter, sucking on her cheeks like she'd swallowed something sour. "I guess I can't complain about that."

Kai returned the razor and braved a gulp of his cocktail. "Fuck"—he swallowed through clenched teeth—"I hate that I like it."

Crowbar cackled as she shelved the bottles. "I've added two novelties to the menu: the Black Wolf and the White Wolf."

Kai examined the verdant glitter as it swirled with the charcoal in his glass. "And those are..."

She smiled sheepishly. "My take on an old fashioned and a white Russian, inspired by my two favorite fluffy friends."

"So, you've turned me and your girlfriend into signature cocktails. You sure you don't need some of my *fur*?" Kai swilled the rest of the tarry liquid as Crowbar threatened him with bodily harm. Promising not to sprinkle his discarded hair into anyone's drink, Kai rinsed out the glass while Miya packed up.

Wrapping a leftover pretzel in a napkin, Miya dropped into a squat and set it on the floor. The house spirit canted his head, opened his mouth, and croaked, "Tha...nk...you."

Miya's eyes widened to saucers, and she slapped a hand over her mouth, waving down Kai and Crowbar. "He spoke English! He's learning English!"

"Oh, good," Kai deadpanned. "It can irritate me in two languages now."

Gavran swooped down next to the domovoy and pecked at the pretzel. The domovoy lunged, guarding his offering from the pilfering raven.

"Hey, leave him alone, you glutton," Miya scolded her feathery companion when he roosted on her shoulder. "You should stay here until Ama comes back. Keep Crowbar company."

Gavran chortled in response, then beat his wings and glided to the till where Crowbar finished counting the cash.

After slipping on his jacket, Kai clinched Miya's under his arm and joined her next to the domovoy. "Ready to go?"

"Sure." She stood and took the garment from him. "You good, Crowbar?"

Their friend waved them off. "Get out of here, lovebirds. I'm ready to call it a night."

And it had been a night; it was nearly one in the morning. Miya tugged Kai's sleeve, her eyes catching the plum shadows mottling his jaw.

His arm coiled around the small of her back as he followed her out, the crisp night air greeting them like an old friend.

THEIR ONE-BEDROOM APARTMENT was as old as the city. Nestled on the second floor of a triple decker, their pad boasted two whole windows and a pink-tiled bathroom that Miya considered a highlight of the janky interior décor. Kai couldn't have cared less about the pastels, but he was a fan of the neighboring twenty-four-hour corner store, complete with a pharmacy and enough snack aisles to satisfy his middle-of-the-night cravings for pork rinds and mayonnaise. Miya preferred the Dunkies across the street, though she sometimes joined Kai only to watch him fruitlessly evade Marty, the store's overtalkative owner.

The apartment entryway opened to a modest living area with an east-facing window, a two-seater, and an old chest that doubled as a coffee table. Kai tossed the keys onto the kitchenette counter—beige laminate from the '80s—and hung his jacket on a hook behind the door. Two of the four elements on their stove were busted, and the inside of the oven looked like it'd endured an apocalypse. Their fridge could barely hold enough groceries for the week, and the microwave took up half their prep space. It wasn't what Miya's parents had in mind when they patronized her about making a life for herself, but it was the happiest home she'd ever had.

"I need a shower," Kai declared as Miya removed her shoes and draped her coat over his. He retrieved his canary yellow hand wraps from his jacket—the ones she'd had custom printed—and carefully set them aside to be washed.

Miya figured slugging people with knuckles swathed in caution tape matched Kai's sense of humor, but she never anticipated how attached he'd become to them. She reckoned they also helped him stay cognizant of what he was coming home to after a night of breaking bones in an underground fight circuit: a person who loved him.

Kai padded down the hall, stripping as he went. He peeled off his shirt, then kicked his jeans up and caught them over his forearm, the taut muscles of his back shifting beneath streaks of scraped flesh. The water started a moment later, and Miya made for the bedroom at the end of the stubby hall.

Their sleeping quarters were cramped, the bed monopolizing almost every inch of floor space. They'd pushed it right up against the window so they could access the closet, which meant Miya had to crawl over Kai whenever she needed the bathroom at night. Luckily, he wasn't a fussy sleeper and merely exploited the opportunity to grope her butt. He only slept for a few hours at a time, and Miya had no intention of getting squashed by him every time he went to raid the fridge after his naps.

Abandoning her jeans and bra, Miya eagerly replaced her day clothes with an oversized T-shirt. She retrieved the note the stranger had given her and set it on the nightstand—a tiny thing they'd picked up from a trash pile outside a nearby building. Throwing herself onto the mattress, she let her eyes drift shut. Late nights were nothing new, and she was grateful that Crowbar didn't need her at the King of Spades until mid-afternoon. Kai was also a night owl, which meant most of their time together was spent after dark.

"Tired?" his voice cut through the quiet.

He was sopping wet and completely naked, rummaging through the closet.

"Why are you dripping all over the floor?" Miya asked with an annoyed huff.

He raised a brow at her as he dried himself off. "Because someone threw my towel in the dirty laundry."

A smattering of blue and plum marked his ribs.

"Oops." She sat up, watching as he dropped the towel and used his foot to mop up his puddle. It'd taken three years of badgering before he started cleaning up after himself—a positive sign that he'd finally adjusted to sharing space with another person. Five years on, and he'd gotten pretty good at it. As far as Miya could tell, the comfort of domesticity had grown on him—that is, so long as he could run amok on occasion.

Miya had made peace with his need to blow off steam with night-long benders and bar brawls, and to his delight, she even participated in his shenanigans when the mood struck. But he always came home, and for all his wild escapades, his loyalty never wavered. He was candid, sometimes to a fault, but after a lifetime of pretense and double-speak, it was the reason she'd fallen for him.

Kai Donovan was her best friend.

He tossed the towel aside and pointed to the faded black T-shirt she'd cuddled up in. "That's mine."

"Is it?" Miya asked innocently, clasping the hem and peering down as though noticing for the first time. "Well, I think it's mine now."

Brazen and dedicated he may have been, but he was also hopelessly competitive, cursed with a pettiness that rivaled a sophomoric heiress at an Ivy League prep school.

"I see how it is," he said drolly as he stalked toward the bed, a smirk playing on his lips.

"You'll pay me for a drink at the King of Spades, but you won't let me wear your shirts?" She pivoted on the bed to mirror his movements.

Not that it would do her much good. Kai dove for her with inhuman speed, his hand closing around her ankle. She shrieked and shrank into the pillows, her outburst devolving into giggles as he flopped on top of her and assaulted her neck with fiery kisses. His hand slid up her stomach, hiking up the baggy garment.

"You look better without it," he said against her ear, his thumb skimming over the peak of her breast. The smell of blood and whiskey was gone, replaced by the pine and spice soap Miya had foisted on him.

She snagged his lips, but when she pressed her palm to his abdomen, he flinched and sucked a sharp breath in through his teeth.

"Watch the ribs," he chuckled, weaving his fingers with hers and pulling her hand from the tender spot.

Miya dropped her head. "You're really getting pummeled working for Sergei."

"I'm fine," he promised, pinning her hand to the pillow. "And Sergei can't force me to do anything I don't want to. He just hooks me up with fights."

Miya fidgeted beneath him, his insistence doing little to mollify her. "I just didn't know ordinary humans could do so much damage to you."

Kai's mouth caressed her jaw. "They're good fighters—still

stronger than the average person. People can hit pretty hard when they're trained right."

"Stop complimenting the assholes meddling with our sex life," she grumbled.

Kai barked out a laugh, his breath glancing off her cheek. "They're not meddling."

"Yeah?" Miya lifted her head, challenge curving her mouth. "Prove it."

Eyes narrowing, his tongue glided over his teeth behind a tight-lipped smile. She was baiting him, but Kai couldn't resist. He rolled back onto his knees, grabbed her thighs, and yanked her lower on the mattress. The shirt she'd stolen from him rode up, and he pulled it over her head before sinking to his elbows, his lips trailing down her belly. His teeth clamped over the band of her underwear as he hooked a thumb under the gaunt fabric.

"Don't rip—"

The words died in her mouth when he tore the lace like a piece of construction paper. His gaze flitted to her face—smug, mordant eyes daring her to protest. Apparently, wrecking her undergarments was an exercise in spite.

Kai tossed her ruined panties aside and turned his attention to the inside of her thigh, his lips skimming higher.

"Taking the easy route, I see," she taunted, her stomach curling when he pushed her legs apart and grazed her center.

"Less exertion."

"I'm sorry," said Miya, "tell me again how your fights aren't affecting our sex life?"

Kai kissed his teeth and ignored the quip as he descended on her, sublimating his irritation with his tongue between her thighs.

"Shit," Miya hissed when he drew a slow circle around her clit, teasing. One hand glided down his arm while the other disappeared in his unruly hair, pushing him closer.

"Greedy," he murmured, his laugh vibrating against her, and she hooked her knees over his shoulders, reeling him in.

The ache for release bloomed in the pit of her stomach, plucking at the strings that would unravel her. Just as her pleasure crested, Kai withdrew, the heat of his hands and mouth maddeningly absent as he steered her from the precipice, leaving her body screaming with unspent lust.

"That's for razzing me." Kai sat up and wiped his mouth, then sucked her arousal from his fingers.

An annoyed whimper slipped from Miya, but she wouldn't let him gloat. "You realize I *do* have fingers I can use myself." As she slid a hand between her thighs, Kai snatched it away. Miya playfully kicked at his ribs, knowing he'd guard his injuries.

"Lambchop," he warned, seizing her calf mid-air.

She struck with her other foot, and he caught that one too. Her revolt was futile but fun, both of them brimming with mirth as a playful tussle ensued. Kai pinioned her to the mattress, and she squirmed beneath him, her impish cackles gradually waning as she nuzzled his neck and wrapped her limbs around him. The hard ridge below his hips pressed against her, and she angled her own in invitation.

His lips branded her skin as their bodies joined, and she clawed him closer, craving his warmth. Her mouth crashed against his, and he groaned against the kiss as his fingers pressed into her thigh. Kai was single-minded when it came to pleasure, and that afforded Miya delicious glee in disrupting him with the occasional hurdle—just to make him work for it. She squeezed her legs around his waist and pushed, forcing space between them that he desperately wanted to devour.

Gritting his teeth, Kai swallowed a frustrated growl. Her goading never failed to rile him into a contest. Fingers threading through her hair, he tugged her head back, his retaliation earning him a satisfied moan. Miya swore as he held her down, her blood thundering through her veins. Basking in their feverish exchange, Kai flashed her a wicked grin when she dug her nails into his bicep. If there was one thing that could make her come on sight, it was that damn look he gave her when they fucked—like the whole world could've been burning, and he'd still choose to be inside her.

Kai slipped a hand between their bodies and drew a finger over her clit, his touch vindicating every teasing stroke that'd left her longing for his tongue. He didn't disappoint. Miya gasped his name as she came, legs clenched around him, nails raking down his back.

Kai didn't even flinch, his gaze molten as he watched her, savoring every tremor and harsh exhale that met his skin. When he'd had his fill, he eased his grip on her hair and fisted the sheets.

His breath hitched, body going taut, and he bit back a snarl as he muffled his release against her neck.

Miya wound her arms around him as he rocked against her, and the tension gradually bled from his limbs. Bracing on one elbow, Kai traced a path from her pulse to her ear with his lips. "It'll take more than a few cracked ribs to stop me from fucking you," he whispered roughly, then rolled onto his back, dragging her with him.

"You did good." She patted his arm, her eyelids heavy with impending sleep.

Kai scoffed. "I thought dudes were supposed to conk out right after."

Miya shushed him and groped at his face in a haphazard attempt to clamp her hand over his mouth. "You barely sleep anyway."

He evaded her efforts to silence him, chomping at her fingers. "But I get to watch you mutter through your wet dreams."

A smile tickled the insides of Miya's cheeks, and she craned her neck to admire the lines of his face. Her touch roamed the length of his torso, carved with lean muscle. "You're sweet."

Kai wrinkled his nose like she'd accused him of something untoward. "Go to sleep, Lambchop. You're loopy."

Miya snickered and snuggled into the crook of his arm, fingers drumming against his chest. "Whatever you say, *Kai*."

Wedging a leg between his thighs, her eyes drifted to their nightstand where she'd set the note. It'd still been damp when she'd pulled it from her pocket. Now, a tiny green sprig with a single clover heart sprouted from the paper, pale brown veins pulsing through the sheet as though it were a living skin. Barely perceptible streaks of blue ink shone through the translucent fibers, the name —*Caelan Carver*—suddenly a frantic question in need of response.

The stranger's request was as sentient as a tree rooted in the earth, and it awaited the Dreamwalker's reply.

3

KAI

KAI WAS RUDELY awoken by the ear-piercing shriek of a distressed Lambchop. Bolting upright, his senses flared with adrenaline. Needle-point legs scratched on wood, and he swung an arm over Miya's torso, bringing his fist down onto the windowsill in a wall-shaking hammer strike.

Soft, gooey liquid caked his fingers as he unballed his fist and turned his hand over. He'd pureed a cockroach. All that remained of the critter was tarry slop and two crooked antennae.

"Oh God—nope, nope, nope." Miya sat up and kicked her heels against the mattress, scooting back until she'd plastered herself to the headboard. She stared at his hand, covered in bug guts, then pointed to the door. "Go wash that off before it drips on me."

Kai sighed and threw his legs over the side of the bed. The room was still dark, silver light slicing through the seam between the curtains. The murk promised a rainy day as autumn leaves ground to mulch. After returning from the bathroom with a pristine hand and a wet paper towel, he picked a ratty pair of gray sweatpants off the floor and pulled them on.

"We have to move."

Kai faced Miya as he tied the drawstring; the elastic in the waistband was shot. "Because of a cockroach?"

"I hate cockroaches." She hugged her knees to her chest. "Where there's one, there's a million. Did you know they can contaminate food with their poop?"

Kai quirked a brow and swallowed the uncharitable retort that rose in his mouth. "We can't move. The rent's cheap, and the land-lord doesn't ask about ID as long as we keep paying in cash." He'd been a runaway since he was sixteen; a life of luxury had long been foreclosed.

"Why did it have to be cockroaches?" Miya whined.

Kai retrieved his hunting knife from the bedside drawer. Crawling onto the bed, he stretched over her to scrape away the rest of the goop with the blade. "Would you prefer rodents that chew through wires *and* shit in your food?"

"At least mice are cute," Miya bargained. "Maybe I'll buy some traps."

Bug traps were useless, but he wouldn't tell her that. Lately, she'd been stalling at every animal shelter they passed. Adopting a cat for pest control would probably appease her; she'd get a furry companion and a mass murderer in a single package.

"I'll deal with it." He wiped the blade clean, and she muttered her acceptance. Kai had a good track record of keeping his word, his assurance satisfying her for the moment.

As Kai sheathed his knife, a knock sounded on the door, and they both froze like squirrels in the middle of a busy road. Kai tested the air with his nose, then groaned at the familiar scent.

"Fuck me." He tossed the knife into the drawer and marched out of the room. Nearly ripping the wooden slab off its hinges, he stood in the entryway and glared down their uninvited guest.

Thick white hair rounded her neck and shoulder on one side, her amber eyes shining under perfectly groomed brows. Ama shifted her weight and rested a manicured hand on her hip as she silently appraised him.

Behind her, their neighbor from down the hall puttered by, her gaze snagging on Kai. "Me-ow," she purred. "Those pants are riding real low, honey."

Ama screwed her face up, then pushed past him into the apart-ment. "I am *so* glad men aren't my only option."

Kai smirked and leaned against the doorframe, glancing down the corridor. Ursula was well into her sixties, but her sassy ass didn't give a fuck. She cursed more than a mobster in a gambling den and was lewd enough to make a cat-calling construction worker sound tame.

"You better get back in there before I take you for myself," she called as she reached her door.

"And what are you going to do with me, Ursula?" he asked playfully.

She exploded into a gravelly laugh as she glided into her apartment, leaving his question unanswered.

Kai snorted and headed back inside. Ursula was a handful, but she brought them homecooked meals whenever they were struggling to keep up, and for that alone, Kai was grateful.

He found Miya perched on the kitchen counter fully dressed in purple flannels and a black long-sleeved T-shirt.

"I looked into the missing person's case," Ama said as she handed her a folder. "It has all the signs of your favorite form of devilry."

Miya held up the note from the weirdo. It was sprouting some creepy magical weed, and as far as Kai was concerned, plant matter budding from stationary was as red a flag as a Ouija board in a horror film.

"What do you know?" Miya asked as Ama inspected the blooming sheet of paper.

Ama plucked the leaf from the stem and ground it between her fingertips. "Caelan Carver, daughter of Lisbeth and Gabe Carver. An odd tidbit: Lisbeth and Gabe didn't have any children until three years ago."

"And...?"

"Caelan is certainly no toddler." Ama flicked the green pulp away.

"How old is she?" asked Miya.

"Fifteen. She's been missing for a few weeks." Ama flipped a page in the folder to a photo of the girl. "It took a bit of schmoozing on my part, but I was able to leech some interesting hearsay from a friend of a friend who works administration at the police station."

"Go on," Miya urged, reclaiming the note before Ama decided to take it apart.

"Apparently, Caelan appeared exactly three years ago, origins unknown. A local man found her wandering naked around Boston Common. She was disoriented and confused. Had no memory of how she'd gotten there. The man who found her gave her his jacket and called child services. After that, she was put into the system."

Kai leaned his shoulder against the wall. The girl's story wasn't all that different from his, though he hadn't materialized out of thin air. Alice found him wandering the woods outside Granite Falls, Washington, ass-naked and covered in blood. Some of it was his, but most of it wasn't. Fortunately, his stint with child services was cut short when Alice decided to take him in. She knew the pitfalls of being shuffled between foster families, and the odds for young boys weren't too hot. Kai was a wreck, biting anyone who tried to handle him—barely ten years old and already a delinquent. Alice figured a stable home would be his best shot, and she was right, but he still grew into a pariah. Between schoolyard brawls and trips to the shrink, he'd convinced everyone he'd be dead by twenty-five. The high school principal suggested he join the military, but his therapist insisted he'd fail the screenings. He couldn't follow orders to save his life. Too much aggression, too little focus. Alice tried her best, and she was probably the only reason he hadn't gone completely rancid, but he'd been a bigger pain in the ass than he was worth.

"Foster family?" Kai asked, nodding toward the folder in Miya's hands.

Ama frowned, surprised he'd care. "No. They adopted her. She seems like a good kid. All *A*s and *B*s on her report cards, no trouble at home. The only thing a little out of place is that she doesn't seem to have any friends."

Miya smiled wryly. "It's not as weird as you might think."

"Most people can't tell friends from pylons," Kai added flatly.

Ama huffed. "I suppose you have a point. There is one other thing, though."

Miya closed the folder. "What is it?"

"It's speculative," Ama started, "but according to station gossip, the Carvers were bickering over a peculiar habit of Caelan's."

Kai grunted dismissively. "What? Did they find porn on her laptop or something?"

Ama rolled her eyes. "Honestly, you could at least try not to be so boorish."

"Why bother?" Kai shrugged. "Niceties are for conmen and customer service."

Ama smiled tightly. "I'd like to think they make life easier sometimes."

Hostility sputtered between them as Kai volleyed her smirk with his own. "You can put frosting on a turd, but it's still a piece of shit." Ironic, since Ama treated him like he was just that. She always had, though he couldn't blame her entirely. He'd gotten Miya into trouble a few times despite his best efforts, though he always busted ass to fix his fuckups. Still, Ama was a ghoulish bestie with a PhD in judgment.

"Enough," Miya cut in, tapping Ama's arm. "What's this rumor you heard?"

Ama glowered at Kai, then turned back to Miya. "A door."

"Beg your pardon?" Miya blinked.

"Gabe Carver told police that Caelan was fixated on finding some kind of door, but Lisbeth didn't think it was relevant."

Kai and Miya exchanged foreboding looks. Mystery doors were never good. They led to ethereal acid trips and hellscapes made of soul-crushing regret.

"What kind of door?" Miya pressed.

"No one could say." Ama pursed her lips. "But I do think it's interesting that the parents disagreed on whether it was a story worth telling."

"Any sense of why Lisbeth didn't think it was relevant?" asked Miya.

Ama hummed and clacked her nails on the laminate counter. "I imagine Gabe was concerned that Caelan might be mentally ill, and the fixation on the door is a symptom. On the other hand, Lisbeth might've thought her daughter's search had some other meaning or purpose. Perhaps Caelan is merely whimsical and eccentric. Or perhaps it's something else."

"She's trying to figure out where she came from," Kai interjected.

Both women's gazes flew to him, their sudden scrutiny clinging to his skin. He set his jaw and trained his eyes on the wall. Normally, he enjoyed attention. At the Confessional, he soaked up the hungry stares, tugging on the thread between fear and temptation. Unslaked desire was a weapon he wielded to earn his keep, so he held everyone at arm's length, offering only a taste to whet the appetite. Men wanted to fight him, and women wanted to fuck him. Kai indulged the former impulse, but the latter was useful; the more people wanted to fuck him, the more they wanted to fight him too.

He loved those nights when he wore his brazenness like an armor made of vice. But the bravado peeled away eventually, leaving him brittle. A probing glance could feel like a knife to his jugular, and he had nothing to dull the blade. With Miya, he was naked. He'd let her into the catacombs of his fucked-up head, and there wasn't space for anyone else. Empathizing with some fifteen-year-old stray made him want to storm out the door and undo himself at the nearest dive bar.

As though sensing him unravel, Miya hopped off the counter, the folder tucked under her arm. She placed a hand on his abdomen and inspected his injuries, her touch soothing the part of him that felt like a wild animal pacing a too-small cage.

"They're healed," he told her, but she grabbed his chin and angled his jaw, checking the side of his face. She'd find only a disappearing scab on his once-split lip. The bruises on his jaw had faded, and his ribs had fused back together, only a faint yellow shadow to show for his pain.

"Yeah, looks like you're good as new." Her tone was clipped. She hated it when he used his freakish healing as an excuse to get beat up more.

Kai's mouth tugged into a frown, and he gestured toward the folder. "You going to chase that?"

"A missing girl who disappeared as suddenly as she appeared and is searching for an inexplicable door?" She sighed, re-opening the folder. "How could I not?"

Miya's entire life had been flipped upside down five years ago when her parents, neighbors, and every other superstitious dipshit in Black Hollow decided she'd been kidnapped and possessed by a malevolent spirit feared by the town for centuries. In a doozy of poetic twists, it turned out that Miya was, in fact, that spirit: the Dreamwalker reincarnated—literally. Both she and Kai were living incarnations from the town's fable: a story about a girl who got lost in the woods, and a god in the guise of a wolf who guided her home instead of devouring her. The actual event had happened lifetimes ago, and the tale should've ended there, but apparently, *not* dying in the woods when you're a woman makes you a devil-fucking witch.

Her own people tried to butcher her, and Kai, the ominous

black wolf who terrorized the town as the Dreamwalker's familiar, only wanted to help her. As with all conflicts Kai volunteered to resolve, things got a little nasty, and the subsequent bloodbath lowered Black Hollow's population by a few dozen dick-bags.

Not that it mattered. Miya was saddled with that trauma for life. Despite forsaking Black Hollow and guarding her full name— Emiliya Delathorne—anything that tickled those harrowing memories blew a hair up her ass until she dove in headfirst, consequences be damned. Missing girls caught between worlds never failed to yank at her heartstrings. Kai still called her Lambchop, and it wasn't just sentimental; after five years of grueling battles, Miya hadn't lost her tenderness. She cared in ways he never could, and although Kai had no desire to share that affliction, a part of him envied her depthless reservoir of fucks to give.

"Seems like a bad idea," he said, though he wasn't one to talk.

"For once, I agree," Ama chimed in. "This case seems like trouble, and I don't like the sound of the man who gave it to you."

"He smelled weird," Kai added, recalling the stench of rotting wood.

Ama placed a hand on Miya's shoulder. "Enough reason to stay away."

"I don't know," Miya ventured, scanning the first page of notes. "He was strange, yes, but I feel like he's desperate for help."

"Did he offer money?" Kai asked.

Miya ducked her head. "No."

His girl was in dire need of a backbone. Amid hundreds of fake psychics trying to peddle people with imaginary family curses, Miya was the only one worth a damn, and she wasn't even psychic.

She fidgeted as Kai and Ama bore into her, disapproval oozing from them both. "He didn't offer anything, and there was no contact information on the note—"

"Exactly." Kai plucked the folder from her hand. "You should drop it. He doesn't want to pay? He doesn't get to use you."

"I...I guess." Miya visibly wrestled with herself, her eyes glued to the documents as Kai considered putting them through a shredder.

"Well, let me know what you decide, but I need to go. Dahlia asked me to buy her some citrus for the bar." She stopped at the door, her eyes shifting to Kai. "Try not to drag her into trouble."

Kai clenched his teeth so hard they nearly cracked. He did a lot of reckless shit, but purposefully sucking Miya into it wasn't on the list. "Fuck off," he barked as she left, but not before she extended him her middle finger.

"Will you two ever get along?" Miya asked.

"Probably not, but in case you haven't noticed, I'm not the one swinging my dick around."

Ama always had a bone to pick with Kai, and she'd taken to taunting and patronizing him since the day they'd met. Mutual concern for Miya was the only miracle that could unite them.

"She's right, though." Kai palmed the back of his neck as he turned the folder over. "This case sounds like more trouble than it's worth."

Miya gently pried it back from him. "Give me some time to think about it. You can't deny it sounds right up my alley. And frankly"—she gestured at his phantom bruises—"that's rich coming from you. Doesn't anyone ever question your supernatural healing?"

Kai made a noncommittal sound. "Wounds heal from the inside out. Important bits first. The stuff on the surface goes last, so I've always got something to show for the pain." He dropped his hand to his side. "Perks of being...whatever the fuck I am."

Miya chuckled. "A literal god incarnate?"

Kai's lips pulled back into a rakish grin, and as though reading his mind, Miya hung her head and groaned.

"Don't—"

"A god in the bedroom, maybe."

She pinched the bridge of her nose. "Don't flatter yourself."

"Don't need to." He leaned over and nipped her earlobe. She lightly shoved him, and he stumbled down the hall, laughing. "You flatter me plenty."

"Put some clothes on so I can flatter you less," Miya quipped after him.

Kai felt a smile tug at the corner of his mouth as he re-entered their bedroom and sifted through the closet for something more presentable. He never imagined himself living with another person —not since he was a teenager slumming in Alice's rickety bunga-low. He'd been on his own since he was sixteen, finding shelter and sustenance where he could. The loneliness had garroted his ability to trust. His connections remained fleeting, superficial—a casual lay for the night or an overstated bond after too many drinks at the bar. Most of his time was spent alone—an extrovert forced into a life of introversion. Bouncing around the west coast, a whole decade passed before he found Miya in Black Hollow. He hadn't realized how desperately he'd craved intimacy all those years, the ache for it subsumed in a bottomless pit of rage and grief.

That cavernous hole in his chest had finally shrunk over the last five years. He still didn't trust, still lost himself in reckless escapades, but he had something—or someone—to anchor him. Alice would've hacked up cigarette ash if she saw him now. Then, she'd sacrifice every firstborn to garner what Miya had done to change him, but in truth, she hadn't changed him. Perhaps she'd lit a fire under his ass, but not even a pack of three-headed hell hounds could force Kai Donovan to do something he didn't want to. Miya simply never expected him to be something he wasn't. She adored his irreverence, but she also gave him the space to be more. He was still himself; he was just better at it than he used to be.

Kai staved off the worst of his impulses because he chose to— because despite spending his life being the asshole, he wanted to be a friend to this one girl. It wasn't that she was special or unique; she wanted him for exactly who he was, and he wanted her for the very same reason.

Besides, Kai was pretty sure he lacked the wiring for romantic love. People asked if Miya was his fuck buddy or his girlfriend, but he didn't understand the distinction. Love was supposed to be the dividing line, yet that line didn't exist for him. Sure, friendship and sex were usually separate, but Miya offered him the best of both. She was his best friend and his lover, and he cherished that more than any bullshit about romantic grandeur.

After dropping his old sweats, he yanked on a pair of dark green cargo pants and a black tank top.

"I'm off to Marty's," he told Miya as he strode into the kitchen. "Need anything?"

She idly stared into the fridge with a pout. "Something for breakfast?"

Kai nodded, "Got it," then headed out the door.

The corner store, creatively called *Connah Store*, was about as clunky and generic as its name. Boasting aisles dedicated to junk food and over-the-counter meds, the shop reserved a meager fridge on the back wall for dairy and stray pieces of fruit. The only drawback was Marty, the overeager owner who responded to warnings about as well as a tub of ferrets. He was a syrupy little man with the complexion of unripened goat cheese and the survival instincts of an end table, but over the last year, he'd grown on Kai.

After collecting what he needed and paying, Kai fled before Marty accosted him. As he stepped outside, a familiar scent struck him—an intrusive, pungent odor that stood out like curdles of mold on a bed of fresh berries. Whirling, he caught sight of a shadowy figure dressed in a long taupe coat. He stood at the edge of the road with his feet firmly planted on the asphalt—a human frame that could barely contain whatever not-so-human thing was inside. Unconcerned with incoming traffic, the man's head quivered and cricked to the left until deep brown eyes settled on Kai, boring into him like alloyed steel drilling through earth.

It was the stranger from the King of Spades.

Kai stepped forward, and the man wandered straight into oncoming traffic. As his ratty fishing boots hit the pavement, a too-warm breeze washed over the street, assaulting Kai with that same fusty stench from the night before. His stomach flipped, and white-hot pain blossomed just above his tailbone, scalding his spine.

Panic set in. It'd been five years since he'd endured this particular torture. The unbidden change was supposed to be a distant memory, yet the mere sight of this creep stirred it to the surface. Kai's tongue scraped over his canines, suddenly longer as they prodded his lip. He thumbed the sharpened point, his face twisting into a snarl when the tooth pushed back against the pad of his finger, fighting to emerge. His skin blazed, every pore prickling as coarse black fur threatened to sprout from his flesh. Kai's chest seized, and his breath hitched in a wild bid to stem the tide. He had to get the fuck out before his body splintered, breaking away the human to remake the wolf.

My, my, a raspy voice invaded his thoughts, abrading his senses like iron wool on rust. *What big teeth you have.*

A car horn blared as an SUV barreled forward and swerved, just barely evading the madman who'd waltzed into the lane. The car skidded by, obscuring Kai's line of sight, though he kept his eyes trained on the spot where the stranger stood. Sweat dribbled over his brow, the heat of it like lava pooling around his eyelids. He hunched over, uselessly gripping the shopping bag as though it would spare his hands from morphing into paws. The car regained equilibrium and pulled over. The road opened in front of Kai, but the stranger was gone. He'd vanished into thin air, and the pain of Kai's transition bled from his bones. The driver of the SUV stumbled out of his vehicle, arms thrust out as he stared at the road, bewildered. Only the faint residue of musky wood and moss remained—anomalies in a city that smelled of fumes and mortar. Whatever traces lingered in the air, they were impossible for Kai to track, dissipating into the wind like a ghost in search of home.

KAI DIDN'T TELL Miya about what he'd seen in the street. Was the stranger following her? Checking whether she'd look for that missing kid? Miya may have been accustomed to occult shenanigans, but her jobs thus far were child's play—mundane hauntings and mischievous spirits rearranging refrigerator magnets. Most spirits didn't mess with the Dreamwalker when she told them to sod off. She wasn't just a witch; she literally straddled realms. Spirits normally didn't have form, but any entity stuck with her was vapor turned to bone. And bones could be crushed, ground to dust.

No one fucked with a woman who could shunt ethereal pricks straight into hell without an appointment. Miya didn't need an invitation; she came knocking on the devil's door when she damn well pleased. It used to scare the shit out of him—seeing what she was capable of—but he'd learned to trust her power, encourage it even. But on this side, she was vulnerable like anyone else. Here, where flesh, blood, and red earth reigned, Kai was the vanguard, and the stranger in the fishing hat had a foot in his domain.

He'd also nearly forced Kai into a transition.

Which was why he kept quiet about what he'd seen in the street. Miya had enough on her plate, and Kai was too freaked out to broach the subject. The last thing either of them needed was another mystery.

They spent the rest of the day watching schlocky horror films on an old laptop and drinking to every cliché in the repertoire.

After guzzling half a dozen shots, Kai fessed up to having another fight that evening—a detail he'd omitted mostly by accident. Miya's mood instantly soured; she'd taken the night off from the King of Spades, leaving Crowbar and Bastien to manage the place by themselves. They bickered about it for a few minutes—something about Kai being inconsiderate and impulsive—then fucked the argument away against the adjacent wall. A neighbor upstairs stomped on their ceiling, yelling at them to knock it off, but that only emboldened Kai to wring his name from Miya's lips.

Sex was his favored method of conflict resolution. Intimacy had a way of blunting his edges, whittling away his stubbornness until he finally puzzled out how to use his words. Miya wasn't wrong; he had a selfish streak and chased thrills when she needed him to hit the brakes.

"I'm sorry," he murmured against her hair as they lay on the couch afterward, limbs tangled and sweaty. He meant it. It always took him a while, but he *really* meant it.

"I know," she sighed, her cheek pressed to his chest. "I just wish you'd told me so I didn't plan my night around you."

"I'll take a break after tonight," he promised. "Payload's double, so we'll be good for a little while."

Miya squirmed in his hold. "Do I need to get another job? I can quit this spirit detective stuff and work retail."

"No." Kai wound his arm tighter around her, staying her writhing. "Do what you love, but for fuck's sake, start charging for it."

Miya snorted on a giggle. "I'm working on it, I swear."

Kai pulled himself up against the back rest, hauling Miya with him. "Fighting at Connor's bar is the only way I know how to make money, but I don't just do it for the cash. I like fighting."

She was silent for a moment, her nose brushing across his collar bone. "I know you do, and honestly, it's fine. I'm not a huge fan of Sergei's schemes—pushing it to three rounds, forcing you to take hits you don't have to—but I know it's a necessary evil, or it wouldn't be convincing. I guess I'm upset it occupies a completely different part of your life."

"You mean that I keep you out of it?" he asked. "Sergei's Russian mob. The less of me they have to exploit, the better."

"I don't hate what you do," Miya clarified, "but I'm not keen on the *mob* part."

"I'm just a fighter." He gave her a light squeeze. "Believe me, there's nothing I'd like more than to show you off at the Confessional."

"You can," Miya insisted. "If the mob wants to find your weaknesses, they will."

Kai tipped his head back, the corner of his mouth tugging into a frown. "I'm trying not to give them a reason to look, Lambchop."

Miya peeled herself from his body, then rummaged through the pantry for a bag of potato chips. "If you're just a fighter," she said through a crunch, "then they shouldn't have a reason to."

Touché. Kai kicked himself off the couch. Unmotivated to pluck his clothes off the floor, he dressed like molasses, then stalked up to Miya and snatched a potato chip from her fingers with his teeth.

"We'll hash something out while I'm on break." He didn't want her to feel like his dirty secret. Snaking his arms around her, he pulled her against his chest—an apology delivered through a flimsy veil of affection. "I'll be back as soon as the fight's over."

Miya nodded, nuzzling his shirt as her hand rustled around the inside of the bag.

After planting a kiss on her forehead, Kai grabbed his change of clothes. The guilt was already creeping in, sinking into his bones where he couldn't reach it—a tarry residue worming around his marrow.

He resolved to tell Sergei that he'd be off for the next few weeks. For the last month, he'd spent almost every night at the Confessional, and it was starting to wear on his closest friend. Kai glanced at her on his way out, returning her tepid smile. Whether it was retribution against a smarmy mongoose at a dive bar or mass murdering cockroaches, Kai always honored his intentions.

For Miya, he'd carve his heart out to keep a single promise.

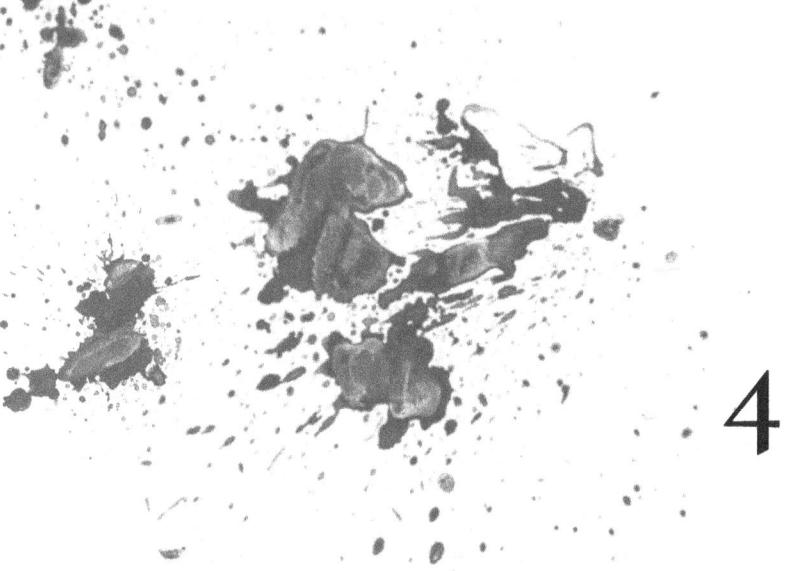

4

THE HAIRS on Kai's neck rose like hackles, his mouth curling into a grimace. Even in his human body, he could tap into that animal sense that warned him when he was being watched.

"Feels weird tonight." Connor shook his head as he surveyed the bar. "The faeries are up to something."

"Faeries aren't real." Kai sipped his whiskey. After shrugging off his jacket, kicking away his boots, and changing out of his cargo pants, he sat lounging at the bar while he waited for his opponent, his caution tape wraps folded next to him on the counter.

Connor's steely gaze slid to his friend. "Should you be drinking before a match?"

"My ribs hurt," he said flatly. "Fractures are healed, but I'm still sore. Whiskey takes the edge off."

"You could've taken an Advil," Connor pointed out, his palm thumping on the counter for emphasis.

Kai pushed the now empty tumbler away and stood. "I'm good."

"You say that a lot."

"And I never lie."

"Doesn't mean you know what you're talking about." Connor tilted his chin. "Hey, Donovan. Be careful. I hear this one's tough."

Kai removed his socks, shoved them into his boots, and stripped off his shirt. "They all are." He smirked, eyes flitting to Connor's. "For humans."

Carol ambled out of the kitchen and behind the counter,

hooting as she wiped the dew from her forehead, then swiped the Jack to pour herself a shot. "It's smokin' for a Sunday."

"See," Connor warned with a wag of his finger, "something's up."

"Weird shit happens every day," said Kai, to which Carol nodded and raised her glass.

"Faeries," mumbled Connor.

Kai snorted, pulled his beat-up phone from his pants pocket, and texted Miya—a small balm for disrupting their night together. Then, he handed the device to Connor—habit to ensure he didn't lose it in the inevitable chaos. The cracked screen and dented corners were lesson enough to take precautions.

The Confessional filled up, the murmurs around him cresting as the door chimes announced new arrivals. A bluster swept through as two men strode in. The first was stout, in his fifties with a loose tie and a balding head. Behind him, a sentient tower of hulking muscles followed, his track suit straining against his bulging quadriceps and impossibly wide back. He wasn't much older than Kai, his hands already balled into fists at his sides, ready to punch holes into anything that moved funny. As the door slammed shut, a chilly gust washed the man's scent toward Kai, raising his skin into gooseflesh. He knew this scent.

The large man's gaze darted up, his dark eyes frigid. His hair was the color of mud, thick tresses tied back in a loose, messy bun. Tension bracketed his mouth as he quashed a scowl, and in the way he moved, Kai detected a barely restrained wildness, a brutality waiting to be unleashed.

The shorter, balding one turned his head and whispered over his shoulder, "Ne otvlekaysya."

Don't get distracted.

Barring traded insults with Sergei, Kai hadn't spoken Russian in years, but he refused to forget it. As a teen, he filched dictionaries from the school library and any piece of literature he could find from garage sales and second-hand stores, determined to cling to the only remaining piece of his old life. Almost everything had slipped away like water through his fingers, but this, he'd guard with everything he'd invested in snubbing his high school teachers.

The two Russians circled around to the far side of the bar, though not before shooting Kai a baleful glower. They knew who he was. Moments later, Sergei made his appearance, his collar wrinkled and his armpits sweat-stained as he removed his coat and slicked back his straw-colored hair. The candied strands had fallen out of place, windswept from the bitter cold.

"Everything all right?" Kai asked, eyeing him warily.

Sergei patted himself down for his wallet, then ordered a drink. After begrudgingly sliding a Sazerac to his nemesis, Connor made himself invisible in the corner, observing the goings-on with his arms crossed tightly over his chest. The air felt heavy, weighing on the skin like a soupy summer fog.

Sergei's attention snagged on the newcomers. "Yes," he answered after a pause. "Are you ready for the fight?"

Kai shrugged. "Ready as ever." He wasn't sure why Sergei expected tonight to be any different, but he chalked it up to those piddly nerves.

The blonde man nodded and let out a shaky breath. "Good. Don't forget, there's a lot on the line. I need this over in one round." He fished a crumpled cigarette box out of his pocket and smacked it against his palm until one of the cancer sticks popped loose.

"So you've said," Kai reminded him. "Relax. He's got tree trunks for limbs. He's probably as fast as a brick on an even surface."

Sergei cast Kai a withering look as he bit down on the cigarette. "You can't joke about everything."

"I'll joke until my dick falls off—"

"And you can't smoke in here." Connor appeared behind them, knocking Sergei on the arm. "Take it out front."

Sergei huffed and snatched the cigarette from his lips, then shoved it into his pocket. "Sorry. Forgot."

Connor threw his arms up. "How the hell do you forget about a law that's been in place for years?"

Kai knew how. Sergei had lost his fucking head. "You need to chill."

"How're your ribs?" the mobster asked, dismissive.

Kai palpated the tender muscles in his abdomen. "Almost fine."

Connor shot him a dubious glare from where he stood behind the counter, but Sergei seemed satisfied.

"Don't fuck up," was all the piss-haired brat had to say.

"Don't shit those expensive pants," Kai sniped back, bumping his shoulder as he shoved past him.

Employees maneuvered the furniture from behind the gated

door, fashioning the makeshift ring. Table legs screeched in protest, and a dozen or so chairs lined the perimeter of the open floor. Kai's foe was seated in one of them, shirt off and legs spread like his dick was too big for courtesy.

There were no referees for the fights—just a well-tolerated honor code that rarely had to be enforced. No one worth a damn wanted to win by cheating, and when someone got knocked down badly enough, their adversary usually knew to call it a day. If things went sideways, Connor was there to interfere. He may have been gentle as cotton ball, but the man was six-foot-four and built like a monster truck. He'd maul anyone who threatened the delicate peace of the Confessional—a neutral territory between different factions in the underworld. Laypeople were still the main clientele, and the bar had a reputation to uphold. Although Connor's family had loose ties to the Irish mob, they kept enough distance to turn the Confessional into a haven. Sure, they hated Bratva, but they had to tolerate everyone. Kai was grateful for it; he made all his money here. He steered clear of Bratva, but for all intents and purpose, he was their fighter through Sergei.

Unlike Cosa Nostra, the Sicilian Mafia that exploited notions of family to keep order, Bratva units were only loosely affiliated with one another and operated independently. Competition and infighting were common, which was likely how he'd wound up in a match against another Russian.

Kai rolled his shoulders back, banishing the tension creeping into his spine. After wrapping his hands, he hopped over a table and through one of the faux windows along the partition, then approached the ring. His opponent rose, body unfolding like a looming portent. He must've been six and a half feet tall. Massive shoulders tapered to a narrow waist, the angle dizzying, and although he wasn't as lean as Kai, he looked like he could stop a train barehanded. Worst of all, the behemoth showed no sign of rampant overconfidence.

His stillness was unnerving.

"Get on with it!" a drunk patron hollered from behind the flimsy barrier.

Scanning their audience, Kai's gaze narrowed when he glimpsed bright auburn hair among the throng—the woman who'd been at the bar last night. Connor said she came to every match, and he wasn't exaggerating.

Kai hooked a foot around one of the chair legs and dragged it aside, then stepped into the ring. His opponent mirrored him, his easy strides eating up the distance until there was barely a foot between them. Kai took in a slow, deep breath, teasing apart the other man's scent. His heartrate was slow, steady, and where others reeked of pungent sweat and fear, this man smelled like winter and smoke and something Kai couldn't place. But what unsettled him most was the roil of familiarity—like some dormant thing lurking in the recesses of his mind had stirred.

Siberia. He smelled like Siberia.

"Your name?" the Russian's voice rumbled like a motor engine. His accent was thick, like he was unaccustomed to the way English fell from the tongue.

Kai quelled the urge to brush him off. Most people didn't care for his name, but he didn't often get to give it either. "Kai Donovan."

The man's thick eyebrows rose just enough for Kai to see curiosity flicker across his eyes. "Donovan..." he trailed off. "An unusual name."

"They're a dime a dozen around here."

The man chuckled under his breath, his mouth barely curving. "Unusual for *you*," he clarified.

Kai set his jaw, unable to volley a response at the veiled remark. "You got a name to give, or are you just here to take mine?"

A divot appeared in the spoke of the man's left cheek as his smile nearly reached his eyes. "Zverev," he said, then languidly backed away to give Kai his space. "Ivan Zverev."

Zverev.

An icy specter coiled around Kai's heart and tore the beating mass into his gut. His stomach churned, and he swallowed through clenched teeth as nausea clawed up his esophagus. Kai only realized he was holding his breath when his lungs began to burn, and he forced the air in through his nose.

Zverev.

He couldn't remember if or when he'd heard that name, but some long-forgotten part of him, locked in the underbelly of his psyche, recognized it—reacted to it.

Zverev.

It was a Slavic surname like any other, yet the mere mention of it was a serrated blade riving him in two.

Zver.

Beast.

Someone shoved Kai from behind, snapping him out of his plummet into darkness. His opponent—*Zverev*—was charging, closing the gap between them fast. Too fast. His elbow pulled back, his torso rotating as he wound up for a downward strike. His entire midsection was exposed, but Kai sensed it was a trap—an enticing target to lure him in.

Kai darted back and twisted out of the way, evading the behemoth's fist by a hair's breadth. It'd come down faster than expected, and Kai felt the air slice past his nose. The big man hit hard.

Sergei wanted the match over in a single round, but Zverev wasn't just big and strong; he was nimble, bouncing on the balls of his feet like a featherweight. Definitely not a brick on an even surface.

Kai risked a gander at Sergei. He was gnashing his teeth, his face red with alcohol and apprehension. Around them, men and women yelped and cheered, egging them on. Normally, fighters charged at Kai like he was a Black Friday sale, but neither he nor his colossal opponent were that dumb. While the first swipe had seemed explosive, Kai knew it was little more than a leisurely test.

Zverev raised his fists and pumped them forward, then circled Kai like a wolf funneling prey into an alcove. The bastard was neither naïve nor scared as he crowded Kai toward the line of chairs. The next swing came faster, but Kai was ready, parrying Zverev's hulking arm and landing a disorienting kick just above the knee. Zverev's leg buckled, but he quickly recovered, pivoting on his stable foot and dashing out of the way. His heel brushed the edge of the ring, and with alarming agility, he leapt forward, throwing a jab at Kai's nose.

A textbook faint, forcing a high block that would expose Kai's injured ribs.

Kai dropped his shoulder and slapped Zverev's fist down as though it were a gnat, his patience whittling down to sliver. "You going to flirt with me all night?"

The behemoth's lip curled at the taunt, his eyes sparking to life.

"What's wrong, *Donovan?*" he sneered the name. "I didn't think you'd be so bashful."

Irritation needled the back of Kai's neck, that low simmer ratcheting up to a boil. He was off his game. His limbs felt heavy, his reflexes tardier than his brain cells the morning after a nasty bender. Something about hearing that name—Zverev—had burrowed under his skin like a festering splinter. No matter how hard he tried to focus, he couldn't salve the unease blossoming in his gut, its slimy tendrils snaking around his bones, bridling him until he was as stiff as a marionette.

"Sometimes I like playing hard to get." Kai flashed him a menacing grin, then shot forward, matching Zverev's uncanny speed. If the big man wanted to dance, Kai would oblige. He may have been smaller, but he refused to believe that a walking dump truck could outmatch his agility. Zverev's arm whaled through the air. It would've been one hell of a bitch slap, but Kai ducked, his torso sailing in a low arc before he popped up next to his foe. Cupping Zverev's nape to lock him in place, Kai whipped an elbow right across his face. Flesh undulated as bone met bone, and the towering Russian stumbled.

Zverev bared bloodied teeth as his head snapped back into place, and he puffed heavily. His brows furrowed, sweat trickling down the side of his face as he reconsidered his opponent.

Then, he smiled.

Not the cocky, shit-eating grin Kai wore like armor, but a beam of genuine, unfettered joy.

"Nakonets!" he bellowed, then slapped both cheeks with open palms, revving himself up.

Nakonets. *Finally.*

Finally, what?

Zverev barreled forward and slammed into Kai, who dropped his center of gravity and braced just a moment too late. Organs rattled between muscle and bone as he nearly flew out of the ring and into a throng of observers. His joints screamed from tension, his heels skidding across the floor.

Shoving Kai back, Zverev dipped low and drove an uppercut into his stomach. Kai torqued his midsection to protect his injured ribs, but the behemoth's fist landed like a concrete slab. White hot pain tore through his abdomen, radiating up his back and along his jaw. He nearly doubled over, black specs dotting his vision. So, this was what it was like to see stars.

Kai fought to stay on his feet, his knees wobbling as he rasped for air and gulped down the bile that bubbled up with a wave of nausea. Slumping over, he fixed his hand against the floor and pushed off, springing out of the way. He'd taken a lot of beatings in his life, but he sure as shit wasn't used to getting hit by someone as tough as him—maybe tougher. Their opening dance had been little more than a courtesy.

It was an unwelcome revelation: Ivan Zverev had been toying with him.

Kai felt a mounting urge to whirl on Sergei and huck a chair at his puny ass. Why the fuck had no one told him that Ivan Zverev wasn't a man, but a monster penned from the same ink as Kai?

Surely, Sergei had known. He'd insisted on caution despite Kai's record, and in his arrogance, Kai had assumed his opponent would be like all the others—an ill-equipped human with too much ego and too little to lose.

Maybe Kai wasn't much different.

He was in no position to stomp his feet and throw a tantrum. The blinding pain in his torso had dulled to a tolerable ache, but Zverev wouldn't let him collect himself. He charged again, but Kai wasn't about to let a two-hundred-and-fifty-pound boulder crash into him a second time. He wheeled around Zverev, using his agility to pivot behind him. Zverev spun, whipping his arm around like a cudgel, but Kai arched back and side-stepped him, then thrust his leg out with a push-kick to the sternum. Thrown off balance, Zverev's heel clipped the floor, and he toppled several of the stools. Before he could orient himself, Kai lunged, mincing every weak point on the human body: kidneys, armpits, the sciatic nerve. Crimson splattered across his neck when his fist connected with Zverev's jaw, but just when he thought the tower might topple, a giant hand clamped down on his forearm.

Kai bit back a grimace. Pulling away was useless; his best bet was to lean into the snare and maneuver with his foe until he found a loophole. On the street, Kai would've sliced a blade straight up Zverev's IT band and left him for dead, but they were at the Confessional where there were rules—annoying, intrusive-as-fuck rules. And Zverev was the fastest heap of muscle Kai had ever shared oxygen with. The behemoth's fist collided with Kai's jaw, jostling his brain around the inside of his skull. Air rushed past his face as gravity betrayed him, and the din in the bar warped into a muffled cacophony.

Don't hit the floor.

Easier said than done.

Don't hit the fucking floor.

Out of sheer spite, Kai willed his body to rotate, but he couldn't stop the fall. He met those rotting old boards on his side, the grains like sandpaper on his skin. Zverev dove for him, and he rolled out of the way. Struggling to his knees, he barely managed to get a foot flat on the ground. His mouth filled with a metallic taste, and he spat it out, spraying the floor in red, but more flowed over his tongue—an unwelcome reminder that he too could bleed. The once-welcome clamor was like knives shoving into his ears. Nausea wracked his body, and the room tilted like a ship in a storm, lights glaring and faces bending.

"Fuck," Kai growled, fingertips pressing into the grimy wood as he tried to drown out the noise, but there was just too much.

"Tap out!" he heard Connor bellow over the crowd. "Tap the hell out, you stubborn ass!"

Nothing ignited Kai's defiance like being told to tuck his tail between his legs. A low, primal sound rippled from his throat as he punched into the floor, planted his foot, and propelled himself upright.

Zverev offered no quarter. He leveled Kai onto his back with a rough tackle, then pinned him down and grappled for a chokehold. Kai lifted his elbows to keep the beast at bay only to take five knuckles to the gut. The air fled his lungs, and a sharp twinge of panic vised around his neck like a living noose. He was trapped.

"You're a scrappy little shit, I'll give you that," Zverev grit through his teeth.

Only a man the size of a skyscraper would have the audacity to call Kai *little*.

Air whistled past his cheek as Zverev's fist wound back for another assault. His giant body unfolded, and Kai glimpsed an opening. Shoring up his strength, he launched his torso off the floor and drove a forearm straight into the behemoth's throat, then clamped his teeth around the soft, pink nub on his chest. Kai jerked his head to the side with a feral snarl, tearing flesh like a rat in a snare—frenzied and drunk on mindless instinct. Blood spattered over his face, coloring his vision scarlet as a bone-cutting scream ripped from Ivan Zverev, and he reeled back, freeing his prey. Kai trundled over and spat out the stray nipple, then clambered to his feet.

A hush fell over the crowd as Zverev's wails filled the void.

"That's a violation!" came the manager's objection as he rushed toward his shambling fighter, now clutching his wounded breast.

Connor was slack-jawed behind the bar, his horror as raw as runny egg whites. Of course, Zverev's handler wasn't wrong; the rules of engagement were simple: no weapons, no eye-gouging, no nut shots, and definitely no biting. Ripping a man's tit off was the equivalent of brandishing a pair of knitting needles and lunging for the eye sockets.

"Animal!" The balding, red-faced Russian thrust an accusatory finger at Kai. "Vanya"—he turned to the towering fighter—"get cleaned up."

Vanya nodded, his gaze meeting Kai's as he sucked in sharp, quick breaths, then shook his head. "You have no self-control."

Kai ground his teeth to gravel. Shame coated his tongue, more bitter than the blood, but he had nothing to wash it down with. After the stunt he just pulled, he doubted Connor would let him anywhere near the whiskey.

Ivan Zverev was right; Kai really had gone off the rails. He'd never met his match, but his opponent had been ready—knew what he was up against. Fight or flight had grabbed Kai by the balls, but he wasn't wired for flight, so he fought, and he fought dirty. Normally, it didn't matter. He was happy to sully his hands in a bar brawl or a back-alley scrap, but in a high-stakes contest with strict parameters, his impulses were hardly commendable. They made him volatile. He'd won the fight, but he'd lost the match, and now he'd pay for his facile victory.

"What the *hell* was that?" Sergei hissed as he yanked Kai away by the arm and spun him around.

Kai whipped free. "Why the hell didn't you tell me what I was up against?"

"What does it matter?" Sergei rebuked. "Do you think he knew what *you* are?"

"He sure as shit seemed to." Rage and confusion roiled under Kai's skin like lava. His voice dropped, low and dangerous. "Tell me who he is."

"Forget that." Sergei waved him off, unperturbed by the boiling cauldron next to him. "He's a freak like you, and that's all you need to know. The point is, you fucked up. You *really* fucked up."

Kai glared through Sergei's skull like he could sear his brains to char. What was he supposed to say? *Oops? Sorry I ruined his symmetry?* "He had me pinned."

"So, you panicked and bit him like some rabid dog?" Sergei seethed as he threw his hands up.

"My bad," Kai grunted, the admission of fault knotting his insides.

Sergei planted his hands on his hips as he paced, scowling into the middle distance. "You have no idea what you cost us."

It wasn't often that Kai felt the weight of dread settle in the pit of his stomach. It was heavier than he expected, like a sack of rocks bound to someone's ankles.

"Fuck." Kai huffed, his shoulders slumping. "How much?"

Sergei whirled on him. "What?"

The back of Kai's neck prickled with a slimy new layer of foreboding. "How much money do I owe Bratva?"

"Money?" Sergei scoffed, shaking his head.

Kai's lips parted, one side of his face scrunching. "Don't I owe you scumbags for the loss?"

The noise of the bar fell away, the air between them curdling like sour milk. Sergei took a harsh step forward and grasped Kai by the shoulder, the tension in his fingers seeping into Kai's bones.

"It's not money you owe, friend."

"I'VE GOT A BAD FEELING." Miya fumbled with her phone, smacking the touch screen until the flashlight winked to life.

Ama swiped aside a low-hanging branch. "Too bad you're ignoring it."

It was well past sundown, and Kai was probably neck deep in bourbon and bar bets. Restless, Miya told Ama she'd decided to take on the Caelan Carver case and would spend her night digging around Boston Common where the teenager had appeared three years ago. Ama tried dissuading her, oscillating between amicable reasoning and maternal scolding, but it only cemented Miya's prerogative. In a gesture of peevish resignation, Ama joined her on the misadventure, poised to mock her poor eyesight.

"You'd think a park would be better lit," Miya grumbled. Boston Common was a spiderweb of walkways that cut across a hilly, tree-speckled field. The paths were lined with benches and lamplight, though half the bulbs were out, leaving the grass between the trees shrouded in darkness. The park was stunning during the day— vibrant gold and vermillion canopies brightening the space as leaves fluttered to the ground with the breeze. But at night, the clouded autumn sky muted those welcoming hues.

Ama flipped her dazzling white hair over her shoulder. "You humans are truly a marvel. So frail, and yet so destructive. You can level an entire city with the push of a button, but you can't even see three feet in front of you."

"To be clear, it's fortunate humans don't share your freakish senses," said Miya. "It must be hard, perceiving so much of what others are oblivious to."

"I enjoy being a wolf among sheep." Ama snapped her fingers to get Miya's attention, then grabbed her elbow and guided her away from a trunk disguised as a shadow.

Miya stumbled past a protruding root. "Sometimes I'm shocked you and Kai live in human bodies, given your contempt for them."

"Kai didn't have a choice for most of his life, and now he has you." Ama glanced her way. Her honey-colored eyes reflected light even in the darkness—one of the many peculiarities Miya first noted about her and Kai. "I prefer this body. So much more fun than romping through the woods. Infinite possibilities to express myself."

Ama—the white wolf with sunlit eyes—had acted as a distant protector since Miya was a child. She still remembered their first encounter: a dreary summer day at the farmer's market, her parents preoccupied with fruit baskets while she propelled herself skyward in a rusty old swing. A wolf had poked its head out from the trees on the border between town and wilderness, seizing Miya amid her desperate flight. She spent years waiting for that wolf to return, to restore some semblance of magic in her life.

But it was Kai, not Ama, who breathed life back into Miya's world. She mistook him for the wolf from her childhood, but while Ama's fur was white as snow and soft as fine silk, Kai's was obsidian black, wild and coarse like bristles. Even their human bodies boasted the same shades and features as their animal selves. Ama, a picture of refined wintry elegance, and Kai, the embodiment of ravening instinct, brazen and full of mettle. They were so alike and yet so different, repelling one another like magnets with the same polarity.

Miya's phone buzzed then, and she swiped past the home screen.

About to break some teeth. Don't hex me.

"Always so ceremonious," Miya chuckled as she composed her reply.

Don't get punched in the dick.

"What did he say?" asked Ama.

Miya shook her head and locked her screen. "Nothing special."

"Does he know you're out here?"

There she was—the devil's advocate. Kai and Ama's baseline had always been hostility, but they were eager allies in one regard: Miya's wellbeing. Yet she hated being coddled. She'd spent her life feeling squashed by expectations of propriety and good decision-making. The freedom to live unfettered had been cudgeled out of her from an early age, and that was precisely why she'd found Kai so attractive; he was everything she'd been denied by her upbringing—a wayward firecracker ruled by raw intention, consequences be damned. Kai emboldened her, and because he liked emboldening her, he rarely stood in her way. Ama, however, was a creature of cold, unyielding logic. Costs and benefits; risks and rewards. She was driven by calculation—by the probability of a desirable outcome. Their approaches couldn't have been more divergent, consensus as rare as a cosmic event.

"He doesn't," Miya replied quickly, shining her flashlight between two trees so she wouldn't trip on a root.

When they stepped into the clearing, Miya was grateful for the level ground and towering lamp posts. Ama stopped next to her, ogling the side of her face with an arched brow. "You're hiding it from him."

"No, I just don't want to worry him right before a fight."

Ama hummed, unconvinced.

Irritation needled Miya's chest. "Maybe I don't want you two ganging up on me."

The mirthful smile fell from Ama's face. "Regardless, I'm glad you didn't go alone."

Miya routinely took risks Ama disapproved of, but the white wolf's tolerance was so low that a turtle could trip the wire. Kai was brash by nature, so if *he* had a bad feeling, maybe this was reckless. Whatever the case, three was a crowd, and the last thing Miya wanted was to feel corralled by two stubborn, overprotective wolves.

A mass of black feathers swooped down from a branch, the telltale caw of a raven signaling Gavran's arrival. Miya extended her arm, and he accepted the roost, his talons biting into her skin as he steadied himself.

"Did you give Bastien a goodbye peck for me?" Miya teased as she wiggled her fingers through his blue-black plumage.

Gavran angled his head back, his throat swelling as he released a happy gurgle, then hopped from Miya's shoulder down to Ama's.

Ama leaned in as he nuzzled her neck, and she cooed, "Are you behaving yourself with the clientele?"

They'd always been inseparable. Ama claimed that Gavran had raised her—a careful truth blurred by omission—but it was clear they'd spent a lifetime together. Gavran now split his time between the Dreamwalker and the white wolf, though Miya could tell Ama missed him when he was gone. Fortunately, she had Crowbar to keep her company when pride kept her from seeking out her feathered friend.

Gavran chortled and beat his wings, then scanned the field, his head canting this way and that.

"All right, what are we looking for?" asked Ama.

Miya peered through the empty park. "I'm not sure yet, but this is the spot Caelan was found."

"It could be a dead end. Three years is a long time."

Miya's hand wandered to the pendant around her neck. "I've got no other leads. Besides, if there are strange disappearances—or appearances—whatever's causing them will leave a trace."

Silence and darkness cloaked the grounds like an unfamiliar vesture, the space made alien without the daytime chatter of congregating denizens. Parks, stripped of their social purpose, revealed a forgotten underside of a city with ancient bones. They were repositories of grim histories—executions, massacres, riots. The soil on which Boston Common stood was anything but pristine—something the trees knew well. Their roots burrowed deep into the earth, drinking the blood of the slain, soaking up the vestiges of their agony.

During the day, parks hosted the living as they searched for solace; at night, they were where phantoms came to mingle, to revel in clandestine mysteries.

Miya traipsed along the grass, guided only by a sense she could neither control nor fully tap into. Then again, it was never about control; it was about trust. Her power would serve her when she required it. The common was mired in a low, fey frequency that quavered beneath her feet and caressed her face like a hyaline mist.

It enveloped her, tugging on those ethereal threads that tethered her to the unseen. Her hand floated up as though steered by spectral breath, and she curled her fingers around the labradorite pendant.

The dream stone always helped her find her way. Dropping into a crouch, Miya laid her palm flat on the grass. Her eyes drifted shut, and she listened until the stone hummed to life, and she felt a slow, steady thrum beneath the soil. In the dreamscape, where all that was solid melted into air, and nothing remained in the same place twice, she'd learned to follow the roots. They were like veins beneath the earth's skin—a map of the very domain that gave them life. That matrix of roads led her where she needed to go. The trick was identifying the correct root—the correct path.

Hunting specters from the waking world wasn't so different. Emotions and energies clung to the land, and the same roots that soaked up agony soaked up other things as well. Miya just had to pick up the trail.

"That way," she said, pointing with her eyes still closed.

Gavran squawked and took off from Ama's shoulder, gliding forward. He circled overhead, then dove toward a rogue tablet in the middle of the grass, fluttering above it before landing.

Ama sidled up to Miya and offered her a hand. "Looks like you found something."

Miya accepted the gesture and hauled herself up. "Let's see what it is."

A rectangular slab of dappled stone lay wedged in the soil, dying grass caressing its hewn edges. A plaque was fixed into it, marking the place where the Great Elm of Boston Common once stood. Miya swept her flashlight over the darkened brass, reading the inscription aloud.

Site of the Great Elm
Here the sons of liberty assembled
Here Jesse Lee, Methodist Pioneer.
Preached in 1790
The landmark of the common. The elm blew down in 1876

—

Placed by the N. E. Methodist Historical Society

A felled tree, its lingering shadow suffused in castaway histories. Miya wondered if a piece of it still skulked underfoot, pulsing with untold stories, clipping at the seams of another realm.

One little tear in the threads, and the whole boundary could unravel.

"It's always a damn tree." Ama sighed loudly, and Gavran thrust his neck out and croaked at her as if offended.

In Miya's hometown of Black Hollow, British Columbia, it'd been a willow known as the Emerald Shade and an ancient redwood that Gavran called the Red Knot. Then there was the Gray Gnarl—a dead elm lost in the swamps near Orme's Rest, Louisiana, from where Crowbar and Bastien hailed. It seemed they had another elm on their hands, though it no longer stood, and Miya had no way of feeling its breath beneath her palm. It was little more than a memorial now—a shade left behind by a living edifice.

Miya wondered if this one still had form in the dreamscape. It was true that things moved, but the sense of place remained. The woods surrounding the Emerald Shade always looked and smelled the same; it was the *where* that changed. Orienting in the dreamscape using laws of physics was like trying to capture mist in a jar. Miya had the roots to guide her, their pulse amplified by the dream stone. It was a fragment of the dreamscape gifted to her by Gavran and cultivated by the Dreamwalker's will. Now, it was a part of her.

Look with different eyes, both Kai and Gavran once told her.

"Surely, you knew this was here." Miya frowned at the raven, who cocked his head in reply.

He beat his wings, protesting her accusation, then buried his beak into his thick plumage.

"The trace is too faint, even for him," said Ama.

"I have a hard time believing that," Miya grumbled. Gavran was a trickster, only ever offering partial truths. He liked watching mortals stumble to comprehension.

Ama planted her hands on her hips and squinted. "You've gotten better and haven't noticed."

If Miya had improved, she was unaware. Her journey from fledgling to fully realized Dreamwalker was tumultuous. Like the dreamscape that'd claimed her, her growth had been chaotic and replete with hurdles. She'd been unmoored, scrabbling for something sturdy to cling to in a torrential sea of unknowns. For the better part of five years, that something had been Kai. She eventually learned to withstand the current on her own, though he was there to anchor her when she needed him.

"That weird energy I felt is pooling here, under this plaque," Miya told them. She ran her palm over the inscription, and something sparked against her skin—a wrinkle in the veil, a fissure in the stitching.

"Shit," she whispered, feeling the crimp like a crack in glass. "The boundary is really weak here. It would take no effort to puncture it and waltz right through."

Miya could access the other realm in two ways. Either she dreamwalked—her spirit temporarily leaving its container—or she ripped a hole through the barrier and physically let herself in. The latter was exhausting, her body screaming for rest before the journey back. This spot, however, was like wet paper. Tearing through would be easy.

Gavran hopped side to side and pecked at the dirt bordering the plaque.

Miya tilted her head toward him. "You sure you didn't feel this?"

He peered up at her, silent, and she knew he wasn't fibbing.

"I barely feel it," Ama confirmed. "Now that you've pointed it out, I can, but I never would've detected it otherwise."

"I guess that tracks. It took me a bit to find it, but now that I'm here..." Miya trailed off, her brow furrowing. "Do you think Caelan Carver might be like me?"

As far as they knew, Miya was the only one who could shred the border between worlds. The Dreamwalker was gestated in the womb of Black Hollow's most intimate terrors, but folklore was vast and versatile; different cultures shared fears, conjured fiends of a similar ilk. What if Caelan represented the same to her own people, whoever they were?

"I need to get closer," Miya declared.

"Dreamwalking?" the white wolf ventured.

Miya shook her head. "I'm going straight in."

Ama's eyes widened in a rare expression of surprise. "Is that necessary?"

Miya gestured toward the plaque. "There's an open door right here. I don't have to chip my way through the wall."

"Do you simply eat a cupcake that's been left on your doorstep?" Ama scoffed.

"Depends on if it's sealed in a box or has a note or—"

"Miya"—Ama pinched the bridge of her nose—"that's not the point." She tapped her boot against the ground and sighed heavily. "Dreamwalk first. Leave your body here and project your spirit through the fault line. There's no need for you to go bouncing between realities. What if you get stuck or wind up somewhere else?"

"I'm not a fly trapped in a lampshade."

"No, you're a living nightmare to a town of benighted fools, but that doesn't mean you can't take precautions. Let me watch over you from this side."

Miya's rebuttal dissipated. She knew Ama was right. It was an unnecessary risk, and yet she still wanted to take it. Ama and Kai were always there to break her fall, robbing her of the opportunity to truly test herself. The wolves were a force to be reckoned with, but so was the Dreamwalker. Her methods were merely different.

Kai at least let her do what she wanted, and she sheltered him from his demons as often as he rescued her from her doubts. He was dauntless where she was incisive, and he trusted her to be as sharp as he was ferocious. They honed each other like blades, their conviction unwavering. Ama tempered that forging fire, barring Miya from potential harm.

And yet...she was right.

"Okay," Miya conceded, then unzipped her mauve leather jacket and laid it over the grass. She was glad she'd layered up, her long cami and fleece hoodie keeping her warm against the autumn chill. Easing herself onto the thin cushion guarding her jeans from the frigid ground, she waited for Ama to join her—their ritual whenever she dreamwalked.

The white wolf plopped down behind her, then guided Miya's head into her lap. Miya waved for Gavran, whose three-pronged spurs found their new perch on her arm. His head dipped, and he playfully plucked at a tuft of loose fleece.

"I'll see you on the other side," Miya told him, then turned her gaze skyward. She drank in the charcoal expanse, void of a single glimmer, then closed her eyes and replaced its darkness with her own.

"You know what to do," Ama's voice echoed all around her, and she tipped her chin in acknowledgment.

Miya's palms flattened against the earth, and the dream stone warmed against her chest like a tiny hearth. The raven's talons flexed against her forearm, and his low purr soothed her into a reverie. Soon, the world would rend open, and the umbral plane would swallow her up. She felt the pull, that limber tether that bound her to the dreamscape growing taught. It beckoned her spirit. All she had to do was answer.

Cradling the Dreamwalker, the white wolf incanted, "Descend, as only you can."

6

WHEN MIYA OPENED HER EYES, she was met with the hanging star—the dreamscape's sun and moon. Rings of amber, marigold, and wisteria pink haloed the luminous white orb, bleeding into the now smoky sky. While Boston was submerged in night, the dreamscape glowed with a pallid fog. Dark, slender shapes like lightning wove through Miya's vision, and after blinking away her bewilderment, she recognized them as tree branches, stretching overhead. They converged at a massive trunk that grazed the crown of Miya's head where bark met earth. A thick, solid mass swung from one of the tree's limbs, and as Miya's gaze trailed up, her breath snagged in her throat.

A body—feet limp, hands bound, and skirts billowing in the breezeless air. The woman's head drooped chin to chest, her neck broken where the noose pulled taut. The rope creaked with strain as the body swayed—the only sound in the silence.

Miya remembered then: Ann "Goody" Glover, an Irish woman who spoke Gaelic, was hanged as a witch in 1684 because she couldn't recite the Lord's Prayer in English. Apparently, God was monolingual. In the dreamscape, Ann still dangled from the elm, and the ancient tree remained, unbothered by its shadow's absence in the physical plane. Miya once believed that only the shadows of things resided here, that they endured despite the transience of their tangible counterparts. Over time, she'd reversed her thinking; the whole of the waking world was the shadow to the spectral realm. Ann was dead, but she wasn't gone.

"Wake up," came a mirthful chime. "It's time to dream."

Miya's gaze skimmed over the rolling hills peppered with maples and oaks, then settled on a boy no older than twelve. Cropped halfway down his ears, his messy midnight hair resembled plumage, flashing with sapphire iridescence. Waxy cheeks stretched open as jagged teeth filled his smile, and his depthless inky eyes tunneled into her soul.

"Gavran," Miya sighed, then slowly sat up.

He thrust out his arms, his feathered cloak billowing around him. "In borrowed flesh."

"Is it really borrowed if you've decided to keep it?" Miya asked wryly.

"Pedantry." Gavran waved a delicate hand, his fingers thin as chicken bones. "The flesh is ash. This is only a facsimile."

An ageless raven spirit hailing from the dreamscape, Gavran had been a companion to the first Dreamwalker. She'd bestowed him his name, and he in turn imparted guidance. After she died, Gavran lost his tether to the physical world and donned a child's cadaver to compensate. It was his corporeal form, but with Miya awakened as the new Dreamwalker, he no longer needed a physical vessel. She grounded him, and yet he'd adopted the lost boy's shape in the ethereal realm too. Miya wondered if he missed his human body.

"I know." She rubbed the balls of her hands together and surveyed her surroundings. The air was dense and musty, like a noxious smog had descended over the plain. She'd never seen this corner of the dreamscape.

Beneath Ann's corpse, a weeping redbud kept the towering elm company. Vivid magenta flowers blossomed along its branches, but as the petals broke off and wafted to the ground, they turned sanguine, their velvety skin liquefying into drops of scarlet that soaked into the soil.

"Do you know where we are?" Miya asked.

Gavran clawed at the rusted earth with one finger, staining his skin copper. "As much as a rock knows flight."

"Right." Miya huffed as she rose to her feet. "Say no more."

Gavran shook off his curved claw and mirrored her. "You're always bigger here than you are there."

Miya blinked down at him. "Bigger? I don't feel any different."

The boy offered her a toothy smile, sharp points clipping his thin gray lips. "Out there, every person is an ant climbing a clump of dirt, yet they each believe they are scaling a mountain. Here, where dreams and shadows reign, things are different. You can bend this world like the sun bends shadows."

Miya plopped her hand on Gavran's head. It always felt like touching a doll, yet she knew he was alive under that eerie pickled skinsuit. "I might be stronger here, but I want to make a difference out there. That's why I'm trying to find this girl. She matters to someone. I want to do for her what no one could do for me."

The boy frowned. He reached for Miya's hand, pried it from his head, then plied her fingers this way and that. "I help," he said quietly, "because they failed you." His abysmal eyes, wide as the sea, met hers. "I won't fail you."

"You never have." Miya smiled, then took his hand in her own. "Let's go."

She squeezed the dream stone with the other, and at her silent command, the pendant floated up and pulsed with life. A lavender glow illuminated the smog, and Miya felt the chain tug at the back of her neck.

"This way," she said, and Gavran nodded, following by her side.

The stone was a lantern in the haze, revealing just enough for them to make their way. Formless shadows danced in the distance, shapeshifting as the hanging star's light moved through the vapor. Trees melded into titans with limbs that could bridge skies, and hills capsized into bottomless gullies. The ground undulated beneath their feet, and while Gavran moved as though gliding, Miya tottered unsteadily beside him, unaccustomed to such lively terrain. It seemed hellbent on impeding her, which meant she was closing in on something that didn't want to be found.

"There," Gavran hissed, his grip on her hand tightening as his feathery hair stood on end.

Miya squinted through the mist. They'd barely traipsed a dozen yards from the ancient elm. Up ahead, a stone arbor teeming with withered vines framed a barely visible path. Now crumbling with ruin, thorned roses and climbing ivy embraced the hewn granite. Beyond it, the tattered road descended into a pool of onyx-colored water, still as a sheet of ice. It glimmered with starlight, the fog parting around its borders.

"So, this is where it hides." Gavran's mouth slithered into a knowing smile.

"It?"

"The thing that lives in the lake," said the boy.

Miya swallowed thickly and scanned the deathly pool, but she saw no disturbances. "Let's get closer."

"Careful," Gavran warned. "Step too close, and it'll drag you under."

"Let it try."

Then, movement behind the gate's heavy gray walls. Slime and bubbling moss coated the stone as something slunk up the granite. Lumpy claws scraped the top of the arbor, and a long reptilian tail flicked against the vines, tearing some of them loose. Branching horns like rotted wood emerged, followed by a gnarled round face with flaring nostrils, deep set eyes marked by yellow slits, and strings of bilious flesh tethering the creature's gaping maw. Fly-infested quills spiked from its hunched back, nodules and boils mottling ash-green flesh. It perched atop the arbor, its grotesquely long tongue darting about as it eyed its new prey.

"Welcome, Dreamwalker," it said, its voice like scraping nails.

"You know me?" Miya halted several feet before the gate.

"Everyone knows you," came its raspy chuckle. "Or they will."

"We've never met," she countered.

The toad-like gargoyle tittered. "Meeting and knowing are not the same."

"It's a bukavac." Gavran smiled widely at the monster. "Makes a lot of noise—the petty thing."

Those unnerving strings of flesh grew taut as the creature's mouth unhinged, and it shrieked. "Come closer, raven, and we'll see who is petty."

"Let's not." Miya raised a hand to broker peace. "I'm only here to ask a question."

"Nothing is free, Dreamwalker."

Of course not, Miya thought drolly. "Name your price."

A wet sound vibrated from the creature, its tongue lashing from side to side. "I yearn to drown something. To hold a life in my hands and feel it thrash against my will. Bring me something to drown—the stronger the better—and I will tell you anything you wish to know."

Gavran bristled next to her, silently imploring her to choose him.

"Tell me what I want to know, and you can have a go at me," she said instead.

Whirling, Gavran gawped at Miya while the monster considered her.

"Think about it." Miya ignored her companion as he tugged at her hand. "Drowning a goat or a child is not much of a feat. But the Dreamwalker? That must mean something here. As you said, everyone knows me."

A low growl warbled in the bukavac's throat. "Fine. I will answer one question."

Miya nodded, accepting the bargain.

"Are you mad?" Gavran hissed.

She narrowed her eyes at him. "You think I can't best an overgrown toad with moldy antlers?"

"Well—"

"It still has its tadpole tail!"

"Fine," Gavran grumbled, pouting.

Worming her hand out of his grasp, Miya ambled closer and peered up at the bukavac. "I want to know if a girl came through here. A human girl."

The creature raised a clawed hand and stroked its pliant chin. "I have been here a long while...watching, waiting. Sometime recently—perhaps a day, perhaps a decade—I saw a girl slip through. Can't say if she was human, though. So many things wear human-like costumes." It tossed Gavran a pointed glance. "Left a tear in the seam, she did. Young thing had no idea how to properly part the curtain between your world and mine. I thought of drowning her, but she was in such a hurry, I hadn't the time to lure her to my waters."

Miya's heart leapt into her throat, her vision blurring with moisture. A girl who tore through the seam of reality. Another who straddled the fault lines between worlds. Even if Caelan wasn't the Dreamwalker, she was something similar.

The prospect made Miya's chest swell with a confusing cocktail of dread and hope. She was no longer alone; she had Kai, Ama, Crowbar, and Gavran, but it wasn't always so. She remembered living like a hangnail in a town where everyone knew their place—or at least pretended to. She remembered the isolation, the terror that gripped her when her abilities burgeoned. What if Caelan Carver was living Emiliya Delathorne's nightmare?

"Are you finished with your reverie, Dreamwalker?"

The creature lunged, nimble despite its size. The gate crunched under its weight as it launched from its perch, hairline fissures skittering through stone. Its jaw unhinged, the strings of tethered flesh stretching like rubber bands, and it soared toward her, tail whipping in predatory anticipation.

"Shit!" Miya darted out of reach, her figure shimmering as the stone at her breastbone hummed with power. It was more than a compass in an umbral world. It was a weapon, and it yearned to be wielded.

Black and violet smoke spiraled over her limbs, rushed up her spine, and contoured over her skull. A cloak of lustrous feathers cocooned her body like a shield, and a raven-beak mask stretched down her nose, the point curling over her lip. Midnight and amethyst swirled over the ivory in a mesmerizing dance, and as the Dreamwalker straightened, she understood what Gavran meant when he said she was bigger in the dreamscape.

The bukavac was gargantuan, yet what it boasted in size it lacked in mettle. In the dreamscape, physicality did not reign. The shadows of long-dead trees lived as towering guardians because they willed it. Ravens took the form of young boys because they desired it. Gods worshipped themselves into existence simply for the pleasure of it. Every being that traversed the dreamscape made itself in its chosen image, and the Dreamwalker had chosen hers because it terrified those who sought to control her—to corral her into obedience. She refused.

While demons fashioned fear from people's nightmares, they were a dime a dozen. Only the Dreamwalker was strong enough—fierce enough in presence and conviction—to brandish death to the deathless.

A slimy tail whipped out and coiled around Miya's body—a vise around her limbs. The creature reeled her in at warp speed, then dove for the inky pond, dragging her into the murk. Her eyes clamped shut, but she could see the faint lavender glow of the dream stone behind her eyelids, illuminating the abyss encasing her. She heard the demon's gargling laugh —felt its glee vibrating through her bones.

She'd agreed to let the bukavac try to drown her, but she never agreed to die.

Feathers sharpened into spurs, slicing along the bukavac's supple tail. A muffled shriek reached her ears, and her bonds slackened just enough for her to free an arm. She closed her fingers around the dream stone and tugged. The pendant came free. Purple wisps lashed from her grip, and the fang-shaped labradorite elongated into a dagger that resembled volcanic glass splashed with gold, violet, and verdant light. The bone haft, carved into a raven, solidified in her hand, its beak at the butt of the knife serving as a small but deadly hawkbill.

Her eyes shot open, and she spared a moment to revel in the silver glimmers of the deep. The opaque water was as beautiful as a night sky on a mountain summit. Her lungs began to burn, and she thrust the blade down into the underside of the bukavac's tail, slitting him open from navel to heart. She felt the rush of viscera against her hand, felt the current as he thrashed to flee. His fear was salt on her tongue—tangible as the cold on her skin. Kicking off him, she threw her arms out and catapulted from the pond. Dark water erupted around her, then plummeted back into the crater in a violent cascade. The bukavac didn't follow.

Miya landed on the cobbled path.

A bewildered and sopping raven-boy stood beneath the stone gate. "That's it?" Gavran asked, shaking off his arms.

"That's it." Miya shrugged.

"What a soft little frog," the boy scoffed, and Miya responded with a giggle.

Kai would've loved to fight a bukavac. She imagined him leaned against a nearby tree with a bored expression, droning at her to watch her left. He'd twirl his hunting knife around his fingers, sigh regretfully, then gripe that he never gets to stab giant murder toads with sloughing antlers and lizard tails.

Next time they were in peril together, he'd have to call dibs.

7
KAI

IT WAS close to four in the morning when Kai returned, his body and ego equally bruised. He didn't have to flick on the light to know Miya was curled up on the couch waiting for him; her anxiety wafted through the air like a bitter odor.

She sat up, the throw sliding from her shoulders. "Where the hell have you been?"

Worry and agitation laced her voice, the latter winning out now that he was home. He hit the switch, and the dull overhead bulb winked on. "Sorry."

She'd probably called a dozen times, but his phone had died while he'd been hashing out the terms of his blunder with Sergei.

Trailing over him with widening eyes, her gaze lingered on his jaw where fresh bruises had bloomed. She flew off the couch and cradled his face between her hands. "What happened?"

He fled her probing stare, fixating on the floor between them. "I met someone like me."

Her fingers stilled against his cheekbones. "What?"

"I lost." It came out strangled, and he chuckled darkly. He really was stunned.

Miya's mouth hung open as she parroted him. "You lost?" She stepped away, hands dropping to her sides. "Back up. What do you mean, you met someone like you?"

"Big Russian guy. Smelled like Siberia. Strongest, fastest motherfucker I've ever seen." He swallowed, fighting against the lump clotting his throat. "Said his name was Ivan Zverev."

65

Miya was silent as she sieved through the information. "Is he a wolf? Like you and Ama?"

"I don't know." It didn't matter. His parents had been like him, but it wasn't just genetic; he was the reincarnation of a god of destruction: Sendoa, the wolf from the Dreamwalker's fable. None of it made sense. Even Ama wasn't like him—a different bloodline, an origin she wouldn't disclose.

Miya sat down on the couch's armrest. "And you said he smelled like Siberia?"

Kai nodded, exhaustion tugging at his bones. "We might be from the same area."

Miya knew he was born in Surgut, Western Siberia to a Russian father and a Tatar mother. They left when he was young, and he remembered only fragments of his life before Alice. Curious about his heritage, Miya had researched the region's history while he feigned indifference, but he'd listened while she regaled him about Tatar and Slav migrations, deportations, and the oil boom of the '60s. In the absence of something concrete, he quietly adopted Miya's theories. They were true for someone, and they might've been true for him too.

"Are you okay?" Her question snapped him back.

"I'm good," he said automatically, then bit the side of his tongue. Connor was right. He had no clue what he was talking about. "I'll be fine," he amended, scooping her from the armrest and planting a kiss on her forehead. He was tired, and he didn't want to talk—a convenient excuse to omit the worst part of his night.

"Are you okay for money?" she asked.

"Money's not a problem." Vague, but technically not a lie.

Miya accepted his evasion and pressed her lips to the uninjured side of his jaw. "Coming to bed?"

"I'll be there after I shower." His hold on her slackened, and she disappeared into the bedroom.

With a heavy sigh, Kai trudged to the bathroom, feeling like a sack of shit. Stripping off his clothes, he gripped either side of the sink and took stock of himself in the mirror. If his ribs were tender before, they were completely mangled now. A mural of blue mottled one side of his abdomen and stretched over his hipbone all the way to his groin. His legs were shredded from the strain, and he'd definitely pulled a hamstring. Shadows clung to the hollows beneath his eyes, the faint purple matching the bruises lining his cheek and jaw. His lip was split again, and he ran his tongue over the swollen scab, iron and salt greeting him. Despite the wraps, his knuckles were scraped raw. Several of his fingers were jammed, and at least one was fractured. Scratching through his disheveled black hair, his hand came away moist with sweat, and he reached into the shower to turn the knob. Normally, he preferred cold showers, but something warm on his skin sounded...nice. He had more than the loss weighing on him, and he was pissed that Sergei hadn't told him the stakes of losing.

Kai closed his eyes and let the water cascade down his back. It took a while for his hair to soak; it was like the double coat that protected him when he was a wolf—coarse and water resistant to guard from the elements. In the dreamscape, he could transition seamlessly between his two forms, but here, restricted by the laws of nature, it was excruciating. Like being broken apart and put back together.

He took his time lathering up, distracted as he replayed the night's events. Apparently, he'd lost something highly coveted by two competing factions of Bratva—one of them run by Sergei's boss, Pyotr. Neither could claim the thing because it'd been discovered on neutral territory. Unwilling to start a turf war, the match at the Confessional was meant to determine who'd claim the prize. And because Kai had squandered the damn thing, Sergei demanded he steal it back before the other faction retrieved it.

So much for a fair contest.

The mission was entirely covert; Pyotr didn't know that Sergei planned to *surprise* him with the retrieval. Kai had refused, but shirking a debt to Bratva wasn't that simple. He could skip town, but he knew from experience that outrunning demons was like pulling a gun on a fruit fly. For the first time in his miserable life, he'd built his own home, and he wasn't alone. He had Miya, Crowbar, and Bastien. They depended on each other, and Sergei made no bones of reminding him.

"We know you've got a girl at home. She works at that bar your friends run, yeah? That's in our territory," he'd said as he snuck a puff of his cigarette. "Is all that worth sacrificing because you don't want to get your hands a little dirty?"

Fuck. Why hadn't Sergei told him that if he lost, his life would change?

Kai rinsed out the suds, then leaned against the cold tiles, enjoying the water a few moments longer. Sergei called it *the forgery*, though he couldn't explain what it was.

"You'll know it when you see it," was all he'd divulged, but he had no leads on where this neutral party was stashing it. The location would be revealed to the winner, and Kai had until the exchange to filch it.

Vigorously toweling off, he stepped out of the steaming bathroom, the cool hallway air prickling his skin. As soon as he crawled into bed, Miya rolled over and plastered herself to him. He wrapped an arm around her and exhaled slowly. He had to tell her. He could excuse not doing it tonight, but tomorrow...

She mumbled, the crown of her head fitting snuggly under his jaw. Guilt settled in the pit of his gut like a stone. He'd messed up. Really, really messed up. He tried keeping Miya out of Bratva business, but he'd been naïve to think they wouldn't eventually leverage her. Her absence from his fights staved off a few prying eyes, but it was impossible to avert every pair.

Kai refused to drag her further into his shit. He'd fix this quickly and quietly, and when he was done, he'd tell Sergei to keep him out of mob business. Anything less would earn him a maw around his jugular.

Maybe then he could show Miya how badly he wanted her at the Confessional with him.

He had to find out where this forgery was kept. Sifting through Bratva was out of the question, but maybe an outside party would be willing to squeal—someone like him. A freelancer.

Kai's heart juddered in his chest. There was, in fact, someone like him.

Ivan Zverev.

He'd probably been contracted for the fight like Kai, which meant he had no real stake in this charade. Mobsters had loose tongues, and Vanya Zverev had sharp ears.

All Kai had to do was sniff out his kin.

His nerves settled now that he had a plan, but the rest of him revolted at having to interact with Zverev.

Zverev.

What was it about those six letters that twisted him up?

Kai let his weight sink into the mattress, his eyelids heavy with exhaustion even as his mind reeled. His thoughts raced in an incoherent blur, and when he could no longer cling to a single thread, his body finally let go.

8

EVERYTHING STANK LIKE SHIT. *His vision was blurry, muffled sobs and desolate keens filtering through his awareness. Traces of manure smeared the floor at his boots. Splintering boards dug into his back, the coarsely woven fabric of his shirt damp with sweat. His skin itched furiously, but he couldn't find the strength to tear the damn tweed from his torso.*

Someone bumped his shoulder, then coughed—too close. He flinched away and grimaced, shoving the invader from his personal space. His hand looked different—smaller, more calloused than usual. Swollen knuckles, a crooked ring finger; the bone hadn't been set right. He stretched his aching legs—hadn't they been longer?

Slowly, the murk thinned, and his vision sharpened. Wooden walls and ceiling. A car of some kind. Cattle train? It sure as hell smelled like it. His gaze wandered. Bodies everywhere. Some were prone, unmoving. Others sat slumped like him, the light stolen from their eyes. Children wailed with fever and reeked of sickness.

Everything reeked of sickness.

He glanced down, evaluating his clothes. A uniform. A mossy shade of green caked in grime. A body that didn't belong to him. Emaciated. Weak.

Panic suffused him.

He tried to speak, but nothing came out. He was trapped in another's flesh. Trapped on a train with people packed together like pickled fish in a jar. They were putrefying—rotting from illness and hunger. He couldn't move or speak—only observe.

But he didn't want *to observe.*

Fuck, fuck, fuck.

Finally, a voice that sounded like his own cleaved through the cacophony. It was inside his head, but it was something.

He had to get out of this husk. Get out of this car. Get off this train. He willed the body to move, straining against the weight of this alien skin on his soul. He was an interloper, but he didn't care. He'd get out.

Finally, movement. A knee bent. A hand braced against the floor, grains of mud and shit biting into his palm. He pushed and pushed until the car tipped, and he found his feet. Searing pain shot through his back, and he limped forward, nudging through bodies that gave way like ragdolls. Some were catatonic, nothing but meat.

Light bordered the slats of a door on the opposite side of the car. A way out. He waded through the limbs—so many limbs—and reached for the metal lever. He pulled, and the door slid open.

Darkness awaited.

When Kai stepped through, he was at his full height. The muscle had woven back over his bones; he'd returned to his own body, but his relief dampened as his attention shifted to his surroundings.

He was where he'd started on the opposite side of the car. At his feet sat the man he'd been one with, his head bowed, his shoulders slumped. Dark, unkempt hair brushed his shoulders. He still wore the uniform, and Kai realized he was a soldier. Then, the man raised his head. His face was gaunt and pallid, shadows collecting in every crevice, but his brown eyes sparked with fire, a red gleam that promised a fight. Those eyes, somehow still burning, flickered to Kai. The soldier's mouth thinned as he stared at the intruder who'd puppeteered him moments earlier. Then, his gaze drifted down the car.

Kai rotated in place, and the cabin chirred. The door at the end of the wagon shrank as the panels stretched and tilted. Meat hooks sprouted on the walls—black iron coated in something sticky. Blood. The train shook, the fragile light guttering. Murmurs rose like a wave, the scent of fear snaking between the passengers, coalescing in the space behind Kai's ribs. Then, the train screeched. The floor pitched forward, forcing Kai to a knee as he fought for balance. Darkness descended, bathing the wagon in a sightless pall.

Kai's heavy breaths thundered in his ears—the sole sound in the deathly train. Saliva filled his mouth as a sour stench washed over him, and the light from outside blinked through the slats.

Human bodies drained of blood hung on the meat hooks like carcasses. Sharp metal lanced their flesh, their necks bent at deviant angles. Broken marionettes. They twitched and squelched with the car's every jostle, and their unblinking, peeled-open eyes bore into nothingness.

Kai had never been squeamish. He'd seen his share of carnage, endured terrors that had no right existing. What lay before him was no more gruesome, but there was a harrowing familiarity—a creeping dread about the train, about the people hanging from its walls—that soaked through his skin and settled in the marrow of his bones.

Maybe he truly was broken.

Kai spun in search of the soldier. He was still there, knees drawn to his chest, eyes fixed on Kai. The train groaned, the wheels shrieking, but the two men remained locked on one another, tethered by an invisible cord.

Finally, Kai permitted himself a breath and asked, "Who are you?"

The man's eyes, dark and red like burnt clay, flashed with recognition, but he didn't speak. He reached into his jacket, the lapels stained crimson, and retrieved a weathered piece of card.

He held it out to Kai, beckoning him to approach.

9

MIYA

THE SOUR SMELL of rot soaked into Miya's pores, repelling her from the darkness ahead. She clapped a hand over her mouth and lurched, her throat tightening as she fought down the sick.

What fetid corner of the dreamscape had she stumbled into? This place was foreign—not her dream.

She straightened and tried to gather her bearings, but the world was bathed in opaque shadow. As she tugged the dream stone from her shirt, its pale lavender light cocooned her in familiar warmth—a comfort against the cold and damp. She unhooked her finger from the delicate chain, and the pendant hovered like an iridescent firefly. Metal and lumber whined like the rusted frame of an old ship. As Miya took a cautious step forward, she realized she was barefoot, her attire mirroring that of the waking world.

"Great, walking through a horror film in my pajamas." Granules of dirt scratched at her heels. Each stride sent a jolt through her skin, but she pressed on until the dream stone illuminated an iron door raked with vicious claw marks.

Fear slithered up her spine at the sight of the gnarled thing, but she knew not to fight the dream. If she fled, it would warp around her, taking her back to where it wanted her. She had to surrender—to relinquish control so the dream could impart its message. She used to wander into people's nightmares unbidden, living their terror until she learned not to stray. Now, it only occurred when the dreamer was nearby and in severe distress.

Miya's hand closed around the icy doorknob—scuffed, black-stained brass that belonged in a centuries-old wreck. It refused to turn smoothly, shuddering as the mechanism squealed from the friction. When the latch came free, she gave the door a small push, and it chirred open. A long, narrow cabin with bloodied wooden walls awaited. Bodies were strewn across the floor—a feast for the flies—and the smell of excrement mingled with the stench of decay. Carcasses hung from sharp hooks on the walls, but Miya didn't dare look. She didn't want to see their faces—didn't want them following her into the waking world.

She had no clue whose nightmare this was, but what they carried was more than a mere burden. It was a devouring thing, winding through their soul and twisting them up.

Miya peered down the aisle, the murk impenetrable save for the occasional glare stealing through the cracks between wooden slats. Shadows danced over the walls with every flash, and at the end of the cabin, a man stood with his back turned to her.

His strong frame and unruly black hair were a blade through her heart. She'd know him anywhere—in any darkness.

"Kai."

He spun at the sound of her voice, shock parting his lips. The unspoken flooded his expression—shame, guilt, confusion, and grief swirling like a vortex that threatened to consume him.

"What are you doing here?" His voice was hard, innocuous words sharpened into thorns.

Miya staggered back, panic vising around her limbs. She was in Kai's nightmare, and he knew it. She'd intruded on a part of him he'd never shown her—a part he didn't even show himself. A half-formed apology seared her lips. I didn't mean to, she wanted to say, but she could only stare at him as he stared back, the distance between them both cavernous and confining.

"I'm sorry," she blurted at last, but Kai made no response. Brow creased, he scrutinized her sudden appearance, and when he squared himself toward her, she noticed someone behind him—a man slumped against the wall, holding something out.

"Miya—" Kai began, but she didn't wait for him to finish.

She squeezed her eyes shut, clinched her clammy fingers around the dream stone, and barred herself from the chilling specter of her lover's inner world.

10

WAKEFULNESS CAME AS A BURNING GASP. The air felt like knives scraping down his throat, cold sweat beading his forehead and jaw. Kai sat up faster than his body was prepared for, the rush of blood to his head leaving his vision mottled with black. He squeezed his eyes shut—squeezed until it hurt—and rubbed away the ache in his temples.

Beside him, Miya started with the same agonized breath, gulping down oxygen until it filled her lungs. He wanted to ask if she was okay, but he couldn't bear to look at her. Not after what she'd seen. She threw the blankets from her legs and reached to comfort him, her warmth nibbling away the chill.

"No." He grabbed her hands, his voice hoarse. "Stay out of my head."

He'd said those words the first time she'd ever seen inside him— pierced through his armor and grabbed his demons by the balls. Unaccustomed to feeling so raw, he'd lashed out, the statement a vicious rebuke. It was the first time they'd fought—the first time he'd felt his blood boil because someone had gotten too close for comfort.

Now, those words were little more than a gentle plea. Kai knew there was no scaring Miya off. He was her protector, but when it came to the monsters he couldn't see, she protected him.

"I'm sorry."

She sounded panicked, guilt lacing every syllable. Her pulse hammered frantically, anxiety seeping into his skin like ink into

75

fabric. He'd frightened her. After five years together, there was still a piece of him that didn't feel safe. He wanted to cut it out like the cancer it was—curb stomp it into an indiscernible slop—but it was like amputating a limb for an infection that'd already spread.

His sickness was systemic.

Kai released her hands, and her fingers skimmed over his cheekbones, raked through his hair. He didn't stop her this time. She pulled him close, and he buried his nose in the crook of her neck, his breath like lava on her skin. She was shakier than he was, her body trembling against his.

"I didn't mean to. It just...happens sometimes."

"I know," he said softly, his arm cinching around her lower back.

Despite the reassurance, she mumbled another apology like he didn't believe her. He knew how much she practiced. She'd gone from stumbling into strangers' nightmares to commanding every ethereal cranny, but the more intense the dream, the harder it was to stay out. And with Kai, it was especially dicey. They were so close—emotionally and physically. He couldn't keep his shit under lock and key when she was right next to him, and it bled through the cracks of his carefully crafted shield. He knew it wasn't her fault, but he hated it—loathed not having a filter between her gaze and the ugliest parts of him.

He felt her throat bob as her arms slid from his shoulders. "We should maybe talk about—"

Kai shook his head. "No."

She bit her tongue and swallowed her objection. Miya knew how much he valued his agency. On this, she wouldn't push him. Instead, she eased herself back down and stared at the ceiling. She was displeased, but Kai wasn't going to budge. He followed her lead and turned onto his side, his palm sliding over her bare stomach under her T-shirt.

"If you think you can seduce me—"

"I'm not trying to seduce you," he chuckled, then welded her against his chest. He swept her hair aside to plant a tender kiss below her jaw. Her hand found his, still pressed to her stomach, and she settled against him, her eyes drifting shut. It was still dark out— too soon for her to give up on sleep.

But Kai had no intention of returning to that train soaked in death. What the soldier wanted to give him, he'd never know.

11

MIYA

"GOT YOUR KEYS?" Miya asked as she wrestled with the front door. The wooden slab sat wonkily in the frame, and she yanked it to force the latch into place.

Kai fished his keys from his pocket and dangled them off his middle finger.

Miya rolled her eyes, then made for the stairs. "You're the one who always forgets them."

He'd been quiet all morning, the vestiges of last night clinging to him like a sticky film. They'd woken up in each other's arms, limbs tangled and hearts heavy, neither saying a word until restlessness whittled away their inertia. Miya wanted to talk about what'd happened—what she'd seen in his nightmare—but Kai had sealed it away by sunrise. He'd stonewalled her.

He smiled wryly. "Left a note on the door to remind myself."

"I appreciate you not having to break into our apartment every other day."

Kai *tsked* half-heartedly. "I could pick the lock with my eyes closed, Lambchop."

"I prefer the notes."

He'd mentioned an ADHD diagnosis from childhood, though it'd fallen by the wayside amid everything else. After Alice found him bloodied and injured in the woods, he barely spoke—refused to talk about what'd happened. Uninterested in other kids, he spent most of his time alone, distrustful of others. Post-traumatic stress disorder seemed the obvious culprit. But when his teachers complained of inattentiveness and months of homework piling up, ADHD was added to his file. Alice drove him from Granite Falls to Seattle every week for therapy despite barely scrounging up the gas money. Defiant to the end, his progress stalled out, and after puberty hit, the therapist tacked on conduct disorder. Apparently, the institution lost sympathy when he didn't grow out of his trauma by his teens.

The labels racked up like my one-night stands, he'd told her the first time they'd talked about it.

The longer Miya lived with him, the more his behavior made sense, from his constant thrill-seeking to his tendency to zone out and litter the apartment with empty candy wrappers. When life was an unyielding bid for survival, he operated on pure animal instinct, but the need to blend into society—to be a part of it— exposed how differently he functioned. It also made his line of work more palatable for her; he couldn't endure ordinary employment even if he had the paperwork to make it possible.

Noticing her withdraw, Kai gave her a sidelong glance. "Lambchop…"

"If you're going to act like everything's fine, then so will I."

He deflated like a party balloon. His arms came around her waist at the bottom of the stairs, and he hauled her close. "I don't know how to talk about it."

Miya slackened in his hold. He was telling the truth. "You'll have to figure out how to talk about it eventually. If you don't, it'll only get worse."

To that he tightened his grip, his fingers threading gently through her hair. He'd always been like this—preferring touch to words. All those sharp edges, tempered by his capacity for affection. She relished the raw intimacy they shared, but it wasn't enough. Ivan Zverev had clearly rattled Kai, but until he was ready to talk, she could only resent his silence.

Miya reluctantly peeled herself away. "I'm meeting Crowbar at the King of Spades."

Kai dropped his arms and nodded. "I'll be at the Confessional."

"Say hi to Connor for me?"

"Yeah, will do."

A smile ghosted his lips as Miya turned to leave, shadows

clinging to the tired lines of his face. Sorrow gathered there, waiting for him to take notice.

Miya tore a piece of garlic bread from the loaf and offered it to the domovoy. He greedily snatched it up and stuffed it down his gullet. Behind her, Bastien carried boxes of produce into the kitchen, yelling for Crowbar to stop dawdling and help him.

"Chill, man, I was fridging the eggs," she griped as she passed him on her way out.

"Still got bottles to bring in," he called over his shoulder, disappearing through the double doors. He was utterly hulking, his head nearly grazing the top of the frame.

Crowbar scoffed and stomped outside, then brought in the last of the boxes. As she unpacked the bottles behind the bar, Bastien joined her. He tossed his bleached dreadlocks over his shoulder and wiped his brow, his dark skin beaded with moisture.

"I've got some new recipes for the kitchen," he said excitedly. "Crab cakes with a southern flare, my custom blend mac and cheese, fried catfish, cheesy grits, cornbread, black eyed peas with ham hock and rice—"

"Easy, man, we don't have the funds for a menu that size," Crowbar dashed his hopes. "Pick three entrees and a few bar snacks, all right?"

Bastien made a high-pitched wail that had no right coming out of a man that big. "Fine. I'll stick with the crab cakes and the mac. Fried pickles and hush puppies for the bar."

The domovoy glanced up, his greasy little paws clutching Miya's last offering of garlic bread. He licked his nose, eager for Bastien's newest concoction. It was a pity no one could see him; of everyone who frequented the bar, the domovoy appreciated Bastien's cooking the most. Kai lived off it whenever he caught the Louisiana chef puttering around, but he was rarely as animated as their little house spirit.

Crowbar nodded. "Maybe some nachos for the basic bros and a fried chicken bucket for the potheads."

The domovoy smacked his lips, and Miya grinned. "You'll have at least one customer."

"Your angry arm candy with a black hole of a stomach?" Crowbar shot Miya a warning glower. Bastien was terrified of spirits, courtesy of his upbringing in the deep south where he oscillated between Louisiana and Georgia. His aunt was a Manbo, and between her tutelage and a community of fiercely devout Baptists, Bastien's respect for the supernatural teetered on fear. Christianity had done a number on him, and his aunt's world was dark and deep enough to instill a fretful reverence for the unseen.

Miya had no idea if Vodou spirits were anything like Slavic ones, but she figured they didn't quibble over national boundaries the way humans did. Ideas migrated like storm clouds, and no culture was insulated from their influence.

"Uh, yeah," Miya feigned. "Kai adores your food. He'd eat a leather shoe if you cooked it."

She didn't mention that the haint blue ceiling had little effect on the domovoy. Of course, it wouldn't; he wasn't a haint, but a docile guardian of the home. At least, while they kept him well-fed.

"Tell him to stop by. I need someone to sample the goods before they go live." Bastien gave Crowbar a hearty slap on the back. "All right, gal, I'll be back tomorrow when this place opens. You two have fun."

Crowbar groaned at the mention of *fun*. The King of Spades was closed on Mondays, which meant they usually spent it on housekeeping. She and Miya would burn the day unpacking stock, re-vamping the décor, and experimenting with different table layouts. Not that they had many tables.

"There's no rush," Miya reminded her as Bastien gathered his things and headed out. "We can take breaks."

"How about a break before we begin?" Crowbar proposed once Bastien was out the door. "I've got a new cocktail for our special menu, and you look like you could use a drink—mornings be damned."

Miya pouted at the callout. She gave the domovoy's furry cat ears a scritch, then headed for the stools. "Do I really look that glum?"

"You look tired," Crowbar clarified. "But now that I know you're glum, what's eating you?"

Grumbling at the giveaway, Miya climbed onto one of the stools. "I'm worried about Kai."

"Uh oh." Crowbar grabbed the white rum and St-Germaine from the shelf and flipped it in her hand. "Is he getting into more trouble than he should?"

"Not exactly..." she trailed off, watching her friend collect a lemon, Angostura bitters, soda water, purple luster dust, and a bundle of herbs. "What is that?"

Crowbar pulled apart the mint. "Hang on, I need the dry ice."

"Sounds fancy..."

The bartender's eye sparked with glee as she measured out the ingredients. "I call it the Dreamwalker. Purple, sweet, but not without some herbal bite and a dry ice smoke show."

Miya felt her heart swell in her chest. "You named a drink after me?"

"Come on, girl. You're a badass. I mean, I had to ask Kai for some of the details about your whole witchy getup. Can't say he's too good at giving descriptions, so if you've got any alterations you'd like to make—"

"No, no, it's perfect."

"I know you like mint, so I found a way to include it." Garnishing the glass with the sage sprig, Crowbar pushed her violet concoction across the bar, the milky vapors wafting from the glass and cascading over the rim like an ethereal fog.

Miya took a careful sip. "Holy shit—that's amazing."

Crowbar crossed her arms over her chest, puffing with pride. "It's going on the menu. Now"—she got to wiping off the counter—"what's up with our prizefighter? Did he lose or something?"

Miya's shoulders slumped as she let out a long sigh. "Actually, yes..."

Crowbar dropped her cloth, "I'm sorry, what?"

Miya chewed on her lip, then took a generous gulp of her namesake cocktail. She relayed what Kai had told her, sparing no detail about his run-in with Ivan Zverev. Crowbar was so stunned that she pulled up a stool, her jaw slack as she stared at Miya, bug-eyed.

"His match with Zverev shook him up—reminded him of a past he has no access to," said Miya.

Crowbar leaned back. "Well, fuck."

"And there's nothing I can do. He's gone for the day, probably hiding at Connor's. I mean, he told me he didn't know how to talk about it." Another hefty gulp.

"He's a cis dude." Crowbar waved a hand. "Asking him to unpack his shit is like trying to get a gaggle of murderous geese to cross the road faster."

Miya nodded, thumbing at the condensation on her glass. "Life's taught him that anger and spite keep you alive. I love his resilience, but trauma doesn't just go away. It's with you forever."

Crowbar's gaze drifted to her knees as she picked at the loose threads of her torn jeans. "He lost his parents pretty young, yeah?"

"When he was ten. He still treats it like some distant event he has no connection to. Doesn't help that Alice died of lung cancer when he was sixteen." Miya smiled softly. "He really loved her, and I think watching the life seep out of her really messed him up."

"Twice orphaned." Crowbar plopped her cheek into her hand. "Think he'd go to therapy?"

Miya shifted on her stool. "Alice took him when he was a kid, but it was mandatory. He doesn't deny the diagnoses, though it took him a while to admit he's still struggling with PTSD. I'm not sure he'd go without a fight."

Crowbar hummed. "It's a tough pill to swallow when you're a rambunctious punk who can't go ten minutes without picking a fight. Must've made him feel helpless."

"Yeah," Miya acknowledged. "Not his style."

"Well, I hope you can get him into therapy. Sounds like he could use it."

"Me too." She sighed wistfully, then snickered after a lull. "Can you imagine Kai in a therapist's office?"

They blinked at each other, then burst into giggles.

"He'd glare a hole right through the shrink's skull," Crowbar gasped.

"And she'd tell him to use his words!"

"I'm sensing some tension right now," Crowbar feigned with rote compassion and a stiff spine.

Tears stung Miya's eyes. "He'd have an aneurism."

"Good thing he heals fast."

Cursing loudly, Miya choked on her drink, hacking as the rum burned her throat. The front doors burst open then, and she half expected an eerie fog to waft into the King of Spades as Ama's perfect silhouette parted the morning glow. She raised her arm and shook a paper bag that dangled from her hand. "I come bearing gifts."

Crowbar's eyes lit up. "Are those—"

"Beignets...a little taste of home." Ama grinned, pleased with herself.

Crowbar leapt over the counter and threw her arms around Ama, then landed half a dozen kisses over the white wolf's face. "I've been *begging* Bastien to make me some of these, but he's been so preoccupied with his menu."

Ama lathered up the attention, playfully whisking the pastry bag out of Crowbar's reach every time she tried to snatch it. "Who needs Bastien when you have me?" She caught the bartender's lips, then surrendered the beignets.

From the corner of her eye, Miya caught Gavran swoop down onto a lamppost outside. He pecked at the window in greeting, and she smiled tenderly and waved in return.

"Anything interesting happen today?" Crowbar asked as she shoved a beignet into her mouth, the tip of her nose stained with powdered sugar.

"No, not really," said Ama. "But there was this scrumptious-looking man at the patisserie..."

Crowbar's cheeks puffed like a chipmunk's as she chewed on her treat. "Stop tormenting me with your bisexual whiles, you vixen."

Ama wrapped an arm around Crowbar's waist and nuzzled her cheek. "Please, Dahlia, men aren't worth the trouble."

They both shot Miya a pitying look, their lips pursed as they held back their titters.

"Hey, I have no complaints," Miya protested.

"Liar," Crowbar accused, and Miya's mouth hung open in affront.

"Well, you already know my verdict." Ama threw Miya a pointed look. "Attractive but insufferable."

Crowbar tutted. "I think he's a good egg. Definitely easy on the eyes, though."

Miya and Ama's eyebrows shot up as they stared incredulously at the barkeep.

"What?" She shrugged. "I'm gay, not blind."

"Nobody tell him," Ama warned, pointing a stern figure at each of them.

A chorus of mirthful laughter erupted throughout bar, warming Miya's bones. She loved Crowbar and Ama. They'd become family —sisters as much as they were friends.

"As if he needs to be told," Crowbar guffawed. "You just don't want to give him ammo in your endless dick-waving contest."

"It wouldn't kill you to be nice to him sometimes." Miya nudged Ama's shoulder.

The white wolf narrowed her eyes. "It's not like *he's* very nice."

"I know this might come as a shock"—Crowbar mockingly squeezed her girlfriend's hand—"but he responds quite well to sincerity."

"Sure, once you get past six feet of snark and fragile masculinity."

Whistling in surprise, Crowbar cast Miya an expectant stare.

Miya flung her hands up. "I'm biased. You defend him."

Crowbar cleared her throat and turned back to Ama. "I've seen worse."

"Oh, good," Ama deadpanned.

Miya smiled ruefully, her finger tracing invisible patterns on the bar top. "He's working on it."

Crowbar reached for the tequila and poured them each a shot, then raised her glass in a toast. "To my favorite women in the whole world, and that hot guy who's working on it."

Miya winced as the liquor burned down her throat. Neither Ama nor Crowbar bothered with the citrus or the salt, so she toughed it out, swallowing until the bitter taste faded.

Ama's bright amber eyes snagged Miya's half-finished drink on the counter. "How's that new cocktail menu going?"

Crowbar slammed her shot glass down and grinned. "Almost finished"—she winked—"and I've finally hammered out the drink named after my beloved: the White Wolf."

Ama's perfect mask of breezy indifference finally cracked as a glimmer of excitement crossed her features. "What's in it?"

"It's basically a birthday cake in a cup, specially brewed to suit your sweet tooth." Crowbar fired off the ingredients, counting them on her fingers. "Kahlúa Salted Caramel, vodka, and heavy cream shaken together, then topped with whipped cream, caramel sauce, and sprinkles."

"Jesus, you're perfect," Ama cooed adoringly. "Make me one?"

Crowbar reached for the vodka. "Anything for you, pups."

Miya privately wondered how Kai would react to being called *pups* and suppressed a cackle. His disdain for domesticated animals was legendary, and while he seemed to maintain a begrudging respect for the occasional feral cat, dogs topped his list of man-made blunders.

Sitting shoulder to shoulder, Miya and Ama busied themselves with drinks that looked far too pretty for consumption. Crowbar sat across from them, her arms folded on the bar top as she scrutinized their reactions.

"So, we're out of leads for Caelan?" Ama asked as she spooned the whipped cream from her drink.

Miya nodded. "I have an idea, though."

"Go on…"

"Anyone who's been touched by the dreamscape leaves a trace in the physical realm." The bukavac had confessed to seeing a girl who fit Caelan's description pass through the dreamscape and into the waking world. "If we swipe a personal item from Caelan's home, I might be able to track her."

"How does that work, exactly?" asked Crowbar.

"The object is like an anchor," Miya explained. "If I plug into it while I dreamwalk, I might be able to pick up on something, like an energetic trace. It's not an exact science; sometimes I get images, memories, but usually, they lead somewhere. Hopefully, we'll find a clue to Caelan's whereabouts."

Ama nodded, taking a hefty slurp of her liquid birthday cake. "A solid plan. How do we get into her home?"

Miya drummed her nails against her glass. "We can talk to her parents. Make up a story about how we're investigating teen disappearances and—"

"Or we can just break in while they're out and grab something from the girl's bedroom," Ama interjected with a casual shrug.

Crowbar snorted but offered no alternative, leaving Miya to fend for herself. "I guess...as long as we don't get caught." She frowned. "Too bad Kai isn't here. He's perfect for breaking laws."

Ama scoffed, downed the rest of her drink, and flipped her hair over her shoulder as she stood. "Please, Miya. I can break laws too, and I'll look twice as good while doing it.

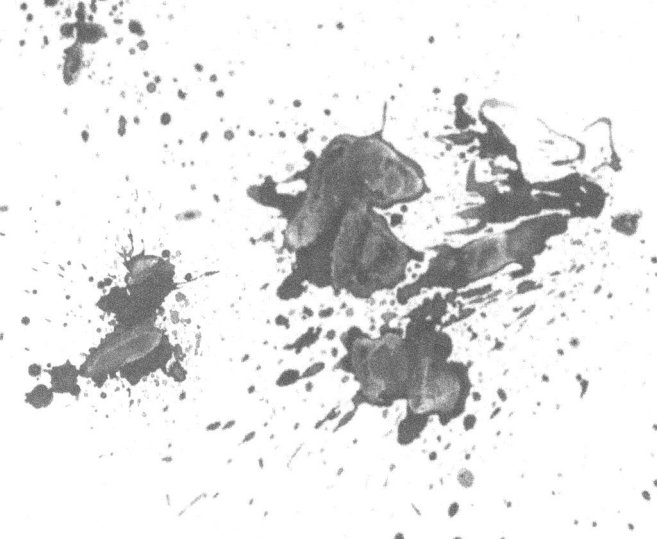

12

KAI

HE COULD STILL SMELL their rotting flesh. The stench of spoiled meat lingered, souring him to the thought of breakfast. A furious itch burned the backs of his eyes, the image of the man on the train etched into his brain like a brand.

He felt like shit. Not just from the nightmare, but from what followed as well. Miya had tried to help him, and he'd shoved her out the proverbial door. She deserved better than that. She deserved better than his fucked-up head, but he had nothing to offer. The best he could do was sort out his shit. Eventually. He had other blunders to deal with first.

Kai had been opaque about his reason for visiting the Confessional. He hated lying, even by omission, which was why he wanted his debt to Bratva cleared by happy hour. Without a word of greeting, he plunked down on the bar stool directly in front of Connor.

"You all right?" Connor asked as he polished a pint glass, his eyebrow quirking.

Kai gave a brittle smile. "Just licking my wounds."

The hulking Irishman grunted and flipped a clean tumbler onto the counter, then grabbed the Writers' Tears. "On the house," he said as he poured two fingers of whiskey.

Kai raised the glass in a gesture of gratitude and promptly guzzled the contents.

"You're off today, aren't you?"

Kai nodded. "No fights tonight."

"A little early for a visit, isn't it?" Connor glanced at his watch.

Kai ground his molars together in deliberation. He trusted Connor, but the less people knew, the better. Safer, too. His body was still bruised, but his heart felt like an open gash. He wanted to cauterize it, seal it shut no matter how badly it hurt.

"I'm meeting Sergei," he said vaguely, feigning ignorance as Connor scowled.

He poured Kai another generous finger. "You got business with that rank weasel?"

"More than I'd like at the moment." Kai swirled the tawny liquid around. Drowning in whiskey was tempting, but running from his demons was a sure-fire way to feed them. The hungry little fucks feasted well when he cast off his plights like a trail of breadcrumbs, and they always came around to puke up their dinner at his feet. In the end, he'd clean up the mess whether he liked it or not.

The door swung open, announcing Sergei's arrival with a conspicuous whine. He was dressed in business slacks and a crème button-up half-obscured by a tweed scarf and a dark jacket that looked too plain for its price tag. Sergei never skimped on clothing, measuring his worth in finery. It was a peculiar contrast to Kai's combat boots and cargo pants with pockets the size of Pennsylvania. The gray T-shirt and worn leather jacket only crystallized their differences—Kai an assemblage of jagged edges to Sergei's polished veneer.

"You look like shit," Sergei said by way of greeting. He offered Connor a terse nod, though the barkeep only sneered and promptly disappeared. "What's his problem with me?"

"He doesn't like it when you're mean to me." Kai refused to acknowledge the jab at his disheveled appearance.

Sergei slid onto a stool and removed his jacket. "I suppose you're a bit sensitive right now, given what happened."

It wasn't just the fight. Kai's nightmare clung to the recesses of his mind like a stubborn piece of gum on the sole of his shoe. He knew it was his own baggage—an unknown past he carried like a rotten keepsake. The corpses strung up on the walls of the train, the soldier huddled in the corner with a molten look in his eyes... what had he tried to give Kai?

It didn't help that Miya had stumbled into his personal hellscape. She was likely wracking her brain on new methods to crack him open and spill his insides out. He probably needed it. He just didn't want it.

"Hey, I have feelings." Kai placed a mocking hand over his heart. There was a sharpness to the words, a menace coating his smile as he showed Sergei his teeth—a friendly assurance and a palpable threat.

"My bad," Sergei droned without a grain of sincerity. He pulled his Zippo from his pocket, knocking it against the counter like it would somehow ease his craving. "What can I do to help?"

That part sounded sincere. Kai reckoned Sergei's ass was also on the line; he had to ensure Kai did his part.

"I need to find Ivan Zverev." That was harder to say than Kai thought.

The Zippo stilled in Sergei's hand. "The man who nearly beat your skull in? Why?"

"I lost the prize to him, didn't I? He might know something about its whereabouts."

"That's reckless," Sergei rebuked, slamming the lighter down.

Kai shrugged, unconcerned. "Everything I do is reckless, and it's the only lead we've got."

Sergei's jaw tightened, his tone coated in ice. "What makes you think he'll talk?"

"I've got a hunch," said Kai. "Call it animal instinct." *Literally.*

Sergei pinched the bridge of his nose and sighed. "Fine, but if you get us into deeper shit—"

"You know I won't," Kai ground out through clenched teeth. "We wouldn't be in this mess if you'd given me information sooner, so shut up and let me do what I do best."

"What you do best is cause trouble," Sergei snapped.

It shouldn't have stung, but it did. Kai caused pain to those he cared about too often. Fortunately, Sergei wasn't one of them. "I'll get it done," he said, then added quietly, "and I won't go down easy."

"Yeah, you're a fucking cockroach." Sergei combed his fingers through his hair, the vein in his temple popping as he weighed his options. He knew Kai was too stubborn to bite it on anyone else's terms. Finally, he leaned back and resumed playing with his Zippo. "You better not muck this up worse than you already have." He rotated to face Kai. "Unlike you, Vanya's a ghost. You've got a reputation around here—partying like some feral animal out of a cage."

Good. Kai wanted people to think he had nothing to lose, and tapping into his wild side did just that. Ironically, the best way to hide his secrets was to act like he had none. "What're you saying?"

"I'm saying that Vanya knows to stay away. He's a hard man to find."

"I'm just looking for a lead," Kai reminded him.

Sergei clicked his tongue. "Lucky for you, I keep my ear to the ground. Rumor has it he hangs around a flower shop."

Kai wrinkled his nose.

"The place is called O'Neil's—a small joint in Charleston," Sergei supplied. "I'm sure you and your...*intuition* will find it just fine."

Kai ignored the pointed comment and stood. "I'll check it out. Keep your shit together in the meantime, *milyy.*"

"What is it with you and nicknames?" Sergei sighed. He loathed being called *darling* more than Miya hated centipedes.

Kai flashed him a fiendish grin. "They make people more tolerable." He shouted goodbye to Connor, then disappeared into the street without a single platitude spared for Sergei.

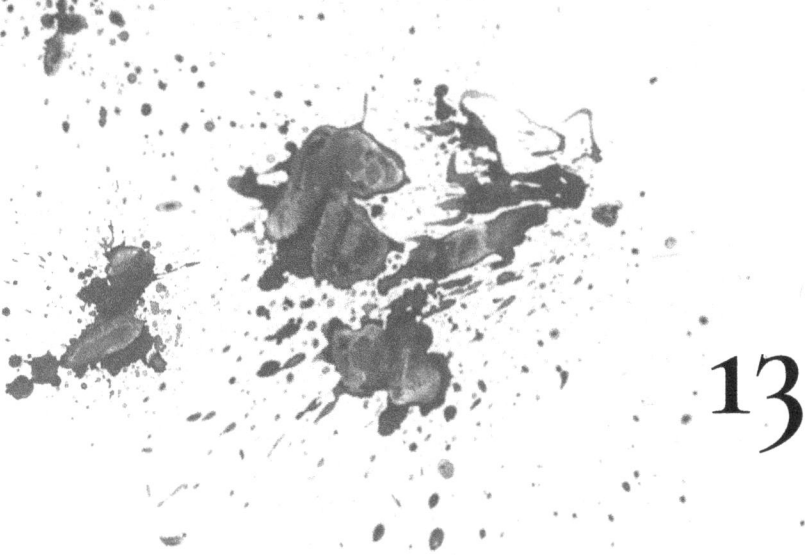

13

WEDGED between a pawn shop and an insurance broker, O'Neil's Florals stuck out like a piñata at a funeral. Pink and green signage framed the window display, a jungle of flowers and potted plants lining the shelves inside. For a Siberian tank affiliated with Bratva, Ivan Zverev kept strange company.

Kai gingerly approached the shop and pushed his way inside. An elderly man sat behind the counter, shaving the thorns off a rose stem. The blossom was a deep crimson, each petal lush and silky as though it'd been bred for a bouquet. Kai's nose tingled from the sweet aroma, leaving him lightheaded. He never fully acclimated to the sheer amount of sensory input he had to sift through, and although the years had taught him to filter most of it out, walking into a hotbox of perfumes still disoriented him.

"Can I help you?" the old man asked gruffly as he smacked his chewing gum, the hints of an Irish accent lilting his question.

There was wariness in his tone. Kai reckoned O'Neil's was known mostly to regulars, so a newcomer was as welcome as a hot turd on fresh asphalt. "Looking for Ivan Zverev," he cut to the chase. Even if he was in hostile territory, the old man would think twice before starting shit with someone he didn't know. The outcome wouldn't be pretty.

The shopkeeper carefully placed his rose on the counter and sheathed his knife. He was practiced with it. "Does this look like a place for one of yours?"

Kai smiled icily as he leaned a shoulder against the wall and crossed his arms. "What gave me away? The lack of translucent skin and pretty blue eyes? Or is it the hair? Too black and pointy?"

The old man's shoulders shook as he laughed like he had pebbles in his lungs. Lifelong smoker, no doubt. "You've got the eyes of a killer. Doesn't matter what color they are."

"Dark and brooding with a hint of hellfire, I've been told."

An unamused grunt. "You don't seem very brooding."

Kai's lips stretched over his teeth in a baleful grin. "I prefer *poorly socialized with a history of violence.*"

The shopkeeper hung his head, suppressing a low chuckle. "You're plucky. I like that." His gaze lifted, and the humor drained from the runnels of his face. "You'll find what you're looking for in the back."

"That's it?" Kai straightened, his hands gliding into his pockets. "Why give up the ghost so fast?"

"Vanya's a big boy. He can take care of himself."

"Fair enough." Kai shrugged. "Try anything and I'll shove a cactus up your ass."

"We don't sell cacti," the shopkeeper called after him.

Kai rolled his eyes on his way to the back room—a dimly lit office with an exit to a loading zone. The door was jammed open, and after a moment, Ivan Zverev strode in with a giant planter in his arms. His hair was tied up like the night they'd fought, and he'd traded out his tracksuit for a pair of worn jeans and an old T-shirt. His eyes slid to Kai, and he nodded curtly before plunking the impressive basket onto the desk.

"I was wondering when you'd show." He wasn't surprised to see Kai. No perspiration, jacked heartrate, or increased blood pressure.

"Didn't realize you were expecting me." Kai kept a respectable distance, hating that he felt the need to.

Ivan gave a half-hearted wave. "Just like you, I have a sense about things."

Kai stomped down the urge to take the bait. He had to focus; he was here for a reason, and it wasn't to pick *Vanya* apart. "What are you doing at an Irish florist's?"

"O'Neil's a good man, and I like it here," Zverev said. "Working with flowers keeps me calm."

A wolf in a fucking flower shop. How quaint. "I thought you work for a Bratva faction."

Ivan grabbed a pair of sheers and began trimming the foliage on one of the plants. "Something like that. It doesn't bar me from being here."

"What are you to them?" A freelancer, Kai was sure, but he wanted confirmation.

Zverev delicately pinched a stem between his fingers. The leaves bore pink and green splotches, reminiscent of the store's sign. "Same as you. Just another body for them to get rich on."

Some of the tension left Kai's shoulders. "Muscle for hire." His hunch had been right. "Your loyalty—"

"Only as good as the money," said Zverev, glancing at Kai.

A true merc, Kai thought. "The prize we fought over—know anything about it?"

"The forgery..." Ivan chuckled, spinning the basket to examine his handiwork. "Well, you know how it is. People talk louder than they realize."

A smile tugged at Kai's lips, and he finally stepped closer. "Any chance you're in a sharing mood?"

Ivan grinned, though his eyes remained on the planter he was dolling up. "Would it console you for your loss?"

A biting remark. "Spare me the participation trophy."

Zverev had no stake in what happened to the forgery; he'd already done his job, making him a free agent. More than that, he and Kai were both freaks in a world that held no space for them. If their positions had been reversed, Kai would've thrown Zverev a bone. He didn't like the guy, but they were of the same ilk, and that meant something.

Zverev finally set down the sheers. "The package is with a third party. They're responsible for brokering a deal with the victor of our contest. Since I won, the prize will be on its way to my employer instead of yours. All I can tell you is when and where the hand off will be. What you do with that information—keep it to yourself. I have no desire to get wrapped up in your crusade."

Kai snorted. It was hardly a crusade. He only wanted to retrieve what he'd lost to keep Bratva off his ass. Still, he couldn't help but wonder why Pyotr and Zverev's employer were fighting over something neither of them actually owned. Those in possession of this counterfeit crap were likely the ones who'd found it. For whatever reason, selling it to the highest bidder would offend the other side, so whoever took it needed a legitimate claim—something agreed upon by all parties. And what better way to settle the matter than through blood sport at the Confessional—the only neutral ground in the city?

"Fine," said Kai. "Tell me where the hand off is."

"No offer?" Zverev smiled coolly. "This information is valuable."

"I've got nothing to give," Kai countered. "Unless you wanted a free drink at the Confessional."

Zverev slapped his bear paw of a hand to his thigh, laughing raucously. "I'd rather have a rematch when you're at your best." He bared his teeth. "When you know what's coming for you."

Kai's lips twitched into something between a smile and a grimace. "You'll get your rematch."

"Good." Zverev nodded. "I trust you'll be itching for it."

Now that they were close, Kai caught another whiff of him— that animal scent invading him like an unwanted memory. He ached to ask about the man standing in front of him, but he didn't dare—not yet. He wasn't ready to dive down that rabbit hole. Ivan Zverev wasn't going anywhere, but the life Kai had built with Miya was a burning carriage headed for a cliff. He needed to grab the reins before they slipped out of reach.

The legacy of his kin could wait. The aching chasm in his chest, the thorn worming through his mind—it could all wait.

Kai tipped up his chin. "What've you got for me?"

14

MIYA

BETWEEN NEWS ARTICLES and the steady stream of neighborhood footage, digging up Caelan Carver's address was easier than it should've been. Her adoptive guardians, Lisbeth and Gabe Carver, resided in a two-story house with slate blue paneling, freshly painted window frames, and storm gray shingles on the roof. Their driveway was empty.

"What if one of the neighbors see us?" asked Miya.

Beside her, Ama remained confident as ever, shoulders back and chin held high. "It's the middle of the workday, and we're just a pair of harmless women. No one will think twice."

Ama was anything but *harmless*. Taking in the white wolf's outfit, Miya marveled at how flawlessly she dressed herself. No one would suspect she was about to commit a crime. Her dark blue jeans clung to her curves like a second skin, yet Miya was sure she could axe-kick a man in the face if needed. Her sleeveless one-shoulder top tucked seamlessly into her high waist jeans, and Miya made a mental note to ask where she found strapless bras that didn't feel like defective suction cups. A thick filigreed silver band that whorled knuckle to knuckle accented Ama's forefinger, her manicured nail tapping absently against her belt.

"We'll be out before you know it." Ama smiled reassuringly. "Gavran will keep watch."

The raven cawed from a nearby maple. Miya glanced up to see him on his perch, his beak tipped skyward in a proud display. He usually oscillated between his roost outside Miya and Kai's bedroom window and a small nook in the attic of the King of Spades, but he was always near—a feathered sentinel keeping vigil. Gavran belonged to the dreamscape, and he took a piece of it wherever he went—a living spirit given corporeal form.

"Let's make this quick." Miya had dabbled in her fair share of law-breaking after escaping Black Hollow with Kai five years ago. By then, he'd had a decade of practice in delinquency. Since the tender age of sixteen, Kai had survived off sheer wits and petty crime while Miya wilted in the comfort of a sterile middle-class home. Her absentee parents provided for her every material need; she never hungered or worried if her toes would freeze off in the middle of the night, though she was starved of affection and approval. Only when she gave up her privileges did she learn how difficult it was to put food in your belly and a roof over your head. Without Kai, she wouldn't have made it, but she had no desire to go back to pickpocketing and pilfering beans from bottom shelves.

Ama gave a brusque nod. Without batting an eyelash, she tried the front door, but the knob only jiggled uselessly. As if feeling Miya's judgmental stare, she shrugged. "What? You'd be surprised how often people leave their homes unlocked."

Miya rolled her eyes. "I hope you brought something you can pick locks with."

"Please." Ama waved her off. "There are half a dozen windows we can try before resorting to pedestrian tactics."

Pedestrian tactics, Miya mouthed to herself, blinking rapidly. A subtle dig at Kai, no doubt, though he would've just elbowed the sidelight, consequences be damned. She decided not to mention that part.

Ama circled the house, scrutinizing every window as Miya dangled several feet behind. "This one." She pointed about seven feet up the side wall. They *could* fit, but it wouldn't be comfortable.

"Why that one?" Miya moaned in protest.

"No mesh, and it doesn't have a lock." Ama turned to her taller companion. "I need you to open it."

Gulping as her stomach flipped into her throat, Miya glanced up at the window. At five-foot-nine, she could easily reach it. "You should've worn higher heels." It would've made up for the three-inch height difference between them, but Ama had chosen a modest pair of tan boots. Practical *and* stylish.

Ama's laugh chimed like a bell. "If you're uncomfortable, I can find a makeshift stool to step on."

"And the stool would thank you for it." Miya wrestled the window open; it was rusty, obviously not in much use. She gave the white wolf a dramatic bow. "You first. If you need a boost, I can—"

Before Miya could finish, Ama jumped and grabbed the windowsill, hauled herself up with the power of an Olympic gymnast, and dove nimbly through the tight space. She landed on the floor without a sound, then called to Miya, "All clear. No dogs or alarms."

Miya huffed, her shoulders bobbing. She tried mimicking Ama's technique, though her ascent was anything but elegant. Her sneakers scraped the paneling as she pried her way up, her forearms hooking awkwardly over the windowsill like gangly mantis legs. Ama caught her wrists as she began to slip and lugged her inside. Miya hit the floor, her arrival announced by a graceless thud.

"You know, you didn't have to do that. I was going to walk around front and unlock the door for you," said Ama, hand perched on her hip.

Miya groaned as humiliation soaked in. "Let's just pretend that was my workout."

The white wolf's pink lips quirked up. "I saw absolutely *nothing*."

It wasn't hard to find Caelan's room. The door was labeled with a custom name plate and outfitted with a silver bell. Like many parents who lacked closure over their child's disappearance, Lisbeth and Gabe kept the teen's belongings untouched—everything in its rightful place. The bed was made but undisturbed, not a wrinkle in sight, the nightstand cluttered with paper, a jewelry box, and a lava lamp that remained plugged in. The mirror atop the oak dresser had collected a thin layer of dust, and a pair of Caelan's jeans were left splayed over the backrest of her chair. An uneven stack of books lined one side of the desk, the rest overflowing from a small shelf tucked against the adjacent wall. Miya perused the titles, searching for patterns. Caelan seemed fond of folktales. Her little library wasn't merely stacked with anthologies of old fables; she also collected research on the topic.

"What sort of object do you need?" asked Ama.

"The stronger the emotional attachment to it, the better," Miya replied. "Since we have an array to choose from, I want to make sure I pick right."

"Take your time," said Ama, posting up by the door.

Miya did just that, sifting through the closet, the wardrobe, and the nightstand. Caelan had no shortage of belongings, but none of them struck her as particularly personal. She sat at Caelan's desk, drumming her fingers along the top. It was plain but functional, a single drawer on either side. She tried to focus, but the entire space was submerged in Caelan's fey energy. There was, without question, something otherworldly about the girl.

"Any luck?" Ama asked from the door.

"Still looking. It needs to be something with sentimental value—something she'd keep tucked away and out of sight," Miya replied.

"What makes you so sure she has anything like that?"

Miya glanced over her shoulder and quirked an eyebrow. She sometimes wondered if Ama had been born a full-grown adult, sprung from some deity's head like Athena. "She's a teenager. Keeping secrets is a big part of claiming your autonomy when you're young."

"If you say so."

Sighing, Miya opened the desk drawers. The one on the left slid smoothly against the runner, then stopped short. It was…shallow. Too shallow. Miya stood and took stock of the desk; it was at least two and a half feet deep, but the drawer didn't pull out that far. The inside was disorganized, filled with random knickknacks: pens, sticky notes, paperclips, and a few stray keychains. Nothing of note. She slid her hand inside and scrabbled around, her knuckles scraping against a solid backing. Crouching, Miya wiggled the drawer loose and yanked it out, then placed it on the floor. She twisted to investigate the desk's interior and found at least a foot of empty space in the back. Reaching into the hollow, her fingers brushed against the edges of a notebook, and she grinned, pulling it free. A red moleskin with bent corners. Many teens kept digital journals, but if Caelan's parents had access to her phone, she might've opted for something more old school. As Miya thumbed through the pages, she saw that it was filled with handwritten entries. She slowed halfway through.

I keep telling Mom and Dad I need to find the door. If

I do, maybe I can fix things. But she knows I'm trying to find it, so I can't go back to the one I came through. She's waiting for me there.

Caelan's parents had mentioned the search for a door. A way back to where she came from, perhaps? The Great Elm was *a* door —likely the one Caelan had come through—and something was preventing her from returning to it. She was trying to find a different one, but what needed fixing? Who was *she?*

"I've got what we need," Miya said, stopping at the final sentences of the last entry.

She's calling me. I can feel her pulling me closer, but I don't want to go. I don't want to answer. I don't even want to think about her. But I don't know how much longer I can resist. What happens when I give in? Will I become a monster?

Miya felt the cold hand of anxiety wrap around her throat. She squeezed her eyes shut and swallowed, breathing through her diaphragm to calm her fluttering heart. Caelan's words were more than just familiar; they were a sharpened spade, poised to excavate demons Miya thought long buried.

"What's wrong?" Ama stepped into the room, sensing Miya's distress.

She handed the journal to the white wolf. Eyes scanning the text, she frowned before shutting the moleskin and returning it to Miya. They exchanged a foreboding look.

"I don't know what to think," said Miya. "It's…a little too close to home."

Ama wove her arm around Miya's and gave her a comforting squeeze. "Don't fret. You'll help this girl before anything goes awry."

Would she? Miya knew all too well how frightening Caelan's experience was. Before Miya knew she was the Dreamwalker, she'd felt the spirit's presence—heard her calling much in the same way. She invaded Miya's dreams, reeling her toward the forest until she'd wake up outside in the dead of night. Sleepwalking robbed her of rest. She was plagued by visions of the Dreamwalker, weeks of her life stained by the persistent drip of fear. She was to be kidnapped—spirited away by Black Hollow's folkloric menace.

Yet it was Miya's own soul from a former life, coaxing her to awaken. There'd been a part of her that *wanted* to be taken, and the Dreamwalker's spirit had only been trying to return to its reincarnated body. But even if Caelan's circumstances were similar, the entity calling to her wasn't necessarily benevolent.

"I'll want to take a closer look at this diary," Miya said when the air in her lungs turned stale.

"Will it do for your dreamwalking plan?" asked Ama.

Miya nodded. "It's perfect."

A chill wound up Miya's spine then—sudden and intrusive—like she was being watched. She locked eyes with Ama, whose lip curled into a sneer. Her snow-colored hair went static, her hackles raised.

On cue, Gavran's warning cry shattered the stillness.

"Window," Ama growled, and Miya pivoted to step out of view, darting to the nearest wall.

She peered out into the street. The neighborhood was empty save for a single figure loitering in the middle of the road. A tattered coat and muddy boots obscured his gangly body. His shoulders hunched forward, a droopy hat shielding his face.

It was the stranger who'd tasked her with finding Caelan Carver.

His head slowly twitched up, the rim of his hat lifting just enough to reveal dark deep-set eyes. They latched on to Miya like fishhooks, ensnaring her where she stood.

"What the hell is he doing here?" Miya hissed.

Ama gathered from context who they were dealing with. "Gavran missed him completely." She sounded flabbergasted—a rarity for the white wolf. "He snuck up on us."

She was right. Gavran had a clear view of the neighborhood, so unless the stranger had appeared out of thin air, there was a pig's chance at flight their sentinel could've been so easily eluded.

"He's definitely not human," Miya muttered, fearful he could somehow hear them. She recalled the slip of paper he'd given her—the way it sprouted by her bedside, beckoning her to respond to his plea. Whatever he was, he had magic in him.

Why, then, did he need the Dreamwalker's help to find a missing girl?

Unless that missing girl had wandered somewhere he couldn't follow.

His head tilted to a harsh angle, and a car came into view, barreling toward him. Miya shifted her attention to the vehicle, though the stranger's stare still seared her. Didn't the driver see someone standing in the middle of the road? She snapped back to the stranger, who seemed oblivious to the incoming death-trap. Then, just as the car reached him, he glided back, seamlessly evading the danger. The car slowed, turning into the driveway.

The Carvers' driveaway.

"Shit." Ama grabbed Miya's hand. "We need to go."

Miya was limp as a ragdoll as she peered at the stranger, now safely on the other side of the road. He tipped his hat to her, a wooden smile cracking his thin lips.

From the nearby maple, Gavran pumped his wings and flew from the branch with a malcontented cry.

15

Miya couldn't decide what to make of the stranger's appearance. Had he alerted them to the Carvers' return to help them escape, or was he cautioning them that the sand in the hourglass had drained to a few precious grains?

Miya groaned and rubbed her palms over her cheeks. She was seeing question marks on the walls, her brain rattling around her skull as the mysteries prodded her. Gavran, for his part, was sulking on a beer tap, using the Guinness as his moping roost.

"Blind bird!" he croaked over and over, staring at his reflection in the brassy handle.

"It's okay," Miya assuaged, giving his neck a thorough scratch. "No harm, no foul."

The raven dipped his head and trilled softly. Miya returned to Caelan's journal, open in front of her on the bar top. She'd flipped through every page, reading the entries multiple times. Caelan's accounts were identical to Miya's experience of the Dreamwalker's haunting: nightmares, sleepwalking, memory loss, visions that blurred the lines between fantasy and reality. The teen recounted terrifying her adoptive parents one night after they awoke to a strange tapping noise in the kitchen.

My forehead was pressed against the backyard door.
Apparently, I was in a daze, my eyes open but glazed over.
Mom says I was clawing at the glass until my fingernails

bled, streaks of red everywhere. I'm so scared, and I feel like a complete freak. I have no idea how I even got down-stairs. Mom thinks I was trying to get outside, but I suck at directions. I don't know which way that door faces, but when I checked online, I knew where I'd tried to go: Boston Common.

This morning, Dad installed a bell on my bedroom door.

Miya remembered that bell. Clearly, it hadn't done its job. Had Caelan let herself out by some other means? Miya had seen the stranger through Caelan's window, which offered a view of the street. The roof sloped gently enough that she could've climbed down without injury. Perhaps she'd been lured out. Had the stranger not requested Miya's help, she would've considered him a suspect. His relationship to the teen was unclear, though Miya reckoned it was supernatural in nature.

The kitchen doors swung open, and Ama leaned out. "Would you like some pecans with your seared Ahi tuna?"

Miya blinked up from the journal. "Sure. And leave a few strips for Gavran." She poked his tail feather, and he twitched. "He's feeling glum."

Ama pouted. "Still?" She shook her head and tutted as she slid back into the kitchen. "So dramatic…"

Gavran gargled in protest, but they both knew he wouldn't refuse a juicy strip of fish. Crowbar had gone to her upstairs apartment for a nap while Ama prepared a quick meal in the kitchen. Even though the King of Spades was closed on Mondays, Miya enjoyed having company on the nights Kai was busy. She preferred the domovoy and her friends to the stillness of her empty home with the occasional cockroach.

Moments later, Ama emerged with dinner, deftly balancing two plates on each arm. She set one down in front of Miya, the perfectly crisped tuna accompanied by a generous portion of spinach risotto. After placing her own serving on the counter, Ama slid a saucer with five strips of fish toward Gavran. He stared at the pick-me-up from his beer tap, his beak hanging open.

The final addition was for the domovoy—a bowl filled to the brim with spinach risotto. Oddly, the house spirit loved his carbs, preferring a vegetarian diet. While Miya was the only one who could see the domovoy, Ama and Kai had a sixth sense for locating him.

"Here you are." The white wolf smiled as she knelt with her offering.

The domovoy made quick work of the food, shoving fistfuls into his mouth until his cheeks were puffed. Miya took a moment to savor his mirth before digging in, the meal perfectly crafted to Ama's exacting standards.

"She was definitely scared," said Miya, leafing through Caelan's journal with one hand.

Ama pushed the risotto around with her fork. "Anything specific about what she was seeing?"

Miya shook her head. "She was struggling to remember things, which I guess tracks. When I went through this, I couldn't remember my own town's folklore. It'd been cudgeled into my brain since childhood, but when I started having nightmares"—she threw her arms up—"poof! Gone." She paused, chewing thoughtfully. "Caelan did mention a shadow self in a few of the entries."

"A shadow self?" Ama hummed, tapping her fork against the plate. "Some oppressive force impersonating its victim, perhaps?"

"Wouldn't be the first time," Miya agreed. Malevolent spirits loved taking the shape of those they tormented.

Ama sighed and waved the fork around. "It doesn't matter. The journal offers clues to her experience, but it won't help us find her."

She was right. Dreamwalking was the only way.

The rest of their meal passed in silence. Miya stacked the plates and returned them to the kitchen, then joined Ama by the bar, her fingers tracing the journal's outer edge.

Ama rose from her stool. "It's been a day. I think I'm going to check on my sleeping beauty upstairs, maybe join her."

"Sounds good." Night had fallen hours ago, and like Kai, Ama kept an irregular sleep schedule.

"You going to hang out here for a bit?" Ama hesitated as she made for the stairs against the back wall—unusual for a bar, but the building hadn't been renovated in decades. They'd installed a door at the top to keep patrons from wandering into Crowbar's living quarters.

"Yeah," Miya replied after a lull, scratching under Gavran's chin. "I might pour myself a drink and peruse the journal a little longer."

Ama nodded. "Let me know if you decide to head home. It's already quite late." Then, she retreated upstairs.

The domovoy's head swiveled as he tracked Ama's footsteps, the floorboards creaking under her weight. She must've been tired; normally, she was silent as a butterfly's wings.

Miya re-focused on Caelan's words. One particular entry kept snagging her attention—a testament to the girl's silent terror, unbeknownst to her parents. Of course, they'd known something was up, but the extent of it was lost on them, impossible to internalize. It didn't matter that Gabe thought Caelan's distress was psychological while Lisbeth believed it was something *other*. In the end, locating a cause wouldn't have mattered if Caelan didn't feel understood.

I'm running out of time to find the door. Every night, I dream of the shadow. It's shaped like me. It's my height and has my way of moving, but it's not mine. It doesn't follow me the way a shadow should. It doesn't follow me at all.

I follow it. I can't stop myself. The shadow scares me, but every time I wake up inside my dreams (weird, I know), I see it in the distance. I walk toward it, and no matter how hard I try, I can't turn around and walk the other way. Sometimes, I can't see the shadow at all, and I panic trying to find it. I'm scared that if I don't catch the shadow, it will catch me. But I don't want to catch it. When I look at her—that dark thing stealing my shape— I'm filled with an awful feeling.

Then, I wake up. Always somewhere I'm not supposed to be. Always confused and with a spotty memory. What else did I see in my dream? I can't fucking remember.

Dad wants me to go to a sleep clinic or a psychiatrist, but we don't have the money. He says he'll take out a loan, *but I know the doctors won't find anything. It'll just put us in debt. Mom wants to take me to a psychic, but those people are scammers. I don't trust them.*

They think they can fix it if they find the right doctor or the right psychic, but doctors and psychics can't help me. Whatever's wrong with me is bigger than what they know—bigger than what they can grasp without breaking.

I know because I'm already broken, and they just can't see it.

Miya's heart squeezed in her chest. Caelan was searching for a way out all on her own. Her parents bickered over which story explained their daughter's struggles, but they were asking the wrong questions, looking in the wrong places. Gabe wanted to know what was wrong with his daughter while Lisbeth wanted to know what was wrong with the world. The truth, however, was somewhere in between. Not every soul could be healed by exorcizing monsters, and not every monster could be placated by a mended soul. Miya knew this all too well. Kai had spent most of his life haunted by specters both literal and metaphorical, and the obsession with carving out a clean division between them was the reason he'd never found the help he needed. Sure, he was traumatized and mentally ill—and that was besides the ADHD—but no one acknowledged that his experiences were *real*. The haunting couldn't be excised from the other things that lingered.

It wasn't one or the other; it was both.

Miya's heel tapped against the stool leg. She was antsy, eager to get to the bottom of Caelan's disappearance. Whether Caelan's shadow was sinister mattered less and less; the teen was obviously afraid, and now she was missing.

Meanwhile, Miya sat comfortably at her favorite bar after enjoying her gourmet dinner when she should've been busting her ass to find a lost girl. Slapping the journal shut, she slid out of her seat. Judging by the entries, the journey into Caelan's inner world would be harrowing.

A shiver raveled up her spine as she recalled Kai's nightmare. The dreamscape laid bare a person's psychological reality; it was completely unfiltered, the mind stripped of its usual defenses. The more intense the denial and repression, the more frightening the visions conjured in the dreamscape, and the harder it became for Miya to resist their pull. Minds were dark places when people harbored secrets, and Caelan seemed to have a few. Just as Kai did.

"We're doing this," Miya said resolutely, her eyes fixed on Gavran.

His head canted to a near ninety-degree angle, and from the corner of the bar, the domovoy mimicked him with a rattling chirp. They weren't so sure, but Miya was. Ama would've wanted her to wait until they were all together, but urgency had its claws against Miya's throat. Sure, it was a little reckless to dreamwalk into unknown territory with only Gavran as backup, but Miya couldn't always depend on others to keep her safe. Caelan needed help, and Miya was the only person with the power to do something. She had to try.

Kai would've done the same.

Miya snatched the journal and strode behind the bar. In Ama's absence, she liked the feeling of being closed in by the counter. Crowbar kept a throw and small pillow for her; it wasn't her first time frolicking around the ethereal realm while at the King of Spades, albeit in less treacherous territory than another person's nightmare. After spreading the blanket on the floor, Miya lay down on her back and fixed the pillow behind her head. Gavran quickly joined her, croaking softly as he hopped around her prostrate form.

"You want to come with?" Miya asked, placing the journal on her abdomen and wrapping an arm around her midsection to keep it secure.

Gavran's head jerked up toward the ceiling as though he were listening for footsteps. When Ama didn't burst through the chandelier, he helped himself to Miya's forearm, using it as a perch. The domovoy too ambled over and nestled in next to Miya, his palms squished into the throw as he kneaded through the soft fabric. He was staring at her, his wide planetoid eyes unblinking, his ears flat against his feline skull.

"I'll be fine," Miya reassured him with a smile. "Just the usual Dreamwalker shenanigans."

It occurred to Miya that foisting her spirit into another realm must've been quite alarming to everyone around her. Even Ama, who'd guided her when she was still a fledgling, treated her out-of-body excursions as a perilous undertaking.

The little house guardian squirmed closer, his shoulders slumped as he watched her warily. He'd grown attached to Miya. She and Gavran were the only ones who could properly interact with him.

"Gavran's coming with me, so I won't be alone," she reasoned. "I'll be back before you know it."

The domovoy huffed in resignation and cast Gavran a sideways glance. Confident she'd quelled his dissent, Miya settled into her throw and closed her eyes, her fingers digging into the journal. Silence rose like a shield, cradling her as the world fell away piece by piece. She focused on the book—her anchor to Caelan. The girl's energy was woven into the ink on the pages, the words vestiges of a stolen soul. As Miya faded, something stirred beneath the earth—phantom roots plying through the fabric of reality. They reached for her, coiling around her limbs, around the journal.

She squeezed Caelan's memories tighter, waiting to be consumed.

16

Miya twisted *as gnarled tendrils slipped over her, groping for what she guarded. She was far from the material plane now, the dreamscape coaxing her to a different kind of wakefulness.*

Follow the roots, *Gavran's voice reminded her, and she reached for one of the snaking things, grabbing hold of it as though clutching the reins on a wild beast.*

It hauled her deeper into the darkness, a carriage bound for the bottom of an abyss. A cacophonous shriek warped the air around her—all bluster. She ignored it and clung to that writhing serpent.

Miya descended until she crashed into something hard and grainy. Stone? No, concrete. She blinked away tears, her vision narrowing on a large crack in the cold gray floor.

Miya groaned as Gavran fluttered down next to her with a playful caw. She pushed herself to her feet and shook the shock out of her limbs, then retrieved Caelan's journal. She knew she was in a nightmare. The dreamscape absent of dreamers rarely had walls; enclosed spaces were the artifice of troubled minds. If she couldn't see the sky and the hanging star cresting the horizon, then she must've stumbled into another's dream...or in this case, their nightmare.

Stained cinder block walls half-bathed in murk surrounded her, and metal beams sprawled across a poorly lit ceiling. A gymnasium or a factory, perhaps? A sliver of light stole out from a fissure in the façade, alerting Miya to a way forward.

She splayed her hand over the gravelly wall and pushed. The light expanded, and the concrete crumbled, revealing a gymnasium with basketball hoops on either side. The netting on the hoops was tattered and brown, the banners along the walls rotted with age. The words on them were illegible, the fabric singed. It was impossible to tell if the gym belonged to a school or something else; the logo was scrubbed from the floorboards, and the paint on the walls had flaked away.

The sound of a basketball hitting the floor reverberated through the empty space. Miya turned in the direction of the dribbling to find three young men frozen in the middle of a game. Arms outstretched, muscles taut, it was as though someone had hit pause on a recording.

Miya felt Gavran's three-pronged grasp on her shoulder, his feathers ruffling in her periphery. She tucked Caelan's journal under her arm and circled the three men, still unmoving, then swallowed a gasp as she jerked back.

They had no faces.

The slopes where their eyes, noses, and mouths should've been were burnished into blank slates. Indiscernible. Unidentifiable. It was as though the nightmare was removing any traces that could lead back to the dreamer.

Gavran's head tilted, and he thrust his neck out. No eyes to peck, he said wryly, his mischievous voice echoing in Miya's mind. He dove from her shoulder, wings sprawling into a robe made of plumage, and his beak retracted to form the angles of a human face. A boy landed on his two bare feet, his inky black eyes and hair stark against waxen flesh. Gavran skirted around the figures, his torso bending sideways as he evaluated them.

"What are they?" asked Miya.

"Memories," Gavran replied. "Muddy like the bottom of a puddle. Faint like a dying breath."

"Maybe she's dreaming about her high school," suggested Miya.

The raven wearing a boy shrugged. "Trifles." His hand shot out from under his feathered poncho, and a bony finger prodded the basketball from the young man's grip.

It hit the floor and rolled toward the bleachers. They were carved out from the rest of the gym by a dark shadow, cast from an unknown source. It was unnatural, defiant of the light. Swallowed away like that, the bleachers seemed more a cage than a boon for eager spectators. Miya trailed the trundling ball with her gaze as it stopped at someone's feet.

A scrawny teen sat on the first-row bench. Short, copper hair cropped midway past their ears grazed heavily freckled cheekbones. Their head hung low, leaving their face obscured. Slouched shoulders fell forward, their elbows resting on grimy flannel pants with holes torn at the knees. They were alone.

"This one's different," Miya said to Gavran, who nodded in agreement. "Not a wraith like the others. This one has bones."

Miya gingerly approached the bleachers, but the teen suddenly stood. Eyes still fixed on the floor, they sped toward the gymnasium doors. Miya cursed under her breath and followed, surprised by how nimble they were.

"Wait!" Miya called after them as they reached for the handle.

The teen half-turned, features bathed in an impending fog. Their mouth opened, but before they could speak, the door whirred ajar. Charcoal brume wafted from the gaping maw. It coiled around the teenager's arm and yanked them into the darkness, their scream snuffed out by the awaiting black.

"Shit!" Miya sprinted after them. The wall warped like a wet painting, the gymnasium melting into a psychedelic mural of brown brick and gray cinder blocks. A navy plaque with crumbling white letters flashed in Miya's periphery before she slammed through the double doors, leaving Gavran behind.

Morton, it read.

She skidded to a halt when the gymnasium disappeared, replaced by a massive factory floor with conveyer belts snaking throughout. Drifting mist devoured Miya's lower half. Rusted metal screeched as the belts jolted to life, and a panoply of shapes emerged from the haze, carried by the assembly line.

Limbs. Arms and legs and torsos and heads. Smooth plastic mimicking human flesh. They bent at impossible angles, mocking the skeletons they lacked. Funneling through monstrous machinery, they vanished only to re-emerge as something resembling a whole. They still lacked features, each of them a carbon copy of the rest.

Miya rotated in place, her breath catching when one of the lifeless figures began to convulse. An elbow snapped, a knee buckled. The neck twisted too far, and something white webbed over the mouth. A muffled shriek caught on the milky film, and the doll tumbled from the line. It crashed to the concrete, and whatever was inside thrashed to break free.

The moment Miya took a step toward the flailing figure, the conveyer belt ground to a halt, and the army of replicas jerked to face their wayward sibling. Fear crawled up Miya's spine, and she snatched at the dream stone hanging from her neck.

"Gavran!" she called, the labradorite humming with a soft lavender glow.

A raven sliced through the fog like an obsidian knife. Wings beating, his talons latched on to the keening doll's jaw. He plunged his beak toward the viscous gag over the would-be mouth and tore it apart like stubborn cobwebs. The scream rang clearer now—sharp and pained. Gavran chipped away at the plastic husk until he met flesh, excavating the prisoner beneath fleck by fleck. Miya glimpsed ruddy, freckled skin, blood pumping eagerly through swollen capillaries. The doll's hostage sat up and ripped at its captor carapace. The bird retreated, evading the frantic swipes of the mannequin come to life.

As the body shambled to its feet, it raised its head and stared at Miya. A jagged line carved the face in two. One storm-colored eye rimmed with tears darted wildly on the human side of the face. Half a mouth was exposed, pink flesh trapped against the confines of the rigid shell. Strands of coppery hair tickled a freckled cheek, and Miya knew she'd found the teen from the bleachers.

Miya raised her hands in a calming gesture, squeezing the journal against her side. "It's okay, I'm here to help—"

A wrinkle formed on the bridge of the teen's nose, and a throat-rending shriek erupted from their barely open mouth. They lunged at Miya, feral in their fear.

The Dreamwalker grabbed the teen's wrists. The sudden collision threw her off balance, and the journal tumbled away. Violet smoke cascaded over her in a protective shield, then morphed into a mantle of iridescent feathers. The tip of her bone mask curved over her chin, the teen's elongated nails striking ivory. Wisps of shadow peeled from her shroud and twined around the assailant to cast them aside.

With a shallow gasp, Miya righted herself before she hit the ground. The factory with its hellish assembly line was gone. Silence—then, the hollow echo of the basketball hitting the gym floor. Cold sweat beaded Miya's temple as her vision closed in on the figure sitting in the stands. Elbows pressed to ripped flannel over bruised knees, head hung like a broken marionette's.

Beside Miya, Gavran gave himself a bewildered once over. He was wearing the boy again. Eyes like pools of ink slid to Miya. "The music here is maddening."

"A broken record," Miya murmured, catching on to his meaning.

"We need to leave," he said with uncharacteristic urgency. "Or we'll become one with the scratches, spinning on and on."

They were in too deep. Caelan's nightmare was a depthless vortex, and it would swallow them if they couldn't find a way to swim—or fly. Miya scrabbled for her pendant, but where she expected the warm, fang-shaped stone with its smooth angles and familiar cracks, she felt only cold, rough edges. Lumps riddled with tiny craters. Miya's gaze darted to her breastbone where she found a knob of coal hanging from rusted wire. It crumbled between her fingers, a soot-like residue staining her skin.

"What the hell?" She staggered back, her breaths ragged as her stomach lurched with panic.

Miya wasn't just in the nightmare anymore; the nightmare was in her, warping her perception.

"Too far, too far," Gavran chanted as the gymnasium began to rumble.

The figure on the bleachers remained unmoving, head bowed, limbs rigid. Miya cast them a cursory glance. Her desire to communicate with the lonesome teen had shackled her to the nightmare. She had to let it go; this was a battle she couldn't win. But how?

Something tender brushed against her thigh, soft pressure kneading into her sore muscles. Miya remembered the domovoy standing guard, keeping their home safe. The King of Spades was their fortress, and the domovoy was its sentinel just as Gavran was the Dreamwalker's.

Who would provide offerings and companionship if not Miya—the one person who could see and hear him? He was counting on her, and he'd already lost his family once. She had to find a route. There were people who depended on her—not just the domovoy, but Crowbar, Ama, and Kai.

Kai. So fiercely independent, and yet they were inseparable, two pieces of a plaited whole. They were bound, as the sky and sea are bound by the horizon.

Miya squeezed the pendant in her palm. It was not a lump of coal, no matter what her senses told her. She focused on where the edges should've been, those sharp cuts forming the lustrous fang. She visualized the brilliant sheen—meadow green, sunset gold, and deep purple melding together as black lightning streaked throughout the labradorite.

"Yes," Gavran encouraged her, his small hand on her back. "Make the world as you envision it."

"This isn't my world," Miya reminded him, the words strained as she fought to preserve the image of the dream stone in her mind's eye.

Talons curled against her spine. "Then take it."

Miya's eyes snapped open, realization surging through her. The realm of dreams was her playground; she could do with it as she saw fit. Violet and midnight shadow spiraled up her limbs, then coalesced at her heart where the dream stone rested. The feathery tendrils swallowed the labradorite, caressing it back to life. Satiated with her magic, the dream stone sang against Miya's palm, and she dropped into a crouch. The wooden floorboards decomposed where she touched them—mere moments rendered into eons—and her fingers sank into the earth, seeking the roots that would lead her home.

They rose like a leviathan from the depths of the ocean, unstoppable as they plowed through soil and concrete alike. Now close to the surface, they mapped a path at the Dreamwalker's command. Lavender light spilled from the pulsing dream stone and seeped into those eternal roots like molten liquid, illuminating the way. They thrummed with life, and Miya wasted no time grabbing hold of that vitality as it pulled her from the quicksand of Caelan's nightmare.

The gymnasium doors split open as the roots roiled beneath the floor, rattling Caelan's conjured world into begrudging submission. Thrusting an arm out to her side, Miya called for Gavran, who'd morphed into his smaller form and dove after his Dreamwalker. He clutched her arm, wings flapping furiously as he fought against the surge. Together, they rode the ancient arteries from beneath the earth's flesh. Miya risked one final gander toward the teen on the bleachers. As their waifish figure shrank into the periphery, she could've sworn she saw them look up, that one storm-colored eye spearing her.

Miya jerked away and ducked as she and Gavran were foisted through the entryway, the momentum sending them sprawling through the air. Gray cinder blocks flashed with white, dissolving into a smooth haint blue ceiling—the color of shallow water. Miya launched upright, rasping for breath. The dreamscape was a sea with no bottom, and no matter how hard she tried staying close to the shore, she wound up tangled in the reeds with nothing but murk below her.

"Shit." She bent over and raked her fingers through her hair, choking back a sob. The nightmares took a toll. It didn't matter that they weren't hers, that the darkness festered in another's heart. Those fetid shadows still reached for her, inviting her into their domain. First Kai, now Caelan. It was too much too quickly—a burden too heavy for the barrow. The dreamers never knew the weight of what they carried.

A throaty croak to her left brought Miya back. Gavran plucked at her pantleg, his feathers ruffled as he too recovered from the unpleasant excursion. Shaky fingers found his plumage, and she felt him tremble beneath her touch.

To her right, the domovoy sat on his haunches, his little paws resting against her thigh as he stared up at her. She'd felt his touch in the dreamscape.

"Thanks, little guy." She smiled and stretched her legs. He'd helped them escape. "I'll get Bastien to fry you a whole basket of fritters."

His ears twitched, and he perked up, his tongue darting out at the prospect of greasy dough. The domovoy backed up as Miya groped for the journal and shambled to her feet, steadying herself against the bar. She was about to call for her friends when the door at the top of the stairs swung open, the knob cracking against the adjacent wall. Ama came thumping down, her face stricken with worry. Like Kai, she awoke without an ounce of bleariness, her senses on high alert.

"What happened?" She strode up to Miya and grabbed her by the shoulders, inspecting her as though she were a prized vase that'd tumbled off its perch.

Miya lazily swatted her away. "I'm fine. I was just doing some investigating."

"In the dreamscape?" Ama asked in dismay.

Crowbar appeared next, eyes half-closed as she clung to the banister for dear life. "What's going on?"

"I didn't mean to freak you out." Miya looked between them, and it was clear that only the white wolf was fuming. "I didn't feel right sitting around doing nothing, so I dove in."

"You should've waited for me," Ama chastised.

"I wasn't alone." The words came out clipped. "Gavran was with me, and the domovoy—"

"This wasn't just a stroll through some scenic knolls," Ama cut her off, her tone waspish. "You awoke in serious distress—enough to rouse me on another floor! You should've anticipated that Caelan's mind would be dangerous. You should've waited for me to anchor you. What if you'd gotten lost or stuck?"

"I have Gavran and the dream stone," Miya asserted without qualm.

Ama turned her balefire stare on the raven, who hid his beak under his wing. "Gavran and the dream stone can guide you, but they can't pull you out from this side. That's my job—my *only* job. I'm supposed to protect you."

"And is that self-appointed or divinely ordained?" Miya challenged, wielding the question like a blade.

Hurt flashed across the white wolf's face, but she wrangled it back down, schooling her features. Ama was practiced in appearances. She was a trickster, never showing her hand. Still, she wasn't unfeeling, and wrath was a difficult beast to tame.

"I've seen what the dreamscape does to you when you're not careful—when you let yourself stray. Kai may be reckless with his body, but you're reckless with your mind, and there's nothing he can do to shield you from the damage. I, however, can." She shifted her stance, her voice brimming with anguish that bloomed from her bones. "Every lashing you take in the dreamscape is a hairline fracture on your psyche. You may not notice the cost now, but one day, you'll splinter like brittle clay."

Sticky heat licked the back of Miya's neck. She did notice the cost, but that was no justification. Harm was inevitable, and she refused to cede her autonomy to a mirage of what-ifs.

"Hey"—Crowbar touched her girlfriend's elbow—"let's just chill out, okay?"

Ama didn't budge, her hair turning static as she glowered at Miya.

"Come on," Crowbar coaxed. "Miya's a big girl. She clearly got out in one piece."

The standoff yawned out until the tension snapped like a tendon, and Ama sighed heavily. "By the skin of her teeth." She circled the bar as Crowbar cast Miya a disapproving glance.

Miya slapped the journal down, though she made no motion to protest. What would it take for Ama to stop seeing her as a child in need of monitoring? She treated freedom of choice the way a parent treated a toddler at a ballot box.

"Want to share what you found in the infernal quagmire of misfit souls?" Crowbar prodded, gesturing for Miya to join her and Ama at the bar.

Gavran squawked in dissent at the descriptor of his homeland, but Crowbar only shot him a slit-eyed glare. "What? You're telling me you're not a misfit soul?"

He puffed up in irritation, then shook out his plumage before fluttering to his favorite beer tap.

Miya slid onto a stool and thumped her forehead to the counter. "It was awful."

When Ama finished rolling her eyes in a wordless *I told you so*, Miya recounted the nightmare—the teen on the bleachers, the ghoulish mannequins, the gym populated by wraiths. Her audience listened as though she were telling a gothic tale, tensing the further Miya drew them into the hellish vision.

"I think I know where that is," Crowbar said after Miya described the facility and the surrounding area. "You said it was a gym, right? Like, a basketball court?"

Miya nodded. "Yeah, like at a high school."

"It's a community center—or was, anyway," Crowbar explained. "You saw a plaque with *Morton* on it, right? That's a street sign. It's in an industrial part of town. The community center there shuttered years ago, but it never got torn down. Neighborhood kids sometimes hang out there—drinking, playing ball, making out. You know how it goes."

"How do you know all this?" Ama asked, looking impressed at her girlfriend's sleuthing.

Crowbar shrugged. "Drunk patron went off about his kid's favorite haunt—kept mentioning a condemned community center on Morton Street. Apparently, he had to rush his kid to the hospital for a Tetanus shot a few months ago after they got high on weed and cut themselves on something sharp and rusty."

"We should check it out," said Miya. "Maybe Caelan ran off with someone. A peer group her parents didn't know about?"

"You think she's slumming around in a defunct gymnasium?" Ama asked with a quirked brow.

"It's more palatable than the alternatives." Based on Caelan's nightmare, Miya would've assumed far worse, but a runaway teen falling in with the wrong crowd was more likely than a supernatural kidnapping. Then again, it didn't have to be one or the other. Caelan could've run away precisely because she knew *something* was coming for her, and she didn't want her family around when it happened.

"I suppose that's true." Ama twirled a strand of ivory hair around her forefinger. "You're right. We should investigate the old community center. The girl might need help." Her eyes glided to Miya. "Are you well enough to go now?"

Relieved that Ama was cooperating, Miya fished her phone from her pocket to text Kai. "I think I'll be sick if I don't.

> I've got a lead on Caelan Carver. I'm checking it
> out ASAP. Might be home super late.

Miya tapped her thumb on the edge of the screen after hitting send. She hoped he wasn't tied up walloping some poor bastard into the floor.

Just as her screen went black, it lit back up and buzzed in her hand.

> All good. I'm working tonight.

Working meant he'd be out until three o'clock in the morning, and he must've been occupied to be so curt. Regardless, Miya didn't have to worry about him getting bored and cleaning out the pantry. Tucking her phone away, she stood from the stool and met Ama's sunlit gaze, the kerfuffle from earlier forgotten. "Ready to go?"

After accepting a quick peck from Crowbar, Ama rose and stretched her limbs, her lips curving into a smile. "I'll get dressed. Pity, though, there'll be no one to compliment my shoes."

Miya chuckled as she thumbed the dream stone around her neck. Gavran hopped down from the beer tap, but Miya stayed him with a look he'd come to know better than the city's canopies. *Stay here*, it said.

As Ama joined her, she wove her arm with the white wolf's and grinned. "Don't worry. There's always someone watching. Even if it's only a ghost."

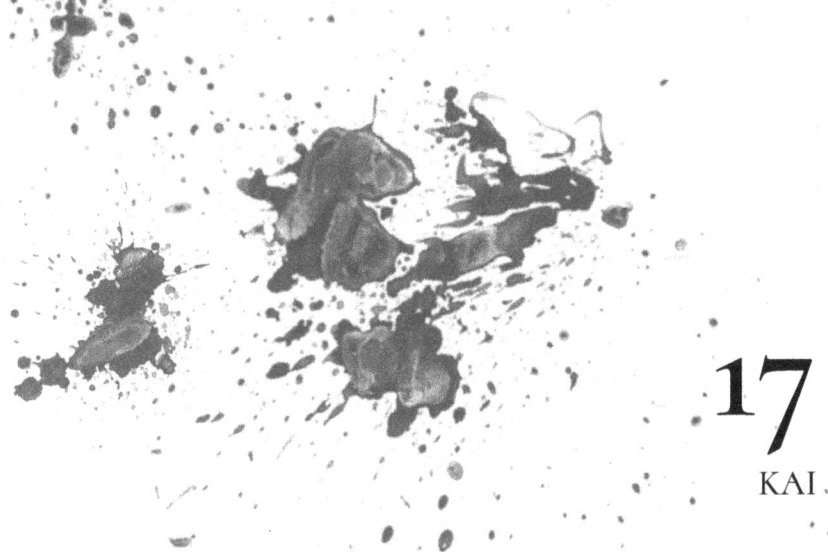

17

KAI

KᴀI sᴛᴀʀᴇᴅ down at the message he'd just sent.

I'm working.

It wasn't exactly a lie, but it wasn't the truth either. Not that it mattered; he still felt like a piece of shit. Dishonesty was cowardice, and Kai hated backing down from an opponent—especially when it was the asshole staring back at him in the mirror. When had he lost his balls to his blunders? He'd always been a fuck-up—never pretended otherwise—but chasing a squandered prize around the city like some indentured errand boy stung more than just his ego. He was risking Miya's trust.

"Fuck." He let his arm flop to his side. He wanted to whip the damn phone into the ether, but he couldn't afford to smash another one. Instead, he switched it to airplane mode and secured it in a zippered pocket in his cargo pants. Bringing a cellphone to a B&E was as dumb as wearing a meat suit to a shark tank, but Kai was sure he'd find only overconfident guppies here.

Standing on an empty street corner in the dead of night, Kai glanced up at the abandoned warehouse. The paint on the overhead doors was scraped away, leaving a thick coat of rust on the exposed metal. The russet bricks had discolored with age and chemical stains, the walls mottled with dark shapes like char after a bad fire. Windows barred and doors chained shut, there appeared no obvious way in or out of the old depot. Kai didn't even know what it'd been used for before the mob got their nefarious little paws on it.

He was...*annoyed*. Normally, he'd tear the lock off and bust in, but this infuriating charade required stealth; he didn't want to get caught and expose his idiot employer—or himself. He didn't even know what he was looking for. Trying to wrangle it out of Sergei was useless; the little turd kept insisting Kai would know it on sight, as if that was supposed to help. How the hell was he supposed to strategize if he couldn't plan for the size of the thing he was stealing? Was it a coin? A fancy pen? Nuclear codes? Some garish sculpture that belonged in a museum?

Grumbling indignantly, Kai stalked to one corner of the building, crossed his arms over his chest, and leaned casually against the bricks. Grains of mortar bit into his bare shoulder as he listened for movement inside. He'd left his jacket behind—it rustled too much and would restrict him in a fight—and opted instead for a black tank. He probably should've worn a long-sleeved T-shirt for more camouflage, but he really couldn't be bothered with the sweat stains. His hunting knife would've also made life easier, but then he'd be tempted to stab people, so he resisted taking it along.

The guys guarding the forgery were a neutral party—unaffiliated with Bratva's inter-faction squabbles. That was, after all, how Pyotr and Zverev's employer wound up beefing over a mystery prize.

Kai's breathing stilled as he counted the hired goons by the cadence of their gaits, each one unique. For those who stood at rest, he waited for the shuffling of clothes or the clank of weapons. They'd be armed to the teeth if they were guarding something important.

Four...five—one of them was asleep—six bodies to incapacitate. The napper was seated close to the window, and the others were making the rounds. The warehouse interior wasn't just open floor; judging by the pattern of footfalls, there were hallways and smaller rooms—offices, perhaps? It would've been easy to hide illegal merch, making the space an ideal criminal outpost but difficult to guard. Too many tight corners, too many shadows to obscure a threat. Perfect for a well-practiced hunter.

Kai knew better than to smash the bars on the window and wake up the snoring bear. Slipping past, he rounded the building and found a back door with a flickering overhead lamp. Eventually, someone would step out for a smoke break. Snatching up a pebble,

Kai whipped it at the light fixture and shattered the bulb, leaving the rear of the depot in complete darkness.

He waited, picking under his fingernails as he rested against the wall around the corner. No more than fifteen minutes went by before the lock unlatched with a loud clunk and the door screeched open. Gravel crunched under heavy boots. A deep voice muttered some vague complaint about the plumbing, and the sound of a fly coming undone raised Kai's eyebrow.

Of course he'd have to knock the bastard out while he was taking a leak.

Kai pivoted off the wall and glided forward. He avoided the pebbles, landing only where the ground was clean enough to cushion his steps. Pressing his palm to the back of the man's head, Kai hooked an elbow around his victim's throat and locked him in a chokehold. The mobster thrashed, but Kai's palm on his scalp pushed him into a constricting elbow—jaws around the jugular. With a pathetic gargle, the man flapped his arms in a wild attempt to thwack Kai in the face, but it reaped only an apathetic eye roll as Kai thrust a knee into the back of the fucker's thigh and buckled his leg. A regular human crashing into him was like a tricycle running into a truck. The guard's resistance ebbed, his dick still flopping in the breeze as he pawed at his assailant's arm once, twice, and then went limp, his weight sagging in Kai's not-so-loving hold.

Kai dragged the man's comatose body several feet from the door and deposited him in the muck next to a dumpster. Then, dusting off his hands, he strolled right into the building and found himself in a dimly lit forked corridor. The navy linoleum floor was at odds with the crumbling brick walls—eighties décor clashing with the industrial revolution. The walls dipped into shadows every few yards. On his right, the hall expanded into an empty shop floor, and the way ahead tapered into a narrow line of doors. The forgery, he guessed, was stashed away in one of those rooms. Kai ducked into the corridor leading to the shop floor where he anticipated scant patrols. He peaked around the corner and was greeted by gruff laughter leaking from one of the rooms midway down the hall. Light flickered from under the door, spilling onto the scuffed-up tiles. The guards who'd been wandering around minutes earlier must've congregated in their makeshift breakroom.

A groan echoed from further down the hall, and the man who'd been dozing by the window rose clumsily to his feet. Judging by his silhouette, he was built from iron and steroids.

Kai retreated against the wall and waited as Big Boris—that's what he was calling him now—started down the corridor with lumbering strides. His advance was torturously slow, but eventually, he reached the juncture where the end of his night awaited. At a whopping seven feet tall, he'd require a...different approach.

Kai darted out into the open like a possum in front of a minivan. Keeping his center of gravity low, he drew his elbow back for an uppercut. All the usual targets—kidneys, liver, sternum—were too well-padded; he'd have to go for the low-hanging fruit. Literally. With a sharp exhale, Kai struck the man square between the thighs, his fist connecting with the only squishy bits left on him. The air left Big Boris in a heaving jerk, and he doubled over with a pained rasp. Quick to exploit the opportunity, Kai spun onto his opponent's back and straddled him.

"Giddy up, big man," he sneered under his breath, then clapped his palms over the muscle-head's ears with a muffled smack.

Disoriented and concussed, the guard wobbled like a two-legged stool, then toppled, barely giving Kai enough time to break the fall. He scooped an arm around Big Boris's collarbone to stop him from crashing against the linoleum, then set him down with a strained grunt.

Now for the rest of the goon squad.

Kai heard cheering from their rumpus room. He guessed they'd cracked open a bottle of booze and were deep in a game of cards, unconcerned with consequences. They were likely some small-time gang clamoring for favor, and once they sold the forgery to Zverev's employer, they'd be swimming in cash.

What could possibly be worth so much? Paying Zverev to win a fight *just* for the right to purchase an obscure relic off some smarmy thugs seemed like a batshit business decision. Then again, the same could be said for Pyotr. Sergei had been ready to pay Kai double to win his match against Zverev, and all that would've afforded Pyotr was a transaction. It made Kai wonder if this wasn't business at all. Maybe it was personal.

But he wasn't here to speculate about a mobster's motivations. All he had to do was retrieve what he'd lost, and he was *so* fucking close. The rest of his obstacles were crowded in one spot—ideal for a brawl but not for stealth. He had to ensure none of them saw his face.

Stalking along the wall, Kai kept out of the scant rays of light peeking through the cracks in the door. The men shuffled in their chairs, muttering and cursing through their game. Kai counted four seated around a table, accounting for all six guards he'd scoped out.

Chair legs scraped the tiles.

"Where you going?" one of the men asked.

Cards slapped onto the table. "I lost, and my legs hurt from sitting. I'm going for a walk."

He had no idea how brief his walk would be.

As soon as he stepped through the door, Kai snatched him from his periphery, clamped a hand over his mouth, and dragged him away. The gangster reached for a pistol holstered at his side, but Kai hammered his fingers and grabbed it first.

"Thanks," he said, then struck the guard's temple with the butt of the weapon. The man slackened in Kai's grasp, blood trickling down his face. After easing him to the floor, Kai unloaded the firearm, dropped the magazine, then strode up to the door and kicked it open. Before the others could turn, he flung the gun at the light fixture, shattering the bulb.

Darkness swallowed the room. Men shouted, chairs tumbled over, and panic thickened the air as they scrambled to gather their bearings. Switchblades flicked open and safeties released, but the wolf was too fast. Kai lunged through the blackness and grabbed the man closest to the door. Palm braced against his target's skull, Kai whipped an elbow across his jaw and knocked him out cold. He shoved the dead weight into a goon fumbling next to him, and as the second guard caught his friend, Kai push-kicked him into the table. Wood snapped, and the iron-like odor of lacerated flesh, sweetened by the guards' wild terror, filled the air. All they saw was a hazy silhouette while Kai remained unaffected. His eyes were sharper, his sense of smell, touch, and hearing heightened as their fear soaked into his skin, waking the predator in him. Sometimes, the scent of blood wasn't enough.

Sometimes, he wanted to taste it on his tongue.

He whirled on the last guard when a deafening crack erupted in the small room. Kai's face twisted into a grimace, his ears ringing as a sharp pain lanced the left side of his core, and he staggered back a step. Wetness spilled through his shirt and onto his hand as he pressed against the wound.

A slow, creeping rage needled Kai's skin. He hated gun-toting, trigger-happy shit lickers more than piss in his whiskey. They were the bane of his life—the reason he'd lost a piece of himself before he was old enough to know wholeness. They were the scourge that'd forced Miya from Black Hollow and shattered her faith in her own kin.

"Motherfucker!" Kai hurled a nearby chair at his assailant. Wood splintered, and the man yelped on impact. Dropping his gun, he fell to one knee.

Kai kicked the firearm out of reach, grabbed the thug by the back of the neck, and yanked him up to the tips of his toes, the movement reaping an agonized wail. With bruising pressure, he dug his fingertips in for emphasis, then slammed the man face-first into the wall, the crunch of bone accompanied by the wet smack of flesh on grout. Blood ricocheted off the bricks and spattered over Kai's face. He didn't even flinch as red oozed down his cheek, then dripped from his jaw onto the floor.

"Where's the forgery?" Kai snarled, the words sounding feral even to him.

The man gave a pathetic whimper. Tears streamed down his face, his gums framed with crimson as his arms hung limply at his sides. "R-room...e-end of the hall," he stammered, copper-laced drool dribbling down his chin.

With a tight-lipped huff, Kai threw the man to the floor and punted him goodnight. Everyone who'd patrolled that night would wake up with a killer hangover, and it wouldn't be from the liquor. Confident he'd remained a blur of shadow and teeth, Kai made his way to the last door.

What he saw, however, made him pause. The door was locked from the outside with three industrial deadbolts. If the forgery was important, wouldn't they lock it from the inside to keep people out?

Kai rested his fingers on the turn piece. Hackles raised, every cell in his body screamed that this was wrong. Who the hell installed a deadbolt on the outside of a room where valuables were held? Was it a vault or a prison cell?

What were they trying to keep in?

Kai leaned closer, and a heartbeat echoed his own on the other side of the door, mimicking the rapid thrum behind his chest wall. It was faint, and only when his breath halted could he home in on the barely perceptible pulse.

A thousand invisible pinpricks invaded him, every instinct revolting against the possibility of what lay ahead. The animal in him knew better than to fuck around and find out, but he'd never been *just* an animal. His abdomen ached from the gunshot wound, and even though the bleeding had slowed, he needed to dig the bullet out soon to avoid infection.

Retreating wasn't an option. Kai rarely got second chances, and when he did, there were strings attached—so many fucking strings. A single misstep would garrot him. The forgery was the fishline around his throat, and the only way to cut himself loose was to open the damn door and find it.

Kai turned the locks. Each bolt shot back into the wood with a reverberating snap, leaving only a flimsy latch between the wolf and his ominous boon—a trojan horse in the middle of a wreckage. His hand, still slick with blood, drifted to the knob.

Turning his wrist, Kai gave the door a small shove.

The room swelled with darkness that spilled into the hall, devouring what meagre light illuminated the crumbling brick and cheap linoleum. It sprawled outward as though yawning after a long sleep, and when it reached the ceiling, the overhead lamp flickered, then fizzled out with a faint buzz.

Kai wasn't sure if it was an invitation or a warning, but it *was* unnatural—a living thing that didn't bend to physical laws. Not that it mattered; he was at home wherever night descended, in whatever shape it took, and he would accept any secrets it cared to impart.

He stepped past the threshold, and the darkness welcomed him inside.

18

MIYA

THE INDUSTRIAL ZONE from Miya's dream was like a graveyard for the city's cast-off neighborhoods, each wall a grim two-story headstone. Some of the buildings were still in use, but the community center remained abandoned, its parking lot overgrown with weeds that'd sprouted from the near-endless cracks in the pavement. As Miya anticipated, it was made of the same gray cinder blocks she'd seen in Caelan's nightmare. The fencing was rusted and bent, the interior dark as midnight waters. Several of the windows were broken—likely the result of a wayward baseball or a rowdy group of teens—giving Miya no illusions about the building's priority to land prospectors.

"I hope you've got an updated Tetanus shot," Ama said wryly as they approached.

"Had my last one eight years ago after I cut my hand on a broken pipe," she replied, tugging at her sleeves. She'd nabbed Kai's oversized black hoodie, which he'd left at the King of Spades several weeks ago—a good disguise should they run into any trouble.

Ama, on the other hand, clearly didn't give a shit about hiding her identity. "Good enough."

"Please don't make me crawl through a window," Miya mumbled as she glimpsed the jagged shards of tinted glass in the window frames.

"Wouldn't dream of it. Come on." Ama led them around to the

front. "I doubt the kids who come here scrape over the glass to get in."

There were no doors—no chains or caution tape or anything to keep people out. "Oh, thank God."

The white wolf chuckled. "I think it'll be a bit easier this time around, no?"

Nodding, Miya made for the doorless entryway. Ama kept stride with her, and they paused only a fraction of a second before crossing into the building. Miya was quick to wield her phone's flashlight, illuminating cobwebbed corners and walls stripped of posters, plaques, and photographs. A half-torn advertisement for a weekly basketball league was still pinned to a cork board, the edges curled from time and moisture. She was certain there was mold lurking along the ceiling—a suspicion Ama confirmed with a displeased wrinkle of her nose.

"We shouldn't stay here too long," she warned. "It's not healthy."

On that they agreed. "Let's find the gym," Miya suggested, and they hurried down the corridor until they came across double doors like those from Caelan's nightmare.

"God, it really is the same." Miya halted, unnerved by the parallel vision. Swallowing her disquiet, she forged ahead, a grimy smear powdering the sleeve of Kai's hoodie.

"This is where the dream took place?" Ama asked as she ambled into the gym behind Miya.

"Yeah..." Miya trailed off as she took stock of the space. "It was...bigger when I saw it. I can't imagine why anyone would be hiding here." The logo was still scrubbed off the floor, and above her, she noted the dark shapes of metal beams bridging the ceiling.

"I don't smell anyone," Ama confirmed grimly. "In fact, I don't think anyone's been here for a while."

Miya did a lap around the perimeter, searching for signs of disturbance, but there was nothing. Only her and Ama's footprints marked the dirty floor. The dust remained settled on every surface. No one had been here in months.

From the corner of her eye, Miya caught the tattered hem of a billowing taupe coat. The heavy thud of fishing boots echoed between her ears, and she spun in search of the stranger. She still didn't know his name, but she knew his presence—the increasing familiarity weighing on her mind. She glimpsed his gangly form slip past another set of doors identical to the ones leading into the gym. These had an emergency exit sign above them, and Miya realized they led to the back of the building.

She'd gone through those doors in the nightmare, chasing after the teen swarmed by shadows.

"This way," she called to Ama, who quickly crossed the floor, her heels clipping the lacerated wood. "I think we're in the wrong building."

As Miya burst through the doors, her eyes landed on an old brick wall that'd browned with age, then drifted to the navy street sign with faded white print.

Morton Street.

It was an old factory building.

The army of faceless mannequins invaded Miya's thoughts—the assembly line, the grisly juddering of artificial limbs.

"Shit, Ama, this is it. I think she's in *this* building." Miya pointed to the street sign as she looked over her shoulder, but before she could meet the white wolf's amber gaze, something cold and rough closed around her wrist.

She whirled around with a staggering gasp, *but the world looked different than it had a moment ago. A milky haze steamed across the brick wall, muting the darkness to a dull, cloudy hue. Deep violet ivy crept along the base of the building, reaching for Miya as a figure filled out the fog. It approached at a languid pace until the mist parted, and the stranger's tall, lanky figure came into view.*

"You." His sudden appearance pushed her back a step. She instinctively reached for the pendant around her neck, its feverish warmth radiating against her hand. The labradorite shimmered through the cracks between her fingers, emitting its lavender light—something that only happened in one very specific reality.

The dreamscape.

With a single touch, the stranger had foisted her right out of her body and into the ethereal realm.

"My apologies," he said slowly, woodenly. "I needed to speak with you, and it appears I am rather feeble tonight."

Feeble *was not a word Miya would've used to describe what he'd just done to her.*

When she made no move to respond, he went on, his words leaving his thin lips more smoothly now, as though he'd finessed the mechanics of human speech. "Normally, I can communicate with the denizens of the physical world, but it is fleeting—a single message, a momentary vision—and it saps my strength." He let out a low warbling sound that dragged into a mournful song. "I need more time."

Spirits usually had no foothold in the physical plane—not without an anchor. Miya speculated that this one attached itself to people only briefly before vanishing. In the dreamscape, however, he had no such limitations. She had no idea how he'd dragged her here against her will, but she doubted asking would prompt a sincere answer. Spirits on a mission rarely understood their own behavior. Besides, finding Caelan was more urgent. The logistics of the stranger's abilities could wait.

Miya continued clutching the labradorite around her neck. "What did you want to tell me?"

"They will come for her," he hissed, and the ivy at his back crawled forward, winding around his ankles. "They will hurt her—all to keep her from herself, to keep her docile, following their rules when they follow none."

"You really care about her," Miya observed, his earnest plea thawing her icy guard. "You're her friend in the dreamscape, aren't you?"

The stranger nodded. "We met when she was traveling through. She became lost. I helped her find her way. Now, I fear, she has become lost again."

A sad smile tugged at Miya's lips. She knew this story too well. It was the tale that defined her and Kai throughout lifetimes. An ostracized girl lost in the woods. A black wolf who led her home. In the end, the fable of the Dreamwalker and her wolf remained woven into the fabric of their identities, their experiences, and it haunted them even now. There was no freedom from the past—only a tenuous peace with its ghosts.

"I can't reach her," the stranger broke Miya from her reverie. "All I can do is touch the living for a moment. To give a message. The closer that person is to the dreamscape, the easier."

Miya's eyes narrowed, his words sparking confusion. "You can't reach Caelan, but you were able to find me without any issues. How is that possible?"

"I cannot find whatever I want," the stranger explained. "Like any being of the dreamscape, I am drawn to specific qualities, and in turn, I *draw them out of others. For some, it is fear, rage, pride, or utter yearning. For me, it is the primordial. The nature in all things. The origin. The stronger one is connected to their roots, the clearer the path to them. And you, Dreamwalker, are your own past made flesh."*

Miya swallowed thickly. He knew more about her than she realized. "Are you saying that Caelan isn't connected to her nature?"

The stranger nodded stiffly. "It's made it impossible for me to locate her. But you...and your wolf..." he trailed off, his gaze shifting to something far away. "Your wolf...I tried connecting with him. But the wolf is too wild. The animal in him revolted, nearly conquered him where he stood."

A fire station's worth of alarm bells sounded off in Miya's head. Kai had never mentioned an encounter with the spirit after they'd crossed paths at the King of Spades, let alone a forced transition. She schooled her expression, but she couldn't keep the rising tide of disquiet from lapping at her tone. "Why did you need Kai? Wasn't I enough?"

"I'll do anything for Caelan," he replied without scruples. "The more allies I rally, the faster she will be brought to safety."

Miya balled her fists and squeezed like she could wring the apprehension from her skin. "You shouldn't meddle with the physical world so much. We have boundaries for a reason; crossing them for personal gain is how spirits go awry."

The stranger's head clicked several notches to the side. "But you can?"

"As you said," she replied stonily, "it's my nature."

He hummed in contemplation. "Yes. Your very existence violates the boundary between worlds. Yet you exist, nonetheless. Surely, someone like you can understand. Rest assured, I do all this for love."

"Love means different things to different people."

For Miya's parents, it meant cultivating the perfect daughter to mirror their values. For Ama, it meant protecting those she loved at any cost. For Kai, love was foreign word—a Rubik's Cube he fumbled with every day. Love wasn't some infallible wall protecting human hearts from evil. It was like water, bending to the shape of those who brandished it. Love could easily be twisted into something thorny—something that could harm.

"You are more jaded than I anticipated." A raspy chuckle. "But there is nothing more to be said."

The rim of his hat tipped up, and Miya glimpsed those earthy brown eyes. They were tunnels into a face streaked with deep-set grooves, giving his skin the appearance of tree bark. The ivy wound further up his limbs, *the rich purple foliage stark against the muted colors of the stranger's clothes and the fog enveloping him. "I will do anything to protect her."*

It sounded like a warning.

Miya braved a step forward only to be jolted back by Ama's voice hewing through the dreamscape.

Miya! Wake up!

"Shit." The stranger watched as she wrestled with herself, curious which path she'd choose. "What's your name?" she asked, realizing he'd never shared it.

"I have no name," he told her. "But your folk have one for me."

So, he was known to humans.

Miya!

*She couldn't linger any longer. With a frustrated huff, Miya squeezed her eyes shut and focused on the dream stone around her neck, willing herself to block out the stranger. She reached for Ama's warmth—amber eyes, snowy hair, a tongue as sharp as a freshly whetted blade. Her fingers twitched, and where she expected to find empty space, she instead felt skin—*the solid shape of a hand.

"Miya!" Ama yelled right in her ear.

Her eyes snapped open after a harsh intake of breath, her limbs turned to jelly, and she stumbled to the side. Without missing a beat, Ama caught and steadied her despite her shorter stature.

"What the hell happened to you?" Her calm shattered like mishandled glass. "You just…fell into a trance!"

"I—I'm sorry," Miya stammered, clapping a hand onto Ama's arm. "He—the stranger—he *pulled* me in."

Ama turned to stone next to her, her irises a pair of thin gold bands around dilated pupils, tension bracketing her mouth as she clenched her jaw. "He must be strong if he can drag you into the dreamscape so easily."

Miya scoffed. "And he told me he was *weak*."

Now on solid ground, she relayed the rest of the encounter as they meandered slowly toward the factory. Ama halted at the mention of Kai—the revelation that the animal in him had revolted against the spirit's influence, forcing him to transition against his will.

"It's some kind of nature spirit. If it draws out the primordial core in whomever it contacts…" Ama glanced at Miya. "For you, it's your dreamwalking abilities. For Kai, it's the wolf."

"He said something similar," said Miya. "And he can't reach Caelan because she's repressed her nature—isn't connected to it."

Ama grabbed her by the shoulder. "You need to be careful. This spirit...it's dangerous. I doubt it's acting in malice, but it will only follow its nature, as it expects others to."

"Do you think it's a leshy—a forest spirit?"

"It could be." Ama's hand fell away. "Human terms don't matter much. They only describe archetypes—patterns—but there is more diversity than mortal knowledge can encompass."

Miya frowned. "It must've traveled far with Caelan. We're in the middle of a damn city."

Ama turned back toward the factory. "It doesn't matter. It's here now, and I doubt it'll stop until it's satisfied with Caelan's outcomes."

"You're right," said Miya, her eyes downcast. "The best way to put the leshy to rest will be to find Caelan and make sure she's safe."

Ama squeezed Miya's hand, then canted her head toward the old building. "Let's go, then."

Unlike the community center lined with windows, the factory was akin to a prison—a sprawling expanse of nothing but brick. Perhaps there were windows on the other side, but the wall they faced was bare. Just as they rounded the corner, Ama dropped Miya's hand and held out her arm in warning.

"Look." Ama tilted her chin forward. She was guarded but calm, assuaging Miya's anxiety.

Up ahead, Miya spotted a human-shaped mass lying motionless on the ground. He was next to a dumpster, several feet from what appeared to be a back door. The bulb overhead was out, which wouldn't have been unusual if not for the glints of glass reflecting off the gravel when Miya swept her flashlight over the area. The bulb was shattered.

"Someone's been here recently," said Ama.

"The leshy said Caelan was in danger," Miya recalled.

"Perhaps that danger was more imminent than we realized."

They exchanged a weighty glance before Ama shook out her arms and made for the door. "Whatever happens, be ready to run."

Miya pouted. "Hey, I can throw a punch."

The white wolf raised a sleek eyebrow. "Kai?"

"Yes."

Ama shook her head. "Strike only as a last resort. Don't try to—"

"Yeah, yeah, hit to disorient, then make a run for it." Miya rolled her eyes. "I know the drill."

"Well," Ama simpered, "at least he taught you that much."

Miya grumbled under her breath. Careful to keep the volume at a minimum, Ama inched her way inside, wary of the whining hinges. As soon as her shoes touched the floor, Miya knew they wouldn't have to worry about being spotted. There, sprawled across the tiles, was another unconscious figure. This one was huge —all trapezoids and lats—but he was knocked out cold, his jaw slack.

"Is he..."

"No," Ama answered her unspoken question. "He's breathing. Probably has a bad concussion judging by the blood leaking out of his ears." Her nose wrinkled, a thoughtful *huh* slipping past her lips as though she recognized something.

"What is it?" Miya probed as she shone her flashlight over the man's stubbled jaw and greasy brown hair. Dark red crusted his earlobes and neck, the trail disappearing into his T-shirt.

"Nothing. Let's move. We don't know how long these men will stay asleep," Ama advised. She scanned the area, a frustrated growl reverberating in her throat. "There aren't many escape routes here."

Nothing my ass, Miya thought, but she wouldn't press the issue while they were in unknown territory. A long corridor with several doors awaited up ahead, and to their right, another hall led into a large open space—a plant floor of some kind? It was too dark to see, and she didn't want to flail her flashlight around. "Is there only one way out?"

"There's a large window at the end of the hall. It's barred, but that won't be a problem."

"How are metal bars not a problem?" Miya asked.

Ama shrugged, stepping over the big man on the floor. "I'll just kick them out of the frame."

Kick them out of the frame, Miya mouthed, balking at the smaller woman. She knew Ama was as capable as Kai, but their sheer physical power never ceased to amaze her. She'd gotten accustomed to Kai's brute strength; he had no qualms throwing his weight around and treated bar brawls as a pastime. Ama, however, preferred the finer things in life. But that didn't mean she couldn't rearrange a man's insides with a well-placed fist.

With a shaky breath, Miya skirted around the man's limp form. She fixed her eyes on the barred window, moonlight filtering through the space between the iron rods. She hoped the dark corridor promised more than a dead end.

19

KAI

I<small>T TOOK LONGER</small> than it should've for his eyes to adjust. The murk in the strange room was like a thick blanket over his sight, dulling his night vision. Gradually, the shadows warped into shapes he could make out.

It wasn't good enough. He should've been able to see *everything*.

Frustrated, Kai ignored the paltry input. He'd spent so much time with humans that their way of understanding the world was rubbing off on him. He'd almost forgotten—he didn't need his eyes.

His preferred senses kicked in like an old habit.

Inhaling, Kai let the room wash over him. The scent of salt and sweat invaded him, and the pulse he'd heard from the hall now thundered in his ears like a war drum. His hand flew to the wall, and after a second of groping, he found the switch. The lightbulb overhead whined, buzzed, then sputtered to life, the dull glow chasing away the otherworldly darkness.

A sharp gasp from the corner of the room guided Kai's attention. Even though he knew exactly what he'd find, it didn't make the discovery any less nauseating.

Bony arms encircled bruised, dirty knees. Short, cropped hair that would've blazed like fire clung to hollow cheeks. The strands were caked in grease, dulled to the color of grimy copper. A face that was more freckles than skin topped a scrawny neck and torso. Eyes like a rainy day, wide with an animal terror Kai knew all too well.

There, huddled on the floor where the two walls met, was a fucking child.

Well, not exactly a *child*.

She looked to be in her mid-teens but was clearly underfed, her collarbones jutting out like dislocated joints. A tattered shirt and flannel pajama pants that'd ridden up and scrunched around her thighs were all that kept her warmer than a corpse.

"Fuck."

The forgery was a person.

Kai's hand dropped to his side. He was welded to the ground, completely and utterly frozen. Fury roiled under his skin. He needed to stay nimble; reinforcements could arrive at any moment.

And yet, he couldn't move.

What the fuck was he supposed to do? Throw a shell-shocked teenager over his shoulder and haul her out of the building kicking and screaming? He may have been an asshole, but he wasn't a complete monster.

Kai swallowed down the sick. Lifting both hands in an awkward gesture of docility, he fought the grimace that tried its damn best to twist his lips.

"Hey…" he started, his voice raw. What the hell was he supposed to say? *I'm here to get you out?* Technically true; still dishonest.

The girl just stared at him, paralyzed. He couldn't blame her. The stench of her fear was stronger than the B.O. wafting off her keepers.

"Are you hurt?" he tried instead.

At that, she blinked, some of the tension bleeding from her expression. Her mouth quirked downward; she probably realized Kai wasn't who she initially thought. Her head twitched side to side, as though she'd forgotten how to move, but the meaning was clear. *No.*

"Okay." Kai exhaled, lowering his arms. "It's time to leave."

That, at least, wasn't misleading.

The girl sat up straighter—guarded but interested. She didn't have to speak for Kai to understand. Body language was his common tongue.

He gingerly approached, watching for signs of panic. When she didn't try to flee, he crouched several paces away, then plopped onto his butt. She'd be more comfortable if they were at eye level and if he wasn't poised to spring at her like a wildcat. He didn't have time to dither, but taking a minute now was better than trying to drag a flailing kid out of a dungeon.

"What's your name?" he asked, annoyed that it came out sounding more like a gruff demand than an earnest question. He'd spent the last half hour beating the brains out of a bunch of muscled blow-up dolls with guns; there was a marshmallow's chance in hell he could wrangle his tone into anything that resembled *soothing*.

The girl's mouth opened, but she quickly clamped it shut. Her eyes widened and darted past his shoulder, dread ensnaring every line on her face.

Kai's gaze narrowed. Had a shadow spooked her? If someone was out there, he would've—

"Shit," he cursed under his breath, rotating as the faint patter of footfalls pierced his awareness.

His eyes momentarily shifted back to the girl. How had she sensed intruders before him?

Kai vaulted to his feet and spun toward the door. No point in slamming it shut—too much noise. Instead, he shuffled back a few steps, blocking the girl from sight. Whatever was headed their way would probably attack him, turning him into the forgery's personal shield. He thought he'd be picking up some cursed object, but this changed everything. While Sergei expected the prize to stay intact regardless of its sentience, Kai wasn't about to let a kid become some trigger-happy thug's pin cushion.

"Someone's coming."

Kai suppressed a shiver. Her voice sounded like air—like the wind straining to speak.

"I know," he groused in reply, ignoring the crawling sensation under his skin.

Focus, he commanded his stupid, scattered brain. He'd never had to defend a goddamn child before. A child he was expected to deliver to the mob like some illicit duffle bag.

He waited for the newcomers to freak out the moment they stumbled upon the mess Kai left behind. The wound in his abdomen ached, the sting worsening as inflammation kicked in, and his body writhed to push out the foreign object. But as the footsteps drew closer, his apprehension dissolved into confusion.

The intruders were smaller than he anticipated, their gait light but careful. When they passed the first body, they paused, but he detected no sign of alarm—no frantic yelling or running amok to investigate. By the time they rendezvoused with the second dead-beat sprawled on the hallway floor, Kai's heart leapt into his throat.

He was so, so fucked.

Straightening from his defensive stance, his shoulders slumped in defeat, but his mind was reeling. He swiveled away from the hall, dropped into a squat, and looked the girl in the eye. "Get ready to go."

Then, the interlopers stepped through the door, their shadows stretching into the room until they melded with his own.

"Kai?"

Miya's voice cut him like a serrated knife. He turned on one knee, meeting her bewildered gaze with a grim stare. Her eyes drifted past him to the girl in the corner, and bewilderment morphed into horror.

"Caelan?" Miya ventured, recognition flooding her features.

The teen's head jerked up, and she peered back at Miya, her heart slamming with such force that Kai thought her ribs might crack. She'd responded to the call.

Kai's jaw clenched so hard he nearly gave himself a migraine; the name Miya had spoken was a hammer to his temple.

Caelan.

The missing teen. The case Miya took from the man who smelled like rotting wood. Kai and Miya were meant to be searching for different things, but they'd been on the same trail all along.

Caelan Carver was the fucking forgery.

"I knew I smelled feral dogshit," Ama snarled from beside Miya.

He'd been ignoring the white wolf, the onslaught of new information cudgeling him from all sides. He kept his focus on the girl—Caelan.

"Can you stand?" he asked, but she was distracted, her gaze wandering between the three strangers.

"Hey." He snapped his fingers. "Focus."

Her pupils dilated, then drifted to his face.

"Can you stand?" Kai asked again and received a curt nod.

"What are you doing here?" Miya's voice was shaky, her shadow growing bigger behind him.

He wanted to tell her. To put the whole mission on hold and explain. But that would've been a stupid decision. He could only hope they'd get a chance to hash it out later.

Kai extended both hands to Caelan, palms up. She hesitated at first, her frantic stare bouncing between the offer and the door. Still as stone, he waited for her to make up her mind even as he counted the seconds in his head. He knew better than to reveal his impatience; it would only demolish any hope of building rapport. He'd been Caelan once upon a time—bruised, bloodied, scared, and distrustful. Her guarded, appraising eyes were a mirror he'd unexpectedly collided with, his child self staring back like a long-neglected friend. That kid Alice found in the woods desperately needed a gentle hand.

Miya seemed to understand his predicament—her compassion transcending his pea-brained grasp—and she hit pause on her pending verbal assault. Finally, Caelan placed two emaciated hands over Kai's. They were so small, delicate as a bird's spine. He was afraid to close his fingers around them. He did nonetheless, and after a gentle squeeze, he rose from his squat and helped the girl to her feet. Then, he turned to Miya.

"This is slowing me down." His voice was steely, uncompromising.

Hurt flashed across Miya's face, carving him out and leaving him empty. The white wolf seethed like an overdue volcano, radiating contempt as she reached for Miya's hand.

An indiscernible twinge wrung through Kai's chest—a feeling he couldn't identify. He thought it was jealousy, seeing Ama's fingers woven with his girl's, until he glared at the white wolf and realized he felt nothing.

The feeling wasn't for her. It was for himself. Ama was there to comfort Miya because he'd fucked up.

Kai wasn't jealous. He was ashamed.

He released Caelan and clasped Miya by the shoulders. Her eyes flew to his, and he withered, yearning for her faith in him more than anything in his life. "You can rip my dick off later, but I'm running out of time."

Her brow knitted as she pursed her lips, then nodded tersely.

Before either of them could speak, a man's voice hollered from outside.

"Company," Ama growled, her attention on the door. "They must've sent backup when the guards stationed here didn't respond."

Miya curled her fingers around Kai's wrist, and he reluctantly let her go. He smiled tiredly. "Is that my hoodie?"

"Yeah," she said, her voice so soft it almost didn't carry. "It's warm."

Fuck, he wanted to die. Guilt gnawed at his insides, and he exhaled forcefully. "Can I borrow it?" He tipped his head toward the shriveling teen. "She's shaking like a chihuahua."

Miya wordlessly slipped out of the baggy sweatshirt and pressed it to his chest. It smelled like her, and for a stupefying moment, he dreaded it would be the last thing he'd have of her.

And there it was—that crippling, bone-deep fear of abandonment rearing its ugly head. He didn't often think about what he carried, but sometimes it grew legs and leapt free from the pits. It took all of him to shove those inconvenient emotions back where he liked them: out of sight.

"I'll see you at home?" Miya's question severed him from his spiraling.

He pinched the hoodie under his arm. "Yeah. Expect a houseguest."

She sucked in an apprehensive breath, then nodded. "Okay."

Ama reached for her hand again. "We need to go. *Now.*"

"I've got the girl," said Kai. "You two get out of here."

"I've got Miya," Ama volunteered, finally acknowledging him as more than a piece of shit.

Miya shot her a waspy look. "I don't need a chaperone."

"Not the time," Ama rebuked, tugging her away from the door.

Overbearing as always. Miya was tired of being mothered by a woman who was supposed to be her friend—her equal. Ama's over-protectiveness would bite her in the ass, but Kai wasn't about to tell her that out of the goodness of his heart. Not like she'd listen, anyway.

Clanking footfalls pummeled the floor as two thugs rushed toward them. Kai yanked his sweatshirt on and flung the hood up over his head, concealing his face from the incoming goons. As

Ama pulled Miya away, he stepped out in front of them, blocking their faces from view. He heard Ama kick in the bars on the window at the end of the hall, then smash through the glass. One of the two attackers skidded to a halt, then reached behind his back. Kai charged, slamming shoulder-first into the man about to draw his weapon. They crashed into the wall, and Kai knocked the assailant's head into the bricks. His companion flinched at the crunch that followed, staggering back to gather his bearings.

He was too slow.

Whirling, Kai drove a forearm into his throat and pinned him to the opposite wall, the claustrophobic corridor working to his advantage. His fist connected with the man's jaw, snapping it out of place. The thug would've screamed, but the concussion got him first, and he crumpled to the floor.

Kai glanced toward the window to see Ama hop through after Miya, her hair like an arctic wind. Unwilling to linger, he stalked back to Caelan's prison cell to find her huddled in the corner, trembling like a mouse. He peeled off his hoodie. "Put this on," he ordered, extending it toward her.

Her eyes meandered to his outstretched arm, and she shuffled away like she was made of brittle shale.

Kai didn't have time to coddle her. "Listen, you don't have to trust me, but unless you want to stay here, I'm your only shot at getting out in one piece."

She was weak and disoriented. Even if she managed to shamble out of the warehouse, she wouldn't get far before collapsing. Dehydration was a bitch. Her captors would catch up, and it would be over. Besides, Kai had a debt to pay, and Miya had her own stake in this girl. What they'd do with her was a problem for later, but Kai refused to hand a kidnapped kid over to the fucking mob.

Caelan balled up her fists and stared at the proffered hoodie. She wanted to take it, but she hesitated. "Where will you take me?" she asked in that same wispy voice.

"My place. You'll have food and a warm place to sleep." His apartment was the most sensible choice for the time being. Until Kai figured out *why* Pyotr wanted her, she couldn't go back to her family. None of them would be safe.

She struggled to swallow, her mouth parched. "Why would I go to some random guy's digs?"

"Do you *want* to stay here?" he challenged, annoyance creeping into his tone. He sighed heavily. "You won't be alone with me. One of the women who stormed in here lives with me, and she's been trying to find you."

Wariness thawing, Caelan pawed at the hoodie, pushed her arms through the sleeves, then pulled the garment over her head. It was massive on her, the hem nearly reaching her knees. Her pajama pants stopped at her ankles, a pair of worn flip flops her only footwear. Kai was increasingly aware of her waifish stature; the poor kid's knobby limbs barely held her upright, and he towered over her by a whole foot. No wonder she was scared.

"Come on," he nudged, gently cupping her arm. Her knees wobbled as she took her first steps, her arm tense in his hold. Progress was slow, but the building was quiet, and he detected no sign of trouble outside.

One painful shuffle at a time, they inched closer to the warehouse doors. Caelan choked back a gasp when they reached the bodies littering the floor—evidence of Kai's own brutal streak. He worried she'd try to book it, but with every set of splayed limbs they passed, her heart grew steadier.

When they found themselves under the broken bulb outside, Caelan's gaze drifted to the unconscious man by the dumpster—the first of Kai's victims that night. She lingered there a moment as though savoring the bedlam, then carefully stepped over the shattered glass.

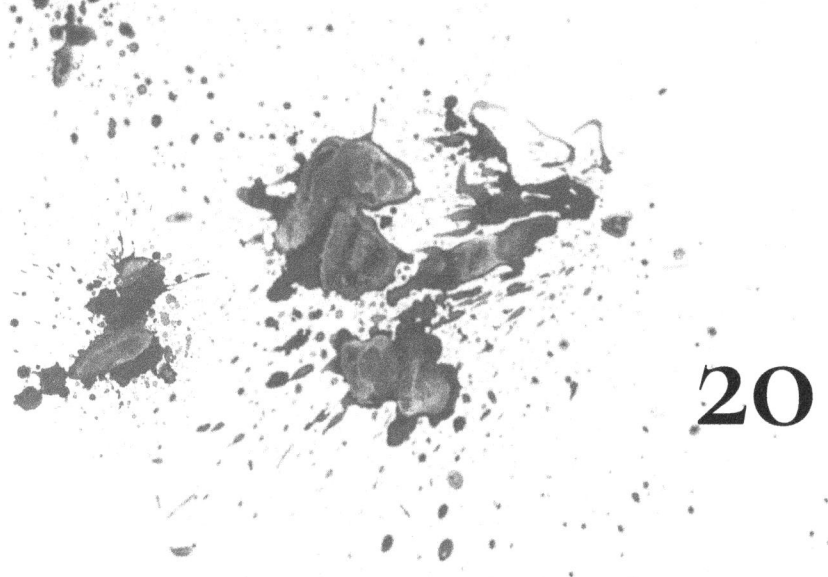

20

THE WAIL of a distant siren cut through the night like a ghost's keen, and fog gathered over glistening asphalt after an unexpected downpour. It'd hit while Kai was in the warehouse, sparing him the additional inconvenience of lugging a sodden, zombified teenager home.

Caelan was walking on her own now, albeit unsteadily. Kai had released her elbow, giving her the space to feel out her own body. She must've been in that room a long time. There were no windows, her senses deprived of the stimuli required to keep her body functioning normally. Now that they were clear of the warehouse, there was no rush, but Kai found himself on edge. The girl either drew trouble or *was* trouble. He hadn't yet decided which was the case. Then again, it could've been both.

"You managing?" he asked as she hobbled next to him.

Caelan nodded. "I'm just weak." After a respectable pause, she risked a gander at her rescuer. "Who are you?"

"Kai," he grunted, unaccustomed to speaking with a teenager. He remembered being one, but he hadn't been a shining example. For six years, Alice raised him in a dilapidated bungalow next to a Mormon church in Granite Falls, Washington. There was no sidewalk, and he had to leap over a ditch just to get to the road. Every Sunday, this girl from the church would try to lure him to service, selling him on some bullshit about inner peace and community. She could tell he was messed up—he'd give her that—but nothing she had to offer would've unfucked him. He wasn't sure anything could.

He glanced down at Caelan. She hadn't badgered him to take her to her family. "Don't you want to go home?"

She shook her head. "I don't have a home."

"Your parents—"

"They're not really my parents," she interjected. "I don't belong with them. I don't really belong anywhere."

He had no idea what she was on about, but the words got stuck between his ribs. Granite Falls had supposedly been home, but it may as well have been an alien planet. His peers treated him like a freak, and it wasn't because of how he looked; it was how he acted. He was erratic, unfocused, always itching to get up and pace around while everyone took diligent notes about Hemingway's angst. The guidance counselor encouraged him to try out for sports teams, but he couldn't remember the rules—hated having to follow them—and it often ended with the coach breaking up fights. Kai rarely started them, but people took his conduct for belligerence. They thought he was *trying* to be a dick. In truth, he just didn't get whatever rulebook they were playing by. Life hadn't sent him a copy.

"We can talk about it later." He didn't care to push the matter. The kid needed food, a shower, and some sleep.

As they rounded the corner, Caelan sucked in a sharp breath and glued herself to Kai's arm. He stopped in his tracks, his spine going rigid as an electric current surged through him. This girl— she wasn't right. Her scent had all the inflections of a human's, but something else lingered under the earthy tones of flesh and blood— a sickly sweetness that clung to the contours of her human-like shape. It was jarring, unfamiliar, and when she touched him, he felt her foreignness claw through his skin.

Pay attention, the wolf warned. *This one's not part of the flock.*

Yet she seemed so fragile. So easily frightened. A pair of flashing headlights were the cause of her sudden start. The car responsible rolled down the empty street, but she skulked into Kai as though she could meld with his shadow and become a part of it.

As the vehicle got closer, Kai let out a defeated groan. It was an unmarked police car, the lettering scrubbed from the sides, but the make and interior partition were unmistakable. As if on cue, the cruiser squealed to a halt.

"Excuse me, sir." The cop circled his showboat after stepping out. "I'd like to see some identification."

Kai sometimes forgot he was as undocumented as Mothman. "Don't need to give you shit. I'm not driving a car." One reason he liked Massachusetts: he legally didn't have to talk to the police unless he was behind the wheel.

Flustered, the cop quickly switched gears and turned his attention to Caelan. "You all right, miss?"

The girl was a block of ice at Kai's side. She didn't move, didn't speak, but he could feel her trembling.

"Miss, please step forward," the officer ordered, alarm shading his voice.

Kai knew how it looked—a scraggly teen in flip flops out with a grown man in the middle of the night. She had nothing on her but pajamas and an oversized hoodie, her face a textbook exhibit of a shell-shocked war survivor.

"She's my kid sister," Kai lied. "Doesn't like strangers."

"I didn't ask you, *sir*." The asshole took an aggressive step toward them, then gestured at Caelan. "I asked the girl to come forward. Release her, now."

Kai hadn't laid a finger on the kid; she'd glommed on to him. She shrank back, her chin wobbling as the officer menaced closer. "She doesn't want to talk to you," he growled, "and she doesn't have to."

"I told you to shut up!" The officer shoved passed Kai and seized Caelan by the arm. A shriek tore from her lungs, and she folded like paper, writhing to get free.

A firestorm snaked through the pit of Kai's stomach, and he grabbed the cop by the throat. It'd been a very, very rough night, and he still had a bullet in his abdomen. Fingers digging into soft flesh, he slammed the officer into the hood of the cruiser. Kai's lips peeled back, teeth bared in a feral snarl. "And I told you, she doesn't want to talk to a pig." He leaned in close as the meat sack kicked uselessly. "You see my face, you look the other way, understand?"

Kai's grip was like a steel vise, and his blood-tinged eyes promised carnage. The cop strained to speak, mustering only a pathetic gag as his chin jerked down. A nod. Knocking him against the hood one last time, Kai released him when his face began to blanche. The officer rolled to his side, wheezing for air.

Kai pivoted and took Caelan's hand. She was shaky but eager to leave.

"I-I guess you're not a fan of the police..." she ventured.

"Never met a law I got along with," Kai muttered as they hurried away. He slipped into a side street to avoid patrol cars. If he was hassled again, Sergei would have to pay off the entire pig pen.

Rummaging racoons and pissing drunks were the only racket in back lanes—innocuous and easy to ignore. Suddenly, Caelan planted her feet and tugged Kai to a halt. Her gaze flew to an adjacent alleyway, the sound of a ricocheting can followed by throaty yowls and feline screeches.

"It's just a cat fight." Kai squeezed her hand and tugged.

"Stop!" She yanked at him again, refusing to budge.

Kai kissed his teeth and rotated to peer into the alley. "They'll sort it out—"

"One of them will get hurt!" Frantic, she pitched toward the darkness, and as she did, the darkness reached back. Shadows that belonged in the slim corridor between buildings swelled into the street, and the lamplight above flickered from the encroaching murk. It was the same ethereal pall from the warehouse, orbiting Caelan like a deathly ring.

It was enough to crush Kai's stubbornness. Cursing under his breath, he dropped Caelan's hand and stalked into the alley. Two grubby furballs tussled between the garbage dumpster and the back door of a fried chicken joint. No wonder it was a match to the fucking death.

One of the cats was definitely going to kick it. Small, orange, and plagued with stubby legs and a long coat, the runt was clearly outmatched but too stupid to back down. Guessing that *this* was the cat whose demise Caelan so brilliantly foretold, Kai bent down and snatched the Cheeto-colored munchkin by the scruff. The cat flailed wildly, hissing in protest as Kai carried him away. Luckily, his legs were too short for him to do any real damage.

"Happy?" Kai sneered, and Caelan nodded, satisfied that he'd prevented a slaughter.

"You can't drop him," she urged. "If you do, he'll just run back and get himself killed."

"What the fuck do you want me to do then?"

"You have your own place, right?" She stared at him expectantly, her suggestion louder than the cat's screeching.

"Fuck tha—" He stopped himself. It was a cat. Cats ate vermin. Their apartment had cockroaches, and Miya was getting fed up. She'd asked to move several times, but the rent was cheap, and their landlord didn't ask questions. He'd been debating gifting her a cat as a compromise, and this one already had a killer instinct. Kai swallowed his objection. "Fine."

With Caelan appeased, the shadows receded. Then, she reached for his hand.

Weird kid, Kai thought as he reluctantly allowed her to curl her fingers around his. The orange tabby continued his futile revolt, but Kai ignored it, holding the cat at arm's length.

Apparently, he'd be bringing home two strays tonight.

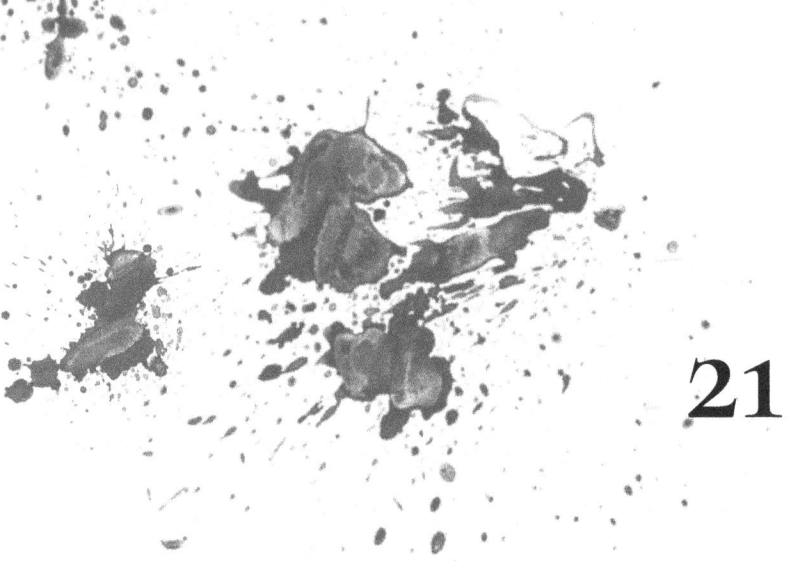

21

KAI WAS SPARED Ama's legendary vitriol. She was gone by the time Miya greeted him at the door, her face stricken with worry that quickly melted into befuddlement as she took in the scene: Kai with a mangled arm and a gunshot wound as he mulishly held a feral cat by the scruff. The damn thing hung limp, growling a low warning tune. His other hand was occupied by Caelan's death-grip. Apparently, she'd taken to him after he scared a cop pissless and saved a flea-ridden furball with too-short legs.

Ushering Caelan inside, Kai shut the door and dropped the cat. He mewled and scurried under the couch where he could safely swipe at passing feet. Caelan stood frozen, absorbing the modest apartment while Miya riffled Kai with her stare. He sighed and kicked off his boots only for Miya to crash into him, her arms snaking around his neck. His nose dropped to her hair, exhaustion and relief sagging his shoulders.

"I've got a bullet I need to dig out," he murmured as he held her tightly.

Miya nodded into his shoulder, then reluctantly withdrew. She looked shattered. "I'll get Caelan settled in."

Once in the bathroom, Kai stripped off his shirt, then whipped it to the floor. Sweat sheened his skin, and he felt warm with impending fever. His immune system was pissed. Blood smeared his abdomen, the area angry and inflamed, and he retrieved the rubbing alcohol and a pair of pliers from under the sink. Dousing a clean towel in antiseptic, he pressed it to his wound, pursed his lips, and swallowed a groan as the sting seared through him. Then, he disinfected his pliers and got to work.

Sticking dull metal into an open wound was about as pleasant as raw dogging a tin can. He tried to relax, fighting the instinct to tense in response to the pain. Jaw clenched and teeth bared, he bit back a snarl as he managed to clip the bullet. At least it hadn't hit any organs. Projectiles rarely penetrated deep enough, and it helped that he beat people up for a living, his body carved from years of hardship.

Kai ripped out the lead nub and dropped it into the sink. A trail of blood speckled the white porcelain where the bullet had rolled to a stop. Kai braced his hands on either side of the sink and hung his head, breathing heavily. Although the wound still throbbed, the sharpness had dulled. The tissue would knit itself back together by morning, leaving only scabs and bruises. After washing the pliers and disposing of the slug, Kai rinsed off in the shower, aggressively scrubbing the grime from his body. He watched the water run brown and scarlet, then swirl down the drain. Toweling off, he yanked on a clean gray T-shirt and black sweats, then stepped into the hall.

"Come on, I'll show you the bathroom." Miya bundled clothes and a fresh towel in her arms as she pushed open the bedroom door. She locked eyes with Kai, then quickly averted her gaze to check that Caelan was following.

Opting to give them space, Kai stalked to the main room and threw himself down on the couch with a heavy sigh. The shower squeaked on, and when the bathroom door shut, Miya padded over to the kitchen. She grabbed a can of tuna from the cupboard, popped the top, and placed it on the floor by the couch. As she straightened, she inspected Kai's arm, covered in scratch marks.

"We can set Caelan up in the bedroom," he suggested. "After she's eaten."

Miya plopped down next to him. "Can you make her something? I'm wiped."

Kai nodded, and they fell into a tense silence. After several long minutes, he angled his head toward her and glimpsed the shadows collecting beneath her bloodshot eyes. His furtive foray into a mob-owned warehouse hadn't just angered her. She was hurt.

"Ama and I fought," she answered his stare.

Kai was the only fissure in their sisterly bond. Ama was clamping down harder than usual with her Mama Bear bullshit, and it was wearing Miya down. He opened his mouth to ask about it when the bathroom door chirred open, and Caelan's wraith-like silhouette skulked into the hall.

"We're over here." Miya waved for her to join them, and as she did, a paw swiped out from under the couch, rattling the tuna can. A chunk of the flakey fish disappeared.

Caelan shuffled into the room, her shoulders slumped and her eyes downcast, though Kai could see her gaze darting around, scoping out every corner, every window and door in search of potential exits. She was drowning in Miya's clothes; her torso swam in a T-shirt with a faded chubby pigeon graphic, and she'd traded her ratty flannels for a pair of fleece pajama pants, the bottoms rolled up to her ankles.

Kai hauled himself to his feet, his limbs like cement. "There's not much in the fridge, but I can make you a sandwich." He grabbed the loaf of bread from atop the microwave and whacked it down on the counter. "You cool with PB&J?"

"Can I have a fluffernutter?" Her voice was so arid, like sand blowing over scorched pavement.

Kai blinked at her. "You want…peanut butter and Fluff?"

Caelan's chin jerked down in a rough nod.

His eyebrow arched as he shot Miya a withering look. "I guess it's a good thing one of us likes whipped marshmallow puke."

Miya managed a strained smile. "It's a delicacy for the finest palates."

Kai shook his head as he grabbed the peanut butter and Marshmallow Fluff, then snatched a butterknife from the dish rack. "You disgust me, Lambchop."

From the corner of his eye, he caught Caelan's mouth quirk. She timidly meandered toward the couch and sat next to Miya, her stare fixed on the coffee table.

Kai vaguely wondered if he was supposed to apply equal portions of peanut butter and marshmallow creme, decided it would be child abuse, and settled for a two-to-one ratio of PB to Fluff. It looked like bird shit. Dumping the sandwich on a plate, he clanked it onto the coffee table in front of Caelan.

"Don't choke on it," he cracked, then smacked a bottled water down next to the plate.

Caelan dug in like a starved hamster, chomping away pieces too big for her mouth. Her cheeks expanded as she struggled to chew, though she eventually managed to get everything down her gullet.

"Should you...make another one?" Miya suggested as the teen scarfed down the fluffernutter faster than Kai could make a shot disappear.

"Sure," he said with a shrug, then returned to the kitchen. By the time Caelan had licked her fingers clean, Kai had dropped another sandwich onto her plate, and she quickly made work of that one too.

She glugged down the water and flopped back against the couch. Her head lolled to the side, eyes drifting between Miya and Kai. "Can I go to sleep now?"

No niceties with this one. Kai liked her.

"Come on." Miya stood and stretched, then led Caelan to the bedroom.

With the bed claimed, Kai yanked the cushions off the couch and unfolded the pullout. He glimpsed the feral munchkin huddled in the base, one tooth poking over his bottom lip as he snarled up at Kai until their line of sight was broken by the thin mattress.

"Don't you dare swipe at my ass," he growled at the cat as Miya returned with a set of sheets. She'd changed into her sleeping T-shirt, which enveloped her torso and upper legs.

"I gave her the spare toothbrush from the dentist," she said as she shoved a pillow in Kai's chest, then spread the fitted sheet.

Now that Caelan was gone, the tension returned like a bad odor. Kai watched stiffly as Miya tugged the corners of the fitted sheet over the mattress.

"Guess you finished your job," Kai commented.

"Yeah, I guess I did." Miya flicked off the kitchen lights, leaving only the table lamp by the couch. "I'll have to ask Caelan about her friend."

"The one who hired you?"

She nodded. "The leshy."

Kai's brow crinkled, and he dropped the pillow onto the mattress. He knew the old man reeked of something that didn't belong. "A fucking *leshy* hired you?"

She yanked the sheet more vigorously than needed and cut him with a look so sharp, he nearly recoiled. "Speaking of—exactly what kind of work are you doing these days?"

Her tone bit deeper than the bullet had, curling his lip into a wince. He'd told her he was working tonight—a misleading half-truth. Miya expected *work* to mean pummeling meatheads at the Confessional, not taking gunshot wounds from mobsters after blasting through their hideout to rob them.

The three feet between them felt like a chasm as Kai mined his thick skull for a coherent explanation.

"That night I lost the fight," he began, "I didn't realize I'd lost something important. I thought it was just money."

Miya crossed her arms and shifted her weight, expectant.

He told her everything—how Sergei roped him into stealing back what he'd lost. How it wasn't money at all, but the forgery. How his collision with Miya at the warehouse wasn't an accident because the forgery wasn't a thing. It was a person, and that person was also the missing Caelan Carver.

Miya sank into the mattress. "I can't believe this." Her gaze hooked into him, cracking him open. "Why didn't you just tell me?"

Shame turned his head. "I thought I could take care of it quickly. Quietly. I didn't want you involved."

"Are you serious?" She spun to face him. He still couldn't look at her, his stare fixed on the window. "When are you going to learn that hiding your problems never ends well? It just makes everything worse. What if something bad happened?"

Anger bubbled under the shame, searing right through it. "And what about you? What would've happened if I hadn't been there to clear a path?"

She flinched back, shock warping her expression before she threw her arms out in disbelief. "I never lied about what I was doing, and I had Ama for backup. Or have you forgotten that she can do everything you can?"

"Not as well. Not with you in the line of fire," he countered.

"Yeah, and you never lost a fight—until you did. And look what that did to your ego." Miya squeezed her eyes shut, rubbing the exhaustion away. "You're not invincible. I thought you trusted me enough not to pretend otherwise."

An acrid taste coated Kai's tongue, burning through his retort.

Miya was right; every time he feigned stability, pretended to have things under control, he hurt those he tried to protect.

"Say something," she pleaded.

Kai threw back the covers, lowered himself onto the mattress, and slid closer to her. What could he say? That he was sorry? He was, but his apology was worthless when he lacked the confidence to know he could choose differently.

"I fucked up," he said when he failed to excavate anything better. "I thought I could take care of it—"

"You would've kept hiding it if it went smoothly?" she interjected, her ire flaring.

He tried swallowing that bitter taste. "I guess I would've."

Tears rimmed her eyes, her hands clasped tightly in her lap as she fought to contain her hurt. Words weren't his forte; he often spoke out of turn, said things that were cruel in their honesty, and forgot that bluntness wasn't always truthful. Sometimes, it was merely scorn masquerading as truth.

"I'm not *trying* to hide anything that matters." He threaded his fingers with hers, drawing small circles with this thumb—anything to keep himself from fidgeting. "I make bad decisions...a lot. You know that. But you don't have to carry the weight of them too."

"I do," she countered. "Sooner or later, it'll catch up to you—and me." She squeezed his hand. "It's not up to you. You don't get to choose what I can handle. Let me make my own judgments. I already have one Ama in my life."

To be compared to that pompous, overbearing—"Fuck."

"I thought that comparison might hit the mark." A tired smile bent her mouth, and she tugged on his hand as she settled under the covers. "We can pick this up tomorrow."

Worn to the bone, Kai peeled off his T-shirt and made to kick off his pants when Miya grabbed his waistband.

"Sorry, hot stuff. We've got a kid in the other room. You probably shouldn't walk around with your dick flapping free."

A frustrated whine crawled up his throat as he threw himself onto his back. He was going to boil to death.

"You'll be fine," Miya dismissed his bellyaching, then killed the table lamp.

The darkness swallowed up what little fortitude he had left. Unable to quell the panic that carved out his ribs and snatched his heart whole, Kai rolled onto his side and curled a tentative arm around Miya's waist. When she neither tensed nor jerked away, he drew her closer, the unbroken seam of their bodies a needed comfort.

Miya turned to face him and pressed her lips to his collarbone. "I love you," she said, the words heavier than anything passed between lovers ought to be.

Kai was made whole and unraveled all at once. The last person to love him died fifteen years ago, when he was too young to be alone but old enough to know what it meant. Alice had given him a second chance at life, and life mocked him by stealing her away. Love was a curse—a harbinger of loss donning a sinister smile. People insisted it was a gift, but to Kai, it was gilded rot.

And yet he wanted Miya's love—had it even. She declared it freely, but he couldn't say the words back. Why could he never say them back?

"I—" The last two syllables died in his mouth. His teeth clamped together, grinding in pathetic revolt. What the fuck was wrong with him?

Miya lowered her head, her arms wooden around his back. He heard the hitch in her sigh, smelled the brine of her tears, and something inside him fractured.

"You're everything to me." The admission left him raw, flayed open. He wove his fingers through her hair, his cheek pressed to the top of her head. She nodded stiffly against his chest, the unspoken tearing at the seam that'd held them together moments ago.

Miya never questioned Kai's loyalty or dedication. He knew it wasn't about hearing the words for the fuck of it; it was about what they carried. It was the surrender that came with the acknowledgment—the acceptance—that the harbinger with a sinister smile was scratching at his door, and he was powerless to look the other way.

22

KAI STARED *at the piece of card proffered by the soldier at the end of the train car. Its edges were threadbare, ragged where the paper was torn. His last dream had ended here, the stench of grime, shit, and blood enveloping him in a nauseating plume. Meat hooks. Bodies. Walls stained with viscera.*

But Miya was gone.

The wagon juddered as metal shrieked against metal, but the soldier was a dark nucleus, those eyes made of fire never leaving Kai's. They beckoned him to listen. The soldier's head swayed with the train's movements, but his arm remained outstretched. He clinched the ratty card between his fingers like he'd gathered his remaining strength solely for this one task. Kai took in the man's appearance a second time—cracked lips, a stubbled jaw, angles carved from hunger, and unkempt black hair that grazed his shoulders. They were alike, Kai and the soldier, though the latter was shorter, slighter, no older than twenty.

Kai's gaze dipped to what the soldier held. The darkness of the train washed out color the way bleach faded blood, but there was no mistaking the pale lilac, the tattered corners, and the creases Kai had made by his own hand, folding and re-folding his most cherished keepsake. The only piece of Alice he had left.

Kai plucked the card from the soldier's fingers, ice coating his veins. "What the fuck is this?"

The soldier stared back, mute. Kai only ever pulled the card from his wallet to remind himself of what belonging felt like—to yearn for its phantom touch. He could do nothing else. Governed by habit, he pressed

open the scrap of card, his eyes tracing every unsteady line of Alice's final gift to him.

Happy Birthday, Kai Donovan.

The day he joined Alice's family and took her last name.

"How did you get this?" He sounded so meek, so unsure of himself. Gone was the man who threatened with a smile and the confidence of a god made flesh.

Still, his question garnered no response, the soldier tranquil in his resignation. This was a dream, after all. The force of Kai's body was useless here.

For the first time since their meeting, the soldier's mouth bent. A specter of recognition curved his flaking lips, and his chin tipped in a gesture that was both a greeting and a farewell.

The train tore from the tracks, blackness stretched above and below, and Kai's stomach leapt into his throat as he fell. He collided with earth that should've been hard, but soft grass and warm fur broke his sudden plummet. When he righted himself, his tail shot out for balance, and he found himself on four paws. He was small, merely a cub, his limbs stout and uncoordinated. With the eagerness of youth, he wove through the meadow toward the scent of his kin.

A woman awaited in a field of cattails. Her features were blurry, though he recognized her long, wild black hair, the shape of her eyes, and the curve of her elbow as she planted a hand on her hip. Behind her, a man peered vigilantly into the woods. Tall, lithe, and broad-shouldered, he was hewn into hard angles and sharp edges. His dark hair wasn't the cool midnight of the woman's but warm and rich like roasted coffee. Kai had inherited the woman's coat—that same disheveled mane as the man on the train car. Her eyes echoed the soldier's, their fiery gleam passed on to Kai so he could one day snare the Dreamwalker with a single searing stare. But Kai also had the watchful man's stature, and the same distrust of what came from the shadowy gaps between the trees.

They were his parents, and they were waiting for him.

No matter how hard Kai paddled his legs, they remained at a distance, ever-patiently expecting him to catch up. He willed himself to move faster until his front paws flew upward, and his back legs lengthened. He pumped his arms—the skinny, unblemished arms of a child—and as his body finally carried him, his parents sank into the cattails like ghosts. Kai stumbled to a halt, his meagre height a hindrance as he waded through the emerald stems. Annoyance morphed into frustration, which mounted into urgency as fibrous blades gave way to more and more and more...until finally, the cattails parted to reveal two large wolves, one pitch black and the other a deep brown. Noticing their son, they trotted into the woods, their boy at their heels.

Kai remembered the incongruence then. He could never stay in step with them. There was always a disconnect, a gnawing rift between who he thought he was and who he ought to be. His parents couldn't decide if he was a firebrand or a trickster, a boy or a god. He was like them yet not, his whole life spent wondering if he'd lost the only people capable of understanding his conflicted nature. It never occurred to him that they weren't conflicted at all. Perhaps being wolves in the shape of humans never daunted them. Kai was born with something else inside him—a legacy that transcended the trifles of species and blood.

A thunderous crackle pierced the sky. A body fell, heavy and limp, and then another beside it. Tattered breaths, tongues lolled, eyes wide open. A furred ribcage straining to hold a racing heart, lungs heaving to pull life back into them as if the air could act as ambrosia.

But Kai knew it couldn't.

He could never stay in step with them. There was always a disconnect, a gnawing rift...

Now, it severed life from death. Child from parents. Human from wolf.

A choked sob snagged Kai's throat as he tripped into the lifeless bodies of the two wolves. Red pooled beneath them, their vitality painting him the color of his ancestor's eyes. Blood flowed free, nourishing the ground in iron.

Teeth clenched into a snarl, Kai's attention snapped toward the source of the gunshots—the scent of death an invisible tether leading straight to his parents' killers. He threw himself down that line, blind with rage. That furious god of destruction Kai carried within him clawed at the confines of his skin, ravenous for vengeance. A grief-stricken roar rent the air as he launched himself at the one holding the rifle. The hunter staggered, and Kai kicked off his slanted thigh to latch on to his torso, one hand gripping a large shoulder while the other raked across the man's face. Fingers dug into flesh, and Kai sank his teeth into the man's neck—a frantic bid for the jugular. Wild, panicked, thoughtless, he gnawed and gnawed and gnawed like he could somehow devour that rift right back. Copper flooded his mouth, but it couldn't quash the pungent taste of sorrow, so he dug deeper, filled himself with more, desperate to drown it out. He didn't hear the man screaming for help, begging for the assault to end. Even if he had, he wouldn't have stopped, but he would've seen the other man coming.

Something hard and flat connected with the back of Kai's skull. Dizzied, he loosened his grip but refused to relent. The stock of the second hunter's rifle slammed down on him once more, and this time, Kai felt the crunch between his ears. His limbs went slack, and he crumpled to the forest floor.

His vision blurred like a greasy film had been placed over his eyes. Gasping for breath, he tried to lift his head, but it was too heavy for a child to carry—heavier than life itself. It thumped back against the ground, sending a wave of nausea and bone-splitting pain through his spine. He tried cleaving through the fog, focused on clenching his fists. They were larger now, knuckles hardened from endless back-alley brawls, palms calloused from years of labor, hands practiced in fighting and fucking. He was a man again, but the man had little left of him.

Jaw set, Kai forced his neck to hold the weight of his skull. He rolled his shoulders forward, battling collapse, and his vision gradually homed in on a small figure.

He saw himself—a boy of barely ten—standing over the two dead wolves.

His parents.

The boy's face was bruised, his hair matted and sticky with blood as it dribbled down his neck and torso. His gaze was far off even as he stared bleakly at the meat left rotting on the ground. Meat that was once something more. Someone more.

The boy too wanted to be meat. But his heart kept beating, kept forcing life and spirit through his veins. That fucking tumor in his chest—that throbbing, malignant mass, violent in its insistence that he live.

Kai's ragged breaths thundered in his ears, his pulse a storm as he writhed against his immobility. He was useless, impotent, a heap of hurt and discord hollowed out by loss. Crushed by an invisible force he could never name, he surrendered to the inevitability laid bare before him. The past clung on, a fishhook in his heart, and it would hack him into pieces.

Kai could only watch, helpless, as the boy bathed in blood turned to greet the man he would become.

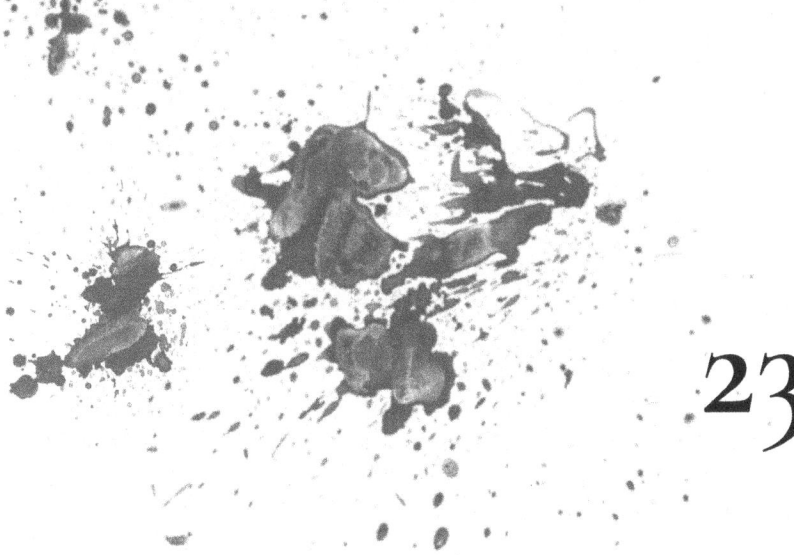

23

WAKEFULNESS SEIZED Kai like a rat trap to the dick. He bolted
upright with a strangled shout, the walls a mural of ghoulish
silhouettes and phantom teeth. His hand flew to his thigh,
searching for his wallet and the enclosed lilac birthday card, though
both rested by the lamp. The afterimages of his nightmare stuck to
his vision like a thick dye. He hadn't relived his parents' deaths in
over a decade; he could barely remember their damn faces. But the
man on the train with eyes like his own...

Miya's touch on his back was his first reacquaintance with reality. He flinched, the sudden contact a jolt of lightning. She'd
awoken with a start; he heard the rapid thrum of her pulse, smelled
her concern—a mawkish sibling to fear.

"Kai?" She shifted closed, her fingers threading through his
sweat-slicked hair.

He clamped his jaw, forcing every inhale and exhale through his
nose. His breaths came fast and shallow despite his efforts to
wrangle his body into submission. Closing his eyes, he banished the
shapes that danced across the room, but the visions didn't stop—
the train, the soldier, the hunters, the wolves, and the boy...

Miya's gasp jarred him from his spiral. Her hand trembled
against the back of his neck, and her eyes guiltily flew to his.

"I'm sorry," she murmured, the apology doubling as a confession. She'd seen the vestiges of the nightmare casting shadows on
the walls of his mind.

Kai shrugged off her touch, realization curdling into anger. He tamped it down, but it seeped through the cracks, corroding his self-control. He whirled on her, face twisted into a snarl. "I told you to stay the fuck out of my head." The outburst verged on a feral growl.

Miya recoiled like he'd flung scalding water at her. Shock skittered across her features before her brow knit, and hurt sharpened into ire. "Fuck you." The rebuke was quiet, hissed through withheld tears. She threw the blankets off her legs and stormed from the bed.

But there was nowhere to go. Their apartment was tiny—five hundred square feet of simmering claustrophobia. Caelan occupied the bedroom, leaving only the bathroom and the kitchenette. Miya paced the six feet of tile, her eyes glassy with moisture. Hiccupping on a sob, she braced against the counter, her urge to flee through the front door palpable as she rocked on her heels.

Mordant guilt abraded whatever wrath lingered in Kai's system. Rubbing his hands over his face, he cursed under his breath, aching to rewind the last thirty seconds. A harsh, humorless laugh clawed up his throat at the thought.

If only he could rewind his whole damn life.

He felt the sting of tears, but the sensation was gone as quickly as it'd come—exiled to the dark pit that homed all his vulnerabilities. He wasn't stupid enough to call them weaknesses, but they left him raw, exposed.

Sodden with shame, Kai crawled from the bed and gingerly approached Miya, her back turned to him. His forehead dipped to her shoulder, and he pressed his nose to the crook of her neck. She was shaking still, anxiety wringing through her body when the stress had nowhere to go—when *she* had nowhere to go. That he was the cause of it knotted him up worse than his nightmare.

Miya rounded on him, her eyes ablaze, her voice like a quiet blade. "Do you have any idea what it's like? Living with a man so traumatized, his pain bleeds out of him while he sleeps? And when I wake up bloodied, he looks at me like *I'm* the one who's crossed a line?" Her mouth clapped shut, a futile attempt to trap the indictment that followed. "A man who, after five years together, can't even tell me he loves me."

Kai bowed his head and swallowed his pulse. "Miya—"

"Shut up and listen. You think if you keep it all inside"—she jabbed his chest—"it's not going to affect me, but you're wrong. All that shit you have locked away rules you, dictating how you feel and behave, how you relate to people. How you relate to *me*. And if you think that doesn't impact me, then you're—" she faltered, her voice breaking. "You're a goddamn idiot."

Unthinking, Kai wrapped both arms around her, a suffocating fusion of terror and desperation propelling him to act—to cling to this person who'd extended her entire life to him. She'd abandoned her home for him, and he was fucking everything up.

"I'm sorry." He held on like she was a ballast, muttering his useless apology. Relief swept through him when the rigidity in her spine gave way, and she slumped in his hold.

She sucked in a ragged breath. "You need therapy."

His head snapped up. "What?"

"Therapy," she repeated into his shoulder. "You need to go to therapy."

Kai stepped back, the declaration gouging his relief.

Her expression was grim, her tone somber. "The past will eat you alive if you don't. And frankly, I'm not sure I want to stick around to watch that happen."

She was being serious. Dead as a fucking fish in the desert serious. Therapy. For Kai Donovan. Or a slow, agonizing trudge to losing his best friend. It wasn't an ultimatum; she'd merely voiced what they both knew. His demons were shearing away pieces of what he'd thought was an iron-clad bond. Eventually, he'd lose her, and it would be his own fault.

His mouth worked, half-formed sounds leaking out as incoherent thoughts pummeled him harder than his regrets. "Who the hell is qualified to deal with"—he swept his arm in front of him—"*this* degree of bullshit."

"Even if they can deal with a tenth of your bullshit, I'll take it." Miya glared, unimpressed. "The fact that you recognize how difficult it'll be to find a qualified professional just proves my point."

Fuck her nerveless retorts. She was right, and there was nothing he could say to weasel his way out. He couldn't pledge an earnest effort to do better because he was doing his best, but his best wasn't enough. He was a trash fire rolling toward a chockful daycare, rancid pieces of him trundling every which way.

The thought of sitting across a therapist made his balls shrivel up in revulsion. He didn't want to talk to a shrink; he'd been down that road with Alice, and it hadn't ended well. He'd narrowly avoided a damning diagnosis of antisocial personality disorder by ditching the clinic while he was still a minor, and he refused to be a case study in a textbook. Scorn burned on his tongue, but he thought better than to give it form. He was hurting the only person who mattered—was incapable of telling her how much she mattered. Even in his most mulish moments, he couldn't deny that she deserved better. He owed her the effort.

With a defeated sigh, Kai slouched his shoulders and nodded. "Fuck me, fine."

"You'll do it?" She perked up, her lungs filling with a hopeful breath.

"You sound surprised."

"Just thought it would take more convincing."

Agitated, Kai averted his eyes and scratched roughly through his hair. "I don't want you to look at me like that ever again," he said quietly, then dropped his hand.

"Like what?"

He clenched his jaw, grinding away his self-reproach. "Like I tore out a piece of you."

She cupped his face between her palms, nudging him to meet her gaze. "Thank you."

His fingers trailed up her arm, and he covered her hand with his own. "Don't thank me yet. The shrink won't."

"Do you want me to come with—"

"No." Too quick. Too stern. He squeezed her fingers as though it would temper the rebuff. "I don't want you there."

He hadn't meant it as a rejection, but Miya shrank away, withdrawing her hand. Kai snatched it back, regret choking him. He reeled her in and smothered her against his chest. "I'll deal with it."

She nodded against him, the bitter undertone of stress and fear melting away. Kai traced the line of her spine, up the nape of her neck, and tangled his fingers in her hair. A sigh slipped from her lips, her gentle curves snug against the rigid plane of his body. It stirred that animal part of him that wanted her on her knees, moaning his name. He hiked up her shirt, roaming her skin with a greedy touch as he walked her back and pinioned her to the counter.

The hard ridge below the cut of his hips pressed against her core. She glanced up, eyebrow raised. "You can't whore your way out of trauma, Kai."

"No shit, Lambchop. If that were possible, I would've fucked my way to enlightenment by now."

The sudden uptick of her pulse betrayed her, but she wore a mask of perfect composure. "Then why bother?"

A wicked smile curved his mouth despite the heaviness in his chest. "I like making you come."

"Does it make you feel better?"

His mirth dissipated, but his lips brushed tenderly over hers as he cradled the back of her head in his hand. "Yes," he half-whispered, half-growled, then devoured the space between them. He meant what he'd said—she was everything to him. The least he could do was show her.

His teeth clipped her lower lip, his mouth a brand on her own. She gasped against the sudden contact, nails raking over the bare skin of his shoulders, his arms, his chest. A low sound rumbled in Kai's throat as he grabbed her by the waist and lifted her onto the counter's edge, his hand smoothing over her thigh.

Miya abruptly broke away. "This isn't getting you out of therapy."

"I know." The challenge in his eyes met the scrutiny in hers. "I just don't want to feel like shit right now."

Her expression softened, and he dreaded glimpsing pity there. Before he could decipher it, her gaze dropped to the scabbing bullet wound in his abdomen, her fingers lightly circling the raised skin. "What about Caelan?"

"What about her?"

"She's in the other room," Miya reminded him.

"And out cold."

"But—"

"Miya, if she so much as farts, I'll hear it."

She took a moment to consider him. "I guess that's true..."

"I can keep quiet." A smirk tugged at his mouth. "Can you?"

Narrowing her eyes, Miya kicked off the counter and corralled him toward the pullout. She shoved him down, and his eyebrows shot up as he fell onto the mattress. Her underwear dropped to the floor, and she climbed onto the bed after him, then gripped his waistband as he propped himself up against the couch's backrest.

Wordlessly, she straddled his hips, then snaked her arms around his neck as his hands skidded up her sides and over the swell of her breasts. He couldn't fuck his way out of trauma, but it sure as hell made everything hurt less.

He let Miya take her pleasure, relishing her ragged breaths, her fingers raking through his hair, her mounting arousal as she chased release. Neither of them bothered removing their remaining clothes—Miya draped in her oversized T-shirt and Kai half-clad in sweatpants. Urgency hooked them both, their desire fueled by woundedness and remorse. If there was a rift between them, their bodies were none the wiser.

Kai didn't care if shame engulfed him whole come the morning. All that mattered was Miya's lips moving in the shape of his name as she unraveled in his arms, and he could, for a moment, allow himself to believe he'd done something right.

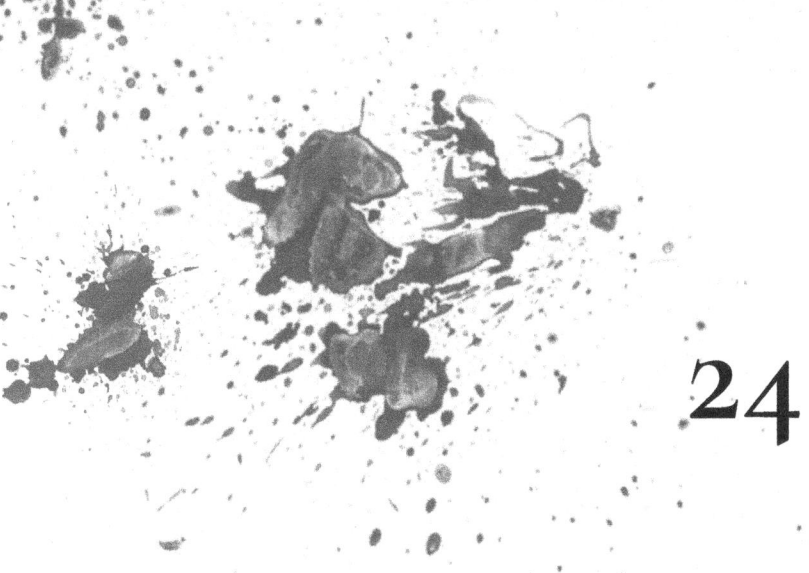

24

THE FERAL MUNCHKIN yowled like he was being skinned alive.

"Shut up, you drama queen." Kai plunked the cat carrier onto the bar top and dropped into a stool. His elbows met the counter, and he ran his fingers through his unruly hair.

"Bro, why do you have a cat?" Connor slid a glass of water toward him and bent over to peer through the mesh door of the nylon bread box.

"That isn't a cat," Kai droned. "It's an orange banshee."

Connor poked the mesh, and the cat shrieked and swiped at him. He snatched his hand back. "Is it Ursula's?"

"I call him Ripper."

"Fitting," Connor laughed.

Maybe Kai should've foisted the furry terror on Ursula. He picked up the glass of water, inspecting it like it was alien goop. "I didn't ask for this."

"You look hung over," said Connor.

Hung over was one way of putting it. He'd woken up feeling worse than that time he'd gotten mauled by a bus. Sure, the sex was great, but it didn't do shit to salve his self-loathing. Guilt spooled in his stomach, his insides a sticky knot. He had nowhere to put that ugly lump—didn't know what to do with it—so it sat idle, growing into something thorny. It didn't help that Miya wore her upset like a pair of manacles. She tried to be pleasant, reassuring him with her affection, but he felt her soreness like the bullet wound in his gut. Her brooding only subsided once she'd found the damn cat skulking behind the microwave. The furball must've fled from under the couch after they'd rattled his safe space, then taken cover behind Kai's favorite appliance.

Caelan was out like a brick all morning, and after checking to make sure she was still breathing, Miya demanded Kai take Ripper to the vet and a groomer. He carried the hellcat under his arm the whole way, ignoring the screeching, biting, and bladed flailing. Horrified, the vet tech donated a carrier, sliding it across the exam table with an awkward smile. Now vaccinated, de-matted, and de-wormed, Ripper boasted a shiny new rabies tag and no longer posed a public health hazard.

"Hey—" Connor waved a hand in front of Kai's face.

Seizing the bartender's wrist, Kai gently pushed him away and gulped down the water. "I'm not hung over." He nodded toward the carrier. "And that…is my new cockroach exterminator."

Connor rubbed his wrist with a frown. "You could choke out a grizzly bear with that grip. Why not just squash the suckers yourself?"

"Too much work, too much mess," said Kai, waving him off. "The cat will kill *and* eat them. Waste management and disposal in one stubby-legged package."

"Right…" Connor trailed off, crossing his arms. "That all?"

Kai shrugged. "A small peace offering to the Lambchop, though it's a work in progress."

"Uh huh," Connor deadpanned. "So that hang over—"

"Yeah, I fucked up a bit."

"A bit…" The bartender raised a brow. "You kidnapped a feral cat, dude. How bad did you fuck up that you figured animal abduction would be a good solution?"

Kai bared his teeth. "Fine. I fucked up big, but I'm dealing with it."

"By…getting your feral cat vaccinated?" Connor ventured.

Kai thumped his forehead to the bar and groaned. "No." He paused, his next words leaving him as a muffled slur. "I need to find a shrink."

Connor choked on his lunchtime beer, then pounded a fist to his chest. "C-come again?"

"You heard me," Kai growled, his head snapping up.

Connor tossed a thumb toward the carrier. "Is your therapy animal not cutting it?"

Kai's eyes narrowed to slits, and he pushed the water glass across the counter. "You think I'm screwing with you, you goddamn potato brain?"

"I think you screwed up, you goddamn cabbage cock."

Kissing his teeth, Kai glanced around the near-empty bar. A pair of men whispered to each other at a corner table, each of them white knuckling their pints like it was a competition. Behind them, Kai glimpsed the woman with the auburn hair—his *fan*—sharing lunch with a guy who looked straight out of a '90s crime thriller. Hardly anyone came around midday, making it the ideal meeting place for illicit business. Connor tolerated it so long as no one started trouble.

"So, you're serious?"

Kai offered a curt nod.

"Damn..." Connor rubbed the back of his head, his hair let down to graze his shoulders. "All right, fine. I might know someone."

"Really?" Kai watched the demonic furball settle into a loaf now that its bread box was on a solid surface.

"There's this woman—forgot her name—but she works with mobsters' wives. A distant cousin of mine's still in the biz—real prick, that guy—but his girl Shawna used to come around here and vent to Carol. Talked about her sessions with this chick a lot."

Kai's face scrunched. "I'm not looking for an aesthetician."

"No, no." Connor waved a bulky hand. "She's the real deal. Clinical psychologist. Her clientele is just...very specific. Confidentiality is her bread and butter. Besides, you know how it is with these ladies. Their lives are rough. Some of them get in real young—think it's glamorous to marry a thug. Their whole world falls apart when they realize they've been duped. Husband's got three mistresses on the side but won't stand for divorce. Lies about what he's up to. Makes threats if she complains too much. Some of them do all right, but a lot of them don't."

The acrid taste of doubt coated Kai's tongue. He was adjacent to the mob, but the proximity was enough to make him sweat. Sergei had already maneuvered him deeper than he wanted to be, and he'd lied to Miya because of it. How long until she became one of those women, purging to a stranger because he'd made her a ghost in their home?

"I'm not a jilted wife," Kai said stonily.

Connor pulled the tap and helped himself to another pint. "Look, there aren't many therapists who'll know what to do with you. You've got problems at home with your girl? Go talk to the woman who's hearing it from the other team. Whatever you're dealing with can't be worse than what a hitman's wife puts up with."

No, it wasn't, but that didn't mean it was good or that Miya should tolerate it. And she wouldn't—not forever. Kai tried imagining his life without her, remaking himself in the shape of solitude. It was a shape he recognized—one he'd owned for the better part of his life. He didn't want it back. Didn't want an existence where his loneliness ate him alive, and his only salve was a parade of sloppy hookups night after night. If Miya left him for her own reasons, so be it, but he refused to be the cause. He just didn't know how not to be, and that scared the shit out of him.

The kitchen doors burst open, and out waltzed Carol.

"Connor!" she barked. "Where the hell's my lettuce order?"

Pint glass raised to his lips, Connor gulped his beer down with his terror. "Should be here—"

"Well, it's not! How am I supposed to make all those salads without lettuce, hm?" She crossed her arms over her chest, ignoring Kai as she drilled holes into her boss.

"All right, fuck. I'll do a store run before the kitchen opens," Connor appeased.

Carol widened her stance. "If I see you lurking around here in twenty minutes, I'll throw a damn skillet at your head."

"Yes ma'am." Connor shook his head, muttering to Kai, "You'd think she owns *my* ass, not the other way around."

Carol's hand came down on Kai's back in a hearty slap. "Damn right I do, boy. This place would do just fine if you were out with a broken skull, but there ain't no Confessional without Carol."

Kai winced as she rattled his spine. "You don't seem like the type to forgive people their sins, you crazy old bat."

"Shut up." Carol threateningly squeezed Kai's shoulder as he snorted on a laugh.

"Speaking of sins"—Connor snapped his fingers—"what was the name of that shrink Shawna used to visit?"

"Shawna!" Carol guffawed. "Yeah, I remember her. She was married to your dingus of a cousin—"

"Second cousin twice removed," Connor corrected.

Carol belched. "Whatever. No wonder she ran away with that hairy Cosa Nostra bastard. Are you thinking of Dr. Krunić?"

"Yes!" Connor jabbed a triumphant finger at her. "That's the one."

Carol nodded, stretching her limbs. "Hristina Krunić. Certified badass. She'll rip your dick off, grill it over some hot coals, then hand it back to you."

Kai scoffed. "How nurturing..."

"Text me her number," Connor said as Carol pivoted toward the kitchen.

"Only if you get me my lettuce," she called over her shoulder.

"Well, you heard Carol. Dr. Krunić will trim off your excess manhood." Connor grinned ear to ear, clearly pleased with himself. "Hey—"

"What?" Kai grumbled, ignoring the conversation that'd transpired.

"I'm proud of you. Getting help takes balls." He leaned over the counter and spread his arms. "Bring it in—"

"Fuck off and get me a drink," Kai snarled, lightly shoving him back.

Connor erupted into raucous laughter, turning a few heads across the dining room. He grabbed the nearest bottle of bourbon and poured Kai a finger, then frowned as the bell on the door chimed.

Kai knew who it was before Connor could sneer the name.

"I thought I might find you here."

Hairs standing on end, Kai resisted the urge to swing an elbow at Sergei's face as he stopped by the bar. He slammed back his bourbon instead.

"I've got to buy that lettuce before Carol chops my fingers off and uses them for croutons." Connor eyed Sergei warily, then tipped his chin up at his friend. "You good?"

"Get me that number. I'll survive the rest." Kai reached around the carrier and slid it toward the bartender. "Take this thing with you. Drop it off at my place."

Connor nodded, then spared Sergei a final glower before he grabbed his jacket and slung the carrier strap over his shoulder. The whole case rattled as Ripper yowled and spun. Once Connor was out of earshot, Sergei helped himself to the stool next to Kai. "So, how'd it go?" he asked as he slipped out of his tweed coat.

Kai stared down his empty glass, debating whether to hop the counter and filch the whole bottle. "It's complicated."

"I don't have time for your deflections," Sergei said impatiently. "I've got business to deal with."

Kai exhaled harshly through his nose, a smirk ghosting his lips. "I thought the forgery *is* pressing."

"It is."

"Then what's got your nuts in a twist? A snitch?"

After some tight-lipped tooth-gnashing, Sergei nodded tersely, his watch clanking as he brought his forearms to the counter. "Where is it?"

"Where's what?" Kai feigned, staring at the wall.

"Don't play stupid. Did you get the forgery or not?"

"It's not a *what*." Kai's grip closed around the empty tumbler. Before he could change his mind, he snatched a bottle from the shelf. "It's a *who*."

Sergei's mouth opened, a strangled sound catching in his throat before shock clamped his jaw. "It's...a person?"

"A kid." Uncorking the bottle, Kai fisted the neck and tilted his head back, chasing down the bitter taste with more bourbon.

"Jesus." Sergei ran a shaky hand through his hair, straw-colored strands tumbling around his face. "They kidnapped a kid?"

"Yeah, you cunt, they did." What did the idiot expect? That his life as a gangster would be clean? Kai dipped into Bratva's shadows now and again, but even that was too much. They were dragging him into their miasma, a phantom quicksand coaxing him further underground.

"I...I don't do that messed up stuff," Sergei said more to himself than to Kai. He folded his hands on the bar top, nails clipping a nick in the wood. "I arrange fights, oversee money laundering and gambling—not human trafficking."

Kai clanked the bottle down and rotated on his stool, leveling Sergei with a withering look. "Who did you think you work for?"

"Who did you think *you* work for?" Sergei shot back, his eyes glassy with panic.

Kai angled forward until they were nose to nose. The mobster went rigid like a piece of brittle wood, and true to nature, he snapped under pressure, cowering just enough to show his hand. He was afraid.

"I never worked for anyone, you shivering little shit." Kai's lips lifted from his teeth. "You know our arrangement. My connection to you begins and ends right here in this bar. You're the one who brought your mess into *my* house."

Sergei was a petty criminal with the fashion sense of a corporate goon. He was squeamish, hiding his gelatinous spine behind busy work in underground fight clubs and gambling dens. Crime was a family business. Sergei may have been born into it, but that didn't mean he was well-suited for it.

"Why does Pyotr want the kid?" Kai asked when the shell-shocked pissant failed to muster a reply.

"No clue." Sergei rubbed his palms over his face, his skin blotchy and red. "Listen, you've got to keep this kid hidden. Don't give them back to their family. If you do, Pyotr will find out, butcher them all like rabbits, then call it a burglary gone wrong." He pressed his forehead to his knuckles. "Just...give me some time. I'll get intel and figure something out."

Kai had no intention of returning Caelan to her family. It would be like herding sheep into a slaughterhouse. "Fine." He passed Sergei the booze. "Guess you're not a steaming wad of phlegm."

He reluctantly accepted the bottle. "That's...very specific."

Kai shrugged. "I like to paint a picture."

Sergei shook his head and handed the bourbon back to Kai, then slipped his arms through his coat sleeves.

"Going after your snitch?" Kai asked, staring down the glass neck as he rotated the base.

"A thorn in my side, but it must be dealt with."

Kai rose from the stool and drained the last few ounces of liquor. Shaking off the sting, he planted the bottle atop the bar. "Let's go for a walk, *milyy*."

Sergei rolled his eyes. "And why exactly are you so intent on joining me?"

Despite the question, he didn't protest when Kai kept stride with him. "A favor for a favor. I'll help you with your rat, and you can't say I owe you for buying the kid time."

"Fair enough," Sergei conceded. "I've always admired your aversion to debts."

Kai's mouth slashed into a chilly smile, and he swallowed down the fury that licked up his throat. "I promise, I pay mine with interest."

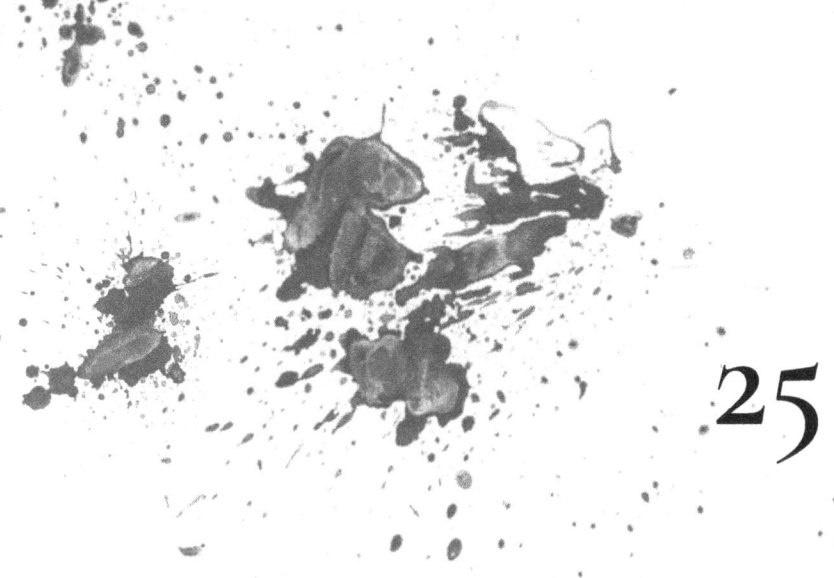

25

THE CORNER POCKET was every cheater's favorite haunt, whether in marriage or a game of poker. A squalid back-alley dive, the bar looked like it could give you a sexually transmitted disease for walking by too slow.

They stopped across the street after Sergei insisted on a smoke, his hand shaking every time he lifted the cigarette to his lips. He rocked from heels to toes as if he could sway himself out of his job. It was remarkable given that he wouldn't have to lift a finger with Kai there to drag the snitch out by the hair.

"So, how badly did this guy shit the bed?" Kai broke the silence.

A plume of smoke rose between them as Sergei exhaled. "Sold some pricy secrets. Got people killed because of it. As if that's not bad enough, a few neighborhood teens were hit in the crossfire. One's dead, and the other will need years of therapy."

An icy tendril unfurled in the space behind Kai's ribs, lashing at his bones until his stomach churned. He shouldn't have been so affected by mundane tragedy—never was—but the phantoms from his nightmares kept threading through his mind, wreathing his thoughts in bramble. He could still smell the copper slicking his skin, making him itchy even now.

"What do you need me to do with him?"

Sergei flicked the embers off his cigarette. "I just need to deliver him to the right person. After that, he'll disappear."

Kai hung his head and laughed darkly. "Delivering him to his executioner. How sweet."

"I'm not a killer," Sergei said, his eyes on the bar across the way.

Kai bore into the mobster, his tongue clicking against the back of his teeth. "I'd have more respect for you if you were."

Sergei stomped on his cigarette. "Men like you and Zverev speak only one language: violence. Makes you useful, but it also makes you rather dull." He smacked Kai on the arm, ignoring his seething glare. "Let's go. You'll have your fill of blood."

Kai followed despite the urge to crush Sergei's skull like a walnut. He didn't care if some self-important goon thought he was dull, but the assumption that he was stupid doggedly followed him through life. Whether it was incomplete homework, his lowbrow pastimes, or his penchant for aggression, people regarded him like he couldn't rub two brain cells together to conjure a single meaningful insight. In truth, Kai spoke many languages. Violence was simply the one he'd become most proficient in.

As they reached the opaque doors of the Corner Pocket, a gaggle of drunk men shambled out. Shadows clung beneath their eyes, their faux-silk shirts and heavy coats suffused with cigar smoke.

"Poker players," Sergei muttered as he stepped aside to let them pass. They waddled by like disoriented poultry headed toward the nearest crosswalk.

The inside of the bar sucked away the daylight like a fog bank at dusk, and the smell of worn rugs and flaking lacquer wrinkled Kai's nose. A counter with stools ran the length of one wall while staggered pool tables commanded the floor space. The shelves were fully stocked with budget liquors, but there was no one in sight.

"Downstairs," Sergei instructed, though Kai didn't need to be told. His ears picked up a heartbeat below the floor.

The staircase was narrow and bare, concrete walls pockmarked with age. Kai was sure they were headed into some kind of cellar when the craggy door whirred open to reveal a decadent room swathed in finery. Burgundy velvet curtains cascaded down black marble walls that were adorned with massive paintings worth more than the building they were in. A fully stocked bar fashioned the basement into an entirely new income bracket, and a felted poker table crowned the stained parquet floor as a centerpiece, one of the six chairs occupied by a man counting chips.

Casually slung back in his seat, he propped a leg up on the table, one pointy snakeskin shoe tip waggling at the ceiling. His salmon-colored paisley print button-up—which he'd failed to button up more than halfway—revealed a thin gold chain navigating a dark thicket on his bare chest. His stubbled jaw ground left and right as he kept his stare trained on the chips, heedless of the two men who'd entered his luxurious cave.

"You didn't tell me he *looked* like a rat," Kai muttered to Sergei.

Sergei refused to dignify Kai's quip with a response. He cleared his throat, drawing the gambler's attention. "Maksim."

The rat shook a greasy lock of hair from his eyes, then tucked it behind his ear. It was cropped midway down his neck, stiff as though he'd christened each strand with pork lard. "Sergei," he drawled. "To what do I owe the pleasure?"

Kai couldn't decide if Maksim was arrogant or lacked discernment.

Sergei's expression turned dour. "No pleasure. This is just business, I'm afraid."

The greaseball flung a chip across the table. It rolled over the felt before wobbling to a stop. "You were always far too serious for this life."

"And you were never serious enough." Sergei gave Kai a weighty look. A bead of sweat trickled down his temple, his spine rigid like he had a fire poker menacing his sphincter.

Too bad. Things were about to get a lot more uncomfortable.

Kai's mouth bent into something not-quite-smile and not-quite-sneer. Sergei wanted him to play errand boy—to leash his boss's rabid hound and wrangle the beast back to a cruel master. Maybe Maksim deserved it, but Kai didn't care about what people deserved. They got what they got regardless of how virtuous or vile they were. Psychopaths helmed governments responsible for millions. Rich kids with a blank cheque for their futures died of cancer. Poor ones with good health got their organs harvested to extend the shelf life of an expiring oligarch. If there was any design to it all, it was a madman's playbook, the rules little more than a gibbering cackle.

Maksim launched to his feet and kicked the chair forward, a nervous laugh skittering out of him as he backed away. At least he knew enough to reckon he'd done something wrong. "What is this,

Sergei? Pyotr snipped your balls, so you brought your pet to do your dirty work for you?"

Sergei's breath hitched, though he remained rooted to the floor, apparently determined to stay and watch as Kai took the bloody reins. "He offered, I accepted," came his quiet reply. "And frankly, I feel no need to vindicate my masculinity to a child killer."

The rat's unruffled exterior finally fractured, and he reached for what Kai assumed was a loaded firearm strapped to his belt. Before he could brush his fingers over the grip, Kai closed in with an easy lunge. He swiped at the inside of Maksim's elbow to halt his scrabble for the gun, then drove a fist into the softness between his ribs. Maksim gagged on a strangled yell, his body folding with the force of the strike. Fingers coiling around the rat's clammy neck, Kai slammed him back into the bar, bottles clamoring as glassware toppled and shattered against the parquet. With his free hand, he hooked the pistol by the trigger guard, casually lifted it from the holster, and tossed it over his shoulder.

"F-freak!" the snitch choked, spit flecking his chin as he struggled to breathe.

Kai slanted his head in consideration. "In the sheets, maybe."

Before Maksim could sling another insult, Kai flung him to the floor like a broken doll. It was so easy, too easy, to take every iota of suppressed rage—rage at himself, his parents, his past carving him hollow—and unbridle it in this putrid corner of the underworld. To unleash every dark impulse on this fragile body animated by a withering soul.

Then again, maybe Kai was no different. Maybe that's why it was so *easy*.

He stalked closer, his shadow swallowing his prey's. And this scrambling meat sack *was* prey. He was sobbing now, his mouth working to form something—anything—that would stop Kai's brutal advance.

"Sergei, call your executioner." Kai's voice was pitiless, resolute.

Eyes wide with realization, Sergei uncrossed his arms and stood pin straight. "You can't—there...there are *methods*," he stammered. "To ensure no one's caught."

Kai's gaze lifted from the quivering heap on the floor to Sergei's dumbstruck face. "You don't have to worry about that."

As his attention slid back to the snitch, a prickling sensation spidered up his spine. It'd been a long time since he'd felt this, though perhaps not long enough. Barring the strange incident with the stranger who'd hired Miya, Kai had complete control over his transition. And ever since he'd acquired that control, he kept the animal locked away.

All with good fucking reason. The change was a saw-toothed blade, his most painful experience—and Kai had experienced a lot. But he wasn't here to be comfortable in his skin. He was here to make a point.

Kai's lips peeled back as he loosened the shackles on the wolf, the predator stirring from its long slumber in the darkest recesses of his being. The animal was a legacy doubly imposed. Once from his parents, and once from Sendoa, the god whose essence he'd inherited. Sendoa died in the shape of a wolf, and those contours plaited with Kai's soul, sinking their teeth into him life after miserable life. Kai didn't know why his parents shared his condition when he harbored the spirit of an ancient deity, but the answers were lost, fractured to pieces and ground to dust by the slow march of time.

It didn't matter anymore.

His head jerked to the side, and a snarl ripped from his throat. That prickle morphed into a simmer, punctuated by a riving along his spine. Pain twisted his face, and he heard Sergei swear while the snitch remained paralyzed—a deer preparing for death. A bone-deep chill quaked through Kai, but his skin felt scalded, screaming for reprieve as thousands of needle-like hairs prodded his flesh from the inside. The wolf twitched and shook, revolting against Kai's flimsy internal cage. Something between a harsh shout and feral growl tore from his chest as a joint splintered, followed by another, until his frame could no longer support his weight, and he collapsed to his knees. His clothes slipped away; they weren't made for these contours. Fingers curled in on themselves, fusing into nubs. Nails thickened into claws, and his canines sharpened, lengthened, biting into his lip as he clamped his jaw to keep from screaming.

What big fucking teeth you have.

Kai sneered, mocking the beast as the pain wrapped him in a savage embrace.

And he welcomed it.

Spiky, disheveled black hair rose to hackles, sprouting along his back and over his limbs, colonizing every inch of skin. His jaw broke, mincing his efforts to contain the agony. The sounds that left him were neither human nor animal—monstrous roars to accompany a monstrous thing.

Every scrap of external stimuli scrambled his senses as he adjusted. Sights were blinding, noises disorienting, smells nauseating. His tail burst from his body like some alien thing racing toward life, and as it swooped low against his haunches, he settled back into his body.

The wolf had always felt like home.

"What the *fuck* is that!" Maksim shrieked, every syllable a stutter as he kicked uselessly against the floor.

Dark eyes haloed in crimson snapped to the bumbling meat sack, a low sound reverberating from behind bared teeth. Kai's muzzle rippled as charcoal lips skinned back, and the cage of white opened, tongue lashing in anticipation of flesh.

Ears flat against his skull, Kai sprang forward with strength that outsized his canine body. But humans bruised so effortlessly under the pin-point pressure of a blunt claw. Maw splitting open in a fiendish grin, Kai locked his fangs around Maksim's jugular. Blood spilled into his mouth, an animal satisfaction purring through him as he rent his victim's neck like a blade through ripe fruit. Maksim lurched, limbs thrashing, his screams devolving into pathetic gargles as his jaw went slack, and his mouth hung open. The tension seeped from his bones, leaving him like limp rubber.

Kai gave the man's throat a final wrench, and his life spattered carelessly across the parquet, staining it in copper. A deep, predatory rumble thrummed out of the wolf, and he finally let go. The rat's body hit the floor with a wet smack, a scarlet mural crowning his rolling head.

His spine had been so brittle, thinner than Kai remembered, the meat encasing it more tender than expected.

Five calloused pads stamped their mark in the blood bridging Maksim's body and his wayward skull. The wolf rotated in placed, nose grazing tail tip like a shadow-inked ouroboros. He retraced his path, prowling toward the only remaining pulse in the room.

Sergei plastered himself against the wall, his breaths drawing shallow as he peered at the wolf stalking closer—a hundred and forty pounds of piercing teeth and palpable terror.

Kai halted several yards from his accomplice. He'd put on a good show, but only half the point had been made.

Before his mastery over the transition, he'd fall asleep a wolf and wake up a man. He didn't know why the reverse metamorphosis was seamless—a shift during slumber—but today, he didn't have the luxury of waiting for that comfort. Today, he'd have to spur the change, will himself to break, to endure the same torture that twisted him from man to beast.

It'd taken him a long time to accept that he was neither one nor the other but both at once. A chimera. A hybrid. He used to think of himself as a wolf clothed in human skin, not unlike Gavran—a raven wearing a boy's corpse. He knew better now. The wolf erupted from the confines of the man, and the man from the shape that made the wolf.

His tail was the first to recede, slipping into the marrow of his spine. Where warmth once cocooned him under his coarse midnight coat, disruptive cold now kissed his naked skin. Fingers unfurled, rupturing from his paws, and his muzzle compressed, forcefully molding into a human-like mandible. There was deafness, followed by a high-pitched squeal cleaving through his ears. A blinding flash of color in a world muted by grays. The wolf standing on four sturdy legs transformed into a man on his knees, his palms flat against a floor mottled in blood, smelling of gore and shit.

Nausea struck like a torrent, and Kai swallowed down the pungent taste of bile. The vinegary lump stuck in his throat, but he refused to allow his body the purge. With an angry shout, he pushed off the parquet and rose unsteadily to his feet. He didn't have time to adjust, didn't care to retrieve his discarded clothes. Balling his fists at his sides, he wrangled his focus into a bullet aimed at Sergei's chest.

Sparing himself one ragged breath, Kai stalked up to the petrified mobster. Red marred pristine white as he grabbed Sergei by the collar, jerked him off the wall, then slammed him back into it. Winded by the collision, Sergei wheezed pathetically. As he sagged, Kai snatched him by the throat and forced him upright.

"Do you know why I won't join the mob?" Kai asked, a vicious snarl still wound into his features.

Sergei tried to shake his head, but Kai's grip was too strong. All he managed was a sorry twitch.

Wrath dammed by a mere sliver, Kai's breath scorched Sergei's face. "It's not because I don't like getting my hands dirty." He smeared Maksim's blood over the mobster's pallid cheek in a gruesome taunt, then leaned closer, the smell of iron radiating from his skin. "It's because I'm no one's bitch. Not yours, and not Pyotr's. You may not be a killer, but I am. You fuck with me one more time —try to threaten my girl or strong-arm me into one of your pissing contests with another faction—and I'll tear your spine out with my teeth." Kai shoved him, the wall juddering hard enough to jostle one of the art pieces off its hook.

"Fuck," Sergei whimpered, his knees buckling in time with the painting's crash to the floor. "What the *hell* are you?"

Seeing Sergei in tatters mollified some of Kai's festering rage. He averted his gaze, his expression mellowing from hellfire to boredom. "I don't know, what the fuck is Ivan Zverev?"

"He's a Zverev," Sergei said stupidly, as though it was supposed to be illuminating.

"Yeah, I gathered that, asshole."

"You've really never heard of them?" Sergei probed like he'd confirmed something he'd long suspected. With a shaky sigh, he unfolded his limbs and dragged himself up the wall. "They're a clan from Western Siberia. Rumor—" he hesitated, then choked on a half-sob, half-laugh. "No, *folklore* has it they're born with bodies hard as granite, unmatched strength and speed. They can smell death before he's honed his scythe and see shadows on moonless nights. Zverevs are hard to come by, and even harder to kill." Sergei's nervous gaze flew to Kai as he confessed, "When I first saw you, I thought you were one of them, but you don't seem to know anything."

Sergei's words abraded whatever slim composure remained on Kai's face. "Western Siberia?" He was born in Western Siberia—in Surgut. He didn't remember any of it; his family had relocated to the United States while he was still a kid. He didn't even know how old he'd been, but he recalled tastes and scents too foreign for a rural town in the Pacific Northwest: sauerkraut, pickled fish, pirozhki. Motes of some vague, elusive memory, but nothing concrete. Nothing that told him anything truly useful. Even his childhood in Washington remained fuzzy, courtesy of the head trauma and repressed memories from the night his parents were killed. They would've been around his age when they died, maybe a little older.

His gut furled into a tight ball, his nerves flayed raw as it dawned on him: Ivan Zverev was likely a distant cousin.

Their botched fight clawed out his insides until he felt empty enough to curl in on himself. He'd relived his parents' murder mere hours before learning that one of his kin wandered the very city where he'd chosen to build a home.

The universe was cruel. Callous, sadistic, and *fucking* cruel.

"You *are* one of them," Sergei whispered, wonder, awe, and horror wavering his voice.

Kai whirled on him, his feet sticky against the wooden floor, his naked body slick with carnage. Behind Sergei, he glimpsed his reflection in the cold black marble wall. Eyes like blood stared back at him, trapped behind an impassable façade.

26

MIYA

BASTIEN PLACED A SERVING plate the size of a flying saucer on the bar in front of Caelan. Three perfectly golden crab cakes and a mountain of fries awaited the teen's shrunken stomach, the fluffernutters from the night before long gone.

"Eat up, kid." He slid her a fork and knife wrapped in a turquoise napkin, followed by a pint of cola.

She didn't need to be told twice. Foregoing the utensils, Caelan dug in with her hands, ignoring the ketchup and remoulade. Miya had never seen someone so ravenous—except maybe Kai, who could endure days without food but griped every hour that passed without snacks. His and Ama's metabolisms adjusted to accommodate their intake, keeping their bodies robust regardless of their environment.

Caelan, on the other hand, was just starved.

Bastien shot Miya a questioning look, and she responded with a rueful smile. Caelan had slept until noon, and after stocking up on junk food from Marty's and buying a pair of cheap sneakers, Miya opted to get the teen some fresh air. It'd taken a while to find clothes that fit her—an old pair of leggings and a cashmere sweater that'd shriveled after a bad stint in the dryer. In the meantime, Connor dropped off Ripper, shrugging noncommittally when Miya asked after Kai. The orange munchkin hid under the couch for another hour before emerging to scarf down some newly acquired cat food. Bolder than the night before, he sniffed at Miya and Caelan, then squatted atop the counter, tail flicking to-and-fro.

Now at the King of Spades, Miya watched Caelan eat her weight in French fries. The bar wouldn't open until four, giving them time to mill about.

"You need anything else, you let me know," said Bastien. "Girl looks too weak to whip a gnat."

"These are really good," Caelan mumbled, her eyes tracking the Gullah chef.

"Those are southern crab cakes. My Mawmaw made those for me any time I was feeling afflicted." His shoulders pulled back proudly. "New England could learn a thing or two about good comfort food."

"We have crab cakes too," Caelan pointed out.

Bastien threw his head back and guffawed. "Not like these, you don't."

Caelan's gaze trailed the length of the bar, then fixed on the shadows beneath the antique mirror.

Bastien's laugh came to a hiccupping halt. "What're you staring at over there?"

Miya glanced over her shoulder. The domovoy sat quietly under the heavy brass frame, staring at the newcomer. His rotund, furry head canted like he was trying to make sense of her, and he chittered softly.

"You can see him?" Miya turned back to Caelan, who nodded curtly.

Bastien threw his arms up. "Shit, no. I'm out. Going to that white lady's crystal shop to buy some overpriced sage." He paused mid-step and squeezed his eyes shut. "...After I finish prepping." Sighing, he bee-lined for the kitchen doors. "Holler if you need anything!"

Miya leaned back to leave the line of sight between the domovoy and Caelan unbroken.

"You can see him too?" Caelan polished off the crab cakes, but the pile of fries was insurmountable.

"He's a house spirit." Miya had never met anyone capable of peering right through the boundary between worlds. Ama and Kai came close—both liminal, both able to sense things beyond the earthly plane. They interacted with the domovoy from behind the veil, tossing hair clippings and breadcrumbs his way, but they couldn't truly see and experience what Miya did.

Caelan was the first.

The teen beamed a smile—something she hadn't shown before. "I thought I was the only one who saw things. I thought I was sick."

Miya clasped her hands together under the bar. Her palms were clammy, anxiety wringing her into restlessness as she wracked her brain for how to engage a traumatized teen. She couldn't approach her like she did Kai, bludgeoning him with what he avoided to force him to look.

So far, so good, she reassured herself, bolstered by Caelan's infectious smile. They were building rapport through the one thing they had in common: contact with the dreamscape.

"I once thought I was being spirited away," Miya told her. "Insomnia, sleepwalking, panic attacks, hallucinations—all of it. Figured I was losing my mind. But I know now there are things out there that don't fit most people's idea of what's real and what isn't. Doesn't matter if you call it *madness* or *haunting*; the experience is real."

Caelan fell silent as she dropped her gaze to her lap. Ocher hair brushed against her brows, obscuring her face. Miya wondered if she was weighing the wisdom of disclosure, but when the lull yawned out into a gaping maw, she snapped it shut with a question.

"Have you ever gone to a place that feels different? Like a dream that isn't a dream?"

"This place used to feel like a dream." Caelan's voice was barely audible. She shifted in the stool, then took a slurp of her soda. "Every place feels that way to me, whether I'm awake or asleep." Her eyes strayed to Miya's face. "I saw you in one of my dreams—a bad one. When you showed up at the warehouse, I wasn't sure if I was still in that nightmare."

It sounded like a riddle, and Miya didn't have the clues to puzzle it out, but the teen clearly recognized her from the hellscape with the doll factory. Miya's own life had once been a waking nightmare, and her conviction that a supernatural entity was out to kidnap her only heightened the unreality of it all, but Caelan didn't seem to suffer the same burden. She wasn't afraid of the dreamscape like Miya had been. Perhaps she simply couldn't decide which world better suited her difference. Whatever the case, she was clearly acquainted with the ethereal plane.

"Do you remember anything from before you were found three

years ago?" A direct question, but one that'd been burning on Miya's tongue. Caelan seemed perfectly socialized, yet she'd appeared out of thin air according to the report Ama dug up.

Caelan ducked a nod. "Sort of. I remember being in a different place. I remember a friend—a spirit who took care of me. We watched this side, learned about it. It's a haze, but once I was here, everything came pretty naturally. I just copied those around me."

The spirit who cared for her must've been the leshy, yet Miya couldn't wrap her head around what, exactly, Caelan was supposed to be. She'd clearly come to the waking world with some knowledge of it, and what she lacked, she learned through mimicry. "What about your parents? They probably miss you."

Caelan worried her lower lip. "I can't go back there."

"Why not?" Miya pressed.

"It's complicated."

"Were you having problems with them?"

"No!" Caelan's head snapped up. "No, nothing like that. They were trying so hard to help me, but...I don't think I can be helped."

"Helped..." Miya ventured. "What do you need help with?"

"Her..." A half-whisper, half-hiss, as though the mere utterance could conjure a ghost.

Miya recalled the presence Caelan had mentioned in her diary. The one calling her. "Is *she* chasing you?"

Hesitation, nervous writhing. "*Pulling* more like..."

Was there really a distinction between *chasing* and *pulling* where haunting was concerned? "And who is *she*?"

A frantic shake of the head. "I don't know. All I know is that if I listen to the call—if I find her—something terrible will happen." The teen released a shaky breath. "I don't want to talk about this. Not right now." She poked at a fry. "How did you find me, anyway?"

"Your friend hired me," Miya said after cudgeling her urge to push the matter. "A tall, elderly man who..." She measured her next words carefully. "He's a foreigner in this plane."

Caelan nodded, drawing figure eights with the French fry. "He cared for me on the other side. The...place you say isn't like anywhere else."

"When did you meet him?"

She paused her tracing on the plate. "I don't know. Time isn't the same over there, but I feel like I've known him for a long time."

"The leshy—"

"Is that what he is?" Caelan sat up straighter. "He doesn't have a name, though it doesn't seem to matter to him." She swung her legs and huffed, her countenance finally loosening. "Either way, I came to this side because I had to, but he—the leshy—he couldn't follow. I miss him."

Alarm spangled through Miya's skull. "What do you mean you *had* to come to this side?"

Caelan's face twisted like a barbed knot had lodged in her throat. "The call," she said, voice wobbling. "I couldn't fight it anymore."

Miya placed a gentle hand on the girl's back, the motion spurring a choked sob. "I'm sorry. We don't have to talk about it." Guilt silenced her, though she'd finally woven several pieces of the story together.

Caelan wasn't being called *to* the dreamscape; she'd been summoned by something on this side. Did she slip into the ethereal plane to escape? To resist this *call*? The leshy may have protected her, given her an anchor so she could battle whatever was trying to bait her. Yet Miya had never heard of spirits trying to lay snares from the earthly realm; they spun their webs in the dreamscape, threading their lures through the cracks between worlds and into the nightmares of their victims, entangling them from afar.

The Carvers said Caelan had been looking for a door. Miya initially suspected that she was re-tracing her steps to the park where she'd first appeared, searching for a way back to her friend. But her pursuer was tempting her to that very spot, as if she knew that intercepting Caelan at the gateway between worlds was the easiest way to corner her.

Hinges screeched from the entryway of the King of Spades, interrupting the tense exchange.

"Miya—I thought you'd be at home." Ama tapped her nails against her belt as the door squealed to a stop behind her, a disapproving frown curving her mouth.

"I decided to take Caelan out for some fresh air," Miya replied, rotating on her stool.

The white wolf's amber gaze slid to the teen, then back to Miya. "That was reckless. What if someone's out looking for her? They might've spotted you."

"She's been cooped up long enough. She deserves to get out a bit." Needled by Ama's admonition, Miya hopped out of her seat. "Would you be scolding Kai if he was the one with Caelan?"

Taken aback, Ama's hand dropped from her hip and flopped against her thigh. "Anyone would tell you this is a bad idea."

"Kai wouldn't."

Ama's stare iced over. "I wouldn't expect otherwise."

An underhanded insult. Miya pursed her lips as Caelan quietly observed the exchange. "I suppose we should go back."

"Who's that?" Caelan leaned over to get a better look. "She was with you that night."

Miya hesitated as the white wolf simmered. "This is my friend Ama. She helped me find you."

Ama crossed her arms over her chest and shifted her weight as Caelan continued to peer at her, unblinking. Finally, she twitched under the scrutiny.

"She's like him," Caelan concluded, severing whatever invisible cord she'd used to reach inside Ama.

"How could you tell?" Miya asked.

"I don't know." Caelan shrugged. "They're just...different. It's like telling cats from dogs."

Ama batted her eyelashes. "Who're the cats in this analogy?"

Caelan puffed up her cheeks, then gave a noncommittal croak. "I don't know what you are. Just that you're not human."

Clearly displeased at the prospect of being either, Ama returned her attention to Miya. "I wanted to make sure you're all right after what happened last night. You seemed...upset."

"We're working it out," Miya said evasively.

The white wolf squinted, unconvinced. "Are you?"

Miya silenced her with a stern *yes*. She didn't want Ama prying —not now. The wolves had always been at each other's throats, though they'd reached a tenuous peace over the last few years. Still, that didn't stop Ama from sniffing out Kai's blunders like a wounded deer's blood trail. The huntress wouldn't dare forego the opportunity for an easy kill.

"I'm taking things slow," Miya said, watching Caelan polish off her remaining fries. "Just keep your eyes peeled for anything... weird, I guess."

Ama arched a perfectly groomed eyebrow. "*Everything* is weird if you stare hard enough."

A chuckle worked its way up Miya's throat, her tone softening. "You know what I mean."

The white wolf half-smiled. "I'll call you later. Try not to get too adventurous." She glanced at Caelan. "Not until we know more."

Miya didn't have the heart to ask the teen about her captivity. She hoped, perhaps foolishly, that Kai would do the work on that front, sparing Miya the uncomfortable task of weeding the truth from Caelan's bleak recollections. She stiffly put on her mauve leather jacket, watching as Caelan layered up with a scarf and a spare coat they'd found collecting dust in the closet.

Offering Ama a reconciliatory hug, Miya led Caelan out the door, the hinges whirring as the King of Spades bid them farewell.

27

FOR THE SECOND night in a row, Kai came home covered in blood. Miya was by the door when he strode in like a portent from the underworld, eyes dark and face spattered in scarlet. She jolted at the sight, swearing at God and the devil alike as he caught her by the arms and held her upright.

"My bad." His voice was low, soft, regret woven into his features.

"Christ—where have you been?" As his grip on her eased, she backpedaled to take stock of the mess.

Kai looked past her at Caelan, who sat demurely on the couch with Ripper curled up in her lap. The cat had taken to her quickly. Both girl and feline perked up, volleying Kai's stare.

"Dealing with Sergei." His gaze shifted back to Miya. "We should talk."

Miya's stomach lurched, her heart dropping through her ribs like a stone. Grabbing Kai's hand, she hauled him toward the bedroom. "Stay here," she told Caelan.

With the plywood door as their flimsy barrier, Miya clasped the knob behind her back. Kai hadn't bothered removing his clothes, which remained suspiciously unmarred compared to the rest of him.

"What happened?"

He stood by the bed, hands shoved in his pockets. "I killed someone."

Miya flattened her tongue against the roof of her mouth to keep the nausea from climbing up her throat. Questions tangled in her mind, but only one broke free. "Why?"

Kai lowered his head, though she couldn't tell if he was worried, ashamed, or something else entirely. "To send a message."

"Kai—" She took a harsh step forward, her hands hovering as a thousand emotions competed for expression. Moral outrage battled her maddening impulse to absolve him—to understand his choices and the ease with which he made them. "I don't understand. What message?"

"Sergei was there." He prowled the room, a predator confined to a cage, gaze fixed on something beyond the wall. "He needed to see it."

"Why?" Miya whispered.

"Breathing room, and Sergei's cooperation. The guy I ended was a rat—a dead one." He stopped, finally looked at her with torrid eyes. "Trust me, it was a mercy killing."

"You wanted Sergei's silence," Miya clarified, "so you killed a man to scare him into shutting up?"

"Like I said, it was a mercy killing." His voice was steady, his posture relaxed. Miya had always known what he was capable of— he'd shown her enough times—but that didn't make it any less unsettling. "If I hadn't done it, he would've been tortured, interrogated, then tortured some more. It would've been slow, painful."

"And you think what you did wasn't painful?" With the blood crusting his neck and the lack of evidence on his clothes, she had a hunch about how this rat died.

Kai shrugged. "It was gnarly, but it was quick."

Miya swallowed down the bile. He appeared so calm—callous even. "Do you really feel nothing?"

He went statue-still, his eyes never leaving hers. He seemed to consider his answer, riffling for a feeling he could point to. When he came up dry, his mouth twisted, and he shook his head. "I killed at least a dozen people to keep you safe in Black Hollow. What's one more?"

"I thought we were past that." Her fists clenched and unclenched as cold settled into her marrow. "Your problems don't have throats you can slit with a knife."

His brows drew together, hurt warping his stoic façade. "It's not like I killed him for fun."

Kai had spent his whole life with a single tool for his quandaries: violence. But it was a broken tool, one that destroyed as much as it resolved. He was still nurturing other ways to cope, and the pitfalls of his aggression were a karmic lesson he had yet to fully learn.

"I know," she conceded. "I just wish you'd told me the truth sooner. Maybe we could've found another way."

His approach was tentative, his hands skimming up her arms when he halted in front of her. He clasped her chin between his thumb and forefinger and gently tilted her head. "Just because spilling blood comes easy to me doesn't mean it's always the wrong choice."

He had a point. Not every instance of violence was a careless indulgence. She'd assumed he'd lashed out, but if it'd truly been a mercy killing, she had no reason to doubt his judgment. Kai lacked social mores, but he knew what propelled people from civility to barbarity better than anyone. Where human decency ruptured, Miya trusted him implicitly. Kai may have appeared utterly wild, but amid pandemonium, no one was as steadfast or as trustworthy.

Her eyes trailed the blood smeared across his jawline. He'd probably wiped it from his mouth with the back of his hand. "You were a wolf."

He nodded. "No way to trace it back to me even with a witness."

Her gaze lifted to his, those mahogany eyes retaining their warmth despite the chill in his voice. "Is it weird that I feel better knowing you killed a man with your teeth?"

At that, he cracked a smile. "Because wolves are supposed to kill, and people aren't?"

"I guess it's pretty stupid when you put it like that."

He ran his thumb over her lower lip, touching his forehead to hers. "I'm a wolf in sheep's skin, Miya..."

"...and I've mistaken you for part of my flock?" she supplied, nostalgia tugging at her lips.

He'd said those words the first time they'd fought—the first time she'd reckoned with who and what he was. He'd been bloody then too, the kill still fresh, the body not yet cold.

"At least you've learned that much, Lambchop."

Miya snaked her arms around his midsection and buried her face in his chest. "I still don't like it."

His nose fell to her hair, and he gave her a gentle squeeze. "I know."

A phone buzzed, and Kai reached into his pocket, one arm still around Miya's waist.

"What is it?" she asked.

Kai stared at what she assumed was a text message, his expression unreadable save for the tiniest twitch of his mouth. Before Miya could ask, he blacked out the screen with a tired sigh. "Looks like I found a therapist."

28

KAI

THE CHAIR WAS TOO COMFORTABLE. Kai seesawed on the edge, seeking a more familiar sensation—a rough plastic lip digging into his thigh, a wobble from a bent leg. But the armchair was a bearhug of soft cushions and round corners—the antithesis to the harsh lines and splintering bar stools he called home.

"Well, this is unusual."

Dr. Hristina Krunić sat across from him in her throne, the backrest wider and taller than any piece of furniture had right to be. She crossed her legs and rhythmically tapped her foot against the table leg in front of her, her hands clasped over a pad of paper backed by a clipboard.

"What's unusual?" asked Kai, stiffer than a bottle of back-alley moonshine. It'd barely been a few days since he'd gotten her number and done the intake forms with Miya's help. He'd hoped for a little more leeway, but apparently, the woman worked fast.

Her mouth twitched into an uneasy smile. "I don't usually get mobsters in my practice."

Kai narrowed his eyes. "I'm not a mobster."

What kind of a therapist opened with *that*? Wasn't she supposed to blather on about safe spaces and free expression? Then again, she seemed about as welcoming as a shark maw—a portrait of icy professionalism: dark hair carefully arranged in a neat bun, thick-rimmed glasses that half obscured her brows, and a sharp navy blue pantsuit that matched the Ivy League frame encasing her PhD diploma.

Her eyebrows raised a fraction. "Really." The word held no inflection. "What are you then?"

Kai considered how to respond, how to make sense of it for her. He could tell her what he'd told Miya—that he was a wolf in sheep's skin—but that seemed a trite half-truth, a crutch he leaned on when he had no interest in justifying his choices. Would she believe him if he told her he was the reincarnation of a dead god no one knew the name of? That the god had a brother who'd followed him across lifetimes as a vengeful spirit made of bottomless spite? Or would she write him off as delusional? Kai's childhood therapist thought the demon tormenting him was a PTSD-related hallucination. He'd railed against the diagnosis, his conviction hinging on a flimsy distinction between literal and figurative haunting. Even if the medical explanation of his experience was wrong, his therapist was right in all the ways that mattered. Angry apparitions aside, he was still fucked up, and that made those forces louder, stronger, more insistent. The ghost left him, but he stayed haunted. A pair of phantom horns in the ass.

And that was why he was here...or so he kept reminding himself.

"I'm...a fighter."

"A fighter," she repeated flatly.

"I fight for a living," he clarified.

"So, you define yourself by your profession?"

Shifting in the chair, he finally leaned back. "Wouldn't call it a profession."

"Then?"

"Just something I do for money." He paused, then added, "I'm good at it."

"Do you like it?" she asked, and Kai was surprised to hear genuine intrigue in the question.

"Well enough." It wasn't a lie, though he'd prefer a real challenge to a performative dance. Zverev had been the first, and now, he was itching for a rematch.

It was the doctor's turn to shift. She tilted her head, her eyes sparking with curiosity. "Mr. Donovan—"

"Kai," he interjected, the formality making his skin crawl.

"Kai," she amended with a polite smile. "Normally, I see the intimate partners of individuals in your line of work. Perhaps you're not a mobster, but you're still involved with the mob, are you not?"

He opened his mouth to protest, then clapped it shut. "Yes."

"And you don't like that," she observed.

"No."

She hummed after a respectable pause. "Organized crime...it draws quite a few possessive personalities."

Kai inhaled slowly, rubbing his palms along his thighs. "I don't like it when people stake a claim to me. I've tried to stay out of it—stick to fighting and taking my cut—but that's not why I'm here."

The sound of a pen scratching against paper. "If the mob isn't the issue, then what is?"

"Someone I care about..." he trailed off, every thought dying before it could gestate into words. "Usually it's fine between us, but sometimes, when shit gets to me, I do things I regret."

"You value this relationship." She tapped the tip of her pen on the pad. "Girlfriend?"

"Sure." A tacit acknowledgment.

Hristina Krunić didn't ask for elaboration. "Did she ask you to come here?"

Grumbling, Kai cast his gaze to the wall, agitated by her precision. "Yes. Offered to come with me too, but I said no."

"Interesting. Why'd you turn her down?"

Kai wracked his brain for a response. He didn't want Miya seeing him like this—awkward, prickly, raw. He didn't know what kind of darkness this little experiment would draw out of him—what he might become excavating the bleakest parts of himself. The shape of his own shadow was a goddamn enigma, and he was terrified that once he traced its contours, he'd find himself staring at a monster. "I didn't think it would help."

He heard a soft exhale—a barely suppressed chuckle—and faced the doctor.

She set aside the clipboard, clasped her knee with both palms, and leaned forward. "What is it that you value most? If you had to pick one thing that matters to you above all else, what would it be?"

He should've picked Miya. A better person would've. But Kai wasn't *better*, and although Miya was his whole world, the question of *value* clipped his tongue short of speaking her name. Yes, Miya was everything to him, and her importance was precisely what'd molded her into a wedge that fit perfectly—painfully—between him and his singular desire to live unfettered, carefree, reckless. In the end, there was one thing Kai Donovan valued more than the bonds that gave his life meaning. "Doing whatever the fuck I want."

"So, your independence?" she rephrased the sentiment.

He grunted as he chewed on a nail—a begrudging admission.

She peered at him as though she could crack through his façade with her will alone. "And do you think you should be allowed to do whatever the fuck you want?"

Sighing, Kai dropped his hand to the armrest. "No."

Hristina Krunić's iron gaze was a fishhook in his temple. After an unbearable pause, she relented, releasing him from her pointed hold. She sat back with a curt nod and smiled. "That must be frustrating."

KAI HAD NEVER BEEN one to tire easily. He'd once evaded three cop cruisers for an entire evening, bar hopping his way through a dozen brawls before going home with one of the losers' girlfriends just to spite him. He'd been twenty-one then—an unscrupulous asshole with a hard-on for delinquency. After Alice died when he was sixteen, he trekked from Granite Falls, Washington to British Columbia on foot, stopping at every major town to steal food, clothes, and start shit for no other reason than to allay his own grief. He'd fought and fucked his way to Black Hollow—a zit lost in the temperate rainforests a couple hundred miles northwest of Vancouver. Miya's hometown. He'd lurked there for ten years before they met, and at the time, he genuinely believed nothing could be more exhausting than making space for another person next to his demons.

He was wrong.

After his first therapy session with Dr. Krunić, he wanted to lie on a cold floor and stare at the ceiling. People yammered on about how validating therapy was, but Kai felt like a deflated tricycle tire after running over a mastiff turd. He wasn't merely tired; he was aggravated from having his secrets wrenched out of the figurative closet and splayed out in front of him. Glancing at them wasn't enough; no, he had to scrutinize them. Study them like artifacts until he could extract some hackneyed meaning from his pain.

Krunić didn't care for his abrasive deflections. She'd caught on to his fatal flaw within minutes—that rabid ache for unconditional freedom he couldn't seem to smother no matter how hard he tried. He'd learned to be selfless when the stakes outsized his ego, but in the daily drudgery of domestic kinship, it was daunting. There were so many opportunities to fail.

Feeling brittle as a sliver of dry bark, Kai nearly snapped when his phone buzzed in his jacket pocket. He reached for the device and found it tangled with his hand wraps. Miya must've slipped them in to make sure he wouldn't forget them for his next fight. Resenting the coil of guilt in his stomach, Kai swiped over the cracked phone screen. It was Sergei, too chicken shit to call after the incident from the other night.

I've got a lead.

The message was followed by a series of brief elaborations.

Someone willing to talk.

Woman named Lidia.

Meet her tonight at Terry's. 9PM.

Kai shot off a quick reply, then opened his conversation with Miya.

I'm working was the last thing he'd sent her—a fucking lie he'd spun while going after the forgery. This time, he told her exactly what he was up to.

She responded immediately, the words on the screen spurring a strangled whine. Miya wanted to come with him to Terry's. She needed a say in how they dealt with Caelan's conundrum, and he was in no position to refuse. Miya told him everything Caelan had divulged; the least he could do was reciprocate. He wasn't thrilled about bringing her into the underworld, but he trusted her to hold her own.

Reluctantly, he agreed, though disquiet clung to his shoulders—

too-long fingers and too-long nails scraping against his skull like a phantom itch. Kai ignored it. He knew that if he scratched, he'd only come away bloodied and unsatisfied.

29

A GRUNGY SALOON with cheap drink specials every night of the week, Terry's was permanently infested by middle-aged men in baseball caps. After squeezing past a herd congregated around a dart board, Kai and Miya slid onto two empty stools at the bar. A small blackboard hung on the wall in front of the shelves, the daily specials scrawled in messy rows of blue and yellow chalk.

As they settled in with their drinks, Miya glanced around. "I guess Sergei's informant will find us here?"

"She'll be easy to spot given the...demographics." Kai finished his bourbon with a pickle back, the sweet, spicy, and tangy combination surprisingly good. Glancing over at Miya to offer her some of his second round, he caught her chugging her vodka mule at alarming speed. "Uh—"

"Sorry." She pushed the tumbler away. "I guess I'm a little nervous."

"You didn't have to come along."

"I wanted to." She spun the glass between her palms. "So, how was therapy?"

Kai awkwardly gulped down his drink. "Fine." It came out terser than he intended. He plucked the shot glass up and set it back down, tapping it against the counter as though he could drum his agitation away.

Miya opened her mouth to respond, but her eyes snagged on something behind Kai. He smelled the presence before he felt the need to turn and look, a syrupy-sweet perfume washing over him.

A woman slid onto the stool next to him, her bare shoulder brushing his arm. He pivoted to find her smiling as she looked him up and down. Dark lashes and smoky eyeshadow framed an icy blue stare. Her long auburn hair was impeccably styled, lush waves cascading over her collarbones.

"Hey," she greeted. "Trouble in paradise?"

Kai recognized her immediately—the woman who came to every one of his fights. "Lidia."

"Sorry to interrupt," she said, sounding very not sorry. Angling her head, she stared down the bar at Miya. "I thought we'd be meeting alone."

"Did Sergei promise you a private audience?" Kai smiled wryly, pushing his stool back to give Miya line of sight.

Lidia waved down the bartender and ordered a Manhattan. "Girlfriend?"

"Partner in crime," Miya replied before Kai could fumble with the question.

"Well, I suppose we should get to business then. You're looking for information about the forgery, yes?" Lidia rolled her eyes as she took a sip of her newly arrived cocktail. "Everyone's after that thing."

"What's your stake in it?" Kai asked.

"Me?" She laughed, the sound like wind chimes. "Nothing, actually. It just so happens my boyfriend's a driver for Pyotr's favorite goon—the one in charge of finding this forgery thing." She scoffed. "Don't know why it's so precious if it's called a fucking *forgery*."

Kai and Miya exchanged a weighty look. Neither Lidia nor her boyfriend knew that the forgery wasn't an *it*.

"Talk to Timur, my other half." Lidia fished her phone out of her purse and flashed them a picture of the man in question—a gym rat with a bad fake tan, too-tight T-shirt, and more gel than hair. "He's at a club called Eden, doing shots with his boys and grabbing some poor girl's ass. He'll squeal if you step on him."

"Wait—you're selling out your boyfriend?" Miya interjected.

Lidia smacked her lips, then withdrew the phone to stare at her boyfriend's picture. "I'm tired of all this."

Kai narrowed his eyes, Connor's words about mobsters' wives pummeling him in the gut. "You want out, and you want him to come with you."

Her lips twitched into an uneasy smile, and she took another demure sip. "If you make him think his balls will end up on a spit, he'll have a reason to leave the country with me, and your identity will be safe." She rotated toward them and grinned. "Win-win."

"He sounds..." *like an asshole*, Kai wanted to supply as Miya trailed off, dumbstruck at the bargain they were making. "Why not just tell him you want to go clean?"

Lidia plopped her cheek into her palm and huffed. "I have. But he just *loves* playing gangster with Pyotr's lackies. Sergei thinks he's a liability, which is why he came to me first. We both want Timur out of the biz."

"Fine." Kai slid his shot glass toward the bartender as he passed them. "I'll scare him off the continent. Fair deal?"

"You're doing me a *huge* favor," Lidia crooned. "Anything I can do to repay you for your...service?"

Miya's jaw dropped in dismay before Kai smelled the irritation billowing off her skin. He couldn't blame her.

He squared his shoulders to Lidia and mirrored her pose. With his elbow leaned on the counter, his mouth curved into a smirk. "Are you offering to buy me a drink?"

"You look like you're having a hard night." She simpered, her lashes lowering as she shifted on her stool. "I'd *love* to make it better."

Kai's lips pulled back into a rakish grin. "Careful. You might regret making that offer."

"Oh, I know a wild animal when I see one. In fact, I've seen exactly what you're capable of at the Confessional." She drew her tumbler through the air. "Go on, order anything you'd like."

Kai canted his head toward the bartender. "I'll have a mule."

The man nodded, and Lidia threw down some cash. When the bartender returned, Kai grabbed the glass and stood, then snaked an arm around Miya's waist, guiding her to her feet. Handing her the mule, he winked at Lidia. "Your boyfriend will be ready to move to the Swiss Alps by morning."

Miya's silent stewing morphed into shock as Lidia's expression took the opposite trajectory. She swore at him as they turned to leave, then shouted at the bartender for another drink.

"That was a dick move," Miya said as they wove through the throng.

"It was," he agreed.

"I mean, she did hit on you without acknowledging my existence," she argued with herself as she slurped up the mule. "But it also sounds like she's stuck in a bad relationship. I feel for her."

A bad relationship. Did people think the same about him and Miya? He hadn't cheated on her, but things were dire enough that she'd forced him into therapy, and all that'd done was gouge a hole through him. It hurt, and he resented it. Kai took the empty glass from Miya and left it on an abandoned high table. Everyone was on the floor now, drunkenly throwing darts or dancing to classic rock music. "Let's go find him."

With the front door blocked, Kai laced his fingers with Miya's and tugged her toward the fire escape. He shoved through the back door, the evening air eating away the dankness of the bar. They stumbled into an alleyway with only a flickering overhead light to illuminate their surroundings. Miya was first to thump down the metal steps.

She peered down the dark lane. "Which way to Eden?"

Kai had no intention of leaving so soon. Frustration was a sticky coat on his skin, his thoughts bouncing to his session with Krunić and everything that'd prompted it. Even in his anger—especially in his anger—he craved Miya's desire for him, yearned to draw it out. As she made for the main road, Kai reeled her into his chest and walked her back until she hit the brick wall by the stairwell, his mouth crashing to hers. Her breath caught, hands hovering before they found his arms. Her lips moved against his, her palms gliding up to his shoulders and around the nape of his neck.

"Someone might come out here on a smoke break," she warned between kisses.

Kai's tongue teased her bottom lip before he clipped it with his teeth. "They can find somewhere else to smoke."

His fingertips stroked along her thigh, following the hem of her jeans. The denim was soft and pliable, and he easily worked his way past the waistband after slipping the button free. He brushed aside the bottom of her panties and hooked a finger along her slick opening, earning a soft gasp as her hips pushed avidly against his hand.

"You better tell me if you hear someone—" Her words died in her mouth when he gently flicked his thumb over her clit. She bit down on her lip and stifled a moan, and he pressed two fingers inside her. Grabbing his wrist, Miya held him steady as she ground against the pressure he offered. She reached between his legs, but he snatched her hand away, pinning it to the wall.

Her eyes darted to his, questioning, and he silenced her with a hungry kiss, her breaths growing labored as she writhed, caged between him and the bricks. Her fingers curled into his hair, and when she told him she was going to come, he pulled away, his hand sliding from her thighs like dead weight.

Her bewildered expression was almost as delicious as the taste of her. Kai casually sucked off each finger, then tugged on the hand he'd pinned to the wall.

"Let's go."

30

AN OFF-KILTER NEON sign marked their destination on a busy downtown road. Eden managed to evoke class and trash all at once —the perfect joint for grunts like Timur.

Kai could feel the questions on the tip of Miya's tongue after he'd stolen her release, but she wouldn't ask—at least not yet— because the answer seemed obvious. He liked riling her up. Krunić was right; he valued his independence more than anything, and Miya had him by the nuts. He was angry that she'd wrangled him into facing his crap, and the fact that she had every right to only intensified his ire. His grasp on his demons was slipping, and Miya blew the door off the cellar where he cured old wounds like salted meat. She made it impossible to look away, unmoored him as much as she grounded him, and this game of denial was the only way he knew to wrest back some modicum of control. He wanted to punish her, make her beg with need for him, and he wanted her to enjoy it.

Eden was a little fancier than their last stop, furnished with dark oak tables, burgundy faux-leather booths, and a stage for local bands and DJs. The bar was tucked in an adjacent room, providing some insulation from the noise. Timur could've been anywhere, but if he loved shots as much as Lidia claimed, he'd worm his way out of the crowd to fetch his booze at some point. They posted up at the bar with another round of drinks, hoping Timur would crawl out soon enough.

With time to kill, Kai coiled an arm around Miya's waist, drawing her close. "You surviving?"

"Surviving, yes." She placed a hand on his chest and pushed him back onto a stool. "Though I'm still annoyed we have to be here at all."

"Consider it a date," he said, watching her step out of reach.

"A date?" She scoffed. "I'm about to watch you threaten a man's life."

Kai flashed her a fiendish grin. "We're doing it for love."

"Not sure I'd qualify Lidia's scheme as *loving*." She stirred her drink, still standing several feet away.

Grated by the distance, Kai curled his finger in a *come-hither* motion. "Blizhe."

Closer.

With a playful eye roll, Miya indulged his command, and Kai hauled her into his lap before she could grab the seat next to him. Her spine straightened as his erection pressed against her backside, and she peeked over her shoulder at him, eyes narrowed suspiciously. He casually spun the stool so they faced the counter, his hand running up the inside of her thigh.

"Aren't you just torturing yourself?" she asked.

"Not as much as I'm torturing you." His fingers brushed over her pelvic bone, tracing the seam that ran directly over the parts of her he'd teased.

Miya held her breath, fighting not to squirm. His hand smoothed over her thigh when she tried crossing her legs, and he pulled them apart under the counter. Her hand slid over his, but she didn't stop him. His touch moved lower, and Miya tried to scoot forward, reaching behind her to either grab or punch him. He wasn't sure which. Kai tapped her hand away, his lips grazing her neck. "Think I don't know how wet you are?"

Her hips inched closer to greet his touch as he stroked through her jeans, and she clasped his wrist, her nails digging into his skin. "Are you *trying* to make me come in public?"

"Not yet."

She forced a harsh breath from her nose, then turned to nip at his jawline. He caught her lips, his tongue dancing across hers as he smothered her whimper. The more she craved release, the more he wanted to deny it, if only to prolong their game.

Miya swore against his mouth, and Kai felt the tension in her core mount. When her pulse grew frantic, plucking at the predator in him, he withdrew his hand and drowned her dissent with a fiery kiss. She fisted his shirt, pressing him for more. A touch, a stroke—anything to slake the hunger.

Her eyes floated past his shoulder. "People are watching."

He knew that already, and he reveled in the greedy eyes drinking them up. Swiveling the stool, he trained his gaze on a group of gawking douchebags that'd sidled up to the bar. One in particular caught his attention.

Timur.

Kai's smile was vicious as he tipped his chin up. "Take a picture; it'll last longer."

Timur fixed a half-drunk stare on Kai, his coifed-as-fuck comb-over so rigid it looked like a block of cement. "Maybe I will."

He slanted himself against the bar and steadied his phone, his friends laughing shrilly at the display. His bronzed skin looked a few shades too orange, his pale blue dress shirt and faded jeans too form-fitting to be comfortable. Timur flashed Miya an alarmingly white smile, his smarmy eyes passing over her. "How many drinks will it take for me to find out if the carpet matches the drapes?"

Kai felt Miya's heart stop, then skitter back to life. "That's him," she whispered to Kai, scooting off him as he stood.

Kai reached over the counter and snatched a bottle of bourbon while the bartender was occupied.

The carroty chuckle-fuck stared at Kai. His snideness melted into confusion, then alarm, and finally, recognition. "Hey!" he bellowed as he stalked up to them. "I know you."

Kai poured himself another drink as if he owned the bottle and the bar. His eyes flicked to Timur, and the edge of his mouth crept up. "Congratulations."

"You fucked up my buddy," came the accusation. "Last month at Wally's."

Miya quirked a brow, probably wondering who the hell named an establishment *Wally's*.

"You'll have to be more specific." Kai winced after a gulp of bourbon.

Timur threw his arms up. "Come on, bro. He was the biggest guy there."

A soft, threatening laugh slipped out as Kai was called *bro*. "A lot of big people left with fucked up faces. Wasn't exactly easy to tell them apart."

"Hey, fuck you." Timur pitched forward, invading Kai's personal space like a French monarch bellying up to a guillotine. "You know who I am?"

Miya turned an icy glare on him. "Someone *very* concerned with the coherence of carpets and drapes."

Kai snatched the phone from Timur's hand, dropped it to the floor, and crushed it under his boot. The crunch was so satisfying, he considered that it may have sounded better than a broken nose.

"What the hell, man!"

Tequila breath washed over Kai, and he shoved the irritant back into a table. His friends caught him by the arms and helped him right himself. Then, he launched forward. Kai saw the blow coming like a bad plot twist, but he didn't budge. Without lifting an arm to defend himself, he angled his head and let Timur's fist glance off his jaw. Knuckles clipped his lip, an iron taste coating his tongue. His head swayed back, and he used the momentum to fling his torso forward like a pendulum.

He really, really wanted to know if he liked the sound of a breaking smartphone more than the crunch of bone.

Kai's forehead connected with Timur's nose, and he homed in on that gratifying snap.

It was a fucking tie.

Timur crashed into the table, his friends failing to catch him this time as they stood frozen in their stupor. Blood pooled around Kai's brows, then dribbled down the bridge of his nose and over his mouth where he caught the stray drops with his tongue. Licking his lips clean, he grinned, menace lacing every word as he said, "Come on, then."

The stampede was...almost funny. The next strike that hurtled toward his face was wide and sloppy, and he easily leaned out of its arcing path. A rush of air swept in from behind, and he side-stepped the buffoon who'd dove for him. Both men nose-dived to the floor, but one quickly rolled into a squat and charged. Bracing for impact, Kai lowered his center of gravity as the man slammed into him. He laced his fingers around the back of his attacker's neck, then flung him aside like a ragdoll.

By now, a crowd had amassed to watch the fray, and a frazzled manager came barreling through the throng. He yelled over the ruckus, demanding that the fighting stop to no avail. Kai glimpsed another fist in his periphery but didn't bother dodging. Using his elbow to bump the inside of the guy's arm, Kai redirected the punch, then thrust a punishing uppercut into his kidney. The man crumpled, retching up overpriced nachos, and Kai finished the job with a light shove to the shoulder that sent him sprawling on the floor.

Kai peeked back at Miya to check on her. She stood by the bar, sipping her drink as she observed the bedlam. He shot her a roguish smile, and she beamed back. After Timur's bullshit, she didn't seem as bothered by Lidia's plan.

As Timur's lackies scattered, Kai clasped him by the back of the neck and drove a knee into his crotch. He keeled over, his shirt stretching over his back so tightly that Kai thought the seams would burst.

"You've got exactly fifteen seconds to tell me what Pyotr wants with the forgery, or I'll tear your dick off and feed it to you like a mozzarella stick."

Lidia's idiot boyfriend cupped his broken nose, crimson rivulets welling over his fingers. "I don't know shit about that—I'm just a driver!"

Kai tightened his grip on the back of Timur's neck. "Keep that up. Ignorance *always* gets people out of dismemberment."

Timur gargled on a curse, his eyes squeezed shut. "Look, I don't know what the forgery is. All I know is that the boss wants it gone. Destroyed. Annihilated. Wiped from existence."

Kai snapped his mouth shut, molten rage scalding his throat. He swallowed it down. Pyotr wanted to kill Caelan. Her death had been brokered by a neutral party because Zverev's employer had use for the girl—probably leverage—and to Pyotr, she was a liability. Something to be buried.

Kai released Timur only to snatch him by the hair. "Why? What's so scary about this forgery?"

"I don't know!" Timur clawed helplessly at Kai's hand. "He doesn't tell us shit!"

A firm yank, and several clumps came lose.

Timur's yowl came out strangled as he waved for Kai to stop.

"There's a rumor that the forgery's a threat to Pyotr's kid. Don't know why, don't know how. It's just something I've heard in my car!"

Sirens blared in the distance, though only Kai heard the far-off wail. They had ten minutes tops before cops swarmed the place.

"One last thing." Kai hauled Timur upright, locking him in with a snarl that promised carnage. "You're done with Bratva. Go home, pack your diapers, and leave. If you're not out of the country by tomorrow night, I *will* know."

Lip trembling, face blotched with tears and blood, Timur's head jerked into a nod.

Kai dropped him like a sweaty gym bag.

In the chaos, Miya squeezed her way through several scrambling patrons and grabbed Kai's hand before anyone else got stupid, dragging him toward the back of the club. She sharply rounded a corner and kicked her way into the restroom, Kai in tow. They tumbled into one of the stalls, and a woman's heels rapidly clicked past them.

Kai *would* have cracked a joke about it, but Miya got to him first. Wrapping her arm around his neck, she wrenched him into a ferocious kiss. He grabbed her waist, marring her clothes in red as he pressed her to the wall. The blood from his cut lip smeared the corner of her mouth, the scent of iron and the sweet, earthy bite of liquor hanging between their ragged breaths. A moan caught in Miya's throat, and her fingers pried past Kai's belt at alarming speed. She actually got into his pants, and as her fingers closed around his cock, he seized her wrist and pinned her hand to the stall, the divider juddering. The sirens were closer now, ringing loud enough for human ears to pick up.

"How long are you going to keep this game up?" she demanded.

Kai choked back a laugh as stern voices flitted around the halls. "As long as I want to play."

Exasperation etched her face. "Can't be that fun blue balling yourself."

He flattened his palm next to her head. "Do you really want to fuck in a bathroom stall during a police raid?"

"Sounds like something *you'd* do."

"I would."

She hesitated, then shook her head. "Not here."

The corner of Kai's mouth tugged into a knowing smile, and he pulled her out of the stall.

WHEN THEY REACHED the secluded park, all pretense of foreplay dissipated. Miya shoved Kai into a tree and clawed off his jacket, her body radiating pent-up lust. The straw-colored grass was still wet from the morning's downpour, but neither of them cared. When she tried to push him again, he caught her wrists and took her down with him. Straddling her hips, he yanked her jacket and shirt off along with her bra. Her hands roamed up his abdomen, scraped over his ribs and around the now-healed bullet wound, her nails threatening to slice deeper until he removed his shirt. After satisfying her silent demand, Kai did away with her jeans and underwear, then unfastened his cargo pants and kicked them from his ankles.

Her legs curled around his waist, throwing him off balance as she drew him in. He barely caught himself, his hands landing on either side of her as his cock pressed against her middle.

"For fuck's sake, Kai." She raked her nails over his backside, pulling on his hips.

With a low growl, he thrust into her, and she jerked with a gratified *yes*. Her thighs clinched his sides, urging him closer, and for the first time that night, he obliged, driving into her with scant gentleness. Fisting the grass by her head, he fucked her as though they'd been apart for years, something inside him splintering as primal want and bone-deep need swirled into an incoherent mass of euphoria and fear—euphoria that he'd finally found something to fill the emptiness inside him, and fear that he could lose it all with one careless mistake.

Kai swore under his breath, hating how helpless he felt. The boundary between desperate longing and impotent rage melted away as he buried himself inside her. Between frantic pleas, Miya tried slipping a hand below her waist, but he intercepted it, pinning both her arms above her head. She wrenched savagely as he held her wrists, and when their eyes met, she gritted her teeth and shrieked in frustration, bucking against him.

She lifted her head off the grass, venom caught between her teeth. "Fuck you."

A slow, wicked smile spread across his face. "I'm the one doing the fucking," he reminded her, then eased his grip on her wrists.

She flew upright the moment her arms came free. Her hand shot out, viper-like, and she struck him across the face. Hard.

Momentarily stunned, Kai reeled back and tongued the inside of his stinging cheek, his skin warm from the impact. His mouth curved into a smirk. He liked her like this.

They were still for a long moment, Kai on his knees and Miya sitting in front of him, the night entirely quiet save for their heavy breaths fogging the autumn air.

"Now what?" Kai asked, his eyes trained on her.

She met his gaze, unflinching, and after ripping up fistfuls of grass, she threw them at him with an exasperated huff. "At least finish what you started!"

A harsh laugh worked its way up Kai's throat as she pelted him with wet lawn. Crawling forward, he helped her to her knees, then circled behind her. From the corner of his eye, he glimpsed yellow fabric poking out of his jacket pocket—one of his caution tape wraps. He leaned over, snatched it free, then folded Miya's arms behind her back and looped the strip around her knuckles and wrist.

Her breath halted. "I forgot I'd put those there."

"What's the saying? No good deed goes unpunished?" He grinned, all teeth and teasing, and bound her wrists together. Curling an arm around her midsection, he hauled her closer, her legs spreading as she straddled him. His mouth traced over her shoulder and up her neck before he clipped her earlobe with his teeth. She shuddered, her anticipation palpable as the curve of her ass ground against his hard length, and she careened forward. Kai caught the wrap woven around her wrists and dragged her back. Her gaze snapped to him, and she jolted when his forefinger pressed to her clit, her knees digging into the earth.

"You done being an asshole?" she asked over her shoulder, and he caught her lips, sparing more tenderness than he had all night.

"Maybe." He rocked his hips forward. "You going to slap me again when I take this off?" He tapped the yellow cotton swathing her hands.

"You seemed to like that."

Kai's grip tightened as he gave the wrap a small tug. "I fucking loved it."

He drew her flush against him, all patience bleeding away as he thrust into her. She gasped and craned her neck, inviting his lips and tongue to trace over every inch of her skin. Moving in pace with him, her head lolled back on his shoulder, her pulse thundering as he held her steady.

"Say my name," he whispered, his breath hot on her ear.

"Go fuck yourself." She strained against his grasp, her limbs fighting to move freely while their constraint only made her wilder.

He'd wanted control—wanted her helpless against him—but he missed the bite of her nails on his skin, hungered for her abandon. Unable to resist, Kai unbound her and wrapped an arm around her midsection, securing her against his chest. Despite her objection, his name left her as a sharp cry, her cunt clenching around his cock as orgasm quaked through her like a torrent. Wreathed in caution tape from knuckles to forearm, she knotted her fingers in his hair, gripping and tugging roughly. He continued stroking her clit, wringing pleasure from her with every utterance of his name until he plummeted over the edge right after her, muffling his shout against her neck as he came. Pleasure flooded his core in brutal waves, and he clung to her as ferociously as she clung to him, the strength leaving him as his muscles turned into a useless heap.

Kai fell back, taking Miya with him as they both trembled, bodies slick with sweat. She slipped free, her knees, elbows, and backside streaked with grass. Kai eased himself down next to her. Lying on his back, he draped an arm over his stomach.

"Hey," he said slowly. "I'm sorry."

"You'll have to be more specific," she managed as her breathing evened out.

"I fucked up." This time, the words came readily. Regret spooled in his gut, spurring him to sit up. "Therapy sucks," he finally answered her question honestly, slinging an arm over his knee. "But I guess that shows how much I need it."

Miya's silence needled him. She usually had something to say—thoughtful encouragement or even-handed reassurance. She shuffled behind him, her arms encircling his neck as she pressed herself to his back. Her warmth salved the curdling tumult between his ribs.

Loosely wound with yellow and black, her hand dangled at his chest, and he enveloped it with his own. "We should get back to the King of Spades," he said.

Miya nodded, reluctant to let go, but Kai's crumbling coping mechanisms could wait. They had a much bigger problem.

Caelan wasn't a lost prize; she was prey.

31

MIYA

The chill hit Miya's skin like a thousand glass blades, and the sweltering heat finally abated. Kai's lips on her own had been torrid, bruising, every unspoken thorn between them coalescing into a chemical eruption that left them both bewildered. He liked to tease—to battle where he played—but in his desperate bid for something resembling control, he'd spiraled right out of it. She knew what he was doing the moment he'd dropped his hand from her thighs in that alleyway. He was angry with her, and this was his catharsis. But their savage lovemaking seemed to have rattled him as much as it'd given him an outlet.

He'd sunk his teeth into her until she gave him what he wanted: a reaction. Slapping his smug, self-satisfied face felt good, and his eager acceptance of her outburst softened the sting of his anger. He had no right being upset with her for strong-arming him into therapy, but he had enough sense not to begrudge her too deeply. Kai preferred hate-fucking to nurturing his resentment, and she figured sex was preferable to pummeling drunks or stuffing his feelings into a metaphorical lockbox. If orgasms helped him process his emotions, she would happily oblige. That is, so long as he stuck to therapy.

Their clothes disguised most of the grass stains as they headed back to the King of Spades. The walk was quiet, contemplative, neither of them filling the space with idle chitchat or rote pleasantries. Miya appreciated that about Kai; he felt no need to break the tension with platitudes. If he wanted something, he'd ask for it.

Kai draped an arm around her shoulders and pressed her to his side. His lips brushed her temple, and she gave his midsection an affectionate squeeze. Before she met him, she rarely thought about how much could be communicated through a touch, a look, a smile. Silences were meant to be awkward, and every emotion required a corresponding name to give it meaning and expression. But she'd learned to listen in other ways—to hear those weighty things whispered by the unsaid. Miya loved words, but there were so many other ways to speak.

As they approached the King of Spades, Kai slowed, his body going rigid.

"What's wrong?" Miya asked as his arm slid from her shoulders.

"It's too quiet, but everyone's awake." He took an anxious step forward, then rocked back, grinding his teeth in apparent indecision. The lights were off throughout the building save for an upstairs room and the vestibule at the bar's entrance.

Miya grabbed his hand. "Come on."

He didn't resist as she led him onward, and the door swung open before they reached it. Bathed in buttery lamplight, Ama stood at the threshold, expectant.

"What happened?" Kai asked gruffly, his hand now on the inside of the open door.

The white wolf cut him with a glare and addressed Miya instead. "Caelan slipped out while you were gone."

Kai opened his mouth—probably to berate Ama about *how* she'd failed to detect this—but Miya pressed her elbow to his ribs, shutting him up.

"Gavran and I tracked her down," Ama continued when the barrage never came. She sighed, hanging her head. "I didn't even notice. She was completely soundless, odorless. We only realized when we found the door wide open."

Kai's mouth snapped shut, and he swallowed his insult. "Where'd you find her?"

Ama gave them both a heavy look. "She was headed for the park. We intercepted her and dragged her back."

"*Dragged?*" Miya echoed, alarm sharpening her voice.

Ama shook her head in apology and stepped aside to let them in. "She fought us. We locked her upstairs in the spare room and barred the window. Dahlia is with her, trying to keep her calm."

Miya's head spun as she rounded into the dining room. Gavran was perched on his favorite beer tap and croaked in greeting while the domovoy crouched in the corner beneath the antique mirror. He appeared restless, shuffling from one foot to the other as he wrung his little paws.

The park. Caelan had a fixation on Boston Common—the place she'd first appeared, seemingly out of thin air, before the Carvers adopted her. Her family said she was trying to find a door, and Miya had all but confirmed that Caelan was searching for a way back to the dreamscape where she could rejoin the leshy. She didn't want to use the gateway at the long-felled Great Elm, yet she kept sleepwalking there. Someone with Miya's abilities could easily tear through the gnarl between realms at the site, and Caelan had done just that when she'd stumbled into Boston's material sphere three years ago, seduced by something on this side—a mysterious *her.* Whoever she was, she was drawing Caelan to the park with increasing persistence, to the place where spirit met flesh and the boundary between worlds remained thin.

Crowbar thumped down the stairs and threw her arms up. "Oh, thank titties, you're back." She looked thoroughly spooked as she glanced between Miya and Kai. "The whole building was going haywire for a solid half-hour."

Kai narrowed his eyes. "The lights?"

Crowbar nodded. "Yeah, the electricity was bonkers—"

"I'm going to check on her," he interrupted, pushing past the bartender.

Miya followed, surprised by his eagerness. Before either of them bounded to the second floor, Kai halted. Caelan stood at the top of the stairs, gripping the banister.

The King of Spades went silent as a grave.

The teen stared down at them as they all stared up in turn. Even Gavran twisted his head around to peek.

Kai's throat bobbed as he swallowed. "You okay, kid?"

Caelan's bottom lip quivered, her grip on the rail tightening. She shook her head, then slowly made her way down the stairs. "I need to go."

Kai placed a gentle hand on her shoulder, stopping her in her tracks. "No, you don't."

"I do." She shrugged him off. "I need to put an end to this."

"Put an end to what?" Miya asked as Crowbar backpedaled to give them space.

Ama snatched her girlfriend's arm, reeling her farther out of the way.

Then, the lights shuddered, a low hum penetrating the quiet. Shadows bled from corners where they ought to have stayed, pooling along the floor like ink.

"I have to go." Caelan's voice filled with urgency, darkness passing over her face as indiscernible shapes scurried along the walls. She took another step, but Kai blocked her with his arm, his palm flat against the opposite wall.

"If you think that because you're scared," he said, "you'll only fuck things up for yourself."

"He's right," Miya agreed. "You don't have to deal with this alone."

"You have no idea what you're talking about," Caelan whispered. She grabbed Kai's jacket sleeve to pull his arm away, but he wouldn't budge. A sudden deluge of anger contorted the girl's face, and she tried shoving past him. He caught her and hauled her back, and a furious shriek ripped from her throat as she began to thrash.

"She's doing it again," Ama warned, shifting to block the door as Crowbar swore loudly.

The room tilted, shadows darting across the walls and floor in a chaotic dance. The bulbs flashed, then faded, their electric whirrs a discordant song. They were like bone spurs to Miya's eardrums. Disoriented, she stumbled to the side and glimpsed Crowbar clutch the bar top for dear life, her knees buckling. Gavran flapped his wings, cawing frantically, and even the wolves fought to steady themselves. Ama widened her stance, and Kai braced against the wall with one arm as the other encircled the teen to subdue her.

It didn't work.

Caelan flailed wildly, landing blows wherever she could. Her elbow clipped Kai's jaw as she twisted in his grasp, and he leaned back when a fist came flying at his nose.

"She's a lot stronger than she looks," Kai said after an annoyed grunt.

Miya believed him. Caelan seemed imbued with supernatural might as she revolted against Kai, clawing and kicking to get free so she could flee the King of Spades.

"Do *not* let her go," Ama yelled across the room, umbral whorls slithering around her feet. "Whatever is calling to her wants this. We can't let it get its way."

Pushing off the wall, Kai wrapped another arm around the girl, locking her against his chest. "I'm sorry," he said through clenched teeth, then lifted his gaze to Miya.

"I'm on it." Gathering her bearings, she navigated toward the center of the room, tracking a web of dark wisps that sprawled across the wall. Light filled the bar for a splintering moment, and Miya realized they were vines, crawling toward the door that Ama guarded. Pivoting, she glimpsed a lumbering silhouette behind the white wolf.

The leshy.

A skitter of fear stippled Miya's spine. What the hell was he doing here? Was he the cause, or had he finally come to collect?

Ama spun and jumped away, her silvery hair static with unease. The stranger floated into the bar, his ratty coat and craggy skin filling the stark shadow in the vestibule. His cedarwood eyes locked on to Miya, and something tugged at her mind, sawing at the tether between her spirit and her body. Black stars bloomed before her eyes.

The leshy was trying to force her consciousness into the dreamscape.

Miya battled the onslaught of sleep when a pair of vicious snarls rived through the chaos. Both wolves doubled over, agony snaring them as they lost their footing. Ama dropped into a crouch, her back arched as her nails dragged down the floorboards. Then, a feral sound tore through the air behind Miya, and she saw Kai crumple as he released a shell-shocked Caelan. With an angry shout, he pounded his forearm to the wall, slamming straight through it as he caught Miya with an anguished stare. His eyes gleamed with fury and blood as he bared his teeth, his canines lengthening into sharp points.

"What the hell!" Crowbar tried to scramble over to them but tumbled to her knees, disoriented.

Ama's head snapped up, her amber eyes as bright as Kai's, her mouth twisted into a pained rictus. Her fingers bent wrong, nails thickening into blunt claws, and she bit down on a whimper, her voice hoarse as she pleaded, "Stay away from it, Dahlia!"

They had no idea what the leshy would do to an ordinary human. It brought out the true nature in things, but it seemed only for the worse. Straining to keep her attention on the approaching spirit, Miya watched as it reached for Caelan, beckoning her closer.

Spellbound, Caelan took a clumsy step forward, and then another.

"Gav...ran..." Miya struggled to call for her familiar, sinking to her knees as her strength seeped away. Through slit eyes, she glimpsed the raven dive for the leshy. The nature spirit swatted the bird away, trapping him in a thicket of foliage that sprouted along the winking sconces. Voluptuous bloodred lilies wriggled from their stems. Petals unfurled like jaws and stuck to Gavran's plumage, blanketing onyx in carmine. A fetid odor oozed from the blooms, and Miya clapped a hand over her mouth to keep from vomiting at the stench, her vision swimming. Gavran beat his wings against his bonds but quickly grew docile, slumping against the sinewy shackles.

Miya had to do *something*. Although the leshy manifested pieces of himself in the physical world, he was still immaterial. If Miya slipped into the dreamscape, she could contend with him on her terms. But it felt like a trap. The leshy wanted her where she couldn't communicate with Caelan and the others. To stop the teen from fulfilling the very portent she resisted, Miya had no choice but to remain physically present. The wolves were paralyzed, powerless against the change being forced upon them. Miya and Crowbar were the only ones left, and the Dreamwalker wouldn't endanger one of her best friends over a mess she and Kai had invited.

Every second that passed dragged Miya further from herself. She could barely stay awake, let alone move. Every weapon in her arsenal was useless or indisposed.

Then, a small round shape streaked past Ama and into the center of the fray. The domovoy planted himself between Miya and the leshy. Hackles raised, he chittered and straightened, balancing on his hind legs. As he rose to his full height, Miya felt the leshy's enthrallment weaken. Her eyelids grew lighter, her body less like lead, and she realized...

The domovoy was defending his home.

His shadow grew, and grew, and grew, until it dwarfed the leshy like a mountain towering over a shrub. Lips pared back from sharp teeth, and the house guardian spread his arms wide, reaching. Those tiny fur-covered arms could grasp only air, but the spectral limbs that mimed the domovoy's movements stretched beyond his natural range, curved shadow claws latching on to the walls.

The sinuous vines squirmed and gibbered in dissent, and the leshy raised his head, the motion slow, stilted. His ancient face was hewn from primordial wrath, every cut in his craggy skin a score against his patience.

Unbothered, the domovoy tightened his phantom grip and pulled.

The interior of the building morphed like a fever dream. The house groaned, the floor roiled, and the walls slid from place like a living maze. With every swipe of his arms, the domovoy maneuvered his colossal shadow and rearranged the bones of the house. The leshy lurched to enter further, but the domovoy stamped a foot, and the floorboards sliced upward, disorienting the invader. He tried shambling forward a second time, but the house warped yet again, erecting walls, shifting tables, and sculpting impenetrable doors at the domovoy's command. The vines that'd snared Gavran stretched, then snapped like bramble under a heavy boot.

With large shining eyes locked on the leshy, the domovoy released a threatening rattle that drowned out the awful squelching of carnivorous flora. His leviathan shadow wielded the home like a fortress and a blade all at once. With a final decree from its small but fierce protector, the house pushed the leshy back into the vestibule, past the threshold, and out into the cold.

The domovoy whipped an arm across his chest, and the door slammed shut.

32

THUMPING her back against the wall, Miya slid into a squat and scanned the bar. Gavran's wing twitched as he struggled to right himself, disoriented from the flowers' toxic fumes. The domovoy's shadow receded, and he ambled over to the raven, grasping a grace-less wing in a good-natured attempt to help. Crowbar wobbled to her feet and stumbled toward Ama. Caelan had collapsed on the stairs, fighting back sobs as she pawed at Kai's jacket sleeve and mumbled apologies.

Like Ama, he was still recovering, hunched over with his head hung and his elbows pressed against his thighs. He clumsily groped for Caelan's hand and gave it a squeeze. "I'm fine." The words came out like gravel, a harsh contrast to the elation they were meant to inspire.

Ama rolled back into a squat and buried her face in her palms as Crowbar fretted, drawing her into a tight hug. "It's okay," she reas-sured, her soft strokes along Ama's spine slowing when she realized that her all-but-titanium girlfriend was trembling.

"I don't remember the last time…" Ama exhaled when she lost the words. She pushed herself up, her expression severe like she'd swallowed a too-bitter pill.

Miya glimpsed wet streaks across Ama's face. The white wolf was rarely helpless—always so controlled, so *in* control—but she'd had her bearings ripped from her faster than she could make sense of it. Ama trusted the safety of her human mask, and the leshy had flicked it away with a mere look, exposing the animal underneath.

Kai was unnervingly accustomed to it. He was as fierce as Ama, yet where she'd acquired mastery, he struggled for autonomy against his demons. The leshy's violation was just one of a thousand gut punches he'd have to walk off.

Miya unglued herself from the floor, walking woodenly to Caelan and Kai. "Do you need anything?"

They both shook their heads, and Miya sighed shakily. She dropped her forehead to Kai's shoulder, and he wrapped an arm around her back.

"What the hell was that?" Ire sharpened Kai's question into a growl.

"The domovoy saved us." Miya turned her head to see the house guardian trundling from one person to the next, anxiously checking to see if they were well. She had no idea if Kai had witnessed what she had—the domovoy's goliath silhouette making quick work of the nature spirit.

"I didn't see dick. Lights flashed, shadows fell off the damn wall, and the old kook in the coat kept loitering by the door. Felt like I was stuck in a fishbowl someone's shitty toddler threw down the stairs." He let her go, his jaw working as he tongued his now blunted canines. "You know the rest."

The haywire electricity and living shadows seemed to be Caelan's doing, but the domovoy existed between planes. Only Miya and Caelan could see him.

"He's not trying to hurt anyone," Caelan insisted. "He's just trying to get me back to where I belong."

"You saw everything?" Miya confirmed.

The girl nodded, then launched into another defense of her friend. "I heard the call again. That's why I wanted to leave. The leshy was trying to help."

"The lights and the shadows...was that you?" Miya asked.

Another nod, slow and ashamed.

So, the foliage was the leshy's doing. Miya smiled weakly. "What he did isn't your fault."

"I'm sorry he scared your house spirit." Caelan glanced between Miya and Kai as they ushered her toward the bar. She dropped onto a stool next to Miya, her shoulders slumping. Having rediscovered flight, Gavran perched on his beer tap and croaked, examining his somber audience.

"What the hell was that?" Crowbar demanded, rubbing the back of her neck.

"Your invisible housecat scared off that bark-faced wilder beast," Kai said dryly. "Apparently, we missed the show"—he gestured at Miya and Caelan—"but these two had front row seats."

"The leshy amplifies the nature in things," said Ama, claiming the stool on Miya's other side. She looked tired, her usually sunlit eyes dull like straw. "For me and Kai, it means forcing our transitions. For Miya, it's shunting her spirit into the dreamscape, leaving her unconscious on this side."

"He doesn't always do it," Miya observed. "This was the first time he let loose on all of us."

Crowbar bee-lined for her moonshine. Uncorking the bottle, she poured everyone but Caelan a generous shot, then offered the teen a soda. "I've had my fill of supernatural shenanigans. Why's some ancient arboreal man trying to activate your powers, anyway?"

"More like cripple us." Ama cast Caelan a dubious glance. She probably wanted the leshy gone for more reasons than one; he threatened her command over her own nature. "I don't think any of us knows what he wants. I suppose it's a good thing the domovoy intervened. Otherwise, our runaway here would be long gone."

"Lay off her," Kai warned. "She didn't ask for this." Leaving his drink untouched, he meandered around the bar and stopped by the wall where the domovoy's shadow claws had latched on. He traced over a deep fissure that hadn't been there before, the marks a battle scar on his second home.

Caelan sat pin straight, fidgeting. "It's getting worse."

"The call?" Miya ventured. Something kept pulling her—an unnamed *she* that seemed to originate from the material plane rather than the dreamscape. An anomaly.

"I've been fighting it for so long," said Caelan. "It used to only get to me in my sleep—that's why I was sleepwalking all the time—but now I hear it even when I'm awake. It's...it's painful."

Kai abandoned the cracks in the wall and hopped over the bar to Crowbar's side. He slammed back his shot, then planted his hands on the counter in front of Caelan, boring into her. "Painful, how?"

Her gaze stuttered from Kai to the shelves behind him. "It feels like my bones are trying to burst from my skin. Like I'm wearing the wrong meat."

Gavran's head angled to a near ninety degrees, and Kai shot him a wry smile. "Gnarly."

"It's true," Caelan insisted. "But I have to fight it. I *know* something terrible will happen if I find what's calling me."

"Why were you kidnapped?" Kai asked without ceremony, spurring a series of slack-jawed glares from around the room.

"I...don't know," Caelan stammered.

Kai raised an eyebrow, drumming his thumb against the counter. "Two competing Bratva factions are trying to get their hands on you, and most of them don't even know you're a person. You're telling me you have *no* inkling about that?"

She shook her head. "I was taken while sleepwalking...because of that freaking call. I thought I was just an easy target. Figured they'd harvest my organs or something."

Miya winced at the girl's nonchalance. She reminded her of Kai when he spoke about his murdered parents—cold, distant. "And you were in that warehouse the whole time?"

"I don't know how long I was in there, but yeah. They fed me twice a day and let me use the bathroom. That's it."

"Three weeks." Kai's gaze dropped. "You've been missing for almost a month."

Caelan's jaw went slack. "Holy shit—"

"It took them three weeks to settle who'd take custody?" Ama's mouth tugged into a disapproving frown. "Sloppy."

"They were probably bickering over how to settle it." Kai scratched through his hair. "Bratva factions don't always play nice. They operate independently, so they butt heads a lot. If one of them realized Caelan was leverage over Pyotr..."

"Why not just take her then?" Ama pressed. "Why the underground fight?"

"She was found by a third party," Kai explained. "Small fry looking for a quick buck. They didn't want to piss off either faction, so they refused to sell unless Pyotr and his rival came to an agreement."

"And that agreement was the match between you and Ivan Zverev." Miya finally reached for her shot. She needed it.

"The broker was smart enough to keep things quiet," Ama realized. "I'm impressed the whole mob didn't know the prize was a person."

"If they yapped, they might've ruined the deal." Kai waggled his fingers for the moonshine. Crowbar passed it to him, and he poured himself more. "I'm guessing they only talked with Pyotr and his rival. As the info went down the food chain, it got twisted up. By the time it reached me and Sergei, we could've been fighting over a deflated soccer ball for all we knew."

Miya rubbed her face and whined. "How'd this third party know Caelan was an asset when they found her? They must've recognized *something*."

"She said she doesn't know." Kai tipped back his drink. "Whatever they recognized—it's not something she's aware of."

"Hey, as much as I love being the center of attention..." Caelan wrung her hands together, then peered up at Kai. "Can I have some fluffernutters?"

Kai's lip twitched. "We're on about mobsters and kidnappings... and you want a fucking sandwich?"

Her chin jerked down, her nod resolute.

Sighing, Kai straightened from the counter. "All right, get your shit. We can go home."

A beaming smile brightened the teen's ruddy face, and she jumped from the stool. When she retreated upstairs, Ama was the first to speak.

"The leshy needs to be dealt with."

A collective groan filled the room, punctuated by Crowbar pouring another round. Their barkeep raised her shot in a tentative toast, and they all clinked glasses.

"We still don't know his intentions," Miya said, smacking her mouth to banish the moonshine's bite. "They might not be nefarious."

Ama picked at a chipped nail. "No, but the impact is. He's desperate to get Caelan back now that you've fulfilled your end of the deal, but for what purpose?"

"Doesn't matter." They all turned to Kai. He stared down his empty shot glass. "Giving the kid to that thing won't stop whatever's got its claws in her. Besides, she's got a family."

"She said she can't go back," Miya said quietly.

"Because her whole life is fucked up." Kai clanked the glass onto the counter. "She can't make that decision until she's gotten rid of whatever's after her."

"That's...oddly mature of you," Ama remarked. Crowbar thwacked her across the arm.

Kai shot the white wolf a venomous glare but waived the chance to spar. "I don't give a shit about what the leshy wants. It's a spirit. It'll do whatever it thinks will help it reach its goal."

"*He* cares about Caelan's safety," Miya countered. "Maybe he showed up because he felt her distress."

"Maybe." Kai's glower softened as his eyes slid to Miya. "Doesn't mean he's actually keeping her safe."

Caelan's footsteps thundered down the stairs before she rounded the corner, bundled in Miya's borrowed clothes. "I'm ready."

She seemed calmer, bouncing back easily after what felt like a night terror made manifest. Miya wasn't sure she would've faired so well at Caelan's age.

Crowbar collected the empty shot glasses. Sidling up to the domovoy's corner, she tilted her bottle and spilled some of the moonshine onto the floor. "Thanks, little guy. I can't see you, but the witchy one says you did good."

Miya smiled in their direction. "I'm glad you two are getting along."

"If he's warding off shit that makes my bar swim like a canoe in a tsunami, he's my new goddamn bestie."

Kai's hand found the small of Miya's back as he steered her toward the door.

"Be careful," Ama warned sternly. "If you need, Gavran can come with you."

The raven pumped his wings and chortled. Miya poked his silken breast, earning a soft purr. "I'm sure he'll do the rounds regardless of what we say."

Gavran squawked in protest, but they all knew he'd spend the night patrolling the neighborhood sky.

Kai grunted Ama goodnight and yelped when Crowbar swatted his ass with a dish towel. After a flurry of friendly threats and a fist bump with the bartender, he hauled Miya and Caelan from the King of Spades. They barely squeezed their way out, pinioning the black wolf in a heap of giggles until he rolled his eyes and steadied them. His arm draped around Miya's shoulders—a familiar comfort —and she reached for his dangling hand, threading her fingers with his.

Caelan shuffled closer to his side, scrounging for security like a small animal caught in the rain. Kai noticed, and a sadness that didn't suit the angles of his face carved his expression into something foreign. His chest rose with a pensive inhale, and after an excruciating beat, he rotated his arm and offered it to the girl.

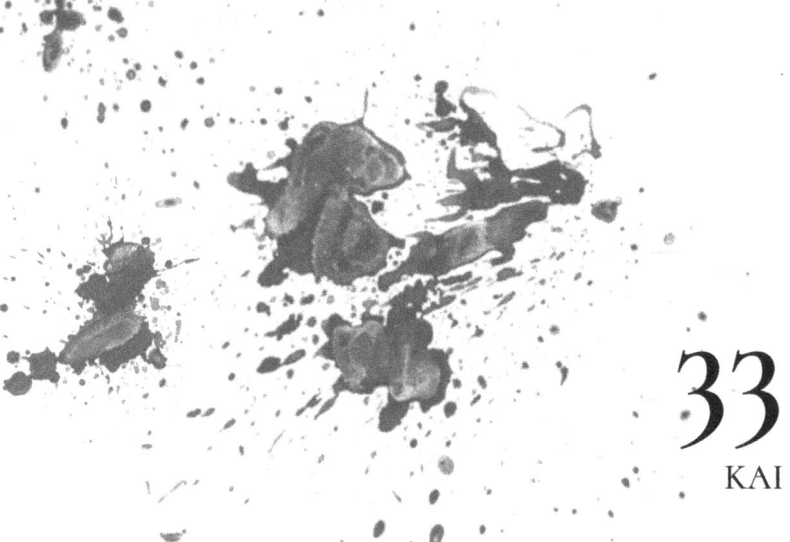

33

KAI

THE LIGHT SWITCHED ON, and Ripper spun to face the bipeds. Half-crouched, he stared at them wide-eyed, a wriggling cockroach hanging from his mouth.

Miya shrieked and whirled from the scene, leaving Kai to contend with the vermin. He didn't have to. The moment he took a step, Ripper slurped up the bug.

"I think it's dead," Caelan offered sympathetically as she unhooked her elbow from Kai's.

Miya poked her head out from behind Kai's shoulder, and the feral munchkin gave a weighty swallow, then gagged. Fortunately, nothing came back up.

"Gross." Miya scowled as Kai removed his jacket and tossed it onto the wall hook.

"At least he's doing his job." He kicked off his boots and made for the kitchen.

"Is *that* why you agreed to bring him back?" Caelan crossed her arms over her chest disapprovingly.

Kai shrugged as he grabbed the jars of peanut butter and Marshmallow Fluff, then snatched the bread loaf from atop the microwave. "It may have crossed my mind."

He glimpsed a smile caress Miya's mouth. Her eyes sparked with knowing as she glanced his way, though she didn't dare say what he knew she was thinking.

You're sweet.

He hated being called sweet. It refuted his entire self-concept—

the devil-may-care persona that followed him from one reckless stunt to another. Yet he wanted Miya to see him as more than an abrasive bastard with a history of delinquency. And she did.

Caelan snuffed out her complaints as soon as Kai began to assemble her fluffernutters. When he finished, she nabbed the plate from the counter and plopped down on the couch. Miya padded off to the bathroom to shower, leaving Kai alone with the teen.

"You sure you're okay?" he asked as she bit through her meal faster than the cockroach had slipped into Ripper's mouth.

This time, she wasn't so quick to confirm, her eyes fixed on the plate. "I don't know what it means to be okay."

The admission came out tentative, as though the words could cut. And they did. Kai felt them slice through his chest and seize the tender parts of him that'd yet to heal. How long had he spent wondering what it meant to be *okay*?

"It's relative, I guess." He reluctantly joined her on the couch, the cushions dipping with his weight.

She tracked his movements as she adjusted her grip on the sandwich. "Relative to what?"

"How fucked up you've been in recent memory."

She stopped chewing, her eyes swinging back to the plate. "I feel less messed up than I did a few hours ago."

Kai plunked his head back, his eyes drifting shut. "That's a start."

He felt wrung out, his limbs like old rubber. Although transitions were always excruciating, he could tolerate the pain when it was a choice. But having every bone in his body broken against his will left him with a little bit less of himself every time. He was depleted, and he lacked the tools to replenish what he'd lost.

Caelan shifted beside him, curling her legs under her. "What happened to you and that other lady back at the bar?"

Eyes snapping open, Kai stared at a cobweb stuck to the ceiling. "We're wolves."

"Like, werewolves?" He heard her heart hammer harder in her chest, excitement lacing her voice.

"No." He sat up with a tired groan. "Werewolves are humans cursed to turn on a full moon. Ama and I...we're different. Like living folklore."

Caelan wrinkled her nose. "Folklore?"

"You know, stories to make sense of the world." He fumbled,

wishing Miya was there to clarify. "Stories people spin about themselves until some of it becomes true."

"Do you and Ama come from the same story?" Caelan asked, oddly accepting of his bumbling.

Kai shook his head. "I don't know why she's a wolf."

Caelan reached for Miya's throw, shoved in the corner of the couch, and spread it over her legs. "So, what's your story?"

Kai narrowed his eyes, weighing if he had the bandwidth for a history lesson, but when he saw her expectant stare and remembered what she'd been through, he folded. "My parents were like me," he began, palming the back of his neck as he settled into the cushions. "I don't remember much about them—they died when I was ten—but some shit just stays with you, burrows in your bones, then leaps out when you least expect it." An acrid taste filled his mouth as his last nightmare came back to him—the sight of his parents' bodies cold on the ground. "They weren't the only reason I ended up like this."

"I'm sorry about your parents," she interjected. "I don't remember mine either—I mean, the ones before…"

"I know," he said quietly, ignoring her condolences. "But the people who give you a second chance are just as important."

She nodded, squirming under the blanket. "What's the other reason you're a wolf?"

The corner of Kai's mouth tugged up. *That* story was more complicated. "Do you think gods are real?"

Caelan pursed her lips, humming. "Not God-with-a-capital-G, but when people believe strongly enough, it's like you said. Sometimes, it becomes real."

"Gods, living spirits, boogeymen." Kai flopped his arms, annoyed at the endless verbiage that existed to describe otherworldly nonsense. "Call it whatever you want. Either way, one of those ethereal assholes is my past life."

Her eyes widened. "Whoa, like, reincarnation?"

"Yeah, I hate it."

"Who was he?" she pressed.

Kai sighed, gesturing vaguely. "Some god of destruction named Sendoa. Had a control freak for a brother who fancied himself the literal fucking creator. Anyway, Sendoa liked prowling the woods as a wolf to scare the shit out of people. Got a real hard-on for the

Dreamwalker after she pissed off the brother with a God-complex—"

"Hold up," Caelan interrupted. "The Dreamwalker...as in your girlfriend?"

"The original Dreamwalker was a different person," Kai explained. "Miya and I—we're reincarnations of those spirits or gods or whatever."

"Okay." Caelan raised a hand to hit pause as she parsed his tale. "You and Miya are the reincarnations of ancient spirits. She's the Dreamwalker, and you're this god of destruction who liked running around as a wolf."

"Sure."

She peered up at him. "What happened?"

"Long story short, things got bloody, and we died. Sendoa was in a wolf's body when it happened, and the Dreamwalker made a pact that they'd find each other in every lifetime until their business was settled." His mouth slashed into a smile. "She got her way."

"And...are you still trying to pay those debts?"

Kai shook his head, the memory of his haunting a permanent stain. Sendoa's malevolent sibling had remained life after life, until it was Kai's turn to contend with their legacy. Since his teens, he'd had a voice in his head, mocking and belittling him. *Auditory hallucinations from PTSD*, the shrink had said. Kai hated the word *hallucination*, like the experience of it wasn't real. But it was.

It took fifteen years for him to accept that it didn't matter whether the ghosts came from his head or his past; the ghoulish fuckery was a perfect symptom of Kai's personal and generational trauma. "Sendoa's brother—*my* brother...he's gone for good."

Caelan smiled timidly, her knees drawing to her chest under the throw. "So, you're with her by choice."

Kai sucked in a sharp breath. He still remembered making that decision. There'd been nothing binding them—no obligation left to keep him by Miya's side. She'd released him, but instead of claiming his freedom, he stayed. He'd cast off the thing he valued most for something he knew was better: companionship. It'd been a missing piece in his life for far too long.

"Yeah, I am."

Caelan tilted her head, curiosity sketching her face. "Do you love her?"

The water in the bathroom shut off as Miya finished her shower. Kai thought of the night she fell asleep in his arms, vacant of the reassurance. Terror curdled in his chest at the thought of speaking those four letters aloud, but when posed as a question, he found himself able to sieve through the turmoil and arrive at an answer. He met Caelan's probing gaze, the ache behind his ribs worse than the leshy's compulsion. "In every way I know how."

His qualification creased the teen's brow. *How do you love?* her eyes seemed to ask, and Kai was grateful when she didn't utter the question. In truth, he had no damn clue.

"So," he changed the topic, "you don't know what's calling you?"

She shook her head. "No."

"But you're sure that if you find it—whatever it is—something bad will happen?"

Caelan plucked Ripper from the floor as he meandered by, scavenging for more cockroaches. She set him in her lap, and Kai was amazed when the feral thing didn't try to claw her eyes out. "It sounds crazy, but it's like being compelled to push a button you know will launch a missile. You don't want to do it, but you can't help it. You've been brainwashed."

"Any idea who brainwashed you?" Kai asked with a balmy smile.

Another shake of the head, and Ripper flopped on his side and began to purr.

"Well, whatever. We'll figure it out." Kai stretched as Miya reappeared, her hair damp and her day clothes traded out for pajamas. It was close to two in the morning.

They exchanged awkward goodnights, and Caelan retreated to the bedroom after brushing her teeth. The cat followed her in, apparently having chosen his person. She seemed more at ease now, and Kai hoped it would buy them a few hours of rest before she busted out of their apartment to chase after some phantom call.

"She trusts you," Miya said with a gleeful smile.

Kai grumbled as he rubbed his eyes. "We're both wounded animals. Like calls to like."

"Give yourself more credit," she chided gently. "You saved her from horrible circumstances, and whether you realize it or not, you're the person she's looking to for some kind of direction."

"Saving her was an accident," said Kai. "If I hadn't been there, you and Ama would've gotten her out."

Miya rolled her eyes and gave his arm a light shove. "Just accept the compliment, you dick."

He smirked at her. "I'd rather you compliment my actual dick."

Miya swatted at his crotch, and he seized her hand and dragged her down with a chuckle. She collapsed onto his lap, and after he wormed out of his day clothes and into sweats, they nestled under the throw in a heap of tangled limbs, exhaustion overtaking them.

If the leshy showed his bark-covered face to change Kai into a wolf in his own home, he'd tear the craggy fuck a new asshole with his teeth.

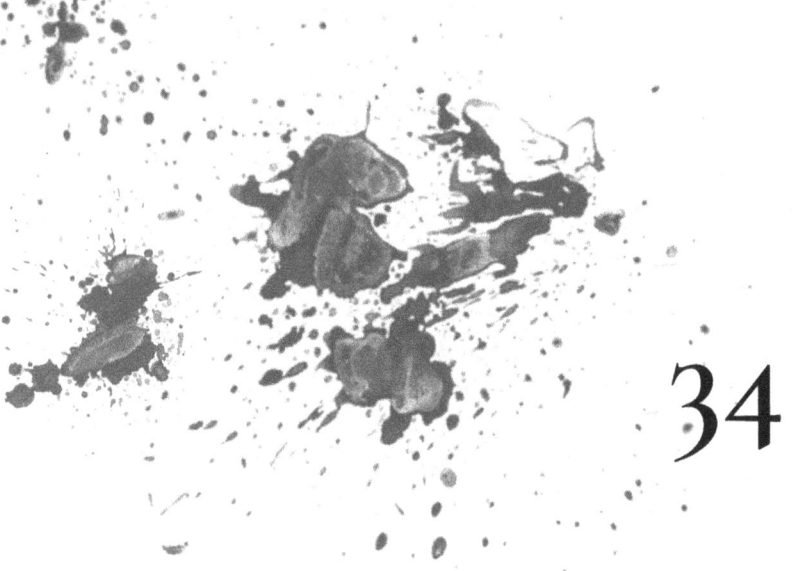

34

KAI AWOKE when Miya's touch danced across his abdomen. She normally wasn't up before him, and as his eyes fluttered open, he saw the sky barely lit with a cerulean glow. Her lips trailed his collar bone, fingers roaming across his hip, then lower, until she took him in her grasp.

"Good morning," she whispered when his breath caught.

"You're...*awake*."

She snickered against his chest, slowly working the length of him. "I couldn't sleep."

He wouldn't complain about her method of killing time. When he grew restless with her tender strokes, he kicked off his sweatpants, and she slid down his body and replaced her hand with her mouth. Kai thumped his head back, fingers weaving through her hair. He loved the feel of her tongue, the heat of her mouth enveloping him—

His phone buzzed, jolting him out of the moment. The cursed device was lost in a pocket somewhere. His clothes were still trapped under him after he'd lazily discarded them the night before, and he managed to shift around just enough to fish the damn thing out. He glanced at the screen.

Sergei.

Agitated, he axed the call and tossed the phone aside. Kai refused voicemail service on principle; people could text if they needed to leave a message. Pleased to be rid of the distraction, he swore under his breath when Miya moaned against him, her tongue sweeping along his hard length.

Then, the fucking phone rang again.

Kai gritted his teeth when he saw the irritant had returned like a mosquito in the dead of night. Snarling, he gently pried Miya off him and sat up. He swung his legs over the side of the flimsy mattress, then barked into the receiver, "What the fuck is it?"

"Did I wake you?" came Sergei's bland response.

Miya raised an eyebrow when she heard who it was, then slipped from the couch and wedged herself between Kai's legs.

Oh, good. She was on her knees.

Kai narrowed his eyes at her, and she flashed him a wicked smile, her hand gliding up the inside of his thigh before closing around his base.

"I *did* just wake up," he said evasively. He squeezed his eyes shut when Miya's tongue swirled around his tip. Gripping her wavy tresses at the roots, he pushed her head down until she'd taken all of him, her soft whimper sending a satisfying shudder up his spine.

"We need to meet," Sergei insisted. "Now."

"Can't." The refusal came out strained as Kai fought to control his breathing. His gaze dropped to Miya, her appraising eyes fixed on him. She wasn't going to stop—and he didn't want her to.

"Why the hell not?" Sergei demanded, his tone sharpening.

Kai tried to conjure a reply, but he couldn't concentrate with Miya's mouth around his cock. He bit back a groan as his focus splintered, his pleasure cresting as she nudged him toward climax.

"Because," Kai said through a growl, "I'm busy getting my dick sucked."

He held down the power button until the screen went black.

Miya choked on a laugh—and what was in her mouth. Grinning down at her, Kai rolled his hips forward and cupped the back of her head, moving with her until he tugged on her hair in warning, and she pulled away to watch him come.

Sergei did little to temper his disgust when Kai finally met with him later that morning. The wolf smirked, reassuring Sergei that he'd eaten well for breakfast.

"I don't understand," Sergei muttered through a scowl.

"Pussy," Kai replied flatly. "I ate pussy."

A flush crawled up the mobster's neck. "Good for you."

"It was pretty damn good for both of us, actually—"

"Shut up," Sergei snapped. "I'm not here to spar with you about your sex life."

"You sure?" Kai deadpanned. "You seemed hellbent on cock-blocking me."

The mobster scoffed and jerked his head toward the street. They were loitering in a back lane a few blocks from the Confessional. "Did you find out what Pyotr wants with the kid?"

"He wants to kill her," said Kai, the playfulness leaving his voice. "Just don't know why yet. The guys he's got looking for her are tight-lipped, and their minions don't know the forgery's a person."

Sergei sighed, shoving his hands into his pockets. "I haven't been able to stick my nose in it much. I'm already in shit for losing the forgery. If I start asking questions, Pyotr will suspect I've got something to do with it."

"But you don't," Kai countered.

"Maybe not directly, but I know where it—*she*—is." He shot Kai a venomous glare. "You've both got me by the balls. If Pyotr finds out I'm covering for you, he'll kill me. But if I tell him where the kid is..."

Kai flashed him a baleful smile. "I'll rip your kidneys out with my teeth."

"There's the threat." Sergei chuckled. "Neither option sounds terribly pleasant, though I'm cooperating with you because I have no interest in becoming a child murderer. The more information we have about Pyotr's intentions, the easier it'll be to untangle ourselves from this mess."

Easier said than done. Kai had already milked Timur dry, but Bratva was a collection of brainless brutes who followed orders, and only the kingpin knew the ropes. Everyone else had partial information, making it impossible to piece the puzzle together from their garbled clues. "Why not ask Pyotr?"

Sergei blinked at him, stunned. "I don't know—why not walk into a snake pit barefoot?"

Kai kissed his teeth, irritation lacing his voice. "You got a better idea? He's obviously good at keeping his secrets, you know, *secret*."

"It doesn't matter," Sergei grumbled. "He's...*summoned* us."

"No one *summons* me, asshole."

"Well, tough shit. Pyotr's getting impatient, and he's shaking down anyone involved in this little charade. Last I heard, he butchered every last one of the mercs holding the forgery for the trade."

Kai raised an eyebrow. "Did he think they'd spill about the kid?"

Sergei shook his head. "They accused him of trying to steal the forgery back after losing the fight. No one realized it was you. I guess that got him thinking about me since I arranged said fight." His eyes swung to Kai. "He wants to meet the man who lost his prize."

So, that's why Sergei wanted to meet so urgently. Kai huffed. "Great. Guess I can ask him myself."

"Don't get cocky," Sergei warned. "That's what got you into this, remember?"

Kai picked at his fingernail, his lip curling into a snarl. "What's he going to do? Kill me? I'm not a pig for slaughter like those deadbeats from the warehouse."

Sergei shoved his shoulder. "You don't know what kind of resources he has or what he's capable of. You're not as invincible as you think, *Kai*," he sneered the name as though it were also a forgery—a moniker used as a facile courtesy. "You don't even know who you are, and all it took was a glimpse at your own shadow to spin you out."

Rage like a firebrand seared Kai's insides, and he grabbed Sergei by the throat in a poor attempt to smother the flame, fingers bruising tender flesh as he seethed, "What the *fuck* is that supposed to mean?"

Sergei grasped Kai's wrist, but he didn't cower, staring back without an ounce of remorse as he wheezed. For once, he'd told the truth, heedless of the consequences.

He was right. The moment Kai came face to face with Ivan Zverev, he'd unraveled.

"My oba znayem...chto tvoye imya ne *Kai*," Sergei managed to choke out.

We both know your real name isn't Kai.

His grip on Sergei slackened, the words a fiercer vise. It was true; he couldn't remember his real name, but there was only one he identified with, and it was the one he'd claimed. The one he'd given Alice when she'd first asked, fitted with the surname she'd bestowed him on his sixteenth birthday.

Kai Donovan.

"When does your boss want to meet?" he asked, suddenly subdued.

Sergei straightened out his collar. "Midnight tonight, at his private club. I'll text you the address."

Kai swallowed down the bitter lump lodged in his throat. "Fine."

With a curt nod, Sergei turned and left Kai to the shadows.

We both know your real name isn't Kai.

Only it was real. It'd been real for the past twenty years—to Alice, to Miya, and most of all, to him.

Kai Donovan was real. He had to be. Because if he wasn't, there was nothing left to stitch himself back together with.

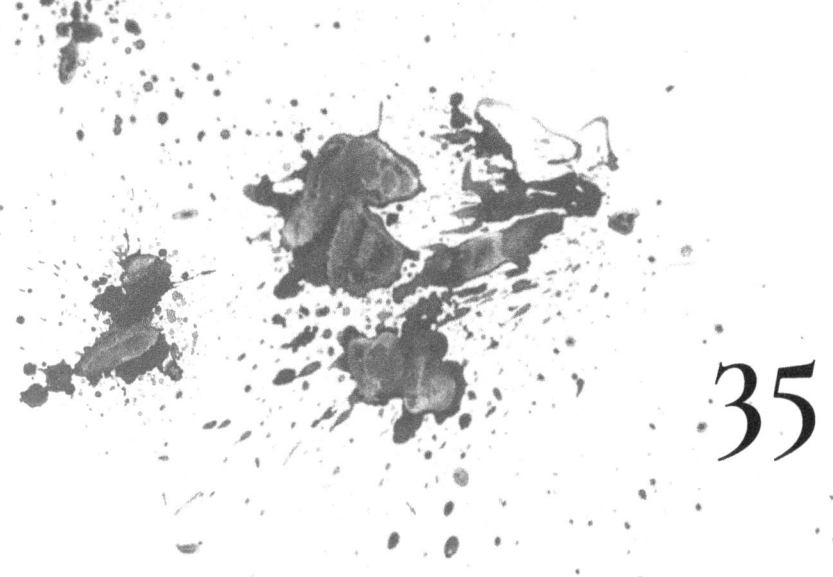

35

CHRYSANTHEMUM WAS as ostentatious as its name. Tucked in an alleyway, the private club colonized a two-story red-brick heritage building. The exterior was unremarkable—no signage indicating that anything worthwhile lurked inside. Despite the windowless steel-reinforced door that looked like it could withstand a siege, a rhino-sized bouncer with an earpiece stood stationed outside the venue.

"I'm here for Sergei," Kai said as he stopped in front of the big man. He was uninterested in dressing for an upscale joint with his combat boots and black cargo pants, but he was ready for a brawl.

The bouncer gave Kai a once-over, squinting vigorously at his worn leather jacket. "Arms up," he ordered.

Kai did as he was told, tolerating the man's bear paws gliding over his sides.

"You're good." He tapped his earpiece. "Someone here for Sergei. Looks like your fighter."

Kai's brow arched over a bored expression. He knew he looked like rabble, but it wasn't like he walked around in boxing gloves.

After a brief exchange, the bouncer smacked his palm on the door with two hollow thuds. As it squealed open, muffled house music bled from the dim hallway, hot air rushing out like a tender sigh.

"Take the stairs on the right to get to the VIP lounge. Pyotr and Sergei are there."

Without a word, Kai slipped his hands into his jacket pockets and stepped into the club. White vapors illuminated by sultry lights wafted past, and heavy bass thundered through Kai's bones like an assault. The smell of pheromones, alcohol, cocaine, and molly invaded him, scrambling his senses until he adjusted. He rounded the corner by coat check and climbed a flight of stairs manned by a pair of bouncers. They stepped aside to let him pass, their hands clasped over their dicks as they tracked him with cautious stares.

A narrow corridor with several rooms awaited on the second floor—probably an office, a restroom, and the VIP lounge the meathead outside had mentioned. Kai didn't have to scope out each one to know where he was headed; the glassy black double-doors at the end of the hall were as loud as the music. He heard no murmurs or chatter filtering through from the other side, which meant the lounge was soundproof. A perfect kill room.

The door opened with a heavy click, and another non-descript bodyguard greeted him with a furrowed brow. He was dressed nicer than the rest, his suit tailored to show off the sharp vee of his torso. His black silk shirt and tie were as impeccable as his ridiculously coiffed hair, though his cauliflower ears suggested his face had endured a less than perfect childhood.

Kai hadn't knocked, though he figured they'd spotted him on the security monitors. As the door swung open, a stocked bar on the far wall came into view, and the bartender—a young woman who looked uncomfortable in her too-tight, too-short dress—shook a cocktail for one of the lounge guests. Decadent leather seating and what appeared to be a hand-carved table populated the dark marble floor, and a pair of chic, velvety curtains framed a large one-way window that overlooked the club.

Definitely a kill room.

Sergei sat on one of the leather sofas, his elbows planted on his thighs as he looked up to see Kai enter. Beside him, another man with thinning brown hair stood before the window, surveying his domain. His broad shoulders were proudly pulled back, his posture at ease as he continued his evaluation of the club in complete stillness, unconcerned with the predator at his back.

"Welcome, Mr. Donovan."

His voice was deep and gruff, like someone had raked his words over coals. The formality plucked at Kai's nerves, set his teeth on edge, but he knew better than to expect otherwise from a man who fancied himself an underworld lord.

"Kai." The word came out low and forceful, like he had to shape it into something familiar before it left him as a threatening growl.

Pyotr unbuttoned the front of his navy pin-striped jacket, then turned to face Kai. He looked to be in his fifties, with graying stubble and thick brows. Deep-set lines bracketed his mouth, intensifying the severity of his expression, though he appeared lithe and nimble under his perfectly tailored suit. "Is there something wrong with your family name?"

The question felt pointed, like he knew about Kai's past—courtesy of Sergei, no doubt.

"I hate formalities," Kai said without elaboration.

"Ah, an insolent one." Pyotr gave a crooked smile as he straightened a cuff. "Customs are important, Mr. Donovan. Whether you like it or not, tradition is the foundation upon which order is built. Identity, too. We are not scraps of wood afloat in a sea, but communities bound by a common set of rules."

Kai swallowed the snort that rose from his chest. He tilted his head, his mouth bent into something mocking. "Do the rules apply to you?"

That seemed to shut him up. Pyotr's gaze narrowed a fraction. "Men of your stature shouldn't get too clever."

"Why?" Kai shrugged. "Does it ruin the order of things?" He meant the question sincerely, though it dripped with scorn. "I knew someone like you once. Obsessed with tradition, order, discipline."

Amusement quirked Pyotr's eyebrow—a momentary intrigue. "Oh? What happened?"

Kai's lips skinned back from his teeth. "I killed him."

Pyotr's head flew back as he burst into a hoarse laugh. "You didn't tell me he was funny, Sergei."

Sergei looked anything but entertained. He grunted in response, but Kai could smell the fear on him. Sweat beaded his temple, his hands clasped between his knees as he observed the exchange.

"You'd make a good jester," Pyotr said with a wave of his hand. "Though unfortunately, you're in a rather serious predicament. You've lost something important to me."

Kai exhaled slowly, steadying his nerves. Caelan.

The bartender shuffled from her post to hand Pyotr his cocktail.

He thanked her with a leering grin, then took a tentative sip. "I'll make you an offer. You find the forgery, bring it to me, and I'll forget your blunder."

Only Kai knew the extent of Sergei's anxiety in that moment. The persnickety bastard was on the precipice of shitting his pants. No amount of humidity could explain away the perspiration on his collar; he was a drop of cortisol from a hypertensive crisis.

"I'll need to know what the forgery is and why you want it so bad," Kai bargained. "Can't find what I don't know I'm looking for." He wasn't normally a liar, but he also wasn't in the business of sending children to a butcher.

Pyotr's hands slipped into his pockets as he regarded Kai with the caution of a predator gunning for oversized prey. "The forgery is a person who must be killed."

"I'm not your personal assassin." *This fucking coward*, Kai thought. "You want someone taken out, do it yourself."

Pyotr waggled a finger at him. "In my faction, we have a policy. My men are not allowed to take wives."

"I'm not your man, and I'm not married," said Kai, derailed by the digression. "Never will be."

Pyotr sneered. "It's a metaphor, you simpleton. Between that buffoon at the Confessional, your dyke friend, and that pretty thing you're rutting, there's a lot for me to work with."

Sweltering heat raveled up Kai's spine, fury gripping the back of his skull. With Pyotr threatening his friends and insulting them in a single breath, he felt the tenuous bridle on his anger slip. "I'll fucking kill you," he snarled, rage shaking the wolf from slumber.

He would've torn Pyotr's head from his shoulders and whipped it at the window when the door behind him cracked open, and a nauseatingly familiar scent wafted through the lounge.

"You could try," said Pyotr, "but what will it cost?"

Kai didn't have to turn to know who stood behind him.

"Good of you to join us, Vanya."

Ivan Zverev glided past to join Pyotr across the way, and Kai's every violent fantasy guttered out like a flame.

"I thought you might be resistant, so I hired Ivan to...assist. I hope he inspires some healthy competition to get the job done quickly."

Kai wasn't listening. He bore into the man with his genetic likeness—a beast trapped in human flesh. Ivan Zverev, for his part, seemed disinterested in sussing out his rival. Maybe he was over-confident, or maybe he was privy to information Kai lacked, but the fact remained that Kai had been forced on his back foot yet again.

"Find me the forgery before he does, and all will be forgiven. Let him win"—Pyotr gestured to Zverev—"and your debt will be far steeper than it already is."

Sergei rose to his feet, stupefied. His mouth opened, but nothing came out.

With a slow inhale, Kai pushed the tension from his body as best he could. He took a menacing stride toward Pyotr, and for a split second, he saw the man's eyes widen before Zverev stepped in to block Kai's path. The loss that'd thrust him into this shitshow descended on him like his nightmares, his body revolting as though he were back on the floor at the Confessional. Even now, he wasn't sure he'd win.

"I forgot to mention…" Pyotr gave Zverev a hearty slap on the back. "Since Vanya here is a free agent, I've taken the liberty of hiring him as my bodyguard. He's *awfully* good at it."

Kai's stomach roiled. For the first time since arriving, he felt something other than anger and contempt. He felt sick. His loss to Zverev was the reason Pyotr believed he was owed anything. Now, Pyotr was shacking up with the man responsible, forcing Kai to play fetch with him. It wasn't merely salt in the wound; it was sadism.

"You've got to be shitting me," Kai ground out.

"I'm afraid not." Pyotr almost sounded regretful.

Ivan Zverev and Kai Donovan locked eyes—wolves among men who wanted to corral them into obedience. Hackles raised, teeth bared, neither dared so much as flinch. There was nowhere to go in this neon cage, the urge to tear through Zverev curdling in the marrow of Kai's bones.

And yet he couldn't move. He was welded to the floor, frozen like a hare in a thicket.

Ivan Zverev was no trifle, and he wasn't just a steel edifice walling Kai from his target. He was a hunter, and soon, Caelan would be his prey.

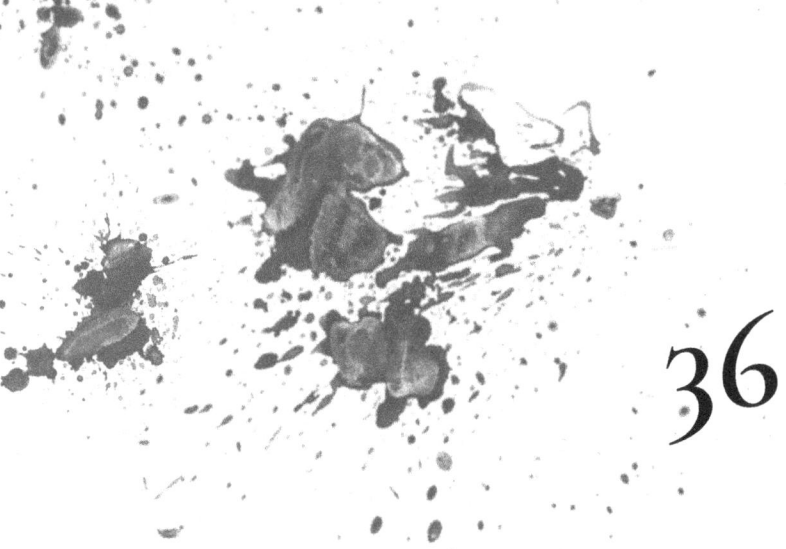

36

KAI HAD NEVER LIKED SILENCE. He gravitated toward bars because of the noise; the din strummed at his bones, leaving him fuller, less alone. Now, in the quiet of Dr. Krunić's office, the stillness spooled into an invisible knot, impossible to untangle. Things unsaid in the quiet of an empty room weighed heavier than the threat of violence.

It'd been three days since his face off with Pyotr at Chrysanthemum, and he hadn't done shit since. Miya said they were laying low, but to Kai it felt like hiding. As long as they had Caelan, she'd bargained with him, Zverev was no closer to finding her. But Kai remained agitated; his instinct was to act, and he wanted solutions *now*. Pyotr wouldn't wait forever—another week, tops. His veneer of control would splinter, and he'd raze the city to get his way. A desperate mobster was an ugly thing.

"How are things at home?" Dr. Krunić asked casually.

To say Kai was *sitting* in the armchair would've been generous. He'd sprawled out sideways, legs akimbo over the armrest. His eyes drifted shut as his neck arched against the curve of the cushion. Why the hell had he agreed to come here twice a week? "Fine."

The shrink narrowed her eyes. "Last time, you mentioned that your partner asked you to come here. Are you communicating with her about our sessions?"

"You mean, is she still pissed at me?" Kai lifted his head and squinted at her. "She's not."

"How do you know?"

Their night in the field flitted through his mind, the sting of Miya's palm against his cheek caressing his mouth into a smirk. "I just know."

"Ah, so you're intuitive."

He wrinkled his nose. *Intuitive* wasn't the word he'd use after a lifetime of being told he was insensitive, emotionally stupid.

"What's wrong?" she asked with an infuriating little smile.

"Don't really see myself that way," he admitted.

"Then what do you think your partner sees in you?"

Kai arched an eyebrow at the doctor. "Damn. No mincing words with you."

She shrugged, twirling the pen around her fingers. "I adjust my approach to my clients' needs. You like directness. No coddling. I can accommodate that."

Smoothly sitting up, Kai planted his feet on the floor and faced forward. What *did* Miya see in him? He'd lost sight of it after five years, found himself wondering if it'd been anything beyond circumstance. They were both outcasts, loneliness cutting to the bone, and she'd been in danger. For once, Kai wasn't the threat; it was everyone else. "She feels safe, I think." He glimpsed Krunić wrestle back her surprise. "I know, sounds batshit. I'm the last person anyone should feel safe with, but things aren't always what they seem."

Dr. Krunić crossed her legs, eyeing him curiously. "How do you mean?"

Kai scraped a fingernail against a callus on his palm. "Wearing a suit and plastering a smile on your face doesn't make you reliable or trustworthy. Your dry cleaning's useless when shit hits the fan. You want someone who's got your back...even if they're a bigger monster than whatever's trying to eat you."

"Do you consider yourself that monster?" she asked without missing a beat.

Kai inhaled slowly. "I'm a monster who knows what people want."

"And what did your girlfriend want when she fell in love with you?"

"To stop pretending." He thought back to the girl he met in the woods of Black Hollow—that unmoored college student crushed under the weight of social expectation. "She just wants to be herself."

"And you give her space for that." It wasn't a question, but a conclusion. She almost sounded smug.

Maybe Krunić was right yet again. He was so plugged into his senses, it was impossible *not* to know what people felt. Even if he didn't always understand it, those insights helped him survive. Kai wasn't completely without charm, and so long as he wasn't possessed by demons or bleeding out in a street gutter, he knew how to turn heads. *That* was the intuition he'd taken for granted since his teens, and it'd helped him cultivate a mask for his basest impulses. He could smell which douchebags to pick fights with so he wouldn't get banned from his favorite dives. Never had trouble getting laid because he knew when a crass word got a woman wet and when it was unwelcome. He paid attention, and he adapted.

"Do you think you're a good person?" Krunić asked, tapping the tip of her pen against her chin.

Kai snorted. "I don't care about being a good person."

She stared at him unblinkingly, her expression deadpan. "A reporter asks an oil tycoon if he thinks his company is good for the environment. The oil tycoon responds that he's not an environmentalist. How does that sound, hm?"

Kai groaned and shifted in the chair, kicking his legs up over the armrest again. "Say what you mean."

"You're evading," she said flatly. "Whether you care about being a good person is irrelevant to my question. In fact, you *must* have an answer to conclude that you don't care. So, I'll ask you again: do you think you're a good person?"

With a glower trained on the wall, Kai gnashed his teeth until his jaw hurt from the tension. He hated how hard it was to form the word—that stupid one-syllable word that made him feel like an ass-naked drunk who'd stumbled into a Sunday cookout. "No."

It came out as a begrudging mutter, but the doctor heard him loud and clear. She nodded like she'd already known, but her features softened as she folded her hands in her lap. "Do you think you deserve to be happy? To have good things come your way?"

His gaze dropped to his hand, splayed casually over his thigh. He'd hurt a lot of people with that hand. Just the other night, he'd beaten a man for a morsel of intel, then threatened his life if he didn't fuck off the continent. He'd also wanted to kill Pyotr—would've if Zverev hadn't shown up to rattle him out of his flaring temper. His apparent cousin had a face as interesting as a bus stop billboard, but a mere whiff of him raised Kai's hackles. Now, he'd have to fend off the beast to protect Caelan. More violence. More bloodshed. He seemed fated to it—suited for it. To say he regretted it would be a lie, but he wasn't proud either. It was just life, and he did what was necessary to survive. He never once thought he deserved all the bullshit the universe rained down on him, but he didn't think he deserved better either.

"No." The admission was quiet, almost reticent. "I want those things," he volunteered, "but I don't think I deserve them. I'm not sure anyone deserves anything."

The therapist canted her head and asked, "What do you mean by that?"

Kai's lip curled as a sliver of irritation needled his chest. "*Deserve* is a dumb word. To deserve something, there needs to be some…" he trailed off, searching for the right phrase, "…cosmic balance. Someone's got to decide, right? People make up these systems—morality, ethics, capitalism, whatever—and they all have their rules. When good things happen, people think it's because they followed the rules. They think they're being rewarded."

He let out a breathy laugh, then twisted in the armchair, his boots landing on the floor with a thud. He'd always been like this—restless, itching for an end to the stillness. Planting his elbows on his knees, he fixated on the stained wood between his feet. "It's all bullshit. When you live outside of it, you know that. People aren't rewarded for anything. Some walk around like they were born with a four-leaf clover up their ass while others are a skidding matchstick in a world made of flint. Some make smart choices, others don't, and sometimes, even good choices bite you in the dick. Hindsight's twenty-twenty. But there's no *deserving* anything. You get what you get, and thinking about whether it's fair is a waste of time." Kai raised his head, boring into her with a seething stare. "So, doc, when you ask me if I think I'm a good person—if I think I *deserve* good—you're asking the wrong question. I'm not good, and I don't deserve good, but none of that matters because it's not about what I deserve. It's about what I want."

He heard her heartrate jack up, her pupils dilating as her breath hitched and she jerked back. Kai averted his gaze; he hadn't meant to scare her.

She cleared her throat, recovering quickly. "Last time you were here, you told me you valued your independence more than anything. That what you want is to"—she flipped through her notes —"do whatever the fuck you want." Letting the page drop, she looked up at him. "And when I asked if you should be allowed to do whatever the fuck you want, what did you say?"

Kai rolled his eyes. "I said *no.*"

Her lips quirked triumphantly. "And why is that?"

He clamped his mouth shut, his impassive expression morphing into something thorny.

She went on, "I accept your critique of cosmic arbitrators, and I agree that the systems in place are manmade smorgasbords that serve some individuals and harm most others. But if you're as amoral as you claim, then wouldn't you do whatever you want without qualms? Why suggest that your ability to pursue your desires *should* be regulated?"

"Because—"

"Because you think some of your desires are bad? Destructive? Harmful?" She clicked her tongue. "Those sound like moral evaluations to me, Kai."

"They have *consequences,*" he ground out.

"Of course they do!" She waved her pen through the air. "But someone who cares only for his wants won't let *consequences* stop him! How do you think we get serial killers? Mobsters? CEOs? Politicians?" She fell back into her chair, her shoulders relaxing. "Why hold back the worst parts of yourself if you don't care about being good?"

Kai hung his head in defeat. He'd momentarily considered giving Caelan up to wash his hands of her. Normally, he'd trade anyone's life for Miya's safety, but he knew that some sacrifices weren't worth the demons. His childhood had been cut short by his parents' murder, and any hope of wholeness fractured with Alice's death. He'd spent the last fifteen years living on pure instinct— unthinking, reactive—but he couldn't survive that way anymore. Miya demanded he look in the mirror, and what stared back at him took the shape of a fifteen-year-old girl with too many secrets for her skinny bones to hold. He couldn't betray her. His reflection would never forgive him, and neither would Miya.

"Good job," he congratulated dryly. "You've convinced me I'm not a total piece of shit."

Hristina Krunić chuckled like she was savoring a secret. "Have you forgotten who comprises my clientele? Trust me. You're not the Big Bad Wolf you think you are."

Kai's lips twitched, and he laughed darkly.

She blinked back. "What?"

"Nothing." He stood from the armchair. "I think we're done for today."

She clicked the top of her pen—a nervous tick, he'd noticed. "All right. I'll see you soon. Same time, I presume?"

Kai nodded as he riffled through his tattered wallet, his eyes snagging on the lilac birthday card. He slapped the cash down next to the candy bowl on the end table, then grabbed his jacket. "See you, doc."

As he disappeared through the door, he felt her scrutinizing the meaning behind his baleful laugh. *No matter*, he thought.

The Big Bad Wolf was a ghost he'd never give up.

37

MIYA

THE LATE AFTERNOON sky hung low and heavy. A gray pall wove around streetlamps and canopies, spatters of rain and hail stippling the small windows of the apartment. They'd avoided Pyotr's notice for several days, though evasion wouldn't serve them forever. Even Miya was getting antsy, frustrated by her lack of inspiration. Conjuring a clever solution to Caelan's plight seemed more daunting than witchcraft, and it was only a matter of time before Pyotr, the leshy, or the teen's sinister caller struck. As Miya stewed, Kai stepped out for supplies after losing three rounds of a macabre card game to Caelan—something about unicorns murdering each other. Miya had no idea where he'd pilfered it from, but she didn't care to ask.

"He's such a sore loser," Caelan said once he was gone. She flopped down on the couch, the orange munchkin between them.

"He's competitive"—Miya shut her book—"and unaccustomed to losing games."

Caelan pulled the throw over her legs. "Didn't think he was the type to like games."

"He's more playful than he looks. Bar bets are his favorite hobby." Miya set her paperback aside and grinned. "So, did you win anything?"

The teen shrugged. "I get to see one of his fights—eventually, that is—and he has to make me fluffernutters on demand for the next week."

Caelan must've liked staying with them if she presumed to hang around for another week. "No wonder he looked like you'd put kale in his whiskey."

Settling back against the cushions, Caelan scratched through the thick fur around Ripper's neck. He leaned into her hand, purring contentedly—a strange sight given his origins.

A knock sounded on the door then, jolting the girl. Ursula had stopped by earlier to gossip, the impromptu visit sending both cat and girl skittering. Loud noises didn't sit well, it seemed.

"It's all right—just Ama." Miya called for the white wolf to enter. "The door's unlocked!"

Ama let herself in and removed her shoes. "Taking the day off?"

"It's been pretty slow." Miya rose from the couch with a long stretch. "And Crowbar insisted."

Ama nodded, her gaze sliding to Caelan. "How are you doing?"

"Okay. Haven't gone sleepwalking since…" Her eyes wandered as she wrestled with the memory.

"Good," the white wolf interjected. "Any bad dreams?"

Caelan sighed. "Yeah. Those are standard."

"Well, I'm here to do something about that." She nodded to Miya. "You went into the dreamscape to find Caelan, and while I found it ill-advised, I can't deny that it worked. What if we do the same for whatever's calling her?"

Miya bristled internally, but now wasn't the time to bicker over Ama's appraisals. She glanced at the teen. "Caelan *would* be tethered to it. I suppose we could try—"

"No."

They both turned to the teen.

Her lips pursed into a thin line. "Please don't dig around my head," she said, her voice tight and small.

Ama opened her mouth to protest, but Miya cut her off. "We'll find another way."

The white wolf's eyes narrowed to amber slits, her expression promising a rebuttal. "Can we have a moment alone, please?"

Caelan's head jerked down in an eager nod, and she fled to the bedroom. Ripper had abandoned the couch with Ama's entry, scampering into hiding beneath the bed. At least he could keep Caelan company.

"This is a mess," Ama said with a sigh, pinching the bridge of her nose. "I know you want to protect her, but you aren't doing her any favors by enabling her avoidance."

Miya wasn't convinced Ama was solely concerned for Caelan's coping mechanisms. She had an agenda, and this was an easy scapegoat—a rationalization for her to get her way. "I'm not going to push her boundaries. She's just barely come around to trusting us." Miya tracked Ama as she circled the cramped apartment. "I know how headstrong you can be about your methods."

"My methods get the job done," came Ama's brusque response.

"And sometimes, you can be too Machiavellian." Miya hesitated, ill at ease making haphazard decisions about Caelan. "We should wait for Kai."

Ama crossed her arms over her chest. "*Kai* is the whole reason we're in this quagmire. He keeps dragging you—all of us—into his messes, and he'll never claw himself out. When are you going to see that?"

Heat crawled up the back of Miya's neck. Yes, Kai had screwed up. Good intentions, perhaps, but old patterns were like scar tissue; they marked you forever. Miya held the white wolf's gaze until the bond between them grew taut—a rope stretched to the point of fraying. "He's traumatized. I don't say that lightly or as an excuse."

"I think that's exactly what you're doing," Ama shot back. "Yes, he's traumatized—more than anyone ought to be. I acknowledge that. But he's hellbent on letting those traumas control him. They give shape to his mistakes. Gargantuan ones."

A scalding lump of coal materialized in Miya's throat. She hated this part of their relationship—despised having to defend the love of her life from a surrogate sister. "If you think he hasn't worked on his problems, you're not paying attention."

"It's not enough," Ama growled back, frustration seeping into her voice. "I'm tired, Miya. I'm tired of worrying when the next calamity will hit. And it always starts with him. I don't want him bringing his demons into our lives—into Dahlia's life."

Miya nearly crumpled under the indictment. Crowbar and Kai were close. He let loose at the Confessional, but he adored the King of Spades, cherished playing guinea pig to Crowbar's cocktails and gossiping about clientele. "This isn't about him, Ama. This is about you wanting to protect the people you love from harm. You're blaming him, but I made choices too. The leshy came to *me* for help."

"Yes, and if Kai hadn't gotten involved with the mob, this would've been more straightforward. We'd only have to contend with spirits, not worry about pissing off gangsters. We could've investigated in peace, sent Caelan back to the dreamscape, and the mob would've been none the wiser." She huffed through her teeth, thrusting a finger toward the bedroom. "Now, Caelan's fate is directly tied to Kai's dealings with Bratva. Now, Miya, we have to fight a battle on two fronts."

She was right. Even if they made Caelan disappear, Kai was still on the hook because of his entanglement with Sergei.

The front door crashed open, striking the adjacent wall. Kai loomed in the entrance, his glower announcing that he'd heard Ama's every charge. He dropped the shopping bag and shrugged off his jacket, his lip twitching into a humorless smirk. Stepping into their circle, his arm brushed Miya's shoulder. She saw the blaze in his eyes as they trailed up to Ama's steely gaze. "Why don't you say it to my face?"

"You heard me," Ama hissed. "It's not like I didn't know you were here."

"Yeah?" He raised both eyebrows. "So, should I keep away from your girl? Fuck off and never set foot in the King of Spades?"

Ama stood her ground, shoulders pulled back. "Preferably, yes."

Miya's head snapped to the white wolf. "You're not serious."

"She's dead serious," said Kai, eerily collected despite the exchange.

"What about Crowbar's opinion?" Miya pivoted toward the white wolf. "You think she won't notice if Kai drops out of her life? You think *I* won't tell her why? You can't make decisions for everyone."

"I'm doing what I think is right," she rebuked, then gestured at Kai. "I don't want him bringing his shit to my doorstep. If that means causing a bit of hurt to someone I love, then so be it."

"But I won't do it." Kai's voice was steady, inflected only by his conviction. "I'm not going to hurt her just because you're obsessed with control."

Anger rippled across the white wolf's face. "What did you say?"

"You're manipulative," said Kai, "moving everyone around like chess pieces, and if they don't obey, you knock them off the board." He stepped past Miya, slicing into Ama's space. "You worry about it, don't you?"

"Worry about what?" she spat, teeth bared.

His mouth cut into a knife-like smile. "That you'll always be second fiddle to everyone in your life. You don't want Crowbar to help her friends if it means you can't get your way, so you try to force a wedge between us."

Ama jerked back, and Kai followed, his shadow devouring hers. "You have no clue if Gavran gives a damn about you, or if he used you to find his precious Dreamwalker." His eyes flicked to Miya's, a dark fire writhing behind them before they returned to Ama. "Do you really care about Miya's safety, or are you scared your raven will fuck off if you don't keep her close?"

Speechless, Ama backpedaled as Kai corralled her further into the room. When she ran out of floor, she shoved him back.

Kai chuckled quietly as he stumbled but caught himself. He always seemed so resigned to her contempt, rolling with every punch she hurled at him. Now, Miya feared the white wolf had bitten too close to the bone.

"You don't know what you're talking about," Ama seethed, her eyes shining with moisture. She was unprepared to douse the flame she'd lit with her own match.

"And then there's me..." Kai spread his arms, irreverent. Agony, self-loathing, and rage curdled into a torrid stare as he snared the white wolf in his maw. "The bad influence." He prowled closer. "The weed choking the flowers in your perfectly manicured garden." Closer. "The traumatized piece of shit who breaks everything he touches."

He leaned forward, a sliver of wrath splintering from his control, lashing his mouth into a snarl. "Judge me all you want, you cold, conniving bitch, but don't hold your breath. You know she'll always choose me because I actually give a shit about what she wants."

Cruel words, thrown out like a shiv to the gut.

A sharp sound like a snapping cord pierced the air as Ama's palm connected with Kai's face. His head whipped to the side, his eyes wide with surprise. As he reached up to caress his jaw, Ama stormed past him. Without sparing Miya a glance, she fled their home and slammed the door behind her.

"Where's Caelan?"

Kai's question was so blasé, Miya thought she'd imagined it. She slanted a look at him, searching for something vulnerable beneath the stony façade. Ama was liberal with her insults—sniped at Kai constantly without compunction. But when she'd directed her scorn at Miya, he'd dispelled the illusion that he'd eat her vitriol forever. Kai was also a wolf, and he too bore fangs. "In the bedroom. Is that really what's important right—"

"She's not in the bedroom."

Miya froze, her heart pummeled by yet another shock. "What?"

"I don't hear her," he said with a weighty glance.

They raced down the hall in unison, Kai a step ahead as he blasted into the room, eyes scanning the half-made bed, the pajamas splayed across the pillow, the sealed closet, and the window...

The window was open.

"Fuck." Kai spun around and left the bedroom, not bothering to examine Caelan's exit point.

Miya thrust her torso out the window and peered into the alleyway. Their building was old, each floor equipped with a fire escape, the black paint on the wrought iron chipped away and mottled with rust.

"I'm going after her while the trail's fresh," Kai said when Miya returned to the living room.

Before he could rush out, she threw her arms around him, and he wrapped her in a tight embrace. "This is my fault. She probably heard us arguing and ran off."

His nose brushed her neck as he exhaled. "It's no one's fault." Reluctantly, he let her go. "I'll get her back."

"How do you know?" Miya asked, wavering with uncertainty.

His grip on the brass knob tightened until the metal squealed. "I don't have a choice."

Desperation was a painful but effective motivator. He offered a weak smile, bereft of reassurance, then disappeared down the stairwell.

Miya shut the door behind him and sank to the floor.

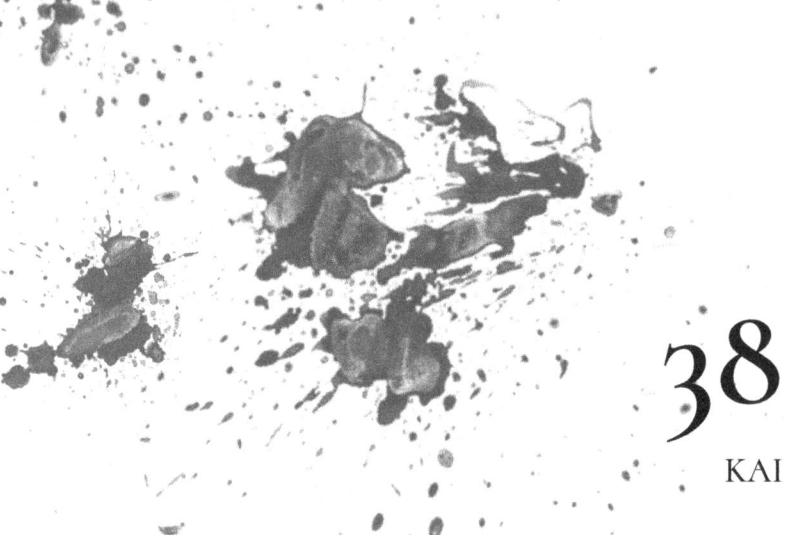

38

KAI

KAI SKIDDED to a stop at the edge of Boston Common. He'd taken too long picking up the trace, circling the block until he found that otherworldly tinge that oiled Caelan's skin. Her scent was unique. Most people were a motley of hormones, sweat, salt, and cosmetics. Each person had a unique undertone, but humans generally smelled alike—different brands of the same product.

The park was massive, and Caelan a wisp in the wind. Dusk darkened the already grim sky—a charcoal expanse choking out the light. As hail pelted the ground, people scattered like autumn leaves, and a frigid wind whipped around the trees with an eerie howl. Boston Common had no hills from the south, offering Kai no vantage point. Every damn gust carried Caelan's scent farther away, leaving him to meander around the Central Burying Ground on the park's southern periphery. As the gale pushed murky clouds across the sky like an ominous carriage, he glimpsed movement in Parkman Bandstand—a round gazebo northeast of the burying ground. Seven brick-laid paths coalesced at the monument like an invitation from every direction. A shadow shuddered from behind one of the stone pillars, and then another, when two figures emerged.

Shock snaked through Kai's middle. It was Caelan, hand in hand with a boy. They were laughing, scantly guarding against the precipitation with a sloppily raised jacket.

It was Caelan, and yet it couldn't be.

The wind made it impossible to catch her scent. But what

unsettled Kai wasn't that she was dressed differently—well-fitted jeans and an emerald cardigan that complimented the cinnamon-colored hair sticking to her ruddy cheeks. It was the smile—a care-free grin that brightened her whole face, made her utterly alien to Kai.

Who the hell was Caelan Carver?

Kai started toward the pair when a familiar malodor halted his steps. Putrid wood. Mildew. Mud. The throes of a dying ecosystem. A stench that didn't belong on the cold autumn wind.

The hairs on the back of his neck rose as he pivoted toward the invader.

A towering figure skulked between the trees, his limbs and torso like a slender trunk, his oversized fishing hat a withered canopy leached of color. Brown like wet mulch. The leshy was easily mistaken for the boughs that disguised him, but nothing could hide his stink. Stiller than the rustling foliage caressing his craggy skin, he lurked mere yards from the giddy couple. Elbow bent, hand raised, his spindly fingers splayed over something at his side. One twitched like a spider's leg, then settled back onto the shoulder he clutched. A shoulder that barely reached his ribs.

Then, they moved in unison, a single stilted step at a time.

Kai's brow knitted, furrowed further, his attention split between the teens wandering closer to the spirit, and the spirit reciprocating their approach. The air thickened with an electric current, and as the leshy emerged with his captive, Kai's stomach bottomed out.

Fuck. Fuck. Fuck.

Caelan. Another Caelan. *His* Caelan. Miya's clothes barely clinging to the jutting angles of a starving girl.

There were two of them. Twins woven from different threads. One made of sunlight, the other stitched from shadow.

The leshy's pupils darted toward Kai. Aural rings wound around umber irises—a peculiar light Kai hadn't noticed before. The creature's grip on Caelan's shoulder tightened, her movements wooden like a puppet with too-taut strings, wielded by a graceless puppeteer.

The girl who wasn't Caelan froze. Kai expected bewilderment, but terror that could only be spurred by recognition twisted her face. She nearly folded as a blood-curdling scream ripped from her throat, and she scrabbled at her boyfriend's arm.

Caelan didn't flinch. Expression neutral, eyes unblinking, neither she nor the leshy slowed their advance.

Fear rooted Kai to the ground. Fucking *fear*. He didn't relate to this dread. He hated spirits. Hated dealing with them. They were Miya's domain—her gift and her curse. But Kai was the only one here; he'd have to bear the burden alone. The two girls may have appeared as halves of a whole, but he knew their union would be a maleficent one. He didn't understand the reasons, but he didn't have to; he trusted his instincts.

With a graveled shout, Kai bolted forward. The moment he reached one of those seven walkways, he felt the leshy's influence strum his bones, pluck at his essence like a sinister harp.

This time, the transition wasn't slow.

His knee blew out like someone had taken a shotgun to it, and he collapsed to the other before it too bent wrong. Crumpling on his side with a roar that rent his throat, his body revolted against itself, denying him even a sliver of mercy. Fur pierced through flesh like a bed of needles, teeth tore through gums, and limbs contorted into impossible shapes. Pain clawed at the borders of his mind, and when his nervous system overloaded, nausea shunted him into a whole new dimension of agony. He bit down and set his jaw when the tremors started, robbing him of control. He couldn't even roll onto his belly when the bile burned up his esophagus and forced its way out. The leshy unleashed on him with a force Kai understood as desperation equal to his own. The spirit was trying to over-whelm him—knock him out before he could recover.

A distant cry. Panicked cursing. The reek of impending death.

The world tilted, but Kai forced himself upright, his legs shaky, uncoordinated. He'd lick Sergei's balls before he'd let a talking shrub in boots lay him out. Untangling his feet from his clothes, his tail swooshed for balance, and finally, his senses stopped swim-ming, the spiraling void in front of him slowing to an irritating sway.

He was salivating, queasy and disoriented, but he managed to focus on the scene ahead, the world reduced to a dichromatic blend of yellows and blues. Caelan remained in the leshy's thrall, obliv-ious to the mayhem around her. The boy yanked at Caelan's look-alike, but she seemed catatonic—jaw slack, limbs like stiff rubber. He tried dragging her away, but she oscillated to-and-fro as though anchored to the earth, her feet made of iron. She was entranced, mesmerized by her own shadow, and as Caelan lifted an arm to reach for her, she reached back, each a mirror of the other.

Kai tripped on his own legs, forgetting how to move with four of them. He burned with fever, though he couldn't sweat it out. This body released heat through breath, and it wasn't enough. He teetered to the side and nearly ate dirt, the sky greeting him when another cry seized his spine, and he righted himself. Hackles raised, ears erect, he forced himself forward, blunt claws scraping the earth. The leshy watched, appraising. He amplified the nature in things; forcing a violent metamorphosis was the only weapon he had. But Kai was already a wolf, and the transition hadn't leveled him like the leshy wanted.

Kai pitched forward as Caelan and her daylight twin drew closer, their fingers a mere inch apart. They both seemed so serene —so at peace with the outcome of their collision course. Muzzle rippling into a snarl, Kai threw himself into the girl he'd stolen from death, side-checking her out of the leshy's grasp and away from the other teen.

Caelan flew to the ground and skidded several feet, flaxen grass marring her too-big flannels. Limbs flailing, she bolted upright and rasped for breath. Wide slate gray eyes swung to the figures around her, searching madly for some inkling of sense. Her gaze snagged on the other girl—an uncanny double, an imitation.

A forgery.

The girl in the green cardigan screamed, falling into her boyfriend's arms as her feet finally came free from the soil.

"Come on, let's go!" the boy yelled, hauling his panicked girl-friend away. They sprinted from the park, sneaking glances over their shoulders. The girl's eyes snapped back to Caelan's. A morbid curiosity.

Trembling uncontrollably, Caelan's breaths came fast and shallow. "What...what's—" Her eyes traced a path to the leshy, her pulse hammering so hard that Kai heard it thundering in his own skull.

With his equilibrium restored, he darted between Caelan and the leshy, blocking the spirit's path. Warm breath fogged the air as the wolf huffed through bared teeth, each canine an ivory dagger. Head lowered, fur raised like stygian blades, Kai flattened his ears and growled in warning as the leshy loomed, barred from his target. Blood red eyes tracked the woodland spirit as it slalomed, and when it dared inch closer, Kai lunged, snapping his teeth. Caelan clumsily rose to her feet, and he herded her away. The leshy wanted to bend her nature into something unwanted—whatever that was.

Her fingers curled into his black fur like she was holding on to him for dear life. His tail flicked side to side, gliding across her shoulder. The predator in him wanted to rip the leshy apart and scatter his limbs like cast-off twigs, but he couldn't leave Caelan's side either—couldn't risk letting her wander. The leshy shuddered and warped like a heat mirage. He winnowed closer, the sudden movement accompanied by a hoarse keen dragged from an unhinged jaw.

Caelan's sharp inhale and the cold hiss of fear coiling around Kai's ribs propelled him to act. The leshy's movements were erratic but confined, like he was trapped in a glass prism. Kai knocked into the leshy and clamped his maw around the creature's brittle leg, gnawing until a satisfying snap cocked his head. But when he veered back toward the spirit, he found the space empty. The leshy was gone. Pincered between Kai's teeth was all that remained of him: a broken tree branch. As Kai slackened his jaw, the stick tumbled from his mouth, shriveling with the fall. By the time it hit the ground, it'd desiccated and moldered away.

Ragged gasps pulled the wolf away from the ashes. Caelan braced against Kai as she collapsed, her arms encircling his broad neck and chest. Burying her face in his fur, she muffled her sharp inhales and muttered, "I didn't want to…I didn't want to…"

Kai plunked down on his haunches, unable to respond. A high-pitched whine leaked out of him, though he didn't pull away as the girl continued to sob, her tears wetting his coat.

"I just kept hearing her call," she hiccupped, "and I couldn't ignore it anymore."

Her call. The girl in the green cardigan—the one who looked identical to Caelan. Somehow, Caelan's double was summoning her, yet she'd appeared horrified at the sight of her otherworldly twin. She may have called, but she hadn't expected an answer.

"It hurt too much to ignore, but this also hurts. Meeting her—touching her—would hurt even more." Caelan's heart slammed so hard against her ribcage that Kai felt it thrumming against his own.

Her body quaked, her face streaked with moisture and heat as she cried and cried like she'd denied herself the catharsis her whole damn life. "Everything hurts," she murmured. "I want it to stop. I don't care if it kills me. Please, make it stop."

Kai pawed at the earth—a nervous reflex. His animal self hadn't honed any sensory barriers. The man was beholden to the walls he'd built to protect himself from overload, but the wolf was a receptacle for everything the environment hurled at him, and Caelan was impossible to ignore. She was in pain. So much pain. As a man, Kai could observe pain at a distance, but the wolf lived it. Pain wasn't an abstraction; it was a barbed manacle locked around his throat.

He needed to change back—needed to shed this hideous instinct that tangled him in another's distress. How pitiful...a hunter who killed without qualm, debilitated by a few shed tears. Besides, he had questions that needed answering, and they could only be asked in a different body. What would've happened if Caelan and her look-alike had touched?

Just as Caelan released him, a figure appeared next to the civil war monument atop a hill to the north. Tall and broad. Legs like steel trunks. Arms like canons. When an angry gust blew in, Kai caught the scent, and his tail lashed anxiously, his soot-colored lips twitching into a grimace.

He locked eyes with Zverev. They remained fixed on one another for a long, breathless moment. Then, Zverev's gaze drifted to Caelan.

Shit.

Kai bumped her legs until her knees buckled and she stumbled in the direction he wanted—away from Zverev, away from the park, toward populated streets where attempted kidnapping wouldn't go unnoticed. He didn't give a damn that he was a wolf; he had to get her to safety.

But where? He couldn't take her home. Zverev would tail them. Even if they lost him, he'd track them the same way Kai had tracked Caelan. The fact that Pyotr's beast managed to pluck the girl's scent from thin air was indication enough that they were fucked.

Kai couldn't hide her, but he could make snatching her more difficult.

He prodded her thigh, pushing her along as gently as he could.

She seemed to catch on. Glimpsing the giant stalking across the field, she cursed, their predicament dawning on her like a spade to the skull.

Kai clamped his teeth on her sleeve and tugged. She broke away from the incoming threat, cool gray eyes meeting the wolf's. Mahogany veiled in crimson, like burnt clay forged in flames.

Run, they said.

39

CAELAN'S TOES clipped the pavement, and she faltered mid-sprint. She was tired, breaths ragged and limbs flaccid. Kai slowed to drag her by her clothes if needed, but she recovered, her hand grazing his ear. Her frantic pulse burst from her fingertips, and he worried she'd collapse. He led her down an alleyway behind the Confessional, ignoring the startled cries of passersby. They probably assumed he was an unusually large lupine dog off its leash, and while the thought would've normally offended him, it was a blessing in disguise. The last thing he needed was animal control shooting tranquilizer darts at his ass.

Caelan keeled over in the alleyway, palms pressed to her knees as she heaved for air. Tracking her from the corner of his eye, Kai backed into a murky corner by the dumpster. They were running out of time. Bracing for the pain, he tuned out the drip of water from the rooftops, the sound of cars sloshing through puddles, the whirr of stale air from nearby vents. He wiggled his toes— short, stubby things with little dexterity—imagined them unfurling into fingers. His bones began to hum, the vibration growing stronger until the tingling morphed into stabbing, burning, maiming. Teeth clamped, he swallowed a whimper, every limb brittle like baked mud as his bones shattered, and he collapsed with a wet smack. A piercing whine lanced his ears, his skull molding itself into something human-like. He caught the edge of Caelan's shout as she bolted over to him, but he couldn't see her through the myriad of reds and greens bleeding into his

vision. Colors his animal eyes didn't perceive. He convulsed as his fur receded, and his body lengthened, the autumn chill scraping his flesh like a dull blade.

Kai pushed off the ground with a determined grunt, and Caelan whirled away to avert her gaze, though he smelled her panic wafting off her skin.

"A-are you okay?" she stammered, peaking over her shoulder.

Kai slapped a palm over his face and groaned, swooning before he regained balance with a stuttering hop. "Fine." He sounded worn. Shambling forward, he pounded on the back door of the Confessional with his fist.

Moments later, it squealed open, and he was greeted by an agitated Carol as she looked him up and down. "Not this shit again!"

Showing up naked in the Confessional's alleyway usually came at the end of a nasty bender—something Carol was accustomed to. But this...this was different. Kai braced his forearm against the frame, his head dangling as though fastened to his neck by a fraying thread. He squeezed his eyes shut, still dizzy from the transition. When the change was forced, returning to his human body hurt twice as bad. "I need my spare clothes." He flung an arm out and signaled for Caelan to come closer. "Lock her in Connor's office. Don't let anyone in."

Carol straightened, her gaze flying to the teen. "Are we kidnapping kids now?"

"The dead opposite." Kai finally lifted his head, his eyes molten beneath a wrinkled brow. "I'm not fucking around, Carol. Do it."

The indignation fell from her face. Mouth clapping shut, she swallowed and nodded. "Come here, kid."

Caelan did as she was told, skirting past Kai and into the bar. Carol let the door slip closed, then reappeared moments later, thrusting a pile of clothes into his chest. "Get dressed," she told him somberly, then retreated inside.

The door clicked into place, but every hair on the back of Kai's neck stood on end as a shadow loomed closer, blocking the light from the street.

"You've had her this whole time."

Sighing as he yanked on sweatpants, Kai ignored the accusation and tied the drawstring to keep the waistband where it belonged, then hung his hoodie off the doorknob. He'd have to return to the park to collect his things. "You're a fucking pest, you know that?"

Zverev pushed closer, his footsteps heavy. "And you're a rat. Pyotr wanted you to find the forgery, but you knew where she was all along. You've been keeping her."

"Yeah, keeping her alive." Kai faced his nemesis, flashing him a barbed smile. "Sorry, but I'm not very trainable."

Ivan Zverev scoffed. "I'd expect nothing less. You lack discipline. It's why you'll always lose when it matters."

A veiled reference. Kai wasn't sure if it was about their match or his entire damn life. Not that it mattered. This wasn't a fight club; it was a grime-covered back alley made of concrete, bricks, and trash. If *Vanya* thought discipline would save him in a street brawl, he had another thing coming.

"You think you're noble? Taking orders from a puckered asshole in a snakeskin suit?" Kai shuffled away from the wall, gauging the space. Claustrophobic. Close quarters. Neither of them would have room to maneuver, which put the big man at an advantage. He was a bulldozer, and the confined lane shackled Kai's superior speed.

"I'm a freelancer," said Zverev, closing in at an unhurried pace. "My livelihood depends on my loyalty to my contracts. I'm reliable."

"You don't think for yourself," Kai rephrased. "Try being reliable to someone who actually needs it."

A low chuckle reverberated from Zverev's throat, his mouth curving into a lopsided smile. "I can't believe I'm saying this, but you're too soft for this business. Sentimentality will get you killed. It's dull."

Kai wiped the soles of his feet with his palms. If he was sentimental, it wasn't because he was soft. "You wouldn't know a sharp object if it stabbed you in the eye."

The smile tumbled from Zverev's face. He stood rigid—a predator in wait. "I suppose I'll consider this the rematch you promised me."

Then, the beast charged.

Kai didn't bother trying to stem the tide of meat and bone barreling toward him. Dropping low, he pivoted out of the way, giving Zverev all the room he needed to waste his energy on a wild swing. His fist connected with a wooden crate next to a dumpster, and the flimsy thing shattered into pieces. Kai only hoped Zverev suffered a few splinters to his hand. Shaking out his fist, the big man turned.

"You can't dance forever, little cousin."

The term twisted a sneer onto Kai's face. "I'll do what I want, you overgrown lapdog."

Corralling Kai toward the corner with the dumpster, Zverev shoved him against the bricks and drove an uppercut into his ribs. Kai tensed his core and nicked the goliath's fist with a defensive elbow, but the punch still landed, rattling Kai's insides like a ripe apricot in a glass jar. Mortar scraped the skin from his back, the sting lashing along his spine. Before Kai could recover, Zverev's knuckles collided with his jaw. White hot pain shot through his skull like a bolt, his vision blooming with stars. He tried shoring up against the wall, but another mammoth fist drove through his mandible again and again. He felt like a nail getting hammered into a board. Iron coated his tongue, the smell of it filling his nostrils as crimson poured over his lip and dribbled to the ground. His vision blurred, the pavement beneath his feet tipping as the world began to swim.

Cursing through a grimace, Kai smashed the crown of his head against Zverev's face, the satisfying crunch stippling his senses. His attacker reeled back with a yelp, blood ribboning between his fingers as he held his palm over his mouth. Kai wasted no time kicking him away, and the giant stumbled, doubling over with an irritated grunt.

Shaking off the blows, Zverev straightened, his dark eyes flashing in time with passing headlights. They shone just like an animal's—just like Kai's.

The black wolf grinned—a mordant smile full of knowing. "Was that soft enough for you?"

Snarling, Zverev reached for a stray bottle off a nearby step and whipped it at full force. Kai ducked as the glass hurtled past his head and shattered against the wall behind him. By the time he looked up, Zverev was in front of him again, forearm to the throat. The breath fled Kai's lungs, his windpipe nearly crushed. Zverev drove him toward the broken glass, jagged pieces littering the ground, waiting to be stepped on.

"Nice touch," Kai strained. He was the one fighting barefoot.

Gathering the copper taste in his mouth, he sprayed the residual blood into the beast's eyes. "You know what really sucks, though?"

Blinded, Zverev roared, warm breath and saliva hitting Kai's cheek.

"Balls."

The goliath jerked back as Kai drove his knee forward and barely missed crushing a pair of gonads. Kai reached into a dumpster and flung whatever he could grasp. Pelted by takeout containers, cold French fries, and grease, Zverev swiped at the offending projectiles. With his attention split, Kai dove low and planted a fist into his thigh, striking the thick band of fibers and nerves that ran from knee to hip. Zverev's leg buckled, and Kai swung an elbow directly across his jaw. His head snapped left, his eyes momentarily blank as he swayed from the concussive blow.

Kai clasped the back of Zverev's head, fingers digging into his scalp. Hauling him close, he locked eyes with his cousin, his teeth set and his lips pulled back in a baleful grin. "Did you think there was going to be a referee to stop me from ripping your other nipple off?"

A gasp caught in Zverev's throat, mouth working in protest. Kai kicked out the beast's other leg in response. Cinching the tender nub between two knuckles, he gave a brutal wrench.

Flesh tore from Zverev's chest—a split second of sweet, silent shock before a harrowing howl obliterated the peace. A car swerved, and murmurs floated into the narrow lane as bystanders puzzled out what they'd heard. Luckily for Kai, most people ignored red flags and moved along.

Wetness coated Kai's fingers as Zverev's shirt blossomed with dark stains. He let go, then snatched the big man's collar. Pulling back his elbow, Kai drove his knuckles straight into Zverev's temple. His limbs went limp, his impressive weight dragging against Kai's hold as his head drooped to the side, his jaw slackened, and he conked out cold.

"Fuck," Kai gritted out, dropping Zverev with a thump. He rolled his shoulders and stretched out his ribs, still cramped from the blow to his middle.

Just as Kai retrieved the hoodie from the knob, the door swung open.

"What the hell are you doing?" Connor threw his arms up as he stepped out. His eyes trailed down Kai's bruised and bloodied torso, then swept to the crumpled mass of muscle lying motionless on the asphalt. "Shit, is he—"

"Dead? Not yet. Help me get him inside." Flinging the hoodie over his shoulder, Kai circled around the behemoth and scooped him under his arms. He *could* carry the bastard by himself, but dead weight was awkward, and Kai didn't want to accidentally snap his head off against the doorframe before interrogating him. "You still got that cable wire?"

"Woah, woah, woah, slow down." Connor followed, alarm lacing his voice. "Forget the cable wire. *Why* are we dragging a Soviet tank into my bar? Is this some whacky revenge scheme?"

"No." Kai's patience was whittling away. How could he explain without demanding blind trust from his friend? Connor would take a bullet for him, but there was no sense in becoming an accomplice without good reason. "That kid Carol brought in? He's trying to sell her to Pyotr."

It wasn't a total fabrication. Zverev *was* given money in exchange for Caelan's return. It was still a transaction, and that was vile enough.

"You're full of shit." Connor's words didn't sound as disbelieving as they should've. "...Are you?"

Kai shook his head, unceremoniously dropping Zverev a second time. "You think I want to be half naked in an alleyway getting my liver pummeled by this"—he gestured flippantly—"tornado for hire?"

Connor pointed at Zverev. "If that's what became of a tornado for hire, what does that make you?"

"Better at street fights," Kai replied dryly.

With a lamenting sigh, Connor grumbled his way to Zverev's legs, grabbed him by the ankles, and together, they hefted him up. "All right, fine, but this better be the last time you shit on my floor."

Kai quirked a brow at the canine reference. He loosened his hold on the turd in question, leaving Connor with the bulk of the weight. Kai watched with vicious delight as his friend's complexion turned eggplant-like, and he struggled to keep his grip.

"Well," Kai grinned wickedly, "aren't you lucky you own a mop."

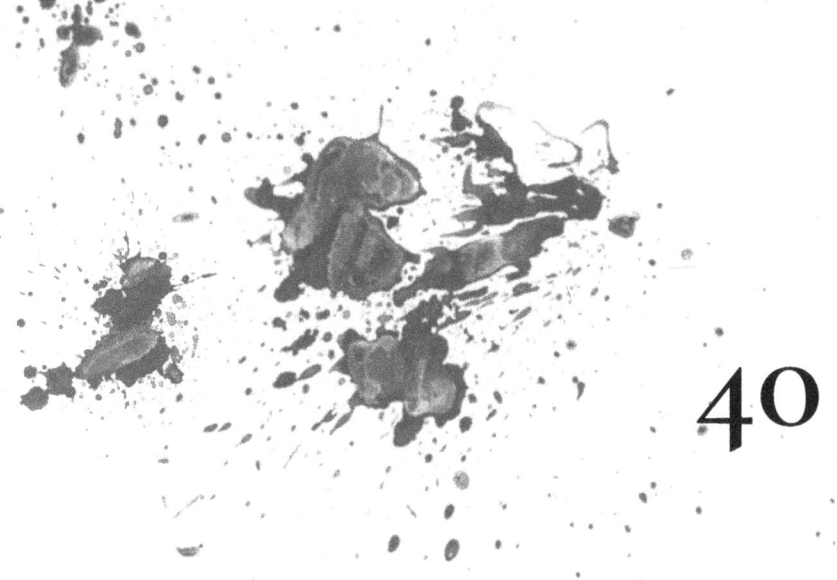

40

THEY DUMPED Zverev in the storage closet next to the office. Kai goaded Connor the entire way, quipping at him for skipping leg day. While Kai preferred more *organic* methods of staying in shape to the tedium of weightlifting, Connor was a zealous subscriber to the bench press.

"Sorry I'm not...a goddamn...werewolf..." Connor panted once they'd dropped off their cargo, a vein still popping in his rouged neck.

"I'm not a werewolf," Kai deadpanned. "Don't blame my genes for your aversion to deadlifts."

"Hey! I do squats!"

"I know a five-foot-six white-haired murder queen who could squat three of you."

Connor shoved the cable wire back into the kitchen nook with the rest of his tools. They'd restrained Zverev's arms and legs, though Connor was displeased with Kai for foisting a bad crime plot on his precious establishment. "What now?"

"I asked Carol to take Caelan home." Kai splashed water on his face in the employee bathroom. The faucet squeaked off, and he ripped free a piece of paper towel to pat his face dry. It came away bloody. "Now that we've got that asshole tied up, we can chat."

"In the damn storage closet?" Connor balked.

Kai rolled his eyes. "Close up for the day. We'll want the place to ourselves."

Swearing to the saints, Connor did as he was told, stomping off to flip the sign in the window. Then, they dragged Zverev into the office and locked the door. He looked pretty messed up, the side of his face that'd met Kai's elbow swelling under a mural of dark purple. Not that Kai looked too hot either. His jaw felt like pulverized meat, but he'd nabbed a bag of frozen peas from the walk-in freezer to nurse his wounds. The cold stung, but it wasn't as bad as the ache in his teeth and the tenderness under his eye. He'd glimpsed a blotch of red around his iris in the mirror—a nasty hemorrhage from the punch he'd stopped with his face. His ribs would need more than frozen vegetables, but Connor wasn't in the business of peddling codeine.

The office was a bland affair—small, cramped, and in desperate need of some color. The room reminded Kai of two closets stitched together. A modest desk, a decade-old laptop, a cork board covered in flyers, and a few shelves stuffed with records, accounting folders, and packs of unopened napkins. Kai leaned against an olive-green filing cabinet near the door, his battered body half-obscured in shadow. The dim glow of the overhead light barely reached him. Connor lurked by the adjacent wall, ready to pounce if needed, though he glanced nervously between the two men. He knew about Kai's unique abilities, that he was something between human and fable. More than likely, he'd surmised that Zverev was another such monster.

"What were you doing at the park?" Kai asked when the behemoth stirred. He tossed the peas atop the filing cabinet, his skin prickling from the chill.

Still rousing from his nap, Zverev weakly tested his restraints. He was slumped against the wall, chin lolling across his chest. His eyes fluttered open, then rose to meet Kai's. Bruised lips skinned back to reveal teeth caked in red. "Look at you. Only a heartbeat from collapsing."

Kai ignored the jibe. Sure, he felt a little ragged after their dumpster duel, but he wasn't fucked up enough to black out like a college freshman during frosh week. "Answer the question."

"I knew what I was looking for," Vanya slurred, rolling his neck with a grimace.

"Don't get cryptic with me," Kai warned, "or I'll slam Connor's favorite kettlebell into the side of your skull."

Zverev choked out a laugh—a painful sound. "You truly are an animal. No regard for the rules of engagement, for dignity or pride. Only survival."

Kai stepped out of the murk, his eyes a scarlet portent as he bore into the man opposite from him. "You said I'd always lose when it matters, but you don't get to decide what matters, *cous*." He bent over to pick up Connor's kettlebell—thirty pounds of pure steel. Adjusting his grip, he gave it a cursory swing as he ambled a few paces closer. "I won't ask again. What were you doing in Boston Common?"

Connor made himself a wallflower, though he watched Kai's every move. He was no rookie to the underworld, but Kai was towing a delicate line. The Confessional was neutral ground; turf wars and vendettas were strictly forbidden, but Zverev violated the pact when he attacked Kai in the pub's alleyway. Dragging Zverev's unconscious ass into the bar was a faux pas, but letting him go without answers would've been worse than breaking etiquette. It would've been stupid. And Kai wasn't about to risk Caelan's life to stand on ceremony.

Zverev sighed, averting his gaze. "Pyotr told me the forgery was someone who looked like his adoptive daughter, Alina. That's who I was looking for. Alina disappeared from school today, so Pyotr had me track her down. He knew I'd find her faster than his best men." He turned back to Kai with a bloodied smile. "I'm sure you understand why."

Kai tightened his hold on the kettlebell. *Of course* he knew why. Zverev was like him—heightened senses, inhuman healing, freakish speed and strength. "The people who kidnapped the forgery—"

"Thought she was Alina. Or a twin separated at birth, raised in a different household." He shrugged. "They were amateurs. Had no idea who they'd taken or that they were handing the girl over to her death."

"You caught up to Pyotr's kid and saw two of her in the field," Kai realized.

Zverev cast Kai a weighty look. "I was surprised to find a whole storybook's worth of creatures."

Kai ignored the meaning woven into that stare, his attention shifting to Connor. He looked uncomfortable—a man pincered between two beasts. The barkeep gave a slight nod of reassurance. Permission to continue.

Exhaling through his nose, Kai wondered if Alina and Caelan were actually long-lost twins. It felt too simple. Too clean. Pyotr called her the forgery for a reason, and everything about Caelan screamed dreamscapes and ethereal devilry. Miya's world—one that terrified him. Kai hated what he couldn't grasp with his own hands. "Why does your boss want the forgery dead?"

Zverev snorted. "I have no damn clue. Clearly, the man thinks this look-alike is a threat to his daughter."

"That makes no sense," Kai growled. "Wouldn't a look-alike be an asset? The perfect decoy?"

Silence. Then, from the wall, "She's a fetch."

Two pairs of otherworldly eyes swung to Connor. Kai frowned. "A what?"

"You said there were two of her, and Pyotr thinks this *forgery*"— Connor emphasized the word—"is putting his daughter in danger. She's a goddamn fetch—a doppelganger."

Zverev scoffed, squirming against his bonds. He winced as the wire dug into his wrists. "Bullshit."

Kai ignored his bellyaching. "If you see your double, it's an omen of your death, yeah?"

Connor nodded. "That's the folklore. They kill and replace you. The Irish call them fetches, but they're pretty much like doppelgangers. Didn't think Pyotr was the superstitious type, though."

"He clearly believes in this asshole." Kai gestured toward Zverev. "Why not a doppelganger or a fetch?"

Zverev laughed sharply. "Pyotr and I are from the same culture." He tipped his chin up at Kai. "It's your culture too, though you've lost your roots. Diaspora will do that." His eyes slid to Connor. "We speak the same language—share an understanding of the world. Pyotr has grounds to believe in me, but a *fetch*?"

"You said his kid's adopted," Kai interjected. "I take it she's not Russian."

Zverev hesitated. "No, she's not. Alina's name may be Slavic, but she's all Celt. Pyotr had her tested."

"Then you have no idea what she has access to, or what has access to her." Kai ran a thumb over his scraped knuckles, something wild and desolate twisting in his middle. Everyone inherited an invisible blueprint from those who came before. A ghost that contoured the world to fit the shape of the past. "My childhood's a blur, but there are…pieces. Things that stay with you like a reflex. I knew what a domovoy was—could explain it when I had to. You don't *lose* culture. It just changes. Imprints differently."

"What're you saying?" Ivan Zverev asked.

"I'm saying that you have no clue what Alina brought with her when your shitty boss adopted her. Sure, he's got his book of Baba Yagas, but maybe he realized his daughter brought her own grimoire into the family. One he didn't recognize." Kai launched himself into an anxious pace, prowling the office from wall to wall. Connor tracked his agitated strides as though he were a trundling grenade with its pin gone astray.

If Caelan was a fetch, then she wasn't the one being haunted. She was the one doing the haunting. *She* was the specter who'd emerged from the dreamscape to prey on the living. Alina—Pyotr's daughter—was the hunted.

The *call* Caelan kept referring to—it came from Alina.

Caelan's garbled resistance made sense now. She didn't want to kill her human counterpart, but the leshy was trying to force her. He amplified the nature in things, and the fetch's was to seek out and destroy its human double. Being around the leshy only intensified the call and Caelan's impulse to answer it.

Kai ceased his pacing, grinding his molars despite the pain shooting through his jaw. Caelan had never wanted to leave the dreamscape. She was pulled out, and yet, Alina was just a girl with an overprotective crime boss for a father. Neither of them wanted this.

Why, then, had Caelan been drawn from the dreamscape in the first place? The answer awaited in an otherworld that terrified Kai, and with a girl on a collision course with death.

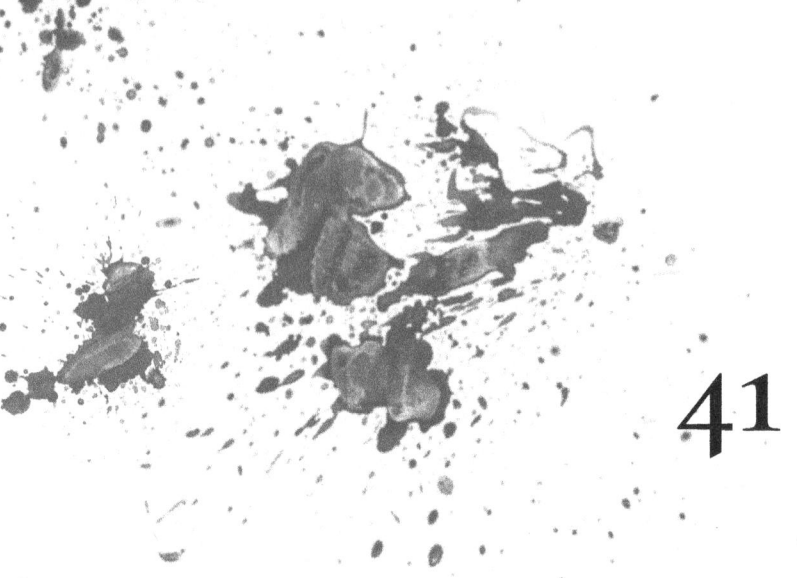

41

THE LINGERING questions sat in the pit of Kai's stomach like an iron ball, the chain running all the way up to his throat until he nearly choked. He hated keeping his uncertainties buried, but he didn't know how to shape them into words. Despite the name of the bar, he had no intention of confessing anything with Ivan Zverev as his witness.

Connor left the office at Kai's request. It'd sounded more ominous than intended, and Kai only noticed when his friend blanched like a block of tofu.

"Now what?" Zverev asked when they were alone. "You're going to kill one of your own?"

Kai snorted, stretching his limbs. "Grisly and tempting, but no." He gently swung his arm, testing a shoulder sprain. Zverev's words needled him, and before he could stop himself, the question sprang from his tongue. "How do you know we're the same?"

"Just like you did when we first met." Vanya shrugged. "You felt it, didn't you? The scent of likeness invading you. One animal meeting another in contested territory."

Kai stilled when Zverev squirmed again, unease coiling behind his battered ribs. If they were truly family—distant as it were— why were they allowing themselves to be pawns in a rich man's game?

"The joke's on me," Zverev continued. "I was warned about you, but I never thought..."

"Thought what?"

"You and I are from the same bloodline. I'm sure you've figured that part out."

"Sergei dumped enough hints for my dropout ass to put it together," said Kai. "So, what? You want me to explore my heritage? Fly off to the motherland and connect with my roots? Forget it."

"You should know your history." Zverev shot him a pointed look. "Our bloodline descends from a forgotten god—a god of destruction who took the form of a wolf."

Only he wasn't *quite* forgotten. Sendoa lived on in Kai, a brand he could never be rid of. "What are you getting at?"

"Gods are everywhere," said Zverev. "They move from place to place, culture to culture, but sometimes, they settle. Our myths say this one died west of where he originated. But the god was ancient even then, and he had lovers before the woman he met his end with."

Of course Sendoa whored his way across the globe before locking up his infernal cock. Kai set his back against the wall. He knew where Sendoa had died, and he was painfully aware of whom he'd died with. The Dreamwalker—the first incarnation of Miya's soul. Just as Sendoa had been Kai's. Their lives ended in the forests near the south Morava River. If Sendoa hailed from farther east, Kai would've wagered a kidney it was from the Western Siberian plains that his family—and Zverev's—called home.

"Get to the damn point," Kai groused.

Ivan Zverev chuckled, his demeanor shifting to something less thorny. "The descendants of that god dispersed—some went west, and some farther east to Siberia and beyond. When the god died, his soul reincarnated again and again, but he preferred the bloodline he created. Children born of his many unions before death."

"Slut." Not that Kai was one to talk.

"Gods have always been promiscuous, in any culture." Zverev sighed, weariness creeping into his voice. "Zverevs are part of that divine lineage—at least, that's what we're taught. The god reincarnates in one person each lifetime, but all his descendants enjoy the benefits of his blood. Strength, speed, healing. Some, they say, can even become beasts."

Apprehension bubbled beneath Kai's skin. He thought he was done with forgotten deities and nascent pasts—done with Sendoa. But his spiritual legacy was also his biological ancestry. He didn't *just* inherit Sendoa's baggage; he'd inherited his goddamn DNA too. A diluted godhood giving vitality to a vessel that homed a primordial soul.

Kai loathed this truth with every ounce of his being. He existed for himself, not to harbor some primeval essence he didn't understand. His whole life he'd battled for autonomy from his demons and his circumstances alike, but the past was a vulture with its talons in his back, its wings a looming shadow that haloed his every step. Each time he thought himself whole, it plucked out a piece of him—raw, tender flesh straight from the bone.

"There was this kid," Zverev began after a heavy pause, "born about thirty years ago. Rumor says he carried the god's soul—had a similar appearance and temperament." He bent his knee with a grimace. "Ethnically, our people are mutts. Slavs and Tatars and anyone who passed through the area. Most of our history is oral, but as we were forced into cities, that history became myth. Details got swapped, altered, so there's no telling if the rumors had weight. Not that it matters. The boy's parents took him across the ocean. No one knows what happened to them, but it was the last sign our people saw of the god, weak as it was."

"Appearance and temperament," Kai mused allowed. "How, exactly?"

Zverev shrugged. "Those stories were lost with the boy's parents and the generation that came before them. We assimilated or scattered. I honestly thought it was bullshit, but..." He cast Kai a nervous glance. "You're about his age, aren't you?"

"My parents are buried far from home," Kai said with a rueful smile. "Shallow, unmarked graves in the middle of the woods. I wouldn't be able to find them if I tried."

A slow, creeping disbelief widened Ivan Zverev's eyes. He swallowed thickly, his face waxen as realization and horror wove into a terrific tapestry. "You're him," he whispered. "You're Mikhail Zverev. The god in mortal form."

Kai would've said he'd never heard the name. Would've cast it off like a pair of rusty manacles. How easy it was to purge one's life of everything but a name. There was so much missing, so much he didn't know, like what to say when the paramedics questioned him after his parents died. He remembered only one thing: *Kai.* His family was a painting marred with dirty water, his life a storybook with half the pages torn out. He knew he'd come from elsewhere and spoke another language. He still held it in his bones—those vital shards that couldn't be excised. His father wanted security. His mother wanted to run. Kai didn't know from what or why, but he cradled her desperation somewhere deep within himself—a strange and delicate thing that lived in him even now, perfectly undisturbed.

But what of his identity? What did it mean to be confronted with a stranger who knew more about him than he knew about himself?

We both know your real name isn't Kai.

Sergei had said as much. Now, it was inescapable fact.

He thought it would be a torrent—an utter deluge spewing from a broken dam—but the memory seeped into him quietly, viciously, so unremarkable yet violent it made him question the reality of it all.

Mikhail.

The K was silent, but when they'd moved to the United States, everyone kept calling him *Me-Kyle.* It sounded so stupid, but they refused to learn—acted like it was too damn hard to omit a single consonant. So, he told them to call him *Kai.* Since they loved that fucking K so much, he would make it his own.

He made everyone refer to him by that three-letter-name—even his mother. The night he made his demands, she didn't bother with *Misha,* the proper diminutive for Mikhail. Instead, it was *Kai* she summoned to join her for dinner.

He was Mikhail Zverev, and yet the moniker rang empty, resonated worse than crumpled tin. It was meaningless to him now —or so he told himself—yet every syllable was a serrated knife sawing through his ribs, poisoning his blood, and overwriting the person he'd spent twenty years becoming.

"You're Mikhail Zverev," Ivan repeated, awe lacing every word.

No. He was Kai Donovan.

"Mikhail Zverev died with his parents."

"What?" The man on the floor peered at him, confusion warping his face.

"That kid," said Kai. "He never left the woods."

42

MIYA

WHEN KAI DIDN'T SHOW by ten that evening, Miya considered launching her own search and rescue mission. Carol stopped by with a distraught Caelan, and although they'd confirmed that Kai was holed up at the Confessional, his continued absence wore on her. After hours of nervous fidgeting, she dragged herself to Marty's menagerie at Caelan's request.

When she returned, she nearly dropped her shopping bags in the doorway.

Kai stood in the kitchen, spooning ice cream straight out of the tub. He stared blankly at the wall ahead as Miya walked in. Still as an anthropologist in an underbrush, she observed silently, wondering if he'd acknowledge her.

"Are you...eating your feelings?" she asked, dumbfounded, then placed her snack haul on the coffee table.

He took a giant scoop and turned the spoon toward her. "Chocolate peanut butter," he offered without inflection.

Caelan sat on the couch, stroking Ripper's back as she too watched Kai. "He's been a zombie since he got in, like, ten minutes ago."

Miya took the spoon he held and swallowed down the ice cream, then dropped the utensil in the sink. Kai looked like someone had carved the fire out of him and dumped a barrel of soil on top. "What the hell happened?"

After a hefty sigh and some impotent puttering, he brought her up to speed, flatly recounting the day's events.

"You just...let him go?" Miya asked after Ivan Zverev. She was clinging to at least three hundred questions about bloodlines and doppelgangers. Kai wavered when the topic of his ancestry came up; there was more to it than he let on, but hearing that Caelan's pursuer roamed free foisted Miya's curiosities onto the back burner.

Finished with the ice cream, Kai nabbed an apple from their depleted fruit bowl and pared off pieces with his hunting knife, casually devouring them straight from the blade. "We came to an agreement."

Miya crossed her arms over her chest as he explained his risky bargain. She expected it to be hairbrained, anxiety balling in her throat. Ivan Zverev couldn't ignore Kai's identity, but he couldn't abandon his contract either.

"He's given me seventy-two hours to find a solution that doesn't end in Caelan's death." Kai's gaze drifted to the girl on the couch. She bowed her head, her fingers stilling in Ripper's fur.

"Or he's coming back for her," Miya surmised.

Kai nodded, his expression grim. "I couldn't hold him hostage. Someone would notice, and I can't put that shit on Connor. He's supposed to stay neutral."

Miya trapped her misgivings behind her teeth. She didn't have a better idea, and Kai had been forced to think on his feet.

"Killing him leaves a bad taste in my mouth." He spoke like he'd considered it. "But I won't let him hurt Caelan either."

A tired smile stretched Miya's lips. "He's not the architect of the problem. Pyotr is. Getting rid of your long-lost cousin isn't a fix."

His shoulders relaxed with her assent. "The deal will buy me time at least."

"What happens if you can't think of anything?" Caelan finally chimed in. "Three days isn't a lot of time."

"He'll come for you again, and I'll just have to send him limping back to Pyotr until something clicks." He sounded so resolute, like beating back an attacker was as common as taking out the trash. "Zverev aside"—he stepped past Miya—"we need to talk."

Ripper jumped from Caelan's lap, stalking across the room to his water bowl.

"Did you know you're a fetch?" Kai asked.

A shake of the head. "I've never had to think about it. I just... existed. And then I was here, trying to find *her*."

Caelan had left the dreamscape to locate her double and replace her. And the leshy, Kai explained, amplified her impulse to do so—strengthened the tether between the two girls and drew it so taut that they'd inevitably collide.

"I think I understand now." Miya circled the tiny island they used for preparing food. The leshy was concerned for Caelan's safety. Miya had assumed something supernatural was pursuing her, but it was the other way around. The girl was an unwilling hunter, but she was also prey—not to some malevolent spirit, but to Pyotr, the adoptive father of Caelan's double, Alina. The leshy wanted to bring Caelan back to the ethereal plane, but that did nothing to silence the call; she'd be drawn into the physical world until she finished what she'd unwittingly started. "The leshy thinks that if Caelan kills her double, it'll put an end to the call. She'll be able to return to the dreamscape and stay there."

Caelan curled her knees to her chest and shrank into herself, wilting like a dying flower. A hiccupping sob shuddered her shoulders. "I can't do this anymore," she managed between sharp inhales. "I can't keep fighting what I am. I didn't understand it—I still don't —but the universe doesn't give a damn about that. It wants me to kill. I knew something bad would happen if I listened to the call, but killing—"

"We'll find a way to stop it," Miya reassured.

"How?" She lifted her head, bloodshot eyes rimmed with tears. "I don't see a way out."

Sorrow was a fist around Miya's heart. She understood this helplessness—had worn it for years. Youth was difficult enough, but bearing a supernatural burden turned hurdles into stone walls. "We're just barely starting to understand this, and we have three days to come up with a plan." She'd call Ama—force her and Kai to reconcile. They needed the white wolf's knowledge about other worlds. Gavran would help too, but he was a wily spirit, frequently speaking in riddles and vanishing for days on end.

Feeling Kai's torrid stare, Miya locked eyes with him. He was suspiciously quiet, his jaw clenched as he parsed something only he was privy to. An imagined scenario. A hypothetical outcome. His brow knitted, the look he gave her both bladed and apologetic.

One of them has to die, it said. A morbid calculation.

An acrid taste filled Miya's mouth, and she gave a slight shake of her head, an outright rejection. "Come on," she said to Caelan, though her attention remained on Kai. "Let's get some air. I think it's getting a little cramped in here."

As the teen rose and joined Miya by the door, Kai's gaze dropped to the knife in his hand. Thumb braced on the haft, he sliced into white flesh, carving out the apple's core.

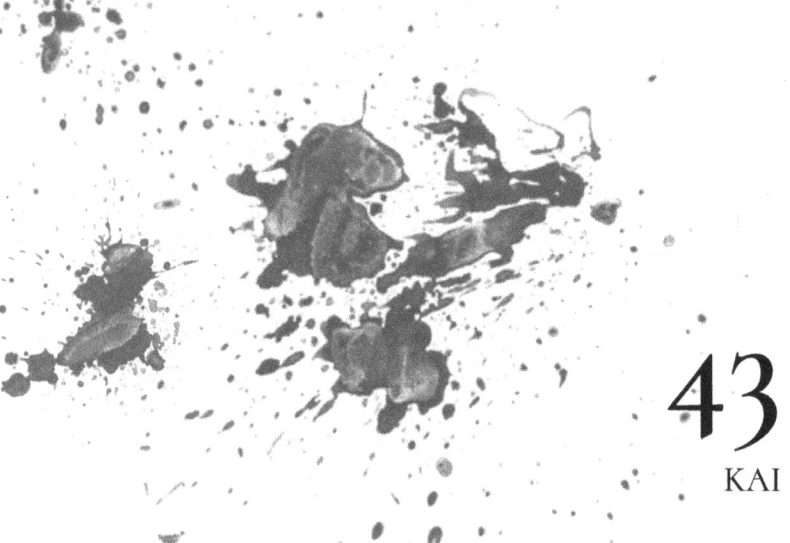

43

KAI

THE LAST THING Kai wanted was to park his ass in Hristina Krunić's too-comfortable armchair. He had less than thirty-six hours to figure out how to save Caelan's life, and each second that passed was a hammer to his temple. Canceling seemed sensible, but he knew that if he did, he might not ever come back. The consistency was the only thing keeping him there, and Miya insisted it would be healthy to stop spinning his wheels for an hour. While dire circumstances warranted professional support, a psychotherapist couldn't do shit about a doppelganger. So, he settled for something more accessible—trauma and all that.

"Normally, a clinician isn't supposed to reveal their personal flaws to their patients." She sat with her hands clasped over her notepad. Always calm, there was something smug and self-satisfied in the way she filled her seat. As if to say knowledge was power, and she had it.

Kai didn't respond, his blasé attitude dissipating. Suddenly, he didn't feel so comfortable splaying his limbs across the armchair like some disgruntled teen in detention.

"There are exceptions to every rule," said Krunić, "and I endeavor to be flexible, opting for an unconventional approach where I believe it is appropriate. In this instance, I'd like to share one of my personal shortcomings with you."

Kai's eyes narrowed to slits. It was only their third session, and she was already switching tactics. That didn't bode well. "You think

I'll spill my guts if you tell me about how Mommy and Daddy messed you up?"

She smiled icily. "Hardly. But I do think you value honesty. So, I'm going to be honest. I struggle curbing my curiosity. You might say that's an asset in my profession, but when pursued impulsively, curiosity can..." She measured her words, twirling a finger through the air. "Get you into trouble."

Kai took a slow, deep inhale. "All right. What'd you do?"

Dr. Krunić flipped open a file that'd been hiding under her notepad. "I took the liberty of digging up your old records. Your intake mentions you're from Washington, and while you're certainly not the only Kai Donovan in the country, there are only a few records on the west coast that correspond to a story like yours." She glanced up at him, gauging for a reaction.

Fingers digging into the leather, Kai swallowed the sharp scrape of nerves in his throat. He'd known this was a possibility. She'd pried out enough for a half-capable detective with resources and a database to piece a story together. Most people didn't care to, but Hristina Krunić wasn't kidding when she said curiosity was her fatal flaw. Those records were legally protected; she must've called in a hefty favor to access them, and she knew he wouldn't tattle. It would only reveal that he was undocumented.

Her attention flicked back to the file. "Post-traumatic stress disorder, attention deficit hyperactivity disorder, conduct disorder, a strong pattern of non-compliance in six years of state-mandated therapy since the age of ten, and then...*nothing*." She smacked the folder shut. "You vanished like a ghost at the tender age of sixteen."

Fifteen fucking years since then. He was legally dead, and he had no intention of changing that. "I lost everything that tied me to that place."

A statement of fact. A thing easily said when he couldn't shore up the courage to utter the quiet part out loud.

"Everything," Dr. Krunić repeated. "Your parents. Then your caretaker. You would've been expelled—likely incarcerated—for beating your classmate to an inch of his life, which I assume prompted your flight from the state."

"He was an asshole," Kai offered with a blithe smile, "and Alice had just died. My application for emancipation was rejected." The assault had also triggered his first transition since his parents' deaths. He hadn't learned to control it—didn't know why it happened or how he was supposed to function in the world. The last thing he'd needed was a stint in juvie. "I had nothing in me but rage."

Krunić nodded—affirmation, cold understanding. "You were mistreated. Your choice to run away was perfectly rational."

Was it? He always thought it was cowardice, an animal instinct to survive. Perhaps he'd thought wrong. Had he stayed and taken responsibility, who, exactly, would he have been accountable to? He didn't owe anyone anything. Alice was dead, and he harbored no remorse for the harm he'd caused to his *class-mate*—an arrogant trust-fund kid who'd tormented Kai since middle school. No one fucked with him now, but back then, Kai had frequently been on the receiving end of cruelty. Bullying. He was an easy target: orphaned, poor, mentally ill, and academically inept.

"That must be news to you," Krunić said when he remained mute. "That you were a victim."

How Kai hated that word—the weight it carried. He'd been wronged and made to believe *he* was wrong. Now he understood. Running away hadn't been selfish. It'd saved him. Surrendering himself to a punitive justice system would've only made him worse —more violent, more anti-social, more disenfranchised. And what good would that've done? Made a pair of soulless yuppies feel better about their son's rearranged face? Was that justice? Flagel-lating a kid who'd lost everything to prove that he was, in fact, a piece of shit who'd never change?

Fuck that. They didn't deserve his pain.

"Like I said, no one deserves a damn thing. You get what you get." His own voice sounded foreign to him, a shakiness to the tenor.

Dr. Krunić nodded. "I understand. If you believe people get what they deserve, then what does that say about you? Not a flat-tering picture, is it?"

"It's all moralistic bullshit," said Kai. "Crap people make up to feel like there's some sense to the world. There isn't."

"Yes, life is quite senseless. You, for example, were ripped from security too soon," she observed. "Everything about your life has been volatile. You learned that you couldn't rely on others, so you fostered independence, self-reliance." She cocked her head. "Sounds nice, doesn't it?"

"It helped me survive. Don't see anything wrong it."

"You told me your independence is the most important thing to you." She tapped the folder. "I believe you. It seems you protect it at all costs, even when that cost is your relationships."

Kai snorted, though he mustered no retort. She was right, and there was no point in denying it. "Not exactly news to me."

"Of course not." She leaned back. "You think your independence is a strength honed through adversity, but have you considered why you guard it so fiercely? What do you stand to lose if you let go a little?"

Kai sat with the question, the answer more a feeling in his veins than a thing he could articulate. Anxiety, unmooring, uncertainty. His mouth opened, his breath halting halfway in before he spoke. "Control."

There it was. That self-satisfied smile. "It's fascinating, isn't it? We associate independence with detachment, individualism, a desire to live and let live. It's the opposite of control. Yet when someone experiences as much helplessness as you have, they become hyper-independent, shed their need of others." She paused, then tossed aside his file. "You're grasping for control in a world where you have none, and the only thing you can control is how much you let others in. The more you allow yourself to depend on them, the more that little boy in you remembers the violence of being torn from those he needed. Parents. Caretakers. Teachers. Doctors. All of them failed you. Now, you refuse to relinquish control even to those you love because you're terrified of reliving that little boy's traumas." She leveled him with a gaze like tempered steel. "Your traumas."

Kai remembered that boy. His blood-stained skin, his skinny limbs and shoulders slouched in defeat. He'd stared at Kai, reckoning with the man he'd become—a man with a different name.

That boy was Mikhail Zverev. Kai wasn't Mikhail, but he carried his corpse in his bones. "I learned something about myself recently," he forced out.

Dr. Krunić raised both eyebrows, and after some waffling, Kai relayed a distilled version of the tale. That he'd forgotten his birth name until recently. That he'd remembered how he came to be Kai, and then Kai Donovan. She listened attentively, her expression a flawless mask of neutrality. He told her about the nightmares—the man on the train, the carcasses adorning the walls, the boy bathed in blood who'd been powerless to save his family.

"And you don't feel like you're that boy anymore," Dr. Krunić said when he was finished.

Kai shook his head. "That kid's gone. Or so I thought. I guess you could say Mikhail Zverev's dead, but his ghost is still around. He's been hanging off my back so long, I've stopped noticing the weight."

"An apt metaphor," she agreed. "I take it these nightmares have been impacting you quite negatively."

Huffing, Kai threw himself back, his ankle resting on his knee. "I started lashing out. That's why my girlfriend made me come here."

"You wouldn't let her look at you when you were in pain." He hated how soft her voice sounded.

"I'm used to being alone when I'm in pain," he said. "And I take care of business on my own."

"It must be frightening, having someone so close." She shifted and ironed out her jacket collar. "That's why you didn't want her coming to therapy with you. Much scarier than going by yourself."

He nodded slowly, the admission providing little reprieve. "It's just who I am."

Hristina Krunić tutted. "Your girlfriend isn't a threat to your independence, Kai. I'm sure you know that, yet you fight her for it anyway."

Kai rolled his eyes. "Yeah, yeah, I get it. Hyper-independence is a trauma response."

"I'm not sure you do get it," she challenged.

"Fine," he sneered. "Enlighten me."

She leaned forward and locked stares with him, fearless in her verdict. "You're wounded, and you're guarding those wounds. Your girl's trying to show you how badly they're festering, and instead of grabbing some damn Neosporin, you're biting her hand off."

You're guarding your wounds.

His mind was a dislocated joint popping into place. A jarring thunderclap of pain seized him as it all settled, and finally, something in his fucked-up brain aligned. He was a frightened animal—a wolf in a claw trap, more afraid of the humans trying to help him than the iron maw sawing through his limb. The more he struggled, the closer those iron teeth got to the bone.

"Your girlfriend's not trying to change you." Krunić's voice shattered his stupor. "Letting the people who love you take care of you won't change you. It'll only give you the space to be yourself."

"I know." The words scraped against his throat like gravel. He felt raw. Unhinged save for a single fraying thread that kept him tethered to the ground.

Miya.

Hristina Krunić smiled, a fleck of warmth sparking her eyes. "What would you rather have independence from, Kai? Your girl? Or your trauma?"

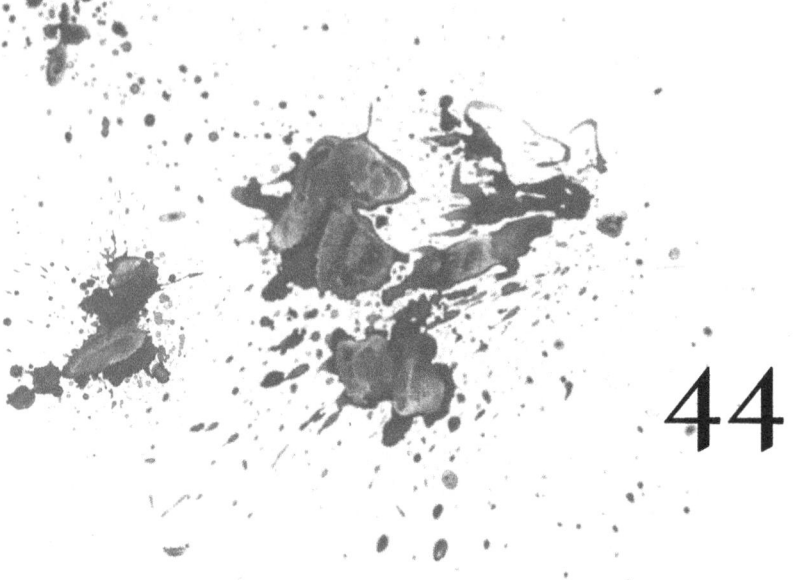

44

KAI NEVER GOT on much with Father Time.

Saturn. Chronos. Death. The reaping of what is sowed.

And Kai rarely reaped well.

When he first fled Granite Falls, he thought he'd be lucky to make it to twenty-five. On his twenty-sixth birthday, he vowed to reach thirty, if only to prove he was capable of surviving. That was the year he met Miya, and once they were bound—tethered in ways he didn't understand—he stopped hedging his bets. He no longer had the luxury of dying young.

Now, he felt the press of time like that teenage boy absconding from the state, unsure of the next meal, the next warm bed, the next anything. Only the dread wasn't for himself; it was for Caelan.

Twenty-four hours left.

Kai shifted on the bench, scanning the mansion half-obscured by a wall of manicured shrubs. He'd burned away the remaining daylight meandering around the city; his head was full of phantoms, and he had no intention of releasing them into his home.

As if yanking every skeleton out of the abysmal closet of his subconscious wasn't enough, he dwelled on Caelan's fate as much as the one he'd evaded. Krunić's insights were a sickle around his throat, and if he didn't tread carefully, he'd lose his head to the reaping hook. He hated how beholden he was to a past he couldn't remember, to an identity he'd lost, and a name he didn't relate to. Kai Donovan had spent two decades wresting control from Mikhail Zverev, sundering himself from the boy who once was.

He'd failed, and it was no wonder. Ghosts were intangible, amorphous.

Wild desperation fluttered in his chest—a frantic bird trapped in a tunnel, longing for the sky. Caelan deserved better than what Mikhail Zverev got. Alina probably deserved better than Pyotr. Both did, irrespective of whether they'd inspired his care or his wrath.

The solution seemed simple: eliminate the common element. Without Pyotr, Ivan would have no contract, and Caelan would be safe. The supernatural shit-fest could be dealt with in peace, and the world wouldn't weep for the loss of another rich sociopath.

There was only one complication. Kai had no desire to orphan another child. No matter which way he angled the problem, saving one girl came at the expense of the other. He didn't particularly care for Alina, but callousness came less readily when he knew the impact of his actions.

He rose from the bench, the mansion an omen and an opportunity. The key to Caelan's freedom awaited inside, as did a damning decision. It was a tight rope—doing the right thing.

Right for whom? Kai wondered in vain—a question trapped within the edges of a churning mind.

It didn't matter. The math was uncomplicated. Pyotr's death spelled Caelan's freedom, and Alina would learn to cope. Her father was a mob boss; an ugly demise was an occupational hazard. Kai just hadn't anticipated that he'd be the reaper at Pyotr's doorstep.

Fuck it.

He was good at getting his hands dirty.

BREAKING in should've been more difficult, but Kai found an ally in Pyotr's hubris. No guards or dogs—only security cameras and sensors evaded like vegetables at a steakhouse. He slipped in through a low window in the back garden. It was cracked open—probably an oversight—though every entry point was disguised by topiary and iron gates. He'd studied the layout of the house before trespassing, gauging its size and scope. Spatial awareness was more important than an exact blueprint.

He landed in a powder room, rubber soles thudding against white marble. Clinical but classy. Ear to the door, Kai found the hall outside quiet. No housekeepers, no bodyguards. Just a too-big house for a man whose wealth outsized his humanity. Judging by the curves of the outer wall, he expected a large office or sitting room in the southeast corner. It wasn't late enough for sleep, and Pyotr seemed the type to while away his evening with overpriced brandy—that is, assuming he had no one's fingers to cut off. Kai knew he didn't—not tonight.

He'd passed Chrysanthemum earlier, and the bouncer from his first visit nodded in greeting. Kai seized the opportunity to pry out what he needed.

"The boss-man doesn't visit mid-week," the bouncer had said with a lazy shrug. "Guy likes routine, and every Wednesday and Thursday, he stays home with his family."

Admirable or controlling—Kai wasn't sure which, but he could hazard a guess.

The corridor outside the powder room was lit only by moonbeams. Ostentatious windows towered from floor to ceiling, showcasing the impressive courtyard at the house's rear. As Kai stalked toward the southeast corner, silver rays passing over him, the sudden thud of a heartbeat rived through his senses.

Someone was nearby.

He could incapacitate them, hide the body in one of the many crannies of the gauche estate. The heartbeat pattered frantically, its owner unmoving around a tight corner up ahead. If they rounded into Kai, things could get messy. He had to strike first. Sliding past the wall, he pivoted into a nook tucked under a staircase, ready to send the poor bastard to bed.

He never got the chance. Shock wove through Kai's bones, freezing him in place—the wolf made a deer in a split second of painful recognition.

Caelan.

No, Alina.

She peered up at him, her face aglow from the phone in her hands. She didn't move, and neither did he. A thousand scenarios roared through Kai's mind, each one starting with Alina's scream and ending with Kai's life.

But the girl didn't scream. She just stared, eyes wide and lips pursed as though she'd caged the cry. Inhaling sharply, her coppery brows knitted as knowing sank into her features.

"Are you Death?"

Kai's mouth opened. He wanted to say *no*, but it felt like a half-truth baked into a larger lie. He was here to end a life.

"You're here to kill me, right?" A demand—calm, untroubled.

"Are you expecting to die?" Kai parried her question with another. Wagering she wouldn't scream for help, he relaxed his stance.

Her gaze shifted to the tiles, unnaturally white in the gloom. "Everyone dies. I guess I just know my time is sooner than most."

"I'm not here for you." Kai's fingers and toes burned to move. He was wasting precious time, but he was also trapped. He wasn't about to threaten a kid, and that left him no choice but to suss out his options while he had her attention. Slanting his body, he angled one ear toward the hall behind him.

The girl tucked her phone into her pocket. Whatever had her heart hammering earlier must've been related. "I saw you in the park before I blacked out."

So, she hadn't seen him shift; her trance must've hit before he'd pretzeled himself into an animal.

"You're with her...the fetch."

"You sound like you're expecting her." Kai shucked away the pretense. "But like I said, I'm not here for you."

"Then why are you here?"

To kill your father. Maybe. I haven't decided yet. Kai swallowed. "Trying to save the fetch. She doesn't want to hurt you."

Alina nodded, backing further into the corner. She plunked down on a bench drilled into the wall under the stairwell—a reading nook with a built-in bookshelf. "I summoned her. I still remember it—that stupid night three years ago."

Exactly when Caelan first appeared.

Kai followed her into the enclave, eager to pull himself out of sight. "What? Did you buy a Ouija board from a garage sale?" Summoning a doppelganger didn't seem like a thing done on purpose.

The girl huffed as she cracked a smile. "No. I just...wished it, I guess."

"You *wanted* your doppelganger to find you?"

She gnawed on her lower lip, palms braced on either side of her as she rocked back and forth. "I hated my life. Still do. This house is a gilded cage. I was homeschooled until last year, and now I'm stuck at a private school where everyone keeps tabs on me. My dad thinks mandatory dinners together twice a week is peak parenting. He says he cares about me, but he's just pruning me to fit his image." A harsh laugh keened from a tight throat. "I wanted someone to take my place. I was just a dumb kid then, so I begged, thinking there was no way anyone out there would listen, but—"

Kai groaned and rubbed his brow with the ball of his hand. "You manifested a fucking doppelganger with the sheer power of your own misery. Excellent." He had no idea how it was possible—how some people gave shape to the unspoken while others drowned in it.

"It was an accident." Her voice was small, timid. "I didn't realize it'd worked."

Alina wasn't unlike the Dreamwalker—a person with gifts no one made room for. How many others were there? How many people had access to things that shouldn't have been real?

"You said you're not here to kill me..."

"I'm not," Kai confirmed a third time.

"Maybe you should."

His eyes sliced into her—all thorns and rebuke. "Don't you have homework to do? Another awkward teen to flirt with? Alcohol to smuggle? Weed to smoke?"

"I'm serious," she hissed. "I didn't mean to summon her. And I sure as hell didn't think she'd be a person who'd have to experience my life if she caught me. I wouldn't wish that on anyone, not even a fetch."

"You should go stay with your boyfriend for a while." Kai didn't care to trip into Alina's emotional quicksand. The important part was that she wouldn't tattle. Her allegiance wasn't to Pyotr; it was to her own pain.

"We had a fight."

So, that's what happened on the phone. "Then make up," he ordered. "Your dick of a father is only going to complicate this, fetch or no. Trust me. You don't want to be here when shit hits the fan, and it will."

She peered up at him, tallying something in her mind. When her calculations stalled out, Kai made himself the variable that would tip her wavering scale.

"You asked me if I'm Death." His shadow darkened the small crevice, foreboding churning the space between them. He was Sendoa's descendent—the stygian wolf marring legends across time, a god of destruction in mortal form. Death was a result, a finality. And the black wolf was never the end. He was the undoing.

"I'm not Death," said Kai. "I'm the fucking calamity that wields it."

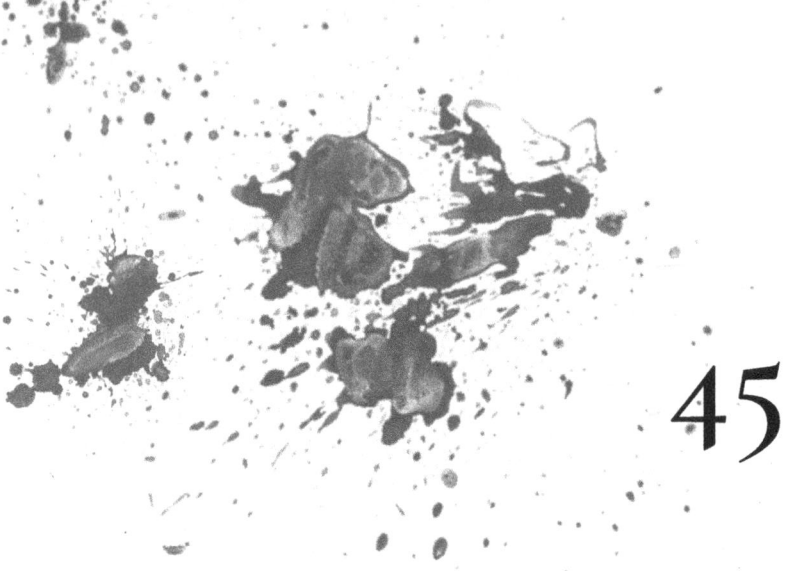

45

W‌HEN K‌AI REACHED the southeast corner of the estate, a pair of oak doors greeted him. Knobs of antique brass waited to be twisted, to unlatch and give way to a fated encounter. Suddenly, Kai didn't feel much like a calamity. Was he being selfish? Going rogue and placing his whims ahead of others? He'd come here without anyone's input, claimed it was the fastest, cleanest road to a solution—one he'd pave himself.

Hyper-independence. That pesky word Krunić used to describe his survival mechanism.

His qualm wasn't with killing. It was killing without Miya's sanction. He'd spent years pretending her opinion came second— that he did what he had to. Why did he act like she'd stop him? If he thought his actions were justified, why didn't he share his convictions with her?

Kai realized, achingly, that he didn't know which of his actions were warranted and which were wanton. He stonewalled Miya not to protect her, but to protect himself.

How pathetic, to learn that all this time, he'd simply been scared.

A wet rustle snapped Kai from his thoughts. Something moved behind the door, blotting out the faint light from the other side. A slither, followed by a creak. The point of a sinewy cord pushed through the razor-thin crack between the doors, a writhing thing that tapered to a mere sliver.

"What the fuck—"

The wood groaned and chittered as vines sprouted from every crevice. Rotten flowers the color of blood—the same ones that'd colonized the King of Spades—bloomed along dark green veins that glided along the doors like a skein of vipers. Before Kai could make sense of it, pain sparked in his skull, mincing his senses. His hand flew to pinch the bridge of his nose, and as he folded, his vision grayed. He knew this agony—the familiar twinge of a forced transition.

Kai shambled back, disoriented. He needed to leave—to get out before he lost control, before his grip on his surroundings slipped.

Then, as quickly as it began, the stabbing in his head stopped. When he glanced up, the flowers and their Medusan stems were gone.

He burst through the doors, but the room was cold and cloaked in darkness. Shelves upon shelves of untouched books, an imposing desk, and an armchair fit for a titan, but no Pyotr, no anything. Only the faint smell of rotting wood.

It was too quiet, the stillness an eerie warning of something amiss, like a forest without birds. What'd changed? He'd been too scrambled from the momentary onslaught to notice the shift in his environment. Kai circled back to the nook under the stairwell but found no trace of Alina. Her phone lay abandoned on the bench, winking to life with unanswered messages. Kai picked up the device and read the text that flashed onto the screen.

> Are you coming over or what?

The frustrated finale to a chorus of pending questions. Alina, it seemed, never got the chance to reply.

46

MIYA

THE PORCELAIN MUG shattered as Caelan's scream tore through the small apartment. Scalding tea sprayed the scuffed hardwood, seeping through the fissures that'd formed with age. Heedless, Caelan stepped over the mess on the floor, her cries punctuated by the crunch of blistering shards beneath her feet. Thankfully, she was wearing shoes. Palms pressed to her temples, she staggered until she curled in on herself with a whimper.

The cacophony cleaved Miya from her seat as Caelan's agony razed the quiet. She rushed over, gently prying the teen's hands from her face. "What's wrong?"

A frantic shake of the head, then, a repeated mutter. "I have to go. I have to go. I have to go." She pulled away, her movements lethargic, and oriented herself toward the door.

The call. Cursing under her breath, Miya side-stepped the broken mug and wrapped an arm around the girl's waist, hoping to stall her. She'd invited Ama over to make peace, yet the forecast proved anything but peaceful.

Unhindered by Miya's grasp, Caelan heaved toward the door. She was so strong, so unencumbered by efforts to stop her. Miya caged the teen in her arms, but it was useless. Fingers rigid, Caelan reached for the door handle with a graveled shriek. Shadows boiled from the floor around her feet, the air crackling with a suffocating, otherworldly static.

A barbed knot twisted in Miya's stomach. She was too weak.

"Stop!" She tried anchoring her feet but slid across the floor, her slippers providing little purchase.

Caelan knocked her knuckles against the brass, bruising, lacerating. Before she could get a grip, the door flew open, a hand splayed on the wood as it crashed into the adjacent wall.

Ama stood at the precipice, her eyes like balefire. Without missing a beat, she locked her arms around Caelan's midsection and lifted her into the air. The teen thrashed, feral in her attempts to break free. Limbs flailing, she threw a careless elbow and kicked at her captors. Pain spangled Miya's cheekbone as she was struck, though she bared down and brushed off the blow.

"Let me go!" A desperate command from a throat scraped raw. "I can't stay here anymore! I can't take it—"

A sickening pop, a scorching scream. Miya's hold slipped as her mind reeled to make sense of what she'd just witnessed. Caelan's arm, warped all wrong. Dark, amorphous shapes leaked from her clothes and skittered along the walls. Umbral creatures gobbled the light as though starved, and for a split second, Miya swore she saw a thousand searching eyes embedded in the shadows. Ravening.

Was there something living inside Caelan, seeking to devour her human double? Had it grown impatient, threatening to consume its own host? Alina and Caelan were a matching pair. Perhaps it didn't matter which of them remained when the dust settled.

Perhaps a forgery could be just as delicious as the original.

Miya flung away the intrusive thoughts, viscous inside her skull. She'd picked up on something—a will that lived within Caelan but was not her own.

They hauled the girl to the couch, holding her with as much tenderness as they could afford. She writhed furiously, her body twisting against the thing inside her—a volition diametrically opposed to her own. A vein bulged in her temple, her face scarlet, contorted. Miya watched, horrified, as her bones bent in ways brittle things ought not to bend. Blood trickled from the corners of her eyes, oozed from her ears, her nose, her gums. Her screams became layered, discordant—a sound from nowhere and everywhere at once.

"We have to do something." Miya locked eyes with Ama. "We have to—"

"Let her go," Ama said, her voice hard.

"We can't—you know that." Confusion scored Miya's features, panic lacing her clipped reply.

Ama shook her head, white hair fluttering around her face. "Keeping her here is pointless if she breaks into pieces. Let her go. We can follow and deal with whatever comes."

Miya choked on her objection when Caelan's back arched, her spine curving until it nearly splintered. Ama was right. This couldn't continue. "Okay," she conceded, her grip on the teen slackening.

Ama faltered, her gaze thawing. "Miya."

She glanced up, the meekness in Ama's voice yet another jolt.

"I'm sorry," said the white wolf. Then, she let go.

Caelan trundled from the couch and limped to the door, her arm and ankle badly sprained, but she paid the injuries no mind, her gaze fixed on something beyond. Entranced, she stumbled out of the apartment, the floor creaking underfoot. At least she wouldn't be difficult to follow.

Miya spared a moment, rotating to face her friend. "Ama—"

The white wolf raised a hand to silence her. "I owe you an apology. I let my insecurity get the better of me. And I—" Her jaw clamped, the words catching on her teeth. "I've been treating you like a child to guard my own fears. It was wrong."

This wasn't the time or the place, but it was needed. Miya's arms encircled her friend—her sister. "Thank you for being vulnerable with me."

Ama returned her embrace. "Crowbar helped," she admitted, her eyes wandering.

Miya waited a moment longer, hopeful for any mention of Kai. When nothing followed, she pushed down the pinch in her chest and turned to the wide-open door. Miya laced her fingers with Ama's and tugged. "Come on. I know where she's going."

Ama shot her a quizzical look, but Miya refused to dither. There was only one place in all of Boston that Caelan kept returning to.

A tangle between worlds.

47

EVERYTHING SMELLED like stale sandalwood and wet earth. Miya flexed her fingers, dirt sinking beneath her nails. With a ragged gasp, she sat up, breath fogging the thick air. A gray mist moved like smoke in the wind, gradually parting to reveal an open field. It was empty save for a leviathan tree—an ancient elm with a wide, gnarled trunk and a crown of jagged boughs. Its roots pulsed beneath the earth, drawing life from the fey soil. As Miya's gaze skimmed upward, she saw the hanging star cresting the tips of the elm's branches. She was in the dreamscape.

She plowed through her memory, retracing each step. After Caelan left the apartment, Ama followed her like an expert huntress. Caelan had ambled clumsily over the grass after they'd reached Boston Common, arm hanging limp as she clutched her swollen elbow. She'd been tranquil, homing in on the felled tree's memorial plaque—a suture between realms. The one she'd ripped through to get to the material plane three years ago. Now, Miya found herself on the other side of reality, wondering how the hell she'd gotten there.

The elm was eternal on this side, needless of a memorial. As Miya re-oriented, her eyes snagged on Ann Glover's swaying corpse. She still dangled from a thick branch, her neck bent where the rope drew taut. A gangly figure in a ratty coat and a tattered fishing hat stood at her feet, staring up at her.

The leshy.

He looked over his shoulder, his head clicking along like a rusty clock hand. As he moved, another figure appeared. A person—no, two people—

obscured by the patchy brown garment clinging to the leshy's angular frame like a sheet on a hanger.

A man Miya didn't recognize, and a girl she did.

They were blurs in the haze, but she knew the shape of the girl—her coppery hair and elfish form. Caelan but not, the original to the imitation, the one who gave the fetch her moniker: the forgery.

The human double, Alina. She jerked away from the man, but he held her by the elbow—the same one that Caelan had injured. She appeared unharmed, but the mirroring between her and Caelan left spider legs crawling up Miya's spine.

Miya shambled forward until the elm's shade swallowed her, and she could make out the fraying threads of the leshy's clothes, the runnels of his craggy face. She stopped beneath the tree's limbs. "Let me out."

The spirit shook his head, the movement stilted. "I cannot."

Denial and confirmation in a single reply. The leshy must've foisted her into the dreamscape after she'd caught up to Caelan. She dreaded to think about Ama, bones snapping as her body twisted into the contours of a wolf. Whatever happened on the other side, Miya had no power. But Alina was there, trapped as Caelan hemmed her in.

"Please," Miya implored, "don't force her to kill."

The leshy tilted his head with a quick jerk, the angle too severe. "This is the only way."

"Aren't you her friend?" she challenged. "You're stripping her of her free will."

"I'm stripping her of a fallacy," his voice rumbled, something discordant warbling between each note. "Peeling away a false skin, like a tree shedding frail bark."

"You're damning her."

"I'm freeing her."

"No," came a familiar drawl, "you're a fool."

Miya whirled, heart nearly crushing her windpipe. A small figure stood at her back, a mantle of dark feathers cloaking the wan body beneath. A corpse worn by a raven. "Gavran."

Lips skinned back from serrated teeth, inky eyes shifting from the Dreamwalker to the leshy. "Deep roots don't always find water, and age is no promise of wisdom."

The leshy was unmoved, attention fixed on the raven donning the boy. "You think I am so foolish that I cannot understand your riddles, bird?"

The boy clasped both hands behind his back, marching forward in an exaggerated fashion. "Youth brings peculiar insight. Unadulterated truths. The wisdom of children, so often overlooked by those courted by their own irrelevance. A pathetic grab for control." His gaze slid over the leshy. "That is the skin you wear, nature spirit. The fallacy which you refuse to shed."

"Speak plainly," the leshy hissed—wind through rustling leaves.

Another slithering smile, iridescent hair ruffling like plumage. "Do you not know what a fetch is, nature spirit? It does not kill for pleasure or to find solace. It kills to fill the space which it has made empty."

"That's right," Miya mused aloud. "The fetch replaces its human double."

"You see," Gavran went on in delighted singsong, "your fetch is never returning home. You could compel her to kill a thousand just like her, and she will remain trapped not only to her instinct, but to the grief it has sown."

Miya glimpsed the waver in the leshy's eyes, echoed by the elm's mournful creak. The spirit shuddered, his edges distorted in the gauzy air. "She cannot return until the mortal is dead. If she tries, she will be called back here again and again. There is no end to it. Only suffering."

"She's suffering because of you," said Miya, her voice coated in steel. "You, who think you know best—exploiting one orphan to kill another. You're supposed to be her ally, not her puppeteer."

"I only want her to come home." To think ancient voices could sound so small. Another tremble, a quake in the earth where the elm's veins snaked beneath the dreamscape's skin.

Miya recognized this feeling—this heaviness that weighed on body and soul. Sorrow like a net of thorns, clinching around the leshy's heart, his realization chased by anguish. No matter what he did, Caelan was lost, enslaved to a nightmarish call or doomed to enact the very horror she fled from: murdering an innocent.

"Let me go," Miya pleaded a second time. "Let me find a way to fix this."

Another shake of the head. "I cannot."

"Why?" Frustration graveled Miya's reply.

"I...cannot," he repeated. "This is my nature, as yours is to dream. We cannot defy what we are."

Gavran's pitch black eyes narrowed, tracing an invisible line to Alina's shadow where she twisted from her captor in a futile dance. He purred in contemplation, then cocked his head with an eerie grin. "I see."

Miya frowned at him. "See what?"

"You must kill it." Gavran's head righted itself, and his expression mellowed. "The nature spirit does not mean to trap you, but he cannot release you either. You must free yourself by force."

Skepticism fluttered in Miya's chest. She looked past the leshy to the spot that had Gavran so rapt—where a shade in Alina's likeness stood as her effigy in the dreamscape. He'd seen something. Miya just didn't know what. "I don't want to kill him."

"You must." Cold certainty, bereft of pity or care.

The leshy lowered his gaze, his broad shoulders flinching into a slouch. "Your familiar speaks the truth."

Miya hesitated, unaccustomed to being beseeched as an executioner. She only ended spirits when she had to—when it was her life or theirs. They never went peacefully, and it helped allay her disquiet. "How can you just accept this?" she questioned. "Don't you want to survive? If you give up now, you'll never see Caelan again. She'll be heartbroken—"

"We each have our individual nature," he interrupted, and Miya could've sworn she saw a smile crack his lips open. "Yet the nature of all things is to die. It is the singular truth shared among everyone in existence. But as you know, Dreamwalker..."

"Everything beats in cycles," Gavran supplied.

The leshy's head jerked down—an uncanny facsimile of a nod. "All that comes apart is remade anew. If my end heralds a new beginning for Caelan, and if you are the catalyst for that beginning, then so be it."

Miya would have to free herself with the leshy's death. Her fingers twitched at her side, her stomach a sunken pit. A chill coiled around her spine, though she felt hot with nausea. This didn't sit right. Her hand flew to the dream stone, its warmth a comfort. It hummed with power, eager to be liberated of its chain around her neck.

Miya tore away the fang-shaped stone. Purple, meadow green, and sunset gold gleamed as the point elongated into a curved blade, and she adjusted her grip around the haft, feeling the carvings scrape against her skin.

The leshy slowly raised his head, his gaze fixed on the harbinger of his end. "Show me your true form, Dreamwalker."

And so, she did.

A shroud of iridescent feathers enveloped Miya whole. Violet and midnight tendrils swirled up her back and over her skull, the shadows coalescing into the bone-beak mask, its ivory point curving over her lip. A mane of plumage billowed out from her dark brown hair in a chaotic dance, irreverent of the windless air.

Surprise widened the leshy's eyes. His chin lifted as he beheld the woman cradling his ruin. "God of chaos," he murmured. "A truly nature-less thing."

"Chaos has a nature." She drew close, then smiled, stopping in front of him. "It's change."

A touch to make the spirit flesh, a swipe of the blade to sever life from its container. The leshy's lips parted, shadows spilling from every cavity and the slash along his barked neck.

"I'm sorry," Miya whispered, her throat tight.

"Keep her safe." The request left him as a tattered sound. His eyes dimmed, and wooden flesh flaked away mote by mote until all that remained was dust.

Miya stood beneath the elm, the dreamscape still as the pile of ash at her feet. How strange—that moment of transition from existence to non-existence. How horrible to be the cause of it. Her hand shook, fingers clasped painfully around the haft of her blade. The leshy had truly loved Caelan, and in the end, love had fashioned his demise. Miya glanced at Gavran, and he offered a solemn nod. He spread his feathered cloak and beat his arms—no longer arms, but wings—his human costume shrinking into the shape of a raven that burst into a charcoal sky.

Miya shot upright, heaving as she took in her surroundings. She was back in the waking world, the cold, wet ground chilling her through her clothes. Boston Common was as dark as the space between stars. The lights were all out, smoke wafting from the glass bulbs—some of them shattered, others stained black. Something had overheated them. The moon, at least, was a silver beacon, promising just enough visibility for Miya to make do.

A canine growl turned her head. Ama, aglow with her snowy coat, barred the path between Miya and the two figures ahead. Her hackles were like lashes, her body coiled, ready to strike. Yet she didn't. Her back leg was curled against her belly, blood matting the fur on her haunch.

Scrambling to her feet, Miya found Caelan sitting in the grass, eyes wide and glassy, a red nick on her arm. A knife wound? A passing bullet? The teen was dazed, and as Miya followed the path of her gaze, she found the scene's architect.

The leshy's fading form tainted the air, but he wasn't alone.

Standing over the elm's memorial, Alina fought a man struggling to restrain her, the spirit's spindly hand barely visible on his shoulder. His collar was soaked in sweat, his slicked-back hair mussed from the tussle as he wrestled the teen with one hand and flailed a pistol in the other.

Pyotr and his adoptive daughter. The leshy had ensnared him—a mobster whose impulse was to achieve results at any cost. The spirit must've amplified his Machiavellian nature, spurring him to drag his own daughter out as bait so he could shoot Caelan himself. And Alina…Simply being near the nature spirit would amplify the call.

The last of the leshy dispersed, leaving only a brown smudge on Pyotr's once pristine shirt. Confusion mellowed his contorted face. His eyes darted around the field, then landed on Caelan.

In the blink of an eye, rage overtook bewilderment. With a vicious jerk, he subdued his disobedient child, then pointed the gun at the forgery.

Miya lunged toward Caelan. Ama shadowed her, slowed by her injury. She wouldn't make it. Neither of them would. It took less than a second to pull a trigger, and as powerful as Miya was in the dreamscape, here, she was only human. All she had was a body she could throw in harm's way and hope that nothing vital got hit.

She tensed in anticipation of pain, either her own or Caelan's. Instead, a feral snarl punctuated by Pyotr's cry and Alina's shriek sent Miya's heart stuttering up her throat. She tumbled onto the grass next to Caelan and grabbed the girl by the shoulders, fragments of the scene battering her awareness.

A dark maw clamped around Pyotr's shoulder. Soft ears flattened against a lupine skull. A deep rumble, vibrating through bared fangs. Crimson eyes like lifeblood blossoming over white silk. A midnight coat, sleek against the lightless backdrop.

Kai had launched himself at Pyotr like a starved marauder, heedless of danger. He'd soared high enough to clear Alina's head, a hundred and forty pounds of claws and teeth. It was awkward, reckless, a frantic bid to save a life. The angle was a bad one, sparing Pyotr his jugular.

He twisted, gun in tow, and fired. Kai's growl hitched as the bullet struck his side, but he refused to let go. With a violent shake, he tore at the muscle around Pytor's neck, blunt claws digging into flesh as the wolf fought to topple his prey. Mad with desperation, Pyotr fired again, this time higher, closer to the heart.

A whimper pierced the air, and Kai fell to the ground with a thud. The blood was invisible on his soot-colored fur, but Miya knew it was there, soaking in. A sharp cry forced its way from her mouth as Kai pushed himself halfway up only to collapse with a ragged wheeze. Ama darted forward, limping, but she wasn't quick enough. Pyotr pulled the trigger a third time.

The gun clicked. An empty round.

With a frustrated shout, Pyotr brought the butt of his pistol down on Kai's head. The wolf roared, wrenching toward his assailant, fangs snapping. Barely evading him, Pyotr snatched his stunned daughter and hauled her away. Ama stumbled as she closed in, the wound in her leg bad enough to prevent pursuit. She planted herself between Kai and the retreating Pyotr, guarding her kin.

Miya hardly noticed how tightly she held Caelan until the teen shifted. Frigid shock filled her veins, slowing her blood. She began to quake, her body refusing to move even as she willed it. She'd been unconscious the whole time, leaving Ama to protect them, forcing Kai to throw himself at a sociopath—to take bullets meant for someone else.

Caelan squeezed Miya's hand, and the trembling ceased. Roused to a nightmare, the Dreamwalker locked an unbidden sob behind her teeth, clenching until the rage grew too monstrous to hold.

Then, she screamed.

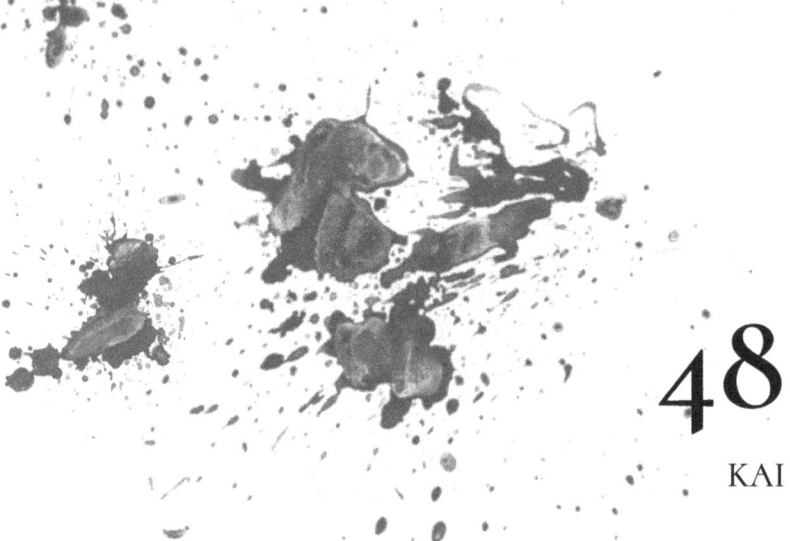

48

KAI KNEW he'd been following the right trail when every bone in his body broke mid-run. After realizing the leshy had come for Pyotr and that Alina was missing, Kai bolted from the mansion without a single fuck given for what the cameras caught. The second he closed in on father and daughter, the transition struck him like a freight train. He didn't bother fighting it. Clothes abandoned, every cell on fire, he pushed past the limits of flesh, bone, and blood. When he saw the gun pointed at Caelan—at Miya—he didn't think twice.

The first bullet went straight through muscle, but the second clipped his lung. That was enough to level him, made it difficult to suck the air back in. Pain streaked through his chest, sawing at his ribs as he battled to stay focused. When that damn gun gave a final impotent click, Kai knew he'd gotten lucky. Another lead nugget to the right spot might've sealed his fate.

Ama was a blur of white, but his ears were trained on Miya. Her raw, throat-rending scream was the last thing he heard before his world went dark.

Kai awoke as a human, no recollection of the transition to naked skin and a voice that formed words. The first one out of his mouth was *fuck*.

He wrapped an arm around his ribs and grimaced, medical gauze meeting his fingertips. He breathed in slowly, one side of his chest tight, achy, still limited in capacity. The torn tissue had likely knitted itself together just enough to stop the air from leaking through his pleural wall and adding pressure to the sad sack that was his mangled lung. It would reinflate by morning, but until then, he'd have the cardio of an eighth-grade asthmatic in gym class.

"You're awake."

Kai's head lolled to the side. Ama sat on the floor of the cramped apartment, her back against the wall. She too had her wounds wrapped, though Kai blinked away surprise at seeing her in Miya's clothes. They were too big, swallowing Ama's limbs. Her legs were bare—easy access to the bandages—and Kai realized that despite their similarities, the white wolf healed slower than he did. Blood had seeped through the gauze around her thigh, and she appeared content to limit her movements.

"I feel like shit." Kai pushed up on one elbow, inching his way into a seated position. Ripper scampered past him, apparently disturbed that he was still alive. Kai realized he was on the floor, towels spread under him to catch the mess. They were soiled, but his bandages looked clean. "What happened?"

"You nearly died." She shrugged. "I had to dig a bullet out of your chest. You're lucky you didn't drown in your own blood."

Kai squeezed his eyes shut and groaned. "Miya and Caelan?"

"Safe," Ama said softly. "Physically, anyway."

"Great." It came out glum. "Can't believe I missed his fucking throat."

"You were in a bind."

Disbelief wrinkled Kai's brow. Had she just defended him?

She sighed, gaze sliding to the adjacent wall. "You did the best you could, and it *was* enough, albeit at your own expense."

Silence curdled the air, all his sharp wit leaving him. "You held the fort down," he finally mustered. "Team effort...I guess."

She managed a half-smile, a lazy curl at the corner of her mouth. Then, she rose, favoring her uninjured leg. "We retrieved your clothes on the way back."

He nodded, tracking her as she hobbled past him and fished his phone out of his discarded jacket. It was the second time his things had to be picked up from that damn park.

"I'm borrowing this," she said. "Crowbar's probably worried."

Kai made no response, accepting her sudden familiarity. It was what Miya would've wanted. He listened for signs of life in the rest of the apartment. Someone was in the shower, and as Ama opened the door to the bedroom, Caelan murmured something and scuttled out, holding an ice pack to her sprained arm.

"Hey," Kai greeted with an awkward wave.

She didn't reply as she ambled closer, then dropped to the floor in front of him, shoulders sagging. Kai shifted his legs and sat up straighter, unsure of what to say to a teenage fetch who kept trying, unwillingly, to kill her human double. She dropped the ice pack and pressed the ball of her hand to the shadows purpling her under eyes.

"Kill me."

A morbid joke, poorly timed. Kai waved her off. "Not worth the jail time."

Her head snapped up. "I'm serious." Her voice was low, shaky, and her throat bobbed before she said again, "I want you to kill me."

This time, he didn't dismiss her. Jaw clamped, Kai fought the pinch of anger that twisted his mouth into a sneer. He trained his eyes on the girl, trying in vain to measure his words. "Why the fuck would you ask me that?"

"Because there's no way out for me." She crossed her legs and rocked forward, the admission strained, the hunch in her back reminiscent of an animal in pain. Back and forth, back and forth, she swayed until she got hold of whatever tore at her insides, then met his gaze. "You're the only one who understands..."

"Understands what?" Kai all but barked.

She was undeterred by his brusqueness, searching for something behind his stony glare—compassion, symbiosis. "That sometimes, doing the right thing feels like shit. Sometimes, you've got to be the bad guy to make things right."

The aloofness he wore like armor cracked, and her desperation lanced through his ribs. The request was earnest, not a dramatic outburst from an overwhelmed child. He realized, to his horror, that she'd thought this through. Sighing heavily, the stiffness bled from his shoulders. "I won't let you kill anyone," he vowed. "I'll stop you a thousand times if I have to, but I'm not going to hurt you. We'll find another way."

"There is no other way!" Her palm hit the floor. "How many times do I have to come within arm's reach of her for you to learn that it's never going to stop?"

"As many fucking times as it takes for your curse to learn that *I* don't stop," Kai snarled.

"That's crazy—"

"No," he interrupted, "it's survival. Life's a mean bitch, and she'll drag you to the gates of hell just to get off, but dying is pointless."

"It's not pointless." Caelan's voice lowered. "It'll save *her*..."

"No, it won't." Arm coiled around his ribs, Kai scooted closer with a wince and clasped Caelan's shoulder. "Your human double? She *wants* to die."

Shock skittered through her features. "But...why?"

"Same reason as you. She's miserable and wants out." Kai gave her a light squeeze, his tone softening. "Your death won't improve her life. It's just an escape hatch for *you*."

Caelan pulled back as if struck, and his hand fell away. She rasped, breaths reedy, and with a forceful shudder, she crumpled to the floor, a desolate keen crawling from her battered bones. Kai noticed the bandage around her arm where one of Pyotr's bullets had whizzed by. He'd missed, and no thanks to Kai. Alina fought her father hard enough to save the person who'd come to take her life. How was it that both girl and fetch wanted to die? And for what? To alleviate the despair inflicted by a soulless tyrant?

"I don't want to kill anyone." Caelan curled into a fetal position, her anguish palpable. "I don't...I don't..."

Kai inhaled shakily, his chest hurting from more than the collapsed lung. "I know you don't."

His entire life was tarnished by violence. Sometimes a victim but frequently the perpetrator, he was intimately aware of how one inspired the other. Round and round it went—a fucked up merry-go-round that spun his entire world on a single axis: trauma. He looked down at Caelan, sobs wracking her whole, despondency brambling her like a thorny rope. He lay a gentle hand on her hair.

"I won't let you walk my path."

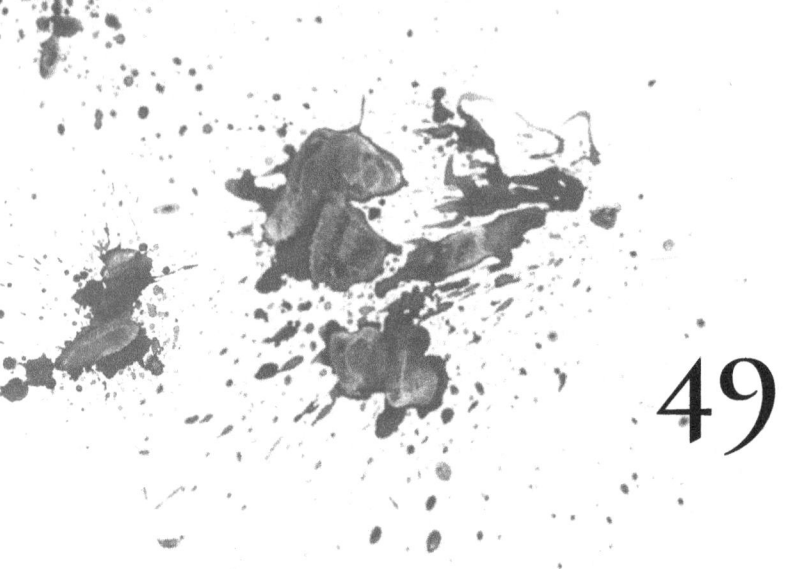

49

TWENTY HOURS LEFT.

They were running out of time, and Kai doubted Zverev granted extensions. After exhaustion pulled Caelan into a listless sleep, Ripper at her side, Kai, Miya, and Ama sat in silence, bled dry of ideas. Eventually, Ama came to the same conclusion that Kai had: one of the girls had to die.

"Gavran saw something," Miya said as though it were a rebuttal. "Right before I killed the leshy, I swear he saw something."

Yet she couldn't impart what, exactly, the damn bird had seen. He'd kept that nugget to himself and was nowhere to be found, an inky blob lost in the night sky. Ama seemed about as optimistic as Kai's deflated lung. Secrets were like shiny bobbles to the raven; if he decided to hoard them, even the devil couldn't pry them from his greedy little talons.

Gavran withheld information for a reason, obscure as it might've been. Perhaps he'd gleaned a way to save Alina and free Caelan, but the cost was too high in his calculation. Gavran was a pragmatist. He loved only Ama and the Dreamwalker, and Kai wagered he'd let the whole world burn to spare either woman an ounce of discomfort.

Whatever solution he'd found wasn't one he thought worth pursuing.

After several hours of puttering, Ama changed and left for the King of Spades, bracing for a scolding from Crowbar, and later, probably Bastien. Kai angrily yanked the pullout free and changed the sheets. When Miya emerged from the bathroom with her day clothes discarded, her forlorn expression seized him like a rabbit snare. She'd shed her armor, all pretense of toughness, and as her gaze caught his, he found himself staring at her shame.

Eyes rimmed with tears, she swallowed a whimper before wiping the moisture from her face.

Shit. Fuck. Shit.

"Sorry," she said through a chuckle, sensing his panic. "I just feel a bit raw."

Limbs stilted beneath her oversized T-shirt, she joined him in the living room. He wrapped both arms around her, and she pressed her cheek to his bare chest, a line of fresh bruises mottling his ribs and sternum.

"You almost died because I fell asleep." The whisper was a self-indictment and a confession.

"You're worse than a Disney princess," he cracked, relieved when she snorted on a laugh, her warm breath tickling his skin.

"I don't know how I'd live with myself if—"

He pulled back and took her face in his hands. "It's not the first time I've sparred with death."

"It's the first time I've conked out in the middle of an emergency," said Miya. "How stupid would that be? If you died because I couldn't stay awake?"

"Pretty stupid," he admitted, then smirked. "But not half as stupid as some of the shit I've pulled." He patted her cheek. "Stop tenderizing yourself, Lambchop."

She nodded, and he reluctantly let her go. He knew there'd be no mollifying her guilt, but he could at least inform her that it was self-inflicted. Kai didn't hold grudges, least of all against Miya. They half crawled under the covers, though neither made to lie down.

"Since you already had a nap today"—Kai grinned when she shot him a lethal glare—"I figured you could spare a few minutes to talk."

She perked up against the couch's backrest, her curiosity palpable. The weight of the last few days had grown too heavy. No matter what he'd endured, some burdens couldn't be borne alone—didn't have to be.

"Mikhail Zverev..." His gaze dropped to his hands as he turned his palms up—always calloused, always marked by hardship. "My own goddamn ghost."

Miya was silent as he recounted his conversation with Ivan, the memory that'd threaded through his bones, the fact that Mikhail Zverev had died in the woods with his parents.

That day, Kai Donovan was born.

"So, the nightmares..." Miya ventured.

"Repressed shit from my past, I guess." He shrugged. "Not all mine. Some of it's...I don't know, ancestral?"

"How do you know?"

Kai scooted down on the mattress and tucked a hand behind his head. "He recognized me," he said of the man on the train.

After a protracted moment, Miya crawled over him, caging his waist with her knees. "There's a lot inside you. Not just your past, but your family's too. You never got the chance to work out what their lives meant—what they gave you. It becomes this...thing in the corner of your eye, always there but just out of reach."

Kai quirked a brow. "You sound like you know about it."

Miya shook her head with a tepid smile. "I'm no expert, but I see it in people's dreams. We all inherit things that don't belong to us. For you, it's a history you were severed from when you stopped being Mikhail Zverev."

The air flowed easier in his lungs now, and he skimmed his fingertips up her thighs. "Want to make me a promise?"

She nearly malfunctioned, unaccustomed to such solemn requests from him. "Um, sure."

He smiled wryly. "No laws will be broken." Kai rarely asked for anything, and it wasn't admirable. He'd glimpsed that same unsavory quality in Caelan, who would rather die than be a liability. The only reason she'd sought Kai's help—if it could be called *help*—was because she'd sensed the same pattern in him. She thought he'd understand, and shamefully, he did.

"Come find me." Mahogany met murky green, imploring. They both knew what he meant, what awaited him on the other side of consciousness. Miya wove her fingers with his, and he brushed his thumb over the back of her hand.

"Next time I'm in hell," Kai said, "help me get the fuck out."

50

THE AROMA *of smoked meat filled the small kitchen. An aged wood table, stone hearth, and a mint green fridge too small for a family crowded the small room. Eggshell walls surrounded him, the plaster stained with time and use.*

Kai looked around the cramped apartment, the ceiling higher than expected. A woman stood at the kitchen counter as she sliced winter salami. Lush black tresses cascaded down her back, untamed and bristly like the shorn hair on Kai's head. It'd been years since he'd trimmed it so short. She turned toward him, her eyes glimmering like garnets, echoing his own.

His mother.

The lines of her face were clear now, like a painting he'd finally gotten close enough to see.

"Misha."

A man's voice—stern but familiar. Kai turned toward the call, some long slumbering part of him stirring. It was the same man from the fields, his face no longer a blur. Hair the color of roasted coffee brushed across severe eyebrows, the rest of it messily cropped around his ears and neck. Broad shoulders, sable eyes, and harsh angles softened by the shadow of course stubble. He extended a piece of dark rye spread with white lard.

His mother gestured with her knife. "Zakonchi svoy obed."

Finish your lunch.

Kai accepted the bread, realizing then how small his hand was. A child's hand, smooth and unblemished by adversity. He raised the slice to his lips, the savory aroma of pig fat dizzying him with nostalgia. A stolen moment. Eyes drifting shut, Kai held the air in his lungs like he was clinging to life itself. Then, he allowed himself a bite. The bread was soft, its earthy flavor complimented by the saltiness of the lard. As the bread's nuttiness rose to the surface, it took on a different taste.

Kai opened his eyes, the colors of his meal reversed—white bread topped with a thick layer of peanut butter.

"Finish your lunch."

The voice was old and graveled, eroding his courage until he barely managed to look up. Alice stood by the window above an old sink brimming with dishes.

Kai soaked up the shoebox kitchen from his seat at the table—gnarled appliances and paltry counter space cluttered with a microwave and a half-busted toaster. Alice raised a cigarette to her lips, the tip aglow before she exhaled, and the smoke filtered outside. She clutched her cane, knobby fingers twitching against the worn grip. The runnels of her face were caked with makeup; she never cared that people thought of her as an old crone in red lipstick. Alice took her time with the bathroom mirror. She wore her age with pride, and she refused to stay out of sight or out of mind.

Kai glanced down at his peanut butter and toast. His hand was bigger now, that of a boy on the cusp of adulthood, but it was too soon...still far too soon. His breath hitched in his throat, dread drumming through his veins. He knew what came next.

"Thought you were fine, huh?"

Alice's words cleaved through him, a sharp, lancing kind of pain.

"What?" The voice was not his own, and yet it was. A sound from the past—something that no longer existed.

Carmine lips stretched thin over yellowing teeth. Her frizzy hair was gray at the roots, the rest of it a faded, brassy orange that Kai knew had once been vibrant as poppies. "It's okay, pup. We're all a little fucked up, but there's still love in the world, isn't there?"

Kai dropped the toast to the table. There was no plate—only a piece of paper towel. "What love?"

Alice canted her head, her pale green eyes drooping with melancholy. I missed you, they said. "She loves you."

"I know."

Her smile turned wistful. "Do you?"

Before he could answer, the house tilted. Chairs slid from the table as Kai's end of the bungalow lifted from the ground, the other weighted by *steel. Scrambling for a handhold, he saw Alice move with the floor as it slipped out from under him. The house lay her down, her body flush with the soil.*

Kai stubbornly resisted the near ninety-degree incline, his feet and elbows shimmied into the crooks where ceiling met wall. He searched frantically for his caretaker, but the kitchen had fallen away, leaving only a bare four-walled box before him. A casket.

Alice lay inside, her hands clasped gracefully across her stomach. Her face was serene but expressionless, her powderless skin wan, and her clothes moth-eaten but respectable. They'd been so poor, and funerals were expensive. Kai hadn't been allowed to arrange it; the local church said they'd take care of it, but something told him it wasn't out of compassion. They pitied him—another lost cause, another drain on their tax dollars. The gesture was little more than a self-aggrandizing pat on the back. No one bothered showing up to the wake, like it was revenge for all the years Alice had refused to play demure, to stay out of sight and out of mind. Now, they were determined to pretend she'd never existed.

Kai's hands shook as he gripped the lip of the casket. Tears gathered somewhere behind his eyes, but he held them back. No one could see him cry; they'd only relish his grief. He balled up his fists and forced the trembling deep into his middle where it couldn't be found—not even by him. With his hand finally stayed, he bowed his head and reached for Alice, eyes squeezed shut as his fingertips grazed her cheek.

"Don't fucking touch me, freak."

Shock flooded him, forcing his gaze up.

Alice was gone.

Blue fabric filled the space where her face had been, and Kai clenched it in a white-knuckled grip. He had someone by the shirt—an old classmate who was sneering, lurching forward. Knuckles connected with Kai's jaw, and he stumbled back, tonguing the sore spot on the inside of his cheek. Rage ignited in his core—that rotten cavity that cradled every shred of grief over Alice. With a feral roar, he threw himself at his assailant. They fell onto the pavement, the boy on his back and Kai on top of him. Teeth bared, the bridge of his nose rippled as he snarled and crushed a fist to the boy's face.

Freak.

He'd show them just how much of a monster he was. A beast. A zver.

Kai knew he was stronger, hardier. He pulled his punches during scraps; a little too much too fast could do more than bruise. This time, he didn't care. He wanted to maim, to flay flesh from bone until only a gritty mass of slop remained—a carcass for the crows.

Blood sprayed across Kai's face, painting him red. The wet smack of pulverized meat was barely audible above the ringing in his ears, but something broke through the fugue—the sudden absence of a hammering heart, the boy's pulse fading to a slow, languid beat. His features were unrecognizable, distorted, limbs splayed, his body still—so completely still —a scarlet Rorschach butterflying across his tattered shirt.

Realization struck with a heavy hand. Kai flew back from the limp body, vision blurring crimson. He knew the boy had lived. The incident spurred his flight from Granite Falls, but the asshole had lived, even if just barely.

You couldn't have known for sure, a voice in the back of his head reprimanded. He could've died just as easily.

For once, Kai had gotten lucky.

"Shit," he muttered, wiping the gore from his face. It was in his eyes, his mouth, the smell of iron dizzying. When he finally cleared enough of it to see again, his hand came away with something clasped between blood-stained fingers.

A piece of lilac card, Alice's words as clear as the day she'd written them.

Happy Birthday, Kai Donovan.

Cruel. Life was so fucking cruel, and it made his mind even crueler.

The pavement vanished. Kai teetered off balance, hitting something with his shoulder. The decayed brown walls of the train encased him, corpses swaying on dull meat hooks with every judder on the tracks. Kai's gaze swung to the soldier who'd handed him the card. He was still seated on the floor, arm outstretched, his red-brown eyes unblinking. He stared at Kai as if waiting for him to realize something. What, Kai didn't know. He was alone—a stranger on a prison train with only a ghost for company.

"What do you want from me?" The words left him as a whisper, barely seeping through clenched teeth. He'd been this man—seen through his eyes. But what was the point?

Slowly, the soldier lowered his arm. His head canted, and he peered past Kai's shoulder at something behind him. Kai whirled into an abysmal tunnel of death and pestilence, the end as distant as the light in a cadaver's eyes.

Then, movement. A shadow blacker than the rest glided forward like a plume of smoke, only it was a solid thing, filling the space between the walls. As it treaded closer, a glimmer of lavender pierced the pall—a mote in the murk. Gradually, edges formed, lines contouring into a familiar shape. A face Kai knew, a scent he sought comfort in.

Miya.

The dream stone hung around her neck—the source of the purple glow. She always said it helped her find her way. Kai never paid it much attention, but now, he understood. It was her lantern in the dark. Her muddy green eyes seemed brighter against the muted backdrop of the train car. They sparked with recognition, but behind her resolve, Kai glimpsed uncertainty about where she'd found herself: the inside of his mind.

The last time she'd stumbled into his dreams, he'd pushed her out—scared her off not with his darkness, but with his refusal to let her see it. This time, there'd be no huffing or puffing, no menacing howl from the Big Bad Wolf.

Little Red Riding Hood was here to stay.

Her fingers threaded with his, her skin somehow warm even in the damp cold of the dream. She squeezed his hand and smiled, then looked around the train car, her expression neutral as she passed over the bodies littering the grime-covered floor. Her eyes fell on the soldier, then tracked to the lilac birthday card Kai held.

"I think we're related." Kai flipped the keepsake between his fingers. "He's not me, but he is—was..." he fumbled. "I don't know."

Miya dropped into a crouch, their hands still linked, and studied the man. "He has your eyes."

The soldier tilted his head the other way, curious about the new passenger on his train. He was so quiet, so docile. Kai had no memory of this person, yet here he was, lurking in the recesses of his mind.

There's a lot inside you. Not just your past, but your family's too.

Miya had said those words to him. He never should've doubted her understanding. She too contended with a legacy disconnected from her by lifetimes—the Dreamwalker's legacy.

We all inherit things that don't belong to us.

Kai's gaze slid to the woman who'd witnessed the worst parts of him and stayed. It wasn't blind loyalty, he realized. She stayed because he'd carved out space for her when his world grew too small, too suffocating. And he'd done it because she'd asked. Because he loved her enough to try.

Kai nearly choked on the word. Love. It stuck in his throat even when it lived solely in his thoughts. Eventually, it would go down easier.

Iridescent feathers sprouted along Miya's spine, her tell-tale shroud enveloping her in a violet and midnight sheen. "Let me help you," she said from behind her bone-beak mask.

A frisson of dread wound through Kai's middle. He clinched Alice's card as though she could give him strength through a ratty old memento. Maybe she could. Hope swelled in his chest, pushing out his resistance. Then, he nodded.

Miya could shatter the boundary between realms. Why not the boundary between past and present?

She adjusted her grip around his hand, and with the other, placed her fingers across the soldier's cheek. He watched, compliant and unconcerned that this feather-clad creature plumbed through his history. The dream stone lit up like a beacon, shimmers of gold, meadow green, and lavender warming the shadows. The cloak around Miya's shoulders lengthened, the plumage extending like a tree sprouting new shoots. They devoured the floorboards sodden with rot, overpowering the scene set by Kai's own mind.

It was terrifying, relinquishing control to the Dreamwalker, allowing her to be his conduit to a past he didn't remember. Except he never did have control, did he? He'd only been hurt and refused to let anyone look too closely at his wounds. It wasn't control, he realized; it was desperation.

The dank walls with their rusty meat hooks dissolved under the shine of violet-black feathers. Kai found himself back in the apartment with his parents, his child's body confining him to his seat at the table. The soldier and Miya had joined him, both standing in the corner behind Kai's father. The soldier's eyes swept over the small room, then stopped at the woman who Kai knew to be his mother.

The rye bread in Kai's hand was half eaten like he'd only been gone for a minute. He took in his mother's appearance again, memorizing the lines of her face, her strong frame, the thin silver chain around her neck. An open locket with a broken clasp dangled at the end of those delicate links, but it was empty.

"Why aren't there any photos?" Kai asked, his voice strange in his ears.

His mother blinked, then pinched the locket between her fingers, smoothing over the engravings on the outer shell. "My parents—your grandparents—gave it to me, but they had no photos to put in it. Everything was burned during the war, and after that, they were too poor to afford a camera."

"Why were they poor?" Kai asked, and his father snorted on a suppressed laugh, exchanging an amused glance with his wife. Something about the bluntness of children, Kai supposed.

His mother dropped the locket and smiled. "Your grandpa was a soldier in the Red Army. One of the best," she said, her face lighting up. "But he was a Crimean Tatar. Many of his people were deported near the end of the war."

Kai's face scrunched, and he folded his legs under him. "Why? Did they do something wrong?"

The woman shook her head, and she looked in the soldier's direction, though she peered right through him. "Humans always fear difference. When times are good, we can suppress that fear and tolerate those unlike us. But in hardship, fear is like a virus, and no one is immune. That's when people show their true colors."

His father chimed in, "It's easy being kind when your life is without worries." He pointed at the half-eaten bread, silently instructing Kai to finish it. "If you want to know how big someone's heart is, watch them when they're in pain. Pay attention when they have something to lose."

Kai's mother fiddled with her locket, her voice somber. "Your grandpa did nothing wrong. He just happened to be a little different at a time when people were scared, suspicious, and their hearts were too small."

Miya wrapped her arms around her middle, pain twisting her face. She met Kai's gaze, and he wondered if this was hard on her—delving into secrets locked away by time and self-defense.

"So, he was deported?" Kai asked after his grandfather.

His mother nodded. "He was exiled to a labor camp in Western Siberia —spent nine years there. When he was released, he went to Surgut, where he met your grandma."

"Was she also deported?"

The woman chuckled. "No, she was a Volga Tatar born here in Surgut."

Kai glanced down at his bread. Only a few bites left. His attention flicked to his father. "Can you beat that story?"

His father threw his head back and laughed raucously, the tenor eerily familiar. Miya twitched in the corner, recognizing the maniacal sound as well.

"No," his father said. "I moved here with my parents when the city was growing. I was just a kid like you. Lots of oil here, so my father got a job in the gas industry, and here we are."

"Sounds boring," Kai yawned. Two bites left.

His father tsked. *"You take after your mother, and she's far more colorful."*

The comment earned him a playful swipe from the woman, who then reached across the table and tapped her son's nose. *"It's true. You have your grandfather's eyes."*

Kai clamped his jaw, his gaze drifting to the ghost in the corner. He peered into the soldier's eyes, seeing in them his mother's garnet stare—a likeness Kai carried since birth. His mother's side had been branded; it was why she'd yearned to flee. He remembered that now—the suffering inflicted from one generation to the next. Through her parents, she'd inherited something unspeakable just as Kai had. But that wasn't all. By law, Kai would've been forced into compulsory military service for a state that'd harmed his mother's family. She wanted better for him, and she wanted to get away. He'd held on to that truth his whole life; he just hadn't known it.

Kai tentatively finished the last of his meal. In it, he tasted not only the flavors of childhood in Surgut, but those of his time in Granite Falls. It was supposed to be a better life, and perhaps it was, but it'd also violently severed Kai from everything he'd known to be home.

As he swallowed the last of his bread, the kitchen faded like wet paint bleeding down a canvas. Only Miya and the soldier remained. The soldier smiled and bid farewell to his grandson, now a man with years of youth unraveling before him.

Where the bread had been, Kai now held Alice's lilac birthday card, no longer stained with the blood from his hands.

51

MIYA

MIYA AWOKE COCOONED in Kai's warmth. A feather-like touch trailed down her spine, the movement languid and gentle—the calm before the storm. Gasping through gritted teeth, Kai's body tensed as consciousness brought with it all the weight of reality, and he fisted the back of Miya's shirt. Only the sound of their breathing filled the silence until finally, his hold on her slackened.

Miya arched her neck, peeking up at him. "Are you okay?"

The days had been filled with lit fuses in a mountain of long-buried memories, bound to erupt eventually. The debris was inescapable, thrusting Miya into Kai's nightmares unbidden. But this time, he'd called to her, invited her in. He trusted her, finally letting her into the dark crevices he guarded with sharpened claws and bloodied fangs.

"I'm fine," he replied, his voice sounding like it'd been raked over coals. His fingertips danced across her shoulder blades, up her neck, combing through her dark brown tresses.

"Do you want to talk about it?" Miya too felt the aftereffects of the shadows he harbored. She'd come face to face with the history that'd cultivated him, but she'd grown bolder in confronting what couldn't be seen—only felt.

"Later."

Protest bubbled up, her desire for closure bumping up against his deflection. "I—"

Kai didn't let her finish. He crashed his mouth to hers before she could get the words out—a firmer refusal, a deferral in favor of more fervent things. Things that were difficult to thwart when they were both so raw. She ran her fingers through his disheveled hair, sweat beading the ends of his bristle-like strands.

"Kai…" she tried again, his breath glancing off her face.

He silenced her with a torrid stare, his eyes sparking red when a passing pair of headlights lit up the room. "Shut up," he said—a quiet desperation, "and let me have this." His hand clasped her hip, slipped under her shirt, singed her skin. He was like fire incarnate, pure heat and hunger that knew nothing of restraint or moderation. And right now, he didn't need words. He needed reprieve.

Miya swallowed her reply and put her mouth to better use. Her back arched when he cupped her breast, calloused palms roaming over her as though for the first time. A strangled sound left him as he yanked off her shirt. The hard plane of his torso moved over her, and his elbows caged her in when she hauled him close. If there was anything they both lamented about the dreamscape, it was the absence of pure physicality. Things were still felt and tasted, but it wasn't the same. Miya understood the ethereal plane, but Kai preferred this one. He'd shown her everything he could through the Dreamwalker's lens, but his world was one of the senses, and he demanded she meet him there.

One arm wound around his neck, and the other dipped lower, fingers prying at his waistband until he kicked off his pants. When he broke away, his thumb dragged across her cheek, snagging her bottom lip, and the other pulled her underwear aside to graze over her vulva. His mouth seared a path over her collar bone, between her breasts, then lower.

Kai spread her legs, his every stroke unhurried, torturous. Miya buried her fingers in his thick hair and tugged, reaping a throaty growl that turned muffled when he finally lost himself between her thighs. Her knees hooked over his shoulders, tattered gasps becoming moans as a familiar tension coiled in her core. When she began to crest, he looked up her body and met her gaze.

"Not yet," he answered her questioning glance, then rose to his knees. "Not unless you want to come for me twice."

She didn't have it in her—not tonight. Not after traversing his memories, feeling everything he'd felt. She just wanted to be close. Her legs encircled his waist, and she dragged him forward. As he fell into her, Miya pressed herself to his chest, every groove and line of his body etching into her skin. Contact. Reassurance. A way to say what couldn't be spoken. Words were imperfect, incomplete.

His mouth was on hers again, teeth catching lips, his tongue rough against her own. Her hips churned to his rhythm, the feel of him inside her as intoxicating as his taste. Kai cursed under his breath, a harsh whisper in her ear. His fingers curled into the sheets as Miya dug her nails into his shoulder, release a promise at the edge of his touch.

Being unraveled was hardly a gentle thing. It was a violent sort of pleasure, an unmooring that flayed you open, stripped you down to your barest parts. How many times had Kai watched her come undone? How many nights had they spent tangled up in one another, drawing out that moment of surrender as though it were the simplest thing in the world? Love and sex were disparate worlds, but entangled bodies sometimes revealed more than lofty proclamations. All Miya had to do was listen.

Kai eased himself down on top of her when that moment ended. He groaned into the pillow, his palm skimming the length of her body. "I needed that," he said through a heavy exhale, then rolled onto his back and draped an arm over his abdomen.

Miya tucked her feet under the tousled blankets and smiled, her pulse still thrumming. "Your steely self-control really fooled me."

He shot her a withering look. "You dig up repressed memories like they're buried treasure, Lambchop."

"Hope we struck the motherload."

"Judging by the post-traumatic nightmare fucking, I'd say you *exhumed* at least a few gold nuggets."

Miya couldn't suppress the snort that slipped out. "Did you just whip up a double entendre about your dead relatives?"

"What can I say"—Kai shrugged—"humor helps me cope."

Shuffling closer, she thumped her head onto his shoulder. "Did you ever meet your grandparents?"

He shook his head, absently lifting his arm for her. "They died before I was born. Bad health, I think. Most of my mom's side got split up, being Tatar and all that."

Ethnic cleansing fractured families for generations, possibly forever. "What about your dad's parents? They were just Russian, right?"

"Well, they weren't shipped off to any gulags, so I always

assumed so." He squinted at the ceiling, then grunted. "I think they kicked the bucket pretty young too. My parents were alone, and that made it easier to leave."

Miya balked at the idiom. *So irreverent*, she thought, then jabbed him in the ribs.

He twitched and glanced down at her with a dark chuckle. He knew what he'd done. "On that topic," he began, "are you going to tell Caelan, or will I?"

Miya blinked, confusion pulling her mouth into a frown. "Tell her what?"

Kai flashed her a wolfish grin, chillingly nonchalant as he said, "That you killed her favorite woodland shit disturber."

Realization sank in like a boulder plummeting to the bottom of a lake. *The leshy*. Whining behind pursed lips, Miya trundled into Kai as he cackled.

He patted her on the back. "Tag team it is."

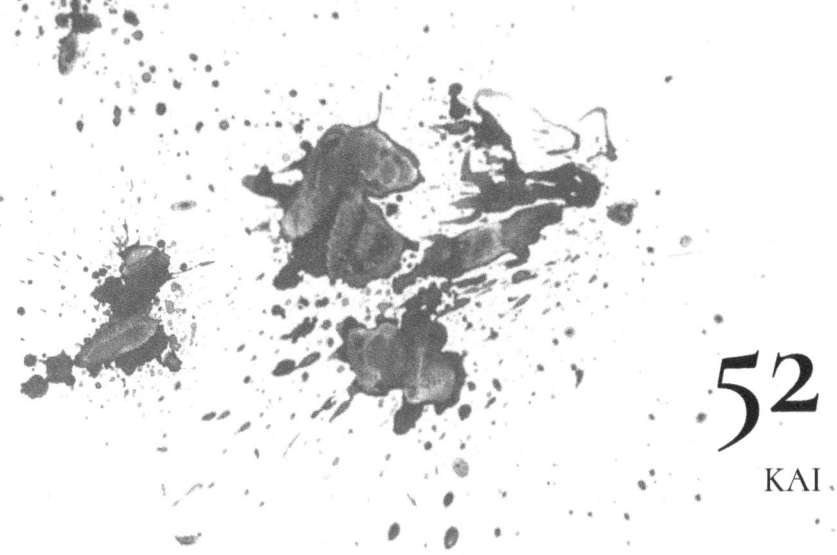

52

KAI

THE TALK WITH CAELAN WENT...FINE. There were tears, group hugs that Kai reluctantly partook in, and a stack of fluffernutters that left the pantry half empty. As if on cue, Ursula slammed a fist on the door with banana bread on offer. She must've smelled the sorrow seeping through the walls.

Kai had never been great at comforting others. His impulse was to shove the pain aside and fill the chasm it left behind with pleasurable distractions. But his approach had little merit with Miya and Caelan. Miya didn't hide her wounds; she ripped deeper into them, sticking her fingers where it hurt most until she located the source of the infection. She interrogated herself constantly, and while Kai didn't envy the discomfort of the process, he coveted the results. She wasn't afraid of her demons, and perhaps that was why he'd kept her from his own.

When Caelan first broke down that morning, Kai wanted to run. He didn't know what to say to make the loss more palatable, and he knew better than to remind Caelan that the leshy brought out the unwanted killer in her. Harsh truths rarely provided refuge from grief. So, they let her cry until she was empty, reminded her that she wasn't alone, then gave her food she loved and a snarling orange munchkin to warm her lap. Small mercies were better than none.

Kai wondered how a fetch could be so human—more human than he ever felt. Did she take on the traits of her double? How did she conceive of herself? He'd always been assured in his sense of self, but his nightmares and ball-crushing therapist taught him that no one existed in a vacuum. No one got sole ownership over their identity.

The alleyway door to the Confessional felt heavier than it should've as Kai pushed his way inside. It was quiet, the bar closed midday, the kitchen empty save for someone prepping before opening. Rounding the corner into the dining room, Kai found Connor stocking liquor on the shelves. Sergei sat at the counter sipping an old fashioned, not bothering to turn when Connor greeted Kai.

"How's the kid?" the bartender asked, and only then did Sergei glance over his shoulder, ears perked.

"Tired." True but evasive. It'd been a rough night followed by a rougher morning. Caelan's mental health was important, but so was her life. They had less than twelve hours to get her off Pyotr's radar.

"Why'd you call me here?" Sergei sounded more cantankerous than usual.

Kai sidled up to them and took the stool next to Sergei. "I don't have enough brain cells to solve my problem." He explained Caelan's origins, his bargain with Zverev, and his ill-conceived plan to murder Pyotr—conveniently foiled by the leshy.

"You think one of them is done for," said Sergei, poking at the orange peel on the rim of his glass.

Kai nodded toward the bourbon behind Connor. "Not sure I like the idea of killing a fifteen-year-old, no matter how badly she wants to die."

"The fetch?" Connor asked, pouring Kai a finger.

"Both of them." Kai dragged the glass toward himself. "They're trapped, both willing to die to free the other."

"How noble." Sergei snorted. "What if there's no other way? You could take the burden off one of them."

Kai's eyes flicked to Connor's disdainful stare. "I could."

"Then what's stopping you? Guilt?" Sergei pressed.

"I can live with guilt. What I can't live with is a shit-stain like Pyotr being the reason for it. He doesn't get to ruin two kids' lives, then make me their executioner." Kai's jaw ticked, and he threw back the bourbon. "Fuck that."

Sergei lowered his gaze. "You're right. They'll be nothing more than casualties. Even if you kill Alina to save your fetch, Pyotr won't stop. He'll hunt that girl to the ends of the earth to sate his pride."

"The only person whose life is worth taking here is your boss's," Connor chimed in. "He's a damn blight, and you know it."

"Agreed," said Kai, lifting his empty glass to Connor.

"It would behoove me to withhold my opinion on that," Sergei grumbled. "Either way, he's only half the picture. Eliminating Pyotr won't stop one girl from trying to kill and replace the other. The only solution would be to murder father and daughter."

Kai's shoulders slumped with another sigh.

Connor hung his head and swore. "Right...and I call myself Irish."

"We all have our flaws—" Kai stopped mid-sentence and sat pin straight. His breath hitched, and his head snapped toward the back door. "Company."

Before Sergei or Connor could ask for clarification, a sound like thunder crashed through the bar. A chorus of footsteps pummeled the floorboards as a dozen armed men filed into the dining room and surrounded them. Kai expected a police raid, but as he scanned the intruders, he didn't see a single one in uniform. They weren't cops; they were mobsters. They'd already unholstered their guns—semi-automatic pistols and revolvers, all of them with suppressors.

Kai's skin prickled with heat, his stomach revolting at the sight of the firearms. He never got over the visceral reaction they gave him—a reminder that his parents were stolen too soon. Pointless. Preventable. He would've traded his soul to forget, to feel nothing, but the pain was a token left behind by Mikhail Zverev.

"What the hell is this?" Connor bellowed. "We're neutral territory, you dumb fucks."

Sergei blanched next to them, his pulse skittering wildly beneath wan skin. He recognized them.

"Not anymore." One of the goons stepped forward. He clasped his hands in front of him, fisting his gun as he tapped the barrel against his navy slacks. His shoulder holster cut across a well-ironed dress shirt, his matching blazer barely obscuring the strap. "This is Pyotr's bar now."

Kai remained seated, calculating. He could beat up twelve men. That they were armed was inconvenient, but eating a few bullets wouldn't kill him so long as they weren't well-placed. His wounds from the park were healing well, and once the adrenaline kicked in, he wouldn't feel them screaming.

Connor's fingers twitched behind the counter. He had a strict no firearm policy. Given the clientele, minimizing the number of triggers seemed wise—not that a hidden rifle under the sink would've done much good against a dozen gun-toting assholes. "Why the hell does Pyotr want my bar? He already owns half the city."

The goon tapping his thigh flashed a crooked smile, his gaze sliding to Sergei. "There's a rat infestation. We're here to clean out the vermin. As payment, Pyotr's installing new management. To ensure things are...up to code."

Kai snorted. *Up to code.* So, Pyotr knew Sergei was conspiring to keep Caelan safe. Maybe he'd gotten sloppy. Either way, the outcome was on their hands.

"I didn't hire any exterminators," Connor shot back, and several chuckles flitted through the pack.

"Community service," replied the mobster, his smile widening.

If Ama were here, she'd goad him for mucking up his metaphor. Community service was free.

"No need. There's already a mouser on property." Kai grinned. "And my teeth are sharp."

"You're still vermin," he spat.

"You sure you're pest control, or are you just here to replace rats with roaches?"

A few of the men pitched forward as Sergei grabbed Kai's shoulder to rein him in. Even if he hadn't lunged for anyone's throat, he lacked the restraint to bridle his tongue.

"You're also coming with us." The leader lifted his gun in Kai's direction. "You had a deal with Pyotr—a job to do. The boss doesn't take kindly to liars."

Kai wasn't listening. The second that fucking barrel leveled at him, carnage painted his vision. "Then catch me if you can," he growled, darting off the stool faster than Sergei could think to stop him.

He closed the distance before anyone could take aim, elbowing the inside of the goon's forearm to slacken his grip. The gun thudded to the floor, and Kai kicked it toward the bar, then grasped the man by his too-gelled hair. With a rough jerk, he forced their gazes to meet. "You want blood?" His voice was feral, graveled by rage. "I'll give you blood."

A strangled rasp was all the man mustered before Kai ripped an oily tuft from the back of his head, then kicked him square in the chest. Kai heard several ribs shatter before the man flew across the bar and crashed into a table, retching as he coughed up his insides. Disbelieving stares whipped toward the mess. Shocked silence. Quiet mutters. Then, the simultaneous clicks of a dozen safety mechanisms going off. Every single gun in the room pointed at Kai.

Reckless? Yes. Satisfying? Also yes. But Kai would rather dig bullets out of his own body than let Pyotr's men abduct him for some perceived slight. They surrounded him, thinking that if they cut him off, he'd have no choice but to go quietly. But all they'd done was aim their weapons at each other. A cocktail of cortisol, sweat, and iron hit Kai's nose, the odor invigorating. They were afraid of him. Pyotr sent twelve men to subdue one because they knew they'd be fighting a beast.

Kai scanned their faces, stopping at the one that stank strongest like chicken shit. Mouth quirking into a smirk, Kai winked, then ducked left. The man panicked. His gun went off, directionless, and someone in the circle screamed, their leg buckling.

Two down, Kai thought, using his momentum to side-check one of the other buffoons straight into the bar where Connor wrapped a dish towel around his neck, wrestling him into a chokehold. Snatching his gun before he could use it, Sergei pistol-whipped the man's face until he crumpled. They both stooped behind the bar, though hardly anyone paid them any mind, their focus on Kai as he pivoted behind a post for cover, then sprang at one of the mobsters, knocking his skull into the floor with a loud crack. Another gunshot went off, muffled by the suppressor, and Kai's arm stung like he'd been struck by a lash.

The bullet had only grazed.

Trapping a snarl behind clenched teeth, Kai spun off another attacker, using him as a human shield. Then, he grabbed the gunner's wrist. With a quick wrench, he snapped the joint, the firearm's clank against the floor drowned out by a pained wail. With a violent shove to the chest, Kai sent the man sprawling, then stomped on his ankle, breaking that joint too.

Five down.

Skirting around the bedlam, Kai smashed his forearm into a man's throat, then hucked his discarded semi-automatic at another mobster's face. He swung an arm around the cunt who'd first fired at him, whispering a menacing *hello* into his ear. The bastard tried to fight, bucking madly, but Kai cinched his carotid with an elbow, relishing the strangled noises that left him as his face reddened, and a vein popped in his temple. As he blacked out, some of the others gathered their bearings. Kai dropped the deadweight and slid behind a table as another bullet flew past. He drove his fist through a chair leg to break off the end, then flung the makeshift stake at the shooter, spearing his shoulder. His pistol tumbled out of his grasp, and he fell into his hollering comrade. Kai didn't waste the opportunity; he bolted forward, unsheathed his hunting knife, and buried it into the second man's gut, twisting before he withdrew.

Both men shambled, one clutching his stomach as blood spilled over his fingers. His expression warped into a sneer as he hurled a few choice words about Kai's mother.

"My mother's dead." Kai raised the knife to his lips. His tongue slid along the blade, lapping crimson from silver. Then, a baleful grin—all teeth rimmed with red. "I'll send you to meet her."

Not a single mobster cocked their gun at Kai as though it were a measure of their machismo. Most of them were injured and had lost their dicks, their weapons scattered around the bar in pieces. The pack leader clutched his ribs and finally hobbled from the heap of chairs he'd hurtled into.

"Don't move!" a shaky voice commanded from the rear of the dining hall.

Kai's stomach bottomed out as he shifted his attention. One of the mobsters had fled, but he'd caught something on his way. Now, he was back for his ransom. He had one arm around Carol's neck, awkwardly forcing her along. With the other, he held a gun to her temple, the barrel digging in as she leaned away. She looked more pissed than scared, barking out threats as she wriggled in his grasp. He twisted her arm, and she yelped, her protests snuffed out.

"Try anything and I'll blow her damn brains out!" His hand shook against the grip.

"Fuck!" Connor nearly threw himself over the bar, but Sergei hauled him back, hissing at him to calm down.

The taste of satisfaction dissipated, leaving only the sour tang of blood in Kai's mouth. There'd been someone in the kitchen. He'd heard them prepping, but the adrenaline erased it from his mind, and by the time Pyotr's men stormed in, Kai had forgotten about the lone employee. He cursed his own lack of forethought—his belligerent refusal to play smart when he would rather play rough.

"Surrender," said the man holding Carol. Meanwhile, Connor stood helpless, his eyes flying to Kai for an answer he didn't have.

Kai squeezed his hunting knife, scanning the room. He was happy to risk his own hide—hell, he'd even give Connor and Sergei a thrill if he'd draw most of the trouble. They knew the life they'd signed up for. But Carol? She never asked for this. Even if he could find a way to maneuver, a gun to her head wasn't worth the risk. Reluctantly, Kai sheathed his knife, dropped it to the floor, then raised both hands and clasped them behind his head.

Two men jumped the counter and grabbed Sergei, dragging him away. His angry bellow was cut short when one of them hammered him on the head, knocking him out cold. The attacker spat on Sergei's shoes, muttering profanities.

Wrath propelled Kai to untether his hands and step forward when something struck him on the back of his skull. Stars bloomed before his eyes as he fought for balance, the urge to open his assailant's veins a furious itch on his palms, but he couldn't fight back. He had to take it. As he straightened, he was hit again, and again, each blow landing with more force than the last until he collapsed to his knees, his head swimming.

"Why won't you go down?" the leader spewed from behind, and Kai turned just enough to see him wind up his pistol, one arm still wrapped around his broken ribs.

A snarl rippled across Kai's face as he bared his teeth, defiance lacing his bones.

"Fucking *animal!*" He whipped Kai hard enough that he fell forward, bracing against the floor with a fist. "Go to sleep!"

Steadying his breaths, Kai clung to consciousness. He couldn't retaliate, but he wouldn't comply either. If they wanted to concuss him into submission, they'd have work for it. Sight bleary and skull splitting with hellish pain, Kai looked up at the mobster, committing his face to memory. Then, he smiled, his blood-tinged eyes a promise of what was to come. "When it's my turn, I won't need a gun."

He saw the waver, the tell-tale flinch as uncertainty snared the mobster by the throat. Then, he lifted his weapon.

The last thing Kai saw was the butt of a gun, plummeting toward his temple.

53
MIYA

THE KING of Spades was a second home to Miya, so when Caelan asked to visit the bar after a morning curled under a blanket with Ripper, she was happy to oblige.

"I owe your friends an apology," the teen insisted. Had it not been for the domovoy forcing the leshy out, then Ama running interference with Pyotr, Caelan would've been on her way to homicide.

Disguised in sunglasses, scarves, and too-large hats, they shut the blinds and flipped the sign on the King of Spades as soon as they arrived, closing for the day. The first thing Caelan did after shedding her getup was offer the house guardian half a fluffernutter. His head tilted as he examined the morsel, unaccustomed to anything quite like it after his many gourmet feasts. Ama joined them at Kai's request—more muscle while he was away. Eyeing the sandwich on the floor, Gavran roosted on his favorite beer tap, and Crowbar sipped on a citrusy gin and soda while shouting at Bastien to stop carrying crates stacked three miles high.

"You'll blow your back out!" She shook her head when he ignored her, shuffling things around in the kitchen.

Caelan took her seat at the counter, timidly apologizing for the trouble she'd caused. Both Ama and the bartender exchanged perplexed looks, then laughed.

"None of this is your fault," said Ama. While she'd blamed Kai, she never held any of it against Caelan. For that, at least, Miya was grateful.

Crowbar whipped out a pint glass. "Relax, girl. You don't have to carry the world on your shoulders." She poured the teen a swallow of beer. "To take the edge off. Just don't tell anyone. Wouldn't want to lose my liquor license."

Caelan's eyes lit up at the illicit beverage. "I can keep a secret."

Ama rolled her eyes. "You barely gave her four ounces."

"So she can gulp it down fast in case the cops come blasting through the door!" Crowbar said with mock offense.

"This is why we should move to Europe," Ama chided. "Far more sensible liquor laws."

The entryway bell gave an eerie chime, the hinges on the door screeching as someone stepped into the King of Spades.

He looked more mountain than man. Broad and muscular with sable hair tied back into a knot, an angular face mottled with fading bruises, and cool umber eyes. He wore no jacket, only a long-sleeved T-shirt, track pants, and broken-in sneakers—like he'd stopped by for a drink in the middle of his daily run. Yet something was off. He seemed uninterested in the establishment and simply stood there, scanning the room.

Ama's head snapped in his direction, her snowy mane suddenly static. Her fingers tensed on the countertop, and the corner of her lip twitched as the man's gaze fell on her, and he slowly inclined his head.

It took Miya all but ten seconds to put the pieces together.

She jumped in front of Caelan, Ama joining her the same instant. "We still have time." Ten hours to be exact, but he must've known that.

Crowbar swore and backed away while Caelan nearly tripped out of her stool. Gavran cawed in warning, and Bastien rushed in from the kitchen, grabbing his friend's arm.

Ivan Zverev smiled—an odd thing on such a terrifying man. It was warm, pitying even, and he shook his head. "Sorry. Plans change. My employer's getting impatient."

"What's the point of a deal if you're going to break it?" Miya challenged.

"I'm a man of my word." The smile fell from his face. "Unfortunately, some things are worth more than my honor."

Ama sniffed. "Money?"

"Not money," Zverev corrected, "but what it buys."

Miya bit down on her lip. Zverev was desperate to close the contract and get paid for a reason. "What's Pyotr got over you?"

He fixed her with a stony stare, and she scrabbled for Caelan's hand, eyes sliding to the domovoy. The house spirit bristled at the intruder, but beyond a bit of mischief, he was powerless against the living.

"Odd...for a human to make a home with monsters."

An evasion, which only confirmed Miya's suspicions. "Not all monsters have claws and teeth." She squeezed Caelan's fingers. Gavran spread his wings with an assenting croak, then glided over to perch on Miya's shoulder. "Some are made from the shadows that live in your dreams."

A muscle feathered in his jaw. "Give me the girl, and I'll leave quietly."

Ama stepped up to bar his path. "You know that's not going to happen."

Miya herded Caelan back where Crowbar intercepted her. "How the hell did he find us?" the bartender asked.

Zverev's eyes drifted to Crowbar, his mouth quirking as he tapped his nose—an answer to her question.

Bastien retrieved a baseball bat they'd mounted over the bar, ready to swing, but Ama shot him a warning look. *Only as a last resort*, she seemed to say.

The white wolf had no patience for idle chitchat. She launched herself at Zverev, fearless of the consequences. A wolf was a wolf, after all. She was almost a whole foot shorter, but that did nothing to deter her, her ferocity outsizing her stature. Zverev braced for impact, expecting a head-on assault.

Ama veered right. Kicking off a table, she rapidly changed her angle, flying down at Zverev with a swinging elbow he couldn't evade. Bone connected with bone, and Miya swore she heard a crunch as Zverev's head whipped sideways, and he collided with the wall. Kai would've quipped about drawing first blood, but Ama had the playfulness of a chainsaw when she fought. Before her opponent recovered, she took out his knee with a punishing sweep, then drove her own into his sternum.

Another crack, a grunt from Zverev. Swooning back, he

grabbed Ama's forearm, then shoved her as he righted himself, the force of it staggering. She flew into the stools, braced her arms against the counter ledge, and flipped over the bar. Reaching behind her, she closed her fist around the neck of a vodka bottle, then flung it at Zverev. He twisted away and blocked the shattering glass, but Ama grabbed another, then another, throwing bottle after bottle until the ground was littered with translucent shards. Little did she care—her boot soles were made like concrete. Snatching the rum, she hopped over the bar again and whaled on the goliath still guarding his face. His arm was bleeding, beads of broken glass embedded in his skin. The bottle smashed against his shoulder as he ducked his head, but Ama wasn't finished. She pulled her elbow back, then thrust the sharpened ends straight into Zverev's side, pushing him toward the wall. No hesitation, not an ounce of compunction.

Teeth bared, his giant hand wrapped around her arm, resisting her as she tried to sink the jagged crown of glass deeper. "You're as vicious as he is," Zverev strained, gradually pulling himself off the bottle end.

"Don't insult me," Ama snarled. "That *puppy* is only vicious when he's angry." Her lips peeled back into a sickle grin, her eyes like amber balefire. "I'm just vicious."

She twisted the bottle, slicing into his inner forearm. He released her, yet he seemed no worse for wear despite the gashes and the stab wound.

"He barely feels it," Caelan whispered, her voice trembling.

Crowbar shook her head—a refusal. "That's not possible."

"He's desperate," Miya realized. "He's not really fighting—doesn't want to—but he can't leave empty-handed."

His eyes flashed to Miya, his lip curling as though her words bittered his tongue. Then, as quickly as Ama had beaten him back, he slammed a fist into her ribs, the smack of minced muscle turning Miya's stomach. Zverev lifted Ama in one smooth motion, then threw her across the bar. The white wolf let out an enraged roar, her spine hitting the ledge of the counter so hard that she lurched, winded by the collision. Blood blossomed on the back of her shirt where she'd struck the hard lip of wood. Forcing air into her lungs with a painful rasp, she steadied herself, determined to chase Zverev away.

"There's no winning this," he told her, his tone absent of triumph. He sounded sad, sorrowful even. Maybe he wanted Ama to win, but some warped honor code dictated he fight.

He was too strong. Ama could take almost anyone—even give Kai a run for his money—but what good was that when a single hit from Zverev could trounce a living god? He'd battered Kai into a sorry state, and Ama wasn't faring much better. Her body was smaller, easier to harm, and Zverev looked like he had steel between his skin and his bones.

"Let's go together." Bastien adjusted his grip on the bat. "I may not be much against *that*, but I'm better than nothing."

"No," Ama growled over her shoulder.

Bastien jumped over the bar, undeterred. "Swallow your pride, Queen. You can't win every battle alone."

Ama clucked her tongue. "Don't you dare get hurt."

"This is crazy!" Crowbar pushed past Miya. "I care about these people. Do you understand that?" She pointed at Ama. "This woman is the love of my life, and you're going to tear through her and my best friend to send an innocent kid to her death? You *should* be stabbed with a bottle, you psychopathic fuck!"

Miya seized Crowbar's elbow, hauling her back. "Let them handle it. Someone's got to protect Caelan if shit goes south."

"But—"

Crowbar's protest was cut off as Ama and Bastien charged, splitting the beast's attention. Bastien took the bat to Zverev's knees as Ama sprang high enough to graze the ceiling. Anchoring herself to his shoulders, her legs wrapped around his neck. She twisted her body as she pincered his throat between her thighs, using the momentum to yank him down with her.

Miya had never seen a mountain fall. With gravity on her side, Ama toppled him to the glass-littered floor like dynamite incarnate, a plinking chorus echoing throughout the King of Spades. Bastien continued his assault, pummeling Zverev wherever he could.

Crowbar pressed her hands over her mouth, muffling a gasp. Even Gavran proved restless on Miya's shoulder, his midnight plumage ruffled from the stress as his beak yawned open, and he released a low warbling squawk. Caelan's breaths grew ragged. She tugged against Miya's hold, her skin clammy.

"It's okay," Crowbar reassured her, bowing over to rub the teen's arms. Her voice shook as she repeated the words over and over. Perhaps they should've fled, but Zverev would give chase, and there was no telling if Ama could keep up. Besides, they couldn't run forever.

The sharp sound of splintering wood snapped Miya from her dreadful reverie. The bat had broken. Swearing loudly, Bastien tossed aside the scraps, then dove for Zverev. Ama struggled to keep him grappled, bending his arm to a near-impossible angle, her legs squeezing his windpipe hard enough to crush bone. Even with Bastien helping her, they could barely keep him down. Eventually, he'd overpower them, and then what?

Miya had to do something.

She was the Dreamwalker. She could traverse netherworlds and nightmares, but in the physical realm, she was powerless against men with the strength of titans—a human girl with a human body, so easily bruised. Gavran stilled beside her, peering at her through an eye like wet ink. Then, the boy's voice echoed in her mind.

You are boundless. A creature of chaos. A thing like water and shadow. Water is not beholden to stone; shadow does not yield to material confines. All things crumble, and all light gutters eventually, but the ocean is depthless, and darkness devours everything it hungers for.

The Dreamwalker didn't care for boundaries. She crossed realms not because she esteemed worldly laws, but because she defied them.

She'd cut the seams of reality to let chaos spill out.

Miya released Caelan's hand and walked into the fray. When Gavran tried to follow, she rebuffed him with an icy glare. *Stay with Caelan.*

"What are you doing?" Panic laced Ama's voice as she tracked Miya's movements.

"Helping." Miya dropped into a crouch, then placed her hands on either side of Zverev's face. Both Bastien and Ama gawked at her, terror leaving them slack-jawed.

"Look at me," Miya commanded, and whether out of curiosity or compulsion, he listened. His gaze met the Dreamwalker's, murky green eyes mining for something to excavate. She wasn't sure what she was doing, but she always followed the roots in the dreamscape. They were like roads, taking her where she needed to go.

People too had roots. Perhaps they led somewhere.

With a steadying breath, Miya imagined herself sinking into the man whose skull she held between her hands—a stone making a new home at the bottom of a dark lake. He was guarded, and she sensed in him a wildness that he'd sealed behind a long-worn mask of human propriety. Yet what surprised Miya was the warmth she felt behind his steely stare. She expected cold but instead found a low simmer of resolve that he'd buried beneath a callous exterior—something to hide his motivations, his weaknesses, the spaces where he invested his care.

And he did care. Otherwise, he wouldn't have worked so hard to disguise it.

"What are you hiding, Ivan Zverev?" A sharp pain lanced Miya's skull as she plumbed deeper, chipping at the emotional wall he'd erected. Darkness peppered her vision, but between the undulating shadows, a shape emerged. A reedy silhouette, a man hunched over a desk as he held a thorny stem. Knife in hand, he plucked off the barbs, each snap crystalizing Miya's vision. A scarlet rose, a small shop, an elderly florist. When the last thorn was removed, the man stared wistfully at his handywork. Then, he lurched, a moist hack muffled by his palm over his mouth. Something dark and viscous spewed from his thin lips, dripped from his crabbed hand, and dyed the blossom black.

Illness. Death. Boundaries even the Dreamwalker couldn't flout. All things ended, and the promise of it was a dual blade that both gave time and stole it—slow suffering married to fleeting joy.

"Get out," Zverev snarled.

Miya dug her nails into his temples, hooking into him like talons piercing through flesh. Something warm and coppery dribbled from her nose, and as she licked her lips, she tasted blood.

"Miya—you're hurting yourself," Ama said, her urgency palpable, but she couldn't do anything to stop her with all her strength poured into restraining Zverev.

"Who's the old man?" Miya demanded, ignoring the white wolf's concern. If she could understand why he was doing this, she could figure out how to dissuade him. There was no stopping him by force. Bastien and Ama couldn't subdue him, and Crowbar had no way of protecting Caelan.

Zverev denied her a response. His thrashing turned frantic as he tried shaking Miya's influence, but she held fast. Blood ribboned over her earlobes, oozing down her neck. She wasn't meant to do this—to violate someone's will so blatantly, to rip the dreams from their mind while they were awake. Dreamwalking was easy; she went to those who reached for her in their sleep, unaware of what they manifested. They didn't know they were calling for help, luring the Dreamwalker into their hidden world. But this...this was wrong, and it revolted her.

"Miya, stop!"

Ama's voice was hazy. Red blurred Miya's vision, her mind and body unable to tolerate invading another person. The image of the old man faded, though she'd grasped enough. He was dying, and Zverev was afraid.

Her grip slipped as Bastien finally caved. With a savage roar, Zverev threw them both off, swiping Miya hard enough to send her crashing into the stools before she hit the floor. Pain shot through her spine, the glass shards a legion of jagged little teeth on her skin. With Ama left as the sole defender, Zverev muscled his way to his feet with the white wolf still clinging to him. He threw his weight into the wall, slamming Ama until she let go and crumpled to floor, heaving.

Miya's organs felt like they were in the wrong place, her ears ringing as she battled a nauseating wave of dizziness. Gavran's sharp caw pierced through the cotton in her ears, but before he dove for Zverev's eyes—a last ditch effort to slow the beast— Caelan's voice shattered the bedlam.

"I'll go with you!" She shrugged Crowbar away as the bartender scrabbled for her. Miya saw the guilt swirling in the teen's expression, and shame quickly followed, seeping into her as she reached for blame. "Please. Just stop hurting them."

Zverev staggered as he regained his balance. He plucked the glass from his hands, his shirt torn from the wound Ama had inflicted. Scarlet crescents pocked his temples, though they quickly faded, his supernatural healing already kicking in.

"Caelan." Miya forced herself into a seated position, feeling bruised all the way down to her marrow. "Don't—"

"Come," Zverev interrupted, holding his lacerated hand out to the girl.

Crowbar grabbed the teen, stuttering over her words to deter her, but Caelan had made up her mind. Squeezing Crowbar's wrists, she shook her head, and the bartender didn't have the heart to fight her. Defeated, Crowbar let go. There was far too much on the line to justify holding on.

Caelan joined her captor, slipping her tiny hand into one that could crush granite. Quietly, they departed the King of Spades, leaving three barren souls and a wasteland in their wake.

54

WHEN MIYA LEARNED that Kai had been taken, she knew the blood soaking the bar towels wouldn't be the last of the night. Her injuries stopped hurting the moment Connor told her. A crushing weight settled over her chest, and she sank to the floor next to the domovoy, tears like lava on her face.

Failure stung like a bitch.

"If we storm Pyotr's compound, we'll be gunned down like ducks." Ama's voice of reason barely filtered through the fugue.

"We don't even know where it is," Crowbar added glumly.

"I can get in." Miya looked up when the crunch of glass subsided. Both the white wolf and the bartender had stopped pacing, turning to stare at her. She'd never seen Ama so disheveled. Gore streaked her hands and neck, her white hair crusted with red and mussed from combat. Bastien left for the nearest corner store, promising to return with first aid and extra cleaning supplies. Miya had used up what'd remained on Ama's insistence, tweezing out glass, disinfecting cuts, and wrapping them with medical gauze.

Crowbar threw her arms out, her face as blotchy as Miya's. "How?"

"I can go through the dreamscape." Miya swallowed, eyes darting to Gavran. "Physically."

Tear the seams of reality.

Ama stalked up to Miya, desolation etching her usually serene face. "You know how hard that is on your body. If you go in there, you'll be in enemy territory. You don't have the luxury of resting."

Miya let out a shaky breath. "I know." It'd been years since she'd had to rend her way through realms. She only ever dreamwalked now, but she was desperate.

"My question stands: how are we going to find them?" Crowbar insisted.

Them. Kai and Caelan. The sting returned, dogged that Miya choke on her blunders. "Gavran can help me."

The raven cocked his head, offering an assured beat of his wings.

Miya pushed to her feet, the domovoy chittering as he fretted. "He's our sentinel—on this side and in the dreamscape. It might take some muddling, but it's our best shot."

Ama and Crowbar exchanged worried glances. After several moments of weighty silence, Ama surrendered to a tired slouch. She wrapped her arms around Miya's middle. "If anyone can do it, you can."

An affirmation, a gesture of confidence—trust that Miya could handle herself without support. "Thank you," she whispered, squeezing the white wolf back. "I promise I'll be careful."

Crowbar hustled in, glomming on with a fierce bear hug. She rested her head on Ama's shoulder, and the white wolf craned her neck to plant an affectionate kiss on her girlfriend's forehead. Gavran too joined them, roosting on their entangled arms and nuzzling their faces. They still had each other—a bond forged from love—and together, they were an ironclad fortress.

As they pulled apart, Miya scratched through Gavran's plush breast while he purred from her shoulder. Odd and willful as he was, he remained with her unconditionally. He'd peck out Kai's eyeballs for stealing one of his peanuts, but in the end, his allegiance was to his family. And Kai was family.

Now, all Miya needed was a ritual. Tearing through space wasn't exactly whimsical, and unlike dreamwalking, it couldn't be done anywhere. She needed to make a door—a gateway. The fallen elm's memorial in Boston Common would've been ideal, but she didn't have time to go there. She needed something here, now. The bar had sold for cheap because it was haunted. It had a history—a tether to the other side.

Miya's eyes settled on the domovoy, then trailed up to the old mirror on the wall.

Maybe there was a way.

Ancient trees were an anchor and a suture between worlds. They were fixed points, something proximate to both sides. The domovoy was a spirit tied to his family and home, but he was also immaterial, invisible to most. Perhaps he too could be an anchor, a stitch between realms. And as far as ritual was concerned, what better to act as a doorway than a mirror?

Gavran hopped off Miya's shoulder when she snatched Crowbar's citrus knife and crouched in front of the domovoy. She opened her palm, face up, and he placed his little paw in her hand.

"I need your help," she told him softly. "Kai and Caelan are in danger. I have to find them, but I need a shortcut to the dreamscape. Do you think you could help me make one?"

The domovoy tilted his head and chirped, withdrawing his paw. He needed strength—more than just carbohydrates. Miya cast Ama a questioning glance, and the white wolf nodded.

Miya brought the blade to her palm, blood ribboning over the swell of her hand. The domovoy bent forward, fixated on the pooling liquid.

"This is my oath," Miya began. "Lend me your strength, and you will be fed in my home for as long as I live. You're no longer tied to this place; you're tied to me."

The domovoy stretched his paw, tentative. He gazed up at her with large round eyes, then flattened his palm against hers. A vow made in blood. Warmth spread through Miya's veins, her pulse singing as newfound power wove through her like sprouting ivy.

"Thank you," she breathed, feeling the domovoy bolster her. They were connected now, and wherever she made her home, the domovoy would follow. For now, it was the King of Spades, but she'd freed him of the four walls that'd sealed him here. He'd outlived his first family and was left confined to their residence without recourse. Now, he'd never be forced into isolation again.

Miya gave the domovoy a tender smile, then rose to face the mirror. She extended her arm, and Gavran eagerly found purchase. Miya placed her cut palm against the cold glass, and a delicate stream of blood leached from the wound, drawing a path through the room's reflection. As the scarlet trail fractured the room in two, the glass roiled like water disturbed by a raindrop. Miya was that disturbance. Gradually, the reflection morphed—no longer the

King of Spades, but a dark corridor lit only by pallid fog. Miya grasped the dream stone, feeling it hum against her skin. That umbral tunnel wasn't her destination, but it was a path forward. With Gavran at her side, she'd find her way.

Zverev had his nose. The Dreamwalker had a bird's-eye view of reality.

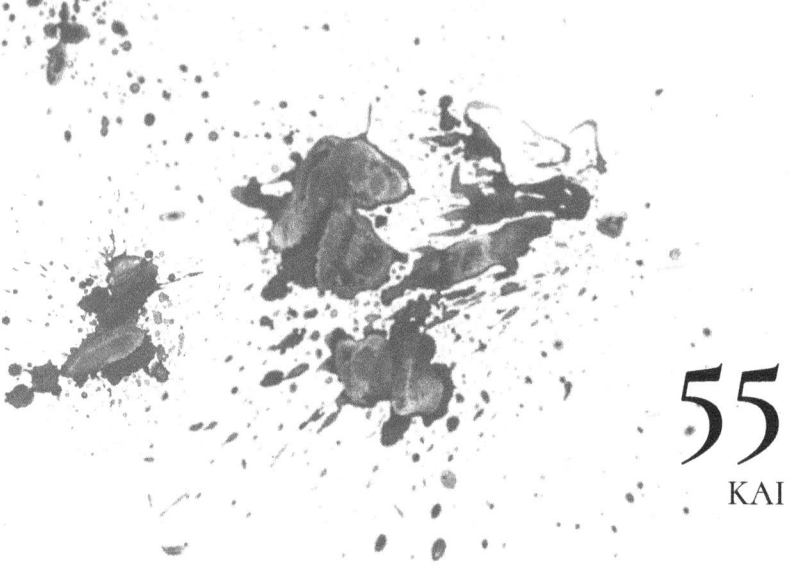

55

KAI

KAI ALWAYS THOUGHT his death would come quick. A bullet to the brain. A well-placed switchblade. A swerving semi on a scantly lit road. But he never imagined he'd wake up to concrete before the grand finale—a prisoner awaiting execution. Gravel bit into his cheek as his face scraped against the floor. He groaned, pushed himself to his knees, then promptly toppled as pain rived through him, splitting his head. Eyes squeezed shut, he waited for the throbbing to ease. No matter how thick his skull was, a concussion was a concussion.

"Fuck." His throat was parched, lightning shooting through his jaw the second he opened his mouth. Judging by the agony he was in, barely a few hours had passed since he'd blacked out. Nausea shredded his gut, and he forced himself to slow his breathing until the tumult subsided. When the hurt grew tolerable, he sat back on his calves and looked around. It was dark save for a hanging bulb that barely illuminated the ground outside his cell. And it was a cell, complete with iron bars and the stench of piss and blood. The piss, at least, wasn't his.

Pressing the ball of his hand to his forehead, Kai massaged the ache away as best he could, then pulled himself to his feet. Nothing was broken, his joints working as intended. He rolled out his neck with a few satisfying pops, then curled his fingers around one of the bars. He gave it a rough jerk. It was sturdy.

"The fuck are you doing?" a voice snapped, and footsteps echoed through the empty corridor. Kai reckoned they were underground in one of Pyotr's illicit torture holes where he sent men to die for displeasing him.

Unmoving, Kai left his hand on the bar. He recognized the voice, and the rancid scent of douchebag followed. His lip curled, the back of his scalp prickling as his hairs stood on end. Moments later, the man who'd beaten him unconscious appeared, shadows clinging to the grooves of his gaunt face. His hair was still too gelled, and his mouth twisted into a sneer upon seeing that Kai was awake.

"Have a nice nap?" he jibed.

Kai tapped his temple with two fingers and smirked. "Helped clear my head, thanks."

"Cocky shit." The mobster kicked the cell door, then spat at Kai's hand. "Hey, paws off the bars."

Ignoring the mucus dribbling down his knuckles, Kai's gaze narrowed into a glare. "Or what?"

Teeth gnashing, the mobster flung his leg forward, aiming for Kai's hand. He missed on the first few stomps. Kai remained motionless, expression bored, watching as this pathetic mass of impotent rage walloped away. The asshole wound back, then threw a wild kick that would've finally hit its mark.

Kai lifted his fingers from the bar and snatched the man's ankle, tugging upward. Losing his balance, the goon fell like a traffic sign knocked over by a storm. His back hit the concrete, a ragged gasp pushing through his lungs.

Grinning fiendishly, Kai flicked off the mobster's dress shoe and yanked his foot through the bars. He yelped, trying to claw his way farther from the cell to no avail. With his knee between two metal rods, Kai snapped his leg to one side, forcing the joint out of its socket, tearing the attached ligaments like a dry rubber band.

A torrid scream filled the concrete cavern, but Kai wasn't concerned. If this was where Pyotr tortured people, it was sure to be soundproof.

"You like power?" Kai dragged him closer, clasping his belt. "You like hurting people who can't fight back?" The mobster's back bent to an excruciating angle as Kai hauled him upright with one arm, then released his belt to grasp him by the collar. With a grip like tempered steel, he pulled the man close, only the bars between their faces. Kai ignored his sour breath, the rim of tears in his eyes, the quiver of his lower lip. He scrabbled for his pistol, but Kai was faster, snatching it from its holster and whipping it at the wall so hard that it broke apart into a useless heap.

"I told you," Kai said through a growl, "when it's my turn, I won't need a gun."

He drew his elbow back as though ripping the spine from a snake. Momentum reeled the man forward, his face slamming into the iron. The satisfying crunch of a collapsing nasal cavity alerted Kai to a gnarly fracture. A strangled keen slipped from the mobster's mouth as his jaw shattered with the second hit, blood pouring from every orifice in his rearranged face. Teeth knocked loose, bouncing off the bars and falling like chips. Still holding him by the shirt, Kai groped around his waistband until he found what he wanted: a set of keys, dangling from a belt loop. Unclipping them, Kai twirled the keyring around his finger, then smiled with all his teeth.

"Sleep well, you shitless brain tumor." One more yank against the bars, one more splinter through brittle bone, and Kai dropped the man to the floor, his head cracking on the concrete. Crimson pooled around his mangled skull, the halo prettier than he ever was.

Kai swooned as he stepped out of the cell, dizziness nearly besting him. He still wore the same clothes—old jeans and a plain gray T-shirt, though his belt was gone, and his pockets were empty. They'd taken his wallet. Searching the mobster, he found his hunting knife strapped to the back of his belt. The dead man must've claimed it as a prize from the Confessional. The walls roiled when Kai tried to rise, and he steadied himself with a hand to the floor. Barking out an angry shout, he forced himself up.

It'd be fine. Fighting with a concussion was just like fighting drunk.

After pilfering the belt and fastening his knife to it, Kai shambled down the narrow corridor, scarcely aware of where he was going. He only noticed his boots were gone when he stepped on a sharp pebble. He could tell he was underneath an old building; the basement was a cellar that'd likely once been used for less nefarious purposes. Now, it was Pyotr's personal prison. Kai stopped to banish the wave of nausea that overcame him as the hall tilted. He lost that battle, doubling over and puking his guts out on the cold gray floor. From behind the wall next to him, he heard a groan that wasn't his and tipped his head to listen. There was a door just a few feet ahead. Kai spat out the bile and wiped his mouth. Pulling himself together, he fumbled for the keys he'd stolen, then tested each one until the lock clicked. The hinges screeched painfully in his ears as he pushed open the heavy metal door enough to squeeze through.

A man sat strapped to a chair, his wrists and ankles bound with rope, a burlap bag unceremoniously tossed over his head. His designer shirt was in tatters, his tie wound around his neck like someone had choked him with it. Poor bastard had gotten his share.

"Sergei," Kai managed through a croak, then tripped further into the room.

The man in the chair stiffened, alert under the bag. He didn't speak as Kai sliced through the bonds with his hunting knife. A bracelet of rope burn marred his wrists and ankles, and as Kai removed the sack, he winced at the sight. Sergei's eye was swollen shut, his nose definitely broken, and his lips split and bruised. When he opened his mouth to speak, Kai saw several gaps in his teeth.

"I've got at least three broken ribs," Sergei rasped, finally shifting to inspect his hands. Several of his fingers were bent wrong.

"You're lucky you're alive." Kai gestured at his co-conspirator. "Can you walk?"

Sergei shook his head. "I'm not going anywhere until it's clear upstairs. Pyotr will put us down like dogs."

"Fortunately, I'm a wolf," Kai cracked, and Sergei threw him a one-eyed glower.

"I can limp," Sergei amended, "but I'm still not moving until it's safe for a snail to crawl through."

Kai nodded. "Fine. I'll go upstairs and clear them out."

"You look like you can barely stand."

"I'm just drunk."

Sergei looked him up and down, then grunted. "You have a concussion."

"I hurled outside your door." Kai shrugged. "It helped." He

wasn't lying. The nausea had abated, and although he was still dizzy, he found it easier to plod in a respectable line.

"There's something you should know," Sergei said as he tested his joints. "I overheard that Zverev is on his way." He looked up at Kai. "He's bringing the girl."

Any iota of steadiness that Kai had clawed back dissipated with Sergei's words. If Zverev was bringing Caelan here, that meant only one thing.

The King of Spades was attacked.

A deluge swept Kai into the wall as he stumbled back. Ama had failed. A surge of anger took her shape, but worry quickly muddled the edges of his wrath. Ama was ferocious. She'd die before letting anything happen on her watch. Kai's insides knotted up until his ribs cramped, his breaths shallowing. He tried to bite them back, but they slipped through his teeth until he fisted his hair in both hands and bowed over, an enraged snarl tearing from his throat.

All he could think about was Miya.

Miya, who embroiled herself in his messes, who threw herself in harm's way to do the right thing. Miya, who gave him the spine to look in the mirror, to carve himself open and see what he was made of.

Miya, his whole fucking world, because without her, he'd be alone.

"What are you going to do?" Sergei's voice cleaved him from his spiraling thoughts.

Kai dropped his arms to his sides and straightened from the wall. He pushed the turmoil under his skin, then deeper, beneath veins, muscle, and bone, far into his marrow where he would keep it locked away until he knew what to do with it.

"What I do best," he said, the revulsion, vertigo, and heartache bleeding out until he felt hollow. It terrified him—that dark void, that absence in his chest—but it was all that moored him now. "Lose my fucking temper."

56

MIYA

When Miya slipped her hand through the fissure between worlds, she didn't know what to expect. She saw the seam from within the fog—a jagged line scoring a path to the physical plane. Gavran had led her to another doorway, and although she had no sense of time in the dreamscape, she hoped it worked in her favor.

Her body moved through space like liquid through cupped hands. Fog gave way to florescent lights, the ground shimmering with the gleam of porcelain tiles. Miya reached and reached until she fell through that crack in reality, tripped over a faucet, and hit the floor.

A bathroom.

Gavran croaked next to her, prodding her with his beak. Miya grimaced, the bandaged cuts on her arms, legs, and hands stinging from the collision. As she clambered to her feet, she turned toward the mirror—pristine save for a pinprick. She stared into it, and that one point erupted into a spider's web that fractured her reflection, the epicenter overlapping the dream stone.

"Let's go," she said to Gavran, then snuck out of the bathroom.

What awaited her was not a compound but a mansion, more museum than home. High arches, floor-to-ceiling windows, soulless décor. A rich man's home, to be sure. Had Pyotr stashed Kai somewhere in his own house?

"Gavran," Miya spoke to the raven on her shoulder, "where are we?"

Exactly where we need to be.

Miya doubted that. Pyotr was smart; he'd keep his business affairs separate from domestic ones. She tilted her head toward her familiar. "Why didn't you take me to Kai? To Caelan?"

It will accomplish nothing, Gavran insisted. *You need both halves to see the whole.*

He didn't normally communicate like this; it sapped his strength, but this wasn't right. Apprehension coiled in her middle. She was losing time. "Gavran, stop—"

There is a way, but it cannot be seen when the parts are disparate. You must bring them together.

She ground her teeth together. "What does that even—"

"Who the hell are you?"

Miya whirled around, her heart stuttering to a halt. Behind the staccato of her pulse, confusion deafened her.

Caelan stood before her, knife clutched in one hand.

"Answer me!" The girl adjusted her grip, thrusting the blade forward.

No, not Caelan. Alina. Miya lifted both hands. "I'm sorry! I'm not here to cause trouble." What was Gavran thinking, bringing her here?

Alina frowned, her gaze drifting from Miya to the raven on her shoulder. "Why the hell do you have a bird?"

"He's helping me find someone." An honest, if cryptic, answer.

Something flashed across the girl's expression—curiosity, or perhaps understanding. She lowered the knife. "I know you. You were with the fetch."

Miya's mouth worked. She was stunned Alina had puzzled it out so rapidly. "You remember me?"

"The mess from the park, yeah?" Alina sighed and slumped her shoulders. "Bits and pieces. Besides, you're not the first weirdo from Team Fetch to bust in here." She shot Miya a sideways stare. "The last guy was sneakier, though."

Miya dreaded to think she meant Kai.

"Do you know where she is?" the teen asked.

The question caught Miya off guard, but she hadn't the heart to lie. "She was taken by someone who works for your father."

The girl's expression sank. "So, you're looking for that asshole, then."

"By asshole, I take it you mean your dad?"

Alina turned and ambled into the kitchen—a white marble masterpiece that boasted more counterspace than Miya's entire apartment floorplan. She set the knife down, then faced her uninvited guests as they tentatively joined her. "I know where he is. I can take you to him."

Miya squinted at the girl. "Or you can tell me where he is and stay out of danger."

Alina shook her head. "Take me with you. I know it sounds reckless—crazy even—but I can't spend another second here."

"You could die—"

"I *want* to die." Alina recoiled at her own words, as though the admission struck a chord she hadn't known was there.

Miya almost flinched. She was no stranger to mental anguish—insomnia, anxiety, and a simmering existential dread that'd uprooted her whole identity, robbed her of motivation to seek joy or even contentment. It was debilitating. Yet even at her worst, she never considered dying. She'd fantasized about disappearing, going someplace no one could find her, but a world in which she didn't exist never appealed to her. The weight of Alina's words settled in her marrow—sticky, stubborn—and for the first time in a long while, she didn't know what to say. "I'm sorry," she tried when nothing else came to her.

"Don't be." Alina sounded so morose, so defeated. She wrung her hands together, scratching viciously at her knuckles. Miya saw they were scraped raw from the habit, probably a form of self-soothing. "My dad doesn't give a shit about me. He thinks he can bide his time because I'm locked up here, under watch like some prisoner. As long as he's in control, he doesn't care about how I feel."

"You're probably right," Miya agreed. Pyotr treated her more like heirloom china than a human being. "He's not fit to care for anyone."

"The point is, my life is meaningless." Alina's lips contorted into a rictus, and she flung her arms out as though she could cast off her despondency. "It's impossible to have friends because I'm barely allowed outside. I had a boyfriend, but he just dumped me because he got sick of sneaking around. Every move I make is sanctioned by *Pyotr*." Her voice wobbled as she spat her father's name, but she quickly regained purchase. "It's death or misery. If I'm going to die, at least let me help someone while I'm at it. My whole life has been in this gilded cage."

"But there's no sense in you coming with me." Miya ignored the persistent rap of Gavran's three-pronged claw on her shoulder. "You could help by telling me where your father is, and once this is over, you can start that search for meaning. Live on your own terms."

Alina drew her shoulders back, her spine rigid. "I won't tell you unless you take me."

"That's just obstinate, Alina—"

You need both halves to see the whole.

Fury sparked the teen's eyes. "I never asked for your help. Who are you to decide my fate? Whatever it is you're doing—how does that help me? Am I to sit here and rot in this mansion until you give me permission to leave? Let me take my life in my own hands!"

There is a way, but it cannot be seen when the parts are disparate. You must bring them together.

Gavran's words echoed in Miya's her mind. She understood now: Alina and Caelan were two halves of the whole. He wanted Miya to bring them together—the very thing they'd fought to circumvent.

Miya sucked in a sharp breath. She knew intimately what it meant to be powerless, to have others dictate your course. If she acted as arbitrator in the name of Alina's safety, then she was no different than her father. A far lesser evil, perhaps, but of the same ilk, nonetheless. Alina would see her only as another dictator presuming to know what's best. What she wanted—what would make her happy—didn't matter.

Miya had no desire to be that person.

"All right." Miya nodded with a slow swallow, and Gavran's scratching abated. "You can come with me. But you should know that I'm not a friend to your father. I'm going in there as his enemy. I just..." She hesitated, searching the teen's eyes. "I don't want you to get hurt."

A wistful smile crossed the girl's lips. "My father has already hurt me plenty."

The words were a curved blade hooking through Miya's chest. Pyotr wasn't just a menace in the underworld; he was vile in his own home too. As Alina dressed for the outdoors, Miya wandered toward the foyer, whispering to Gavran, "How do I fix this?"

A low rattle reverberated in the raven's throat, his blue-black plumage ruffling as his head canted. Eyes like tiny pools of ink fixed on the girl who'd summoned the reaper in her own likeness.

There is no fix, Dreamwalker, but there is always a bargain. You simply may not wish to pay the price.

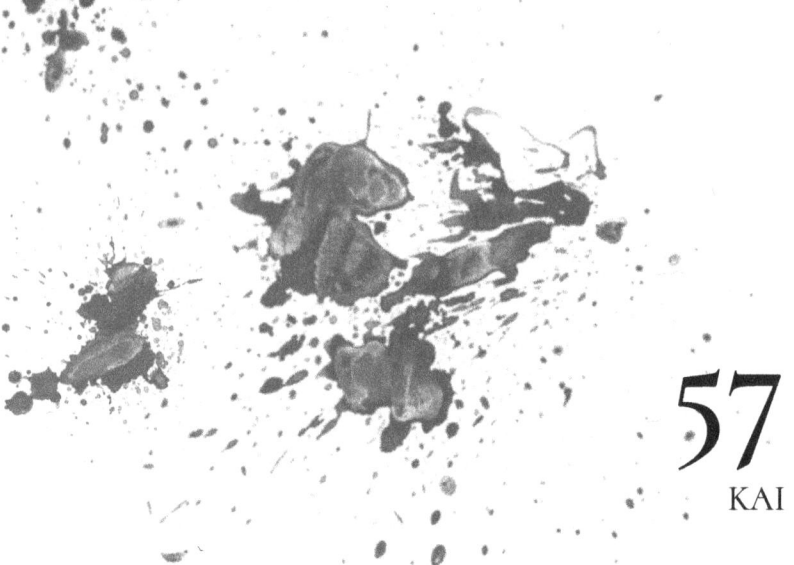

57

KAI

A DISMEMBERED arm was surprisingly hefty. With a dull thud, Kai dropped the limb to the floor and stepped over its writhing owner. It'd made a decent weapon, but he preferred his hunting knife. His shirt was doused in viscous red after the carnage, the blood smeared over his arms, neck, and face. Pyotr's goons had come at him the second he'd emerged from the basement, and Kai had no qualms removing their appendages. Who needed fingers, anyway?

A mechanical thumping pummeled his already battered skull. A laundromat. He was in a *fucking* laundromat. At least it disguised the ruckus he'd caused, though he wished Pyotr would've picked a less cliché front business. Stripping off his shirt, he threw it into one of the still-running washers and slammed the door. It was getting crusty, hampering his movements.

The place was old and stank of mildew, piss-colored florescent lights flickering over stained vinyl. A doorway on the back wall led to the offices, and Kai glimpsed one of Pyotr's overinflated body-guards rushing from his patrol in the cramped corridor. The last man standing.

Dressed in a too-pricy suit, the man barreled forward. As he closed in, Kai headbutted him in the nose, then clapped a palm over his mouth, muffling his scream. Blood gushed from the wound and ribboned over Kai's fingers as he drove the bodyguard into a dryer. Panicked, the man reached for his gun, but a hand closed over his wrist, halting him. Kai shook his head and *tsk*ed, then clamped his teeth around the man's ear.

He ripped the fleshy shell clean off.

The bodyguard collapsed to the floor, cupping the side of his head before blacking out. With the last hurdle discarded, Kai moseyed into the office, a trail of viscera following him.

Pyotr sat calmly at his desk, flipping through the contents of Kai's wallet. It was a modest space—cream walls, filing cabinets that looked decades old, and drapery in desperate need of a dry clean. Pyotr paid no attention to the intruder, unconcerned with the mayhem the wolf had wrought. A caged animal let loose in his home, and he didn't even twitch.

Kai spat the ear out onto Pyotr's desk.

Finally, the mobster's gaze lifted, and he smiled, cold and humorless. He leaned sideways to peer past Kai at the man sprawled unconscious on the floor, blood pouring from his face. Beneath Pytor's white dress shirt, Kai saw the bandages around his mangled shoulder—a parting gift from the wolf.

"How easy it is for you…to tear through meat, to kill. Most have to snuff out the person in the mirror before they can butcher so unflinchingly. But you?" Pyotr laughed, low and dark. "It's as though you were made for this world."

Pyotr had no idea how wrong he was. If Kai had been made for this world, his existence wouldn't be marred by so much pain—senseless, meaningless pain. There was no justification, no grander purpose to it. No, he'd ended up here precisely because he *wasn't* made for this world, and he suffered for it.

He may have been a killer, but he refused to be a weapon for anyone but Miya.

Kai nodded toward the wallet. "That's mine."

"So it is, Kai Donovan." Pyotr tossed it onto the desk next to the dismembered ear. "An unusual name for a Russian."

That his mother was Tatar never seemed to matter. No wonder she'd wanted out. "Not my given name."

"Ah, your chosen name, then?"

He supposed that was true. Even after remembering Mikhail Zverev, it didn't resonate. Kai was a name he'd chosen as a child—a reconciliation between the place he'd come from and the one where he'd found himself. A testament to being diaspora. Donovan wasn't inherited either. Alice had offered it to him, and he'd accepted.

"Dead men shouldn't be so curious." Kai refused to answer. Every so often, his mind flicked to Miya, to Crowbar, to Bastien and Ama. He didn't think Zverev would kill them, but the merc had violated their agreement. If the King of Spades had put up enough of a fight, driven the beast into a corner, who knew what he'd do?

Kai felt the weight of his own blood trail like a manacle. He'd been driven into a corner too.

Pyotr chuckled, the threat rolling off him like his moral compass. "Fools shouldn't try to tell the future."

Before Kai could snipe back, a door wedged between two shelves at the rear of the office swung open. From the alleyway outside, Ivan Zverev stepped into the claustrophobic room, and he wasn't alone. Caelan followed, Zverev's bear-like hand clamped on her shoulder. He didn't seem to be forcing her, but he wasn't taking his chances either. He was badly scuffed up, his shirt bloodied where he nursed a stab wound in his side, though it did little to impede him.

Kai swallowed the bile that seared up his throat, his stomach lurching at the sight of the girl. "Caelan—"

"They're safe," she said as though it were her foremost thought, then took stock of his grisly appearance. "I'm sorry. This is my fault."

Somewhere in the maelstrom rending Kai's mind, the pieces slotted into place. She'd given herself up to protect them. His heart twisted behind his ribs, shame gnawing away the rage that'd fueled him to this point. Kai had failed her. They all had. And Zverev had catalyzed it. Accusation curdled on his tongue, but he didn't dare wield it. He wasn't about to feed Pyotr information, though he would've relished the opportunity to tear out Zverev's jugular.

"Vanya, I'm disappointed," Pyotr's smooth voice cut through the tension.

Eyes fixed on Kai, Zverev guided Caelan in front of him. "I apologize for my tardiness."

Pyotr wagged a finger and shook his head disapprovingly. "You know I don't care for apologies, Vanya. I expect results. You put my daughter at risk. You knew where the forgery was for three days and did *nothing*."

That moved the behemoth. His head turned toward his

employer. "Why do you want this kid, anyway? She's a threat to no one."

"Her captors used her as leverage against me," Pyotr scoffed. "Obviously, I'm going to get rid of her." His eyes slid to Kai. "Besides, you think I don't know that she appeared out of thin air? That her sleepwalking—all over the news when she went missing, by the way—didn't coincide with my daughter's own...experiences?"

Caelan hadn't been the only one under a supernatural influence; Alina must've shown signs too. No matter how desperately she tried clutching her secrets to her chest, Pyotr found a way to wrench them out.

"You're mad," Zverev growled.

"You get half the money for half the work," Pyotr said with a swipe of his hand.

Zverev visibly stiffened. His grasp on Caelan tightened, and a muscle feathered in his jaw as he suppressed a scowl. "My methods were never up for negotiation." He pushed the teen forward a step. "You still got what you wanted."

Pyotr turned his chair to face Zverev fully, crossing an ankle over his knee. "You're soft, Ivan. You think I don't know why you need that money?" A slow, snake-like smile spread over his face. "Chemo's expensive in America, but trying to save an old man from cancer is like trying to drain the ocean of salt."

Shock replaced ire, Zverev's throat bobbing as he choked something back. Kai watched the exchange, his mind racing for a way to pry Caelan from Zverev's maw. If he acted now, it would force Zverev's hand, but Kai wanted to take advantage of whatever conflict was brewing between the two men. Sweat trickled down Zverev's temple, the scent of cortisol wafting off him like garlic breath. Someone Zverev cared for was slipping away, but Kai hadn't pegged him as the type to flirt with futility. Cancer was often a death sentence in the elderly; he knew that intimately.

"You meddled in my business?" Ivan finally spoke.

"I don't hire strangers," Pyotr chided, "and I know all about you, Ivan Zverev." He chuckled, standing from his chair. "O'Neil's Florals. What would a man like you possibly get out of working for a fossil like O'Neil? Unless, of course, it was sentimental." He slipped his hands into his pockets, eyeing Zverev as though he were a slab of meat to be minced. "The old man saved you, gave you a place to call home." He shot Kai a pitying look. "An orphan's story is a dime a dozen."

Kai kissed his teeth, but uncertainty wrung him out like a used washcloth. He'd visited O'Neil's—met the snarky old man trimming thorns off a rose. It was odd, finding a Russian merc arranging flower baskets for an Irishman, but it made as much sense as Kai and Alice had. A crochety old woman raising a fucked-up kid who'd lost his home and family. When Alice had been sick with cancer, Kai would've bargained with any devil for an extra year of life. He wasn't ready to be alone, and something told him Zverev wasn't either.

"You're a piece of shit," Kai snarled at Pyotr, no longer able to bridle his tongue. He had no love for his distant cousin, but he understood what it meant to sell your soul only to come up short. The sheer helplessness, the offense of it all—it turned his insides into lava, scalding his veins.

"You and your kind are all dogs in the end. You just need the right master to be obedient to." Pyotr gave Kai a once over, then reached behind his back. "Though I didn't expect you to escape your crate. Now I have to decide which of you to put down first."

Kai's gaze flitted to Caelan, who peered back at him with wide, stormy eyes. Fear had finally crawled inside her, a slight tremor working through her spine. With nothing to offer her, his attention shifted to Zverev, and they exchanged a weighty look.

He'd been demoted, and his new cut wasn't enough to buy old man O'Neil an extension on his expiration date. No amount of stoicism could mask the despondency etching the lines of Ivan Zverev's face. For a moment that felt too long, too laden, the earth stopped on its axis, and indecision thickened the room. Each of them had a choice to make, and none would be without a heavy cost.

A sickening click punctured the silence as Pyotr aimed a gilded revolver at Zverev's head. "Go on, beast. Earn your pay."

58

MIYA

When Alina promised to reveal her father's hideout, Miya hadn't expected to find herself loitering outside Piggy Bank's Coin Laundry. It was shuttered for the day, a piece of cardboard shoved haphazardly in the window, the word *closed* scrawled on it in permanent marker. Gavran perched on the shop sign's P, squawking triumphantly.

"That's weird. Usually when he's here, there's someone inside watching the door." Alina cupped her eyes and pressed her forehead to the tinted glass. "It looks empty."

Miya wondered if Kai got loose, but that was no guarantee that he was alive. "How do we get inside?"

Alina didn't respond. Her face was still pressed to the window, her hands sliding down the smooth glass with a low squeal. Her eyes were peeled open, and she stared into the laundromat as if searching for something—or someone.

"Hey..." Miya placed a tentative hand on the girl's shoulder, and she jumped, blinking away her stupor. Perhaps Caelan was nearby, influencing her double.

"Sorry," Alina muttered, straightening. "Must've zoned out." She reached into her pocket and fished out a key, presumably for the door.

"He just gave you a key to his multipurpose butcher shop?"

Alina snorted. "Are you kidding? I stole this from his desk."

"Doesn't he lock his office door?" Miya pressed.

The teen shrugged. "He locks everything, which is why I took up lock picking. How do you think I get out of my room?"

Miya tried to school her features, tempering her horror. "He locks you in your room?"

Alina gave her a dark look, then turned the key in the knob. "I wasn't being cute when I said my house is a prison."

No shit. Pyotr used the fetch to justify his Rapunzel-like treatment of his daughter, but he'd be an abusive dickweed regardless of the circumstances.

The door chirred open to the sound of running machines. "I thought it was closed," Miya said as she gingerly stepped inside, Gavran gliding in behind her. The lights were off, yet the washers and dryers were all on.

Alina's expression was grim. "He's trying to cover something up."

Miya grimaced as a series of macabre images flitted through her brain. No one could hear a person scream over the cacophony of a dozen laundry machines. They needed to slow down and figure out a plan. Even if Alina felt safe prancing around her father's illicit empire, Miya did not. Pyotr's men wouldn't hurt his daughter, but a civilian who'd gotten her nose into their business was fair game. "We should—"

Alina's gasp interrupted her. A shadow moved toward the rear of the laundromat, and the teen booked it toward the figure, leaving Miya paralyzed by the front door.

Gavran was the first to give chase, the blur of feathers shaking Miya loose as she too bolted after Alina. From the corner of her eye, she glimpsed a crimson puddle, an arm that didn't lead to a body, waxen skin bereft of life.

Miya clamped her mouth shut and forced down the sick, then skidded to a halt as she caught up to Alina, now standing in the doorway to an office.

Long shadows stretched into the small space, and as Miya followed the gore painted over the tiles, she found Kai at the end of the grisly path. Scarlet streaked his arms, torso, and neck, his hands stained from fingernails to wrists. Dried blood trickled from his scalp, matting his dark hair—a nauseating clue to how he'd been taken.

He pivoted, wild eyes snapping to Miya as his lips parted in surprise. She saw the relief wash over him the moment his body caught up to his brain. Sorrow constricted around her heart; Kai hadn't any inkling of her fate. For all he knew, she could've been dead in the King of Spades. Behind him, Pyotr pointed a gun at Zverev, who held a shellshocked Caelan by the shoulder. The girl's gaze drifted, then settled on Alina.

Fetch and human peered into one another, utterly transfixed. Gray, determined stares, focused yet distant all at once. Then, the simultaneous tap of their soles against the floor closed the gap by a single step.

Pyotr roared, shifting the barrel from Zverev's head to Caelan's. A deafening bang rang out in the small space, and Miya clapped her hands over her ears as Kai lunged. The sound must've been excruciating, but he only winced, heedless of the damage to his eardrums. From the corner of her eye, Miya saw Caelan fall, her face eerily neutral, empty of emotion.

Then, a grunt.

Zverev stumbled back, hand flying to his ribcage. He'd shoved Caelan out of the way just as Pyotr pulled the trigger, rotating his body to protect his vitals. Pyotr had aimed for Caelan's head, which was nowhere near Zverev's. The bullet could scarcely hit him anywhere lethal.

Kai grabbed Caelan as her hands and knees hit the floor. Her head hung between her arms, juddering like a marionette's. As Kai pulled her up, Miya felt every fiber in her body wretch with terror.

Caelan's shadow hadn't moved.

As the teen rose, her umbral counterpart twitched as though testing its bonds. An elbow snapped, and its neck twisted, the dark shape of the head rotating toward Alina. Then, it crawled forward and reached for its twin.

Breath hitched in Kai's throat as he saw the thing move. He reeled back, Caelan in tow, and darkness spewed from the writhing shade, slithering everywhere until even the windows were eclipsed. The overhead light flickered, and with each sputtering blink, a shadowy maw yawned open, devouring the room. When it could unhinge no further, the fangs broke away and skittered along the floor, the walls, the ceiling. Unwieldly teeth took the fetch's shape, every one of them mirroring their sibling on the floor.

Pyotr howled like a madman, and Gavran dove from his hiding

spot atop a shelf, clawing at the mobster's hand until the revolver tumbled from his grasp. Zverev leapt for the weapon despite the panic, then slammed his employer into the wall. Pyotr lurched, the air fleeing his lungs with a wheeze. Zverev's fingers curled around his throat like a vise as he drew close and growled through bared teeth, "Watch your daughter die."

Miya snatched Alina's arm to guide her away, but the girl wouldn't budge. She was rooted to the ground like an ancient tree, her shadow stretching toward Caelan's. It was as though she existed in two worlds at once—part of her in the physical plane and the rest of her tangled in the dreamscape.

Caelan's eyes flashed to life as Kai hauled her back. With quick, ragged breaths, she tracked the darting shadows. She fought against Kai's hold, her body pushing her forward against her say so.

"Make it stop," Caelan wailed in a moment of lucidity. Agony warped her features, and she bucked and thrashed to kick herself free. "Please, just make it stop."

Miya wrapped both arms around Alina's torso, lowering her center of gravity and drawing on every ounce of mortal strength to move the immovable. Then, a chilling whisper spilled from Alina's lips.

"Do it, do it, do it, do it," she hissed, eyes wide and bloodshot, her bones vibrating beneath skin and muscle.

The fetch's thralls writhed and shuddered like ravening ghouls, their arms lengthening into wisps as they grasped at their human twin. The one that'd separated from its master jerked closer, straining until Caelan's silhouette met Alina's, their arms plaiting into a cord. Color flaked from Alina like scorched paper. Her skin blanched, the vibrant cinnamon of her hair draining away, the strands parched and brittle. Behind the sea of shadow, Caelan grew impossibly brighter—a star in a midnight sky. Her hair lengthened, lush and fiery like an amaranth sunset. Her cheeks flushed, and her eyes morphed from a stormy gray to the vibrant blue of a summer afternoon. She was stealing Alina's vitality, remaking herself into the keeper of not one life, but two.

Gavran sliced through the air, then hooked his talons into Alina's shoulder, his outline joining with hers. The contours of the raven bloomed into that of the boy, his shadow spilling to the floor next to the girl's. The raven cocked his head, and the boy mirrored him.

They were all connected by what they cast—a chimera of things both human and not. Miya traced the stream of darkness that bound Alina and Caelan, their limbs fused in a spectral tether.

A tether that'd just formed.

Disparate parts must be brought together, Gavran's voice reverberated from the walls.

He'd told her as much, hadn't he?

You need both halves to see the whole.

"I need to cut the tether," Miya resolved, her eyes fixed on Gavran's shadow. "That's what you saw in the park, isn't it? You saw their shadows merge." She gritted her teeth, realization spuming into anger. "Why didn't you tell me?"

The boy's head clicked the other way, and so too did the raven's.

The cost, Dreamwalker. Not every solution is worth the price.

"What the hell does that mean?" Her muscles ached from the strain, her vocal cords sounding shredded.

What you call a tether is in fact a limb, and what you seek is not a release, but an amputation. If you sever the cord, you'll sever a piece of the fetch. An essential part of her will die with her bond.

His words were a dagger through her middle. No matter what she did, something would be lost. Still, burgeoning fury shackled her in place. "You should have told me! It could've been a clue, a way forward!"

Gavran's wings fluttered, and the feathers of the boy's cloak ruffled with them. *Tethers are not to be trifled with. They are living things, and their instinct is to survive at all costs. Hacking one to pieces has unforeseen consequences, but letting nature take its course is simpler, more sensible.*

Miya understood now: the tether was the thing inside Caelan, forcing her closer to Alina even when she fought to stay away. It was what broke her bones and tore her open when she wouldn't obey. Now, it was bursting free, determined to finish what it'd started.

Gavran should've told her. He should've let them decide together. It was information they could've forged into knowledge, and knowledge offered solutions.

"We could save two lives!" she reasoned.

Or you'll damn both with your refusal to sacrifice one for the benefit of the other.

Miya buried her face in Alina's shoulder. She wanted to wilt, every untenable outcome lancing her skull as she grappled with what to do. They were out of time. If they let Caelan overtake Alina, they'd condemn her to a fate she would've died to avoid. But if they honored Caelan's wish and killed her first, they would save no one. Between a father who caged his daughter like a prized canary and a fetch who would take her place, Alina's life was forfeit.

Desolate, unmoored, Miya searched for the one person who could ground her—weave her weakness into strength. He was indomitable, a ballast in any storm. Feeling her silent plea, Kai's mordant gaze found her like a compass needle pointing north. He was losing his own battle, but he refused to let Caelan go. Miya knew he'd heard every word, the fetch's fey magic splintering the boundary between worlds until Gavran's voice penetrated both.

Jaw set, Kai bowed his head, the burnt red of his irises glinting to the flicker of fluorescent lights. Ever the blade in Miya's hand, he unsheathed his hunting knife.

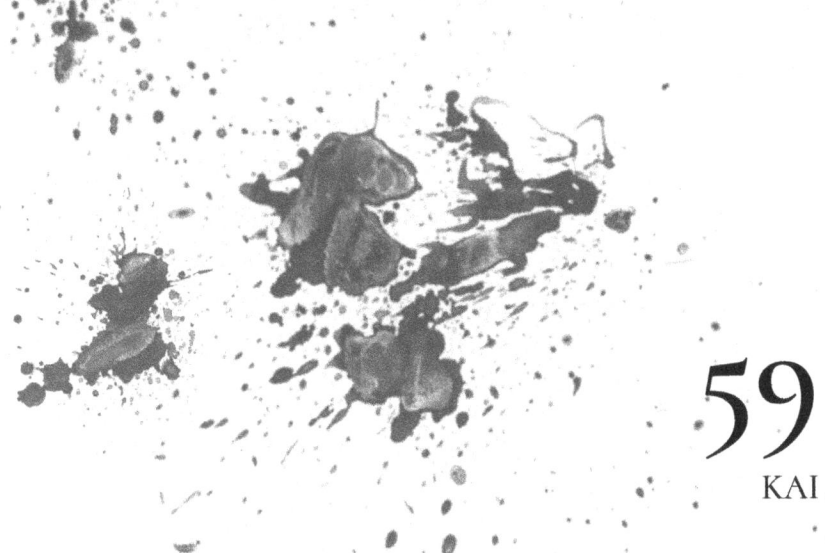

59

KAI

KILLING HAD ALWAYS COME EASY. It was like casting off a weight, the discarded obstacle doubling the satisfaction of taking life to conquer death. It'd rarely been a burden—a decision Kai had to measure against an uncertain outcome. He didn't think about his victims, what they'd lose, or who would lose them, but he also didn't make victims out of anyone. The math was supposed to be easy, but people didn't fit into simple equations.

Hristina Krunić had been right. Kai wasn't as heartless as he wanted to be.

His arms drew tighter around Caelan as she dragged him forward, the few feet between the fetch and her double a scant shield as the shadow drained Alina's vitality. Kai sensed the phantom could only do so much; it still needed Caelan to close the gap and seize her twin's life.

He couldn't stop her. As strong as he was, the thing inside Caelan was stronger, and Zverev was occupied with Pyotr. Miya clung to Alina, and as Gavran's voice invaded them, Kai knew the barrier between the physical world and the dreamscape was crumbling to rubble. Miya met Kai's gaze, her expression forlorn, hopelessness hewing her face into something that tore him in two. They both knew that a blade to Caelan's heart was the only guarantee of freedom. It didn't save Alina from her father, but that was a problem with a different solution.

Kai had no intention of leaving Miya alone with this burden. He didn't want to harm a girl who'd been given only hurt, yet doing nothing was harmful too. Cutting the tether was a risk, but was it worse than death? The latter was final, but it was also a remedy to any affliction. If severing Caelan from a rotten limb changed her into something worse, there would still be blood to spill. And Kai had always been good at getting his hands dirty. Why not once more? If it spared someone pain, if it honored their wishes, why not be the monster they needed?

"Kill me," Caelan sobbed, her knees giving out even as her shoes slid forward, the friction scraping rubber off her soles. "I don't want to be broken."

She'd heard Gavran too.

"I'd rather die than be broken." She seized Kai's forearm, clawing into his skin. Her nails were sharper, her hair the color of blood. She leaked the very life she stole, but the tether was craven, insatiable.

Kai summoned every scrap of might he could muster and spun around the teen. He stepped on her shadow and pressed a palm to her collarbone, pushing her back. In his other hand, he gripped the hunting knife until his knuckles turned white. "Listen to me." His voice came out graveled, his teeth clenched as he tensed every muscle to keep himself rooted. "It's better to be broken than dead."

She shook her head, and as the shadow reached back with its free arm, Caelan's hand clapped down on his bicep, squeezing hard enough to bruise. "You don't know that." Her voice came out layered, discordant. "You don't know what it's like. All I have is myself, and I'm not going to lose what makes me who I am."

An essential part of her will die with her bond.

Kai winced, her fingers on his arm like hot coals. "I don't know what it's like to be you, but I know what it means to be broken." He adjusted his grip on the knife, desperate to keep the girl inside the monster alive. "There's no *essence* to lose. You're not some chipped vase missing a bit of porcelain. You're a person, and as long as you're alive, you *are* yourself—no matter how much you change, no matter how different you feel." His voice lowered, the words spoken for himself as much as they were for Caelan. "We all change. It doesn't mean we're gone."

"There'll be nothing left to salvage," she said, her throat bobbing. "I'll be a husk."

It was ironic, hearing such bleak words from a body so vibrant with color. But Kai knew the feeling better than his own reflection —better than the scars on his blackened soul. He'd spent years trying to give the shell substance, filling it with rage and resentment, violence and sex. He'd poured and poured and poured until he teemed with nihilism and apathy—a lit fuse that left him imploding until there was nothing left of him to destroy. Yet here he was, alive and unyielding, carving out his heart to make space to care.

"There's nothing to salvage but your future," he told her, pleading and convicted all at once. "Even when you're broken, even when you're shaped by the emptiness inside you, it's worth it. You find other things to fill that fucking void." His breath caught, the words stuck until he forced them loose. "I'm not Mikhail Zverev. I'm Kai Donovan. I lost who I was, but not who I am."

"What if I hate who I am?" A frightened murmur, an admission that left them both tattered. Her confession was met with a screeching roar from all around them, the tarry scourge in the walls and floor gibbering as though mocking Caelan—feeding on her self-loathing like a vulture feeding on carrion.

"Then hate yourself," Kai urged, and he meant it. "If that's how you really feel, hate yourself until you're ready to become someone you can stand."

Self-delusion was easy. How quaint—to gorge on vapid affirmation until the lie was buried too deep to notice. But Kai knew firsthand that it didn't matter how much he was loved, how badly he was wanted. He'd continue to maim himself in the name of some facile independence, and nothing Miya did would be enough to stop him because he believed his own bullshit. Lies were a palatable poison, but the truth was a scythe to the soul.

Kai wasn't guarding his independence; he was simply wounded and afraid. The Big Bad Wolf was also a whimpering bitch, and that was okay.

"What if I can't?" Caelan finally replied. "What if this hunger gets worse—hollows me out until I'm a black hole, and all I want is to consume, to take, to kill? What if I become something that *shouldn't* exist?"

Kai clamped his jaw. He couldn't ignore the possibility. Not all life was sacred. The world was an endless parade of birth, suffering, and death, and neither man nor nature cared for every pulse strumming its tune. He lifted his hunting knife, angling the blade. "This won't get dull overnight." His other hand shifted to her shoulder, and he squeezed, his words a promise. "I've got you."

Her scalding touch on his arm eased, and her eyes locked with his as if testing his sincerity. Then, she nodded—an almost imperceptible jerk of her chin.

Kai squeezed his eyes shut and exhaled, then half turned to Miya. "Do it."

Her spine straightened, surprise lacing her features before she homed in on the knot of shadows on the floor. With her arms still around Alina, she garnered her resolve, and Kai watched, rapt, as the Dreamwalker ignited the room.

A lustrous cloak of violet and black plumage erupted around her, gathering her up in a protective embrace. Ivory cradled her skull, rich purple and azure swirling over the bone like oil in water as the raven-beak mask drew over her face, then sharpened to a vee that curled past her lips. Iridescent feathers wove through her hair, billowing in an otherworldly wind. Around Miya's neck, the dream stone thrummed, bathing Alina's shoulder in a lavender glow. Miya yanked the pendant from her neck, the fang-shaped labradorite lengthening into a dagger. It shimmered like volcanic glass— amethyst, emerald, and gold broken only by inky veins that pulsed across the blade.

He'd only ever seen her like this in the dreamscape—in the haze of fantasies and nightmares. Now, in the clarity of the waking world where his senses came alive and desire curled ravenously around his heart, he saw her as if for the first time.

She was stunning.

Miya dropped into a crouch and drove her blade through the shadowy tether, her mantle sweeping up behind her like a midnight wave. Kai expected to hear the clang of metal on concrete, but a wet, fleshy smack sickened his ears as the dagger struck something he couldn't see—something beyond.

Caelan's heart-rending scream ripped Kai from his revulsion. Her legs gave out in front of her, and she sagged in his arms, convulsing as the shadow on the floor began to warp and shudder. Zverev and Pyotr rotated toward them, their faces stricken with horror as they watched the girl writhe.

Miya's head shot up, her blade still piercing the shadow, and she looked to Kai for guidance.

He didn't know what to do. He sank to the floor with Caelan, her weight dragging him down. Holding her as best he could, he tried to soothe her, smoothing sweat-slicked hair from her face. She whipped her head to the side and shrieked, and Kai's hand came away stained with crimson that shed from her like a mist.

"Stop!" Saliva dribbled from her mouth, and she lurched, folding as though each of her ribs were being broken one by one. "Kai, please—"

The blade of his knife stayed flush against his forearm. As Caelan flung her head in violent rebuke, he clutched the back of her neck to keep her from injuring herself.

Miya viciously sawed through the phantom cord—an aberrant thing with the density of cartilage. It bubbled up around her hand, fusing as quickly as she took it apart. From the thrashing shadow, a dissonant squeal deafened Kai to Caelan's cries, but when the ringing in his ears subsided, the sound she made nearly wrenched his heart from his chest.

"End it." Caelan's fingers raked over his arms, her joints locked from sheer agony. The words left her as stuttering rasps. "Please, please, just make it stop."

Kai shook his head, his grip on the knife like steel to curb the trembling. "Don't make me do this," he whispered, though he readied himself even as he begged. He pressed the flat of the blade to the side of her neck, though everything inside him revolted. Her eyes rolled to where she felt the cool metal on her skin, and she twisted toward it, but he'd turned the edge away. He'd promised her he'd do it himself.

"I told you I'm not going anywhere," he said. "I'm not moving until this is over—"

Her spine bent back as another scream tore through her, all the hues she'd sucked from Alina bleeding onto the floor in a ghostly pool. The glacial blue of her eyes faded to the stormy gray Kai was familiar with. Across the room, he heard Gavran caw, beating his wings from his perch on Alina's shoulder.

Kai hooked his stare into the Dreamwalker, and she met him with her own, the symbiosis between them a salve against the onslaught.

Tendrils like black tar whipped up from the floor in a desperate assault, but Miya's cloak was an ethereal armor, her feathers piercing through the globs until they splattered into muck. With a final tug and a war-like shout, she sliced the blade through the sinewy shadow, and the tether snapped. The cord retracted, a festering death rattle shaking the room. The bulbs in the ceiling sparked, then shattered, the army of spectral teeth receding to their source. Alina's shadow shrank back, and so too did Caelan's, the thing on the floor withering away until it sank into the vinyl like an old stain, then vanished.

Alina crumpled in a daze, her eyes darting around as though she'd woken from a fitful sleep. Then, her gaze fell on Kai and the fetch. Caelan went rigid. A breathless keen slipped from her mouth before her limbs went slack, and she wilted in Kai's arms.

For an excruciating moment, he was paralyzed, decades of survival and quick thinking crushed in panic's vise grip. Caelan's neck craned back, her eyes half-open, glazed over and dull. Even with his breath held, Kai couldn't hear her heartbeat. He pressed two fingers to the girl's pulse, each half-second an eternity until he felt the faint patter under her skin. Weak but persistent. His shoulders slumped with relief, and he glanced at Miya, whose feathered mantle dispersed into a cloud of smoke. She checked on Alina, then nodded to Kai. She was fine.

Caelan's fate remained unclear. She was alive, yes, but in what state? Who would greet Kai when she awoke—the kid he knew, or one he had yet to meet?

On the other side of the room, Zverev released Pyotr, both men too stunned to intervene. They'd witnessed a collision of worlds, a severance of bonds made from shadow.

"I'll kill you all," came Pyotr's impotent threat. He thrust an accusatory finger at Kai. "You, that witch of yours, and that fucking forgery!" Then, he whirled on Zverev. "You'll join them...you're dogmeat, and that worthless geriatric—"

"Shut up!" Alina pulled herself to her feet with Miya's help, her chest heaving. "You piece of shit—you're no father. You never have been." Tears welled in her eyes, her face ruddy as the color returned to her skin and hair. "I hate you. I wanted to die because of you, and I'd still rather die than go back to that prison you call home."

Pyotr's mouth hung open, his brow knitting as his daughter's reproach sank in. "You don't know what you're saying. Everything

I've done is for your safety. You don't know how horrible the world is—"

"It's horrible because of people like *you!*" Rage scraped her voice raw. "You keep saying this is all for me, but you're a liar."

Shock morphed into anger as Pyotr's hissed, "You're naïve, disobedient—a brat still."

"Is that what you think parenting is?" Miya stepped in front of Alina, shielding her. "A way to force someone who's powerless to obey you?"

"Don't speak to me, you whore—" Pyotr's venom was cut short when Zverev drove a fist into the mobster's gut, and he doubled over, clutching his ribs.

Kai was as torn as he was surprised. He wanted to pummel the man himself, but he appreciated the spontaneous act of chivalry. Muscles sore and bones aching, he rose to his full height, Caelan cradled carefully in his arms. He turned to Zverev. "I know what you did. If it weren't for the fact that you took a bullet, I'd carve out your jugular."

Zverev snorted. "You still want to carve out my jugular."

"I do, but I won't today, because you're taking Caelan, and you're helping Miya get Alina out of here."

Zverev sighed and tipped his head, his eye on Pyotr. "What about him?"

Kai's glower darkened. "He and I have unfinished business." Zverev opened his mouth to protest, but Kai cut him off with a snarl. "He's mine. You owe me that much."

Zverev shut his trap and nodded, then gently took the girl from Kai's hold. He had no grounds to refuse; he wasn't getting the payment Pyotr had promised him. All he could do was make amends for the harm he'd caused. His eyes flashed with guilt as he peered down at both teenagers. Caelan never should've been a means to an end, and he likely regretted taking so long to accept it. Ivan Zverev couldn't have stomached the sacrifice; the chemotherapy would've cost more than blood money. Wordlessly, he carried Caelan to the door where he waited for Miya to join him.

Gnashing his teeth, Pyotr wedged himself in his cranny like a wet turd. His eyes were trained on his daughter, who didn't spare him a second glance. Gavran roosted on Alina's shoulder, his beak yawning open as he thrust his head forward to menace the mob boss.

Battered and exhausted, Kai locked eyes with Miya, but he didn't dare take a step toward her. He wasn't done yet. Pyotr was a loose end, and Kai was determined to tie it into a noose fit for the mobster's neck. The bastard had no reason to pursue Caelan further, but he was proud, arrogant, obstinate. He'd force Alina back and hunt Caelan mercilessly. A fruitless, belligerent undertaking that would only end in flames.

"I'll see you soon," Miya called, the words laced with questioning.

The corner of Kai's mouth quirked into a tired half smile. "You'll see me soon, Lambchop."

He heard her heart settle. Then, she took Alina's hand and pulled her from the office, leaving the wolf alone with his prey.

60

PYOTR DIDN'T BOTHER REACHING for his gun. Instead, he kicked it toward Kai, the weapon skidding to a stop at his toes. Kai stared down at the revolver, its gilt doing nothing to blunt the heat of sickness tingling along his spine.

"Not going down swinging?" Kai asked, his eyes still glued to the firearm.

"I'd rather not look like a fool." Pyotr straightened out his collar, still fixated on some pretense of decorum. "At this distance, the odds of a headshot are miniscule, and anything less will only make you more savage. I'd prefer a clean death."

A smirk crawled up the side of Kai's face. That Pyotr presumed to negotiate anything was evidence of his hubris. Kai picked up the weapon, weighing it in his hand. "Looks valuable." He traced the ornate embellishments etched into the metal. Perhaps he'd get Sergei to pawn it once they were out of here—compensation for his...*services*.

"It's worth more than your whole life," Pyotr sneered. "Come on, then. Get it over with, boy."

Kai arched a brow as he glanced up at the mobster. Despite being two decades younger, he wasn't half as childish. "Up to the bitter end, you can't help yourself, can you?" He stalked closer, unhurried as he scored Pyotr with a seething glare. "You think insulting me is going to make your death less humiliating, old man?"

Pyotr's jaw tightened. "A bullet to the head is as dignified as it gets in this business."

Kai's smirk widened into something wicked. He pushed out the cylinder and ejected each bullet. They cascaded from his palm, chiming as they ricocheted off the floor. Then, he tossed aside the gun. "Who said this would be dignified?"

Another languid advance, and Pyotr finally faltered. "What, then?" He nodded to Kai's belt where he kept his hunting knife. "You plan on slitting me open from navel to throat?"

Kai chuckled darkly, then unsheathed the knife only to place it on the desk next to his wallet. "No."

A beat of silence passed, a moment of suspension as Pyotr waited for some elaboration—some clue to his fate. When none came, he straightened his jacket and swallowed.

Kai relished the slow creep of fear on the mobster's face. "Groom all you want. You'll scream just the same."

Determined to confront his demise head on, Pyotr tilted his chin, likely thumbing through every grisly method of execution he'd employed during his illustrious career. Kai doubted that Pyotr's lackluster imagination could conjure what he had in mind.

"You should know something before we get started," said Kai, gleefully omitting what, exactly, he meant by *get started*. "You're a fuck up of a father. I don't know why you chose to adopt a kid, but you could've given her a family, a good life."

Indignation seized Pyotr's expression, and he threw his hands out. "I was keeping her safe."

"From what?" Kai challenged. "Your kid hated her life before it was ever in danger. The shit you thought you were protecting her from only showed up because you were an asshole." Pyotr had trapped his daughter in his warped version of reality, and her desire for freedom manifested the fetch. "Caelan was her way out, and you were going to destroy that too. Your daughter asked for death, and you decided you'd kill someone to keep her in a position that makes her want to die."

"The forgery is an abomination," Pyotr ground out. "An affliction on my home. That she would take my daughter's place—"

"Caelan was never a forgery," Kai cut him off. "She's just another person—a random life in a sea of accidents."

"That *thing* isn't supposed to exist."

"And half your men are spunk breaking through an expired condom," Kai told him. "No one is *supposed* to exist. We just do."

Pyotr *tsked*. "Such a nihilist."

Kai shrugged, meandering close enough to push the mobster back a step. "Nihilism ain't so bad, old man. It just means you get to decide what matters."

"As if anything matters to a man like you," Pyotr mocked. "All you do is kill and destroy. I built an empire, made myself a god in this city, and seized what I was owed to forge the life I deserved."

Kai stared down the meat sack gloating in the corner of a tattered room. If this was what Pyotr called an empire, it was an empire of gutters—bloody, shit-stained, and sodden with decay.

"No one's owed life." The wolf flashed a baleful grin. "But even gods die."

A snarl ripped through Kai as something in his spine snapped, and his chin jerked down. Baring his teeth, he rolled his neck to the side, elongated canines digging into his lower lip. Yelping like a hare, Pyotr tried jumping away, but his back was against the wall.

The god of gutters should've kept his gun.

A familiar prickle sent a shudder through Kai, his skin searing. His knees and elbows bent out of place, and every joint in his hand dislodged, bones shrinking and fusing into paws. He splintered with pain he knew he'd never adapt to, yet the sound of a blubbering god was nothing short of succulent to a predator's ears. His clothes shed away, and black fur sprouted over naked flesh, his body quaking as a series of feral growls clipped his throat. His jaw unhinged and pushed forward, making space for a growing tongue. Saliva hung from sharpened fangs as Kai's heavy breaths fogged the air—the sound purely animal—and his tail lashed free of his vertebrae.

Eyes rimmed with crimson rose to greet the architect of Caelan's suffering. Pyotr slid down the wall, gasping helplessly as he stared at the wolf. Rivulets of sweat poured down his face, his mind fracturing from what he'd witnessed. But Kai had no interest in Pyotr's comprehension; he wanted to rip him open—to see what this self-proclaimed god was made of. Charcoal lips skinned back over a gleaming white cage, muzzle rippling into a beastly rictus that promised carnage.

Kai descended on Pyotr like a calamity. Ravenous, he tore at that shoulder wound first, remaking every puncture and gash from the night in the park. Savaging Pyotr twice over, Kai repaid him for the gunshot wounds that'd nearly leveled him. An eye for an eye as it were, and Pyotr seemed the Old Testament type. Kai let him scream—let him thrash and kick under the weight of hell itself. When the mobster clawed at the wolf's mane, Kai bit his fingers clean off, blood spewing from the joints, disappearing in his dark fur. The dismembered nubs dropped to Pyotr's chest, and Kai wound back to drink in his prey. He wondered if Pyotr still thought himself a god, or if pain reminded him that he was a lump of spoiled meat. When Pyotr dared a gander at his executioner, Kai knew he wouldn't see a boy.

The stygian wolf was a harbinger of ruin, a thing of ravage.

As another wail curdled in Pyotr's chest, Kai locked his maw around the man's throat and wrenched. Pyotr's scream faded into a pathetic gargle as blood flooded his mouth, bubbling over his lips. Scarlet dribbled down his chin and stippled Kai's muzzle as he continued to rend the life from Pyotr's body, sawing through cartilage and muscle until he clamped down on the bony cord he'd been mining for. With a violent twist, Kai severed the god from his empire, his legacy a crimson puddle spattered across the floor. He released his hold, and Pyotr's head trundled from the rest of him, his mouth agape, his soulless eyes trained on the wolf. In the end, he was just as brittle as the others.

Withdrawing from the mangled heap, Kai left his mark in the gore. Let them think it was a rabid dog. Bracing for another brutal transition, he coaxed the wolf into its den and surrendered to the agony that shaped him back into a man. When his fur receded and his naked limbs stretched across the tarnished floor, he rasped for breath and struggled to right himself, then fumbled for his discarded jeans. Once he remembered how his legs worked and stuffed them into his pants correctly, he snatched his hunting knife and wallet from the desk. Scooping the gilded revolver and the six stray bullets from the floor, he staggered out of the office, stepping over the corpses as he went. Once he reached the basement door, he leaned against the frame until the world stopped spinning, and the iron faded from his tongue. Divinity tasted like shit.

Kai thumped down the stairs to retrieve Sergei, making sure he saw the bodies on his way out.

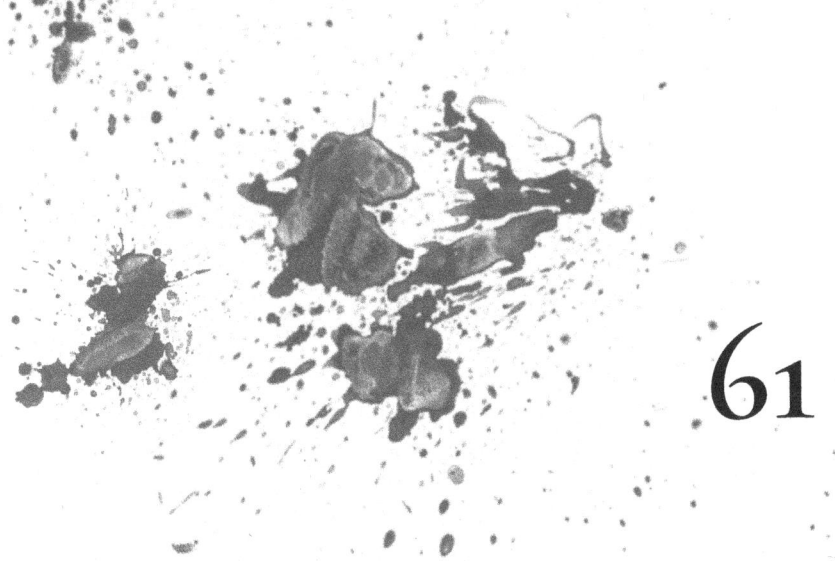

61

WHEN KAI STUMBLED into the King of Spades, a silence heavier than granite greeted him. Miya sat at the bar, her face buried in her hands and an untouched glass of gin between her elbows. At the chime of the bell, she spun on the stool, the despair bleeding from her murky green eyes.

"You look like shit." Her voice wobbled as she clapped a bandaged hand to her mouth, but Kai could see the smile through her fingers.

"I feel like shit." The words came out raspy, and he swallowed down the soreness in his parched throat. With a grumbling sigh, he worked his fingers through his unruly hair, thoroughly matted with blood. His T-shirt was the only thing that didn't look like it'd been dragged through mud, courtesy of a vigorous cycle at the laundromat-turned-crime scene.

"Sergei?" Miya asked as she kicked off the stool.

Kai locked the door and joined her. "At home being a stubborn cunt." He shrugged. "Doesn't want to go to the hospital."

"No more of a stubborn cunt than you." She threw her arms around him, burying her face in the crook of his neck. Exhaling shakily, she ran her hands over his sides to make sure he was in one piece.

He pressed his cheek to the top of her head and curled his elbow around her waist. "I'm fine," he promised. "Just a little bruised and concussed." The sound of pattering footsteps on the second floor snagged Kai's attention. He broke away, his eyes turning to the ceiling. "Where are the brats?"

Miya played with the end of his belt, her gaze averted. "Upstairs with Crowbar and Ama. Ivan behaved himself—dropped Caelan off, then skulked out of here with his tail between his legs. I asked for some space while I waited for you." She looked up at him. "Did you want to see them?"

"Later." He gently moved her aside. "First, I need a shower. Then, I need a drink. After that, a solid nap or a raucous fuck. I can't decide which yet."

Miya choked on a snicker, some of their usual levity returning. "One, then the other."

She hadn't asked about Pyotr. Kai didn't know if he should confess or if she already knew. "About Zverev..." he began.

"I don't think he'll be bothering us," said Miya. "I'm still not his biggest fan, but I know what grief does to people." She sighed, leaning back against the bar. "I saw what he was after. When he attacked us, we threw everything we had at him. I even..." She swallowed as if it left a bad taste in her mouth. "I invaded his psyche. I never want to do that again."

Kai raised an eyebrow. "Have you graduated to mind-reading?"

Miya shook her head. "It wasn't that. I ripped into his subconscious and yanked out his fears. I saw this old man...I think he was sick?"

"O'Neil," Kai guessed. "Owns a flower shop in Charleston. Looks like he means something to Zverev, and Pyotr promised him money for chemo."

Miya's brows drew together, her lips forming a silent *oh*. "I guess O'Neil's not going to make it."

"No," said Kai, his chest feeling tighter than it should've. "But even if Zverev got the money, there wouldn't be any guarantees. He's a grown-ass man. He needs to cope with the loss—use the time he has left instead of stitching together a few extra months."

He remembered Alice's final weeks. She was in agony—unable to laugh without a morphine drip. Even if chemotherapy eked out a paltry deferral on death, it seemed cruel, more for the living than the doomed.

"You're right," said Miya, her validation followed by a wavering pause. "So, Pyotr..."

Kai met her gaze, resolute. "How much do you want to know?"

"Did he suffer?"

"Yes."

Her chest rose and fell with a stifled breath, and she nodded her acceptance. "I'm not naïve enough to think there's a moral high ground here."

Kai broke into a crooked smile. "He still has eyeballs if Gavran wants to peck them out."

"Let's keep that between us." Miya wrinkled her nose.

He chuckled ominously, then headed for the stairs. "If I'm not out of the shower in twenty minutes, come slap me. I probably blacked out from the concussion."

Miya started after him, utterly aghast. Before she could berate him about getting medical attention, he disappeared into the upstairs hall, his maniacal laughter echoing throughout the King of Spades.

Everyone knew Kai Donovan was home.

IT TOOK three rounds of aggressive shampooing and half a soap bar to scrub out the blood and grime that'd accumulated. Although Kai had joked about passing out, he did swoon a few times when the water got too warm. His brain felt like scrambled eggs in a steamer. At one point, he had to sit his ass down in the tub and let the water run over him like some melancholic freshman who'd just gotten dumped. He passed those moments of vertigo brushing his teeth and spitting out the coppery remnants of his deicide. Fortunately, by the time the drain ran clear, the dizziness subsided.

He kept a spare set of clothes at Crowbar's for the same reason he had them squirrelled away at the Confessional: he expected trouble. It wasn't a bad impulse, but in hindsight, he realized it was a little fucked up. While limping back, Sergei told him he was done with organized crime, though he wasn't stupid enough to think he'd ever be free of the underworld.

"What'll you do?" Kai had asked, only half-interested at the time.

"Partner with the Confessional," he'd said. "I'll set up fights, work as an independent contractor. You could continue your business without worrying about less savory entanglements."

It wasn't a bad plan. Kai liked knocking out overconfident cockblossoms for cash, and a manager free of the mob cut him loose from any dangerous strings. After the stunt Pyotr pulled with Connor, Kai doubted Bratva would be allowed anywhere near the Confessional. The fact that a dozen of Pyotr's men bit the dust while storming the place sent a warning to other factions about violating neutral territory. The message was clear: fuck around and find out.

When Kai dragged himself downstairs, the whole gang had piled in around the bar. Half the shelves were empty, a bin of broken bottles tucked in one corner. Remnants of the brawl with Zverev, no doubt. Alina and Caelan sat next to each other, both alive and nursing a beer—courtesy of a naughty bartender perched in Ama's lap behind the counter. Gavran roosted on a beer tap in front of Miya, and she plucked a nacho off a plate that Bastien had left for them to snack on. The chef stood by the kitchen doors, wiping off his hands. His forearms were covered in medical gauze, and as soon as their eyes met, he shook his head and unleashed a flurry of Louisiana gibberish Kai was glad he couldn't make sense of.

"You better bring me some more respectful customers next time," Bastien threatened, then grabbed his jacket. Giving Crowbar and Ama a tight hug, he told the raven to behave himself, then rounded the bar to slap a hand on Kai's shoulder. "I'm clocking out. If another one of your cousins comes barreling in, I expect you to handle it. Family business and all."

Kai groaned through a reedy laugh. "I owe you."

"Damn right, you do." Bastien gave him a light shake, then left the building with a parting holler.

Kai glanced at Ama, offering a curt nod—a silent thank you. She smiled in turn, a glint of apology in her sunlit eyes. Then, all attention shifted to the fetch and her human double.

Alina was the first to speak. "Miya told me about my dad."

Nausea churned in Kai's stomach. He didn't regret what he did, though he hadn't expected it to hit him so hard when faced with the kid he'd orphaned. He shoved his hands into his pockets, not knowing what else to do with them. "Yeah, I killed him." Unceremonious but honest.

"I know."

He ground his teeth behind pursed lips, then met the girl's probing gaze. "You're not angry."

"I'm sad," she confessed. "I hate that I'm sad. He was the only parent I knew, though I don't remember ever liking him. I hated him, but it still hurts."

"It will," said Ama, her tone wistful. "But it will also get better."

"You can stay here," Crowbar chimed in. "There'll be police investigations and all kinds of nonsense in the meantime, but you're old enough and smart enough to apply for emancipation if you'd like. We'll help take care of you until you figure out what you want to do."

"You two in the market for more strays?" Ama asked, looking between Miya and Kai.

"No," said Kai, "though I'd like to talk to one."

At that, Caelan looked up. She'd been mousy the whole time, her beer barely touched while Alina's was half empty. Kai thought the girl who'd lost her father would be more of a mess than the one who'd axed a demonic bungee cord, but loss was a complicated thing. Alina was grieving, yet she could taste her freedom. She really believed she'd be okay one day. Caelan was also bereaved, though she should've felt free. But by the slope of her back and the sag in her shoulders, Kai knew she'd never felt more trapped.

"We'll be outside," Crowbar said, then pulled Ama from the bar. Alina made to join them, but Caelan grabbed her wrist, shooting her a pleading look to stay. They barely knew each other, yet something still tethered them—a strange comradery shared from a common crucible. When the door clicked shut, the King of Spades thickened with unbearable quiet.

"I can't feel it," Caelan whispered, flexing her fingers on the counter.

Kai frowned, glancing to Miya for a hint.

"The dreamscape," Miya supplied. "She's been cut off from it."

Kai blinked, unsure of the problem. If that was the only consequence, it seemed like a win. "I guess that...must be weird?" he offered uselessly.

"You don't get it." Distress was a fog over Caelan's eyes. "It feels like I've lost one of my senses—like I'm missing a limb. I can't see the domovoy. He could be anywhere or gone completely, and I have no way of knowing. The leshy too. He was my friend, and now he's dead. Even if he weren't, we'd be separated forever. Everything is just"—her eyes scanned each of them, searching—"muted, less vibrant. I don't even know what I am anymore."

Alina halted the fetch's spiraling with a gentle touch on the arm. "I can't even pretend to know what you're feeling right now, but what you're saying—the world being muted, losing its color—I get that. I've felt that way for a long time." She hesitated, clenching and unclenching a fist in her lap. "I lived my whole life under Pyotr's thumb. To be honest, I don't know who I am either, but maybe we can find out together." Gingerly, she took Caelan's hand. "Like sisters."

Kai wanted to tell Caelan that the domovoy was still there, still obnoxious, and still solely concerned with his next pretzel. Only Miya could see him now, but Kai felt him like a shade without substance. His gaze trailed down the length of Caelan and Alina's stools, something on the floor snagging his attention. He saw the elongated lines of wooden legs, the warped oval of the cushion, but only one was filled with the shape of a person. The other was empty.

His eyes drifted to Miya, who wore a somber expression. She knew exactly what he'd seen.

Caelan didn't have a shadow.

The fetch took a deep breath, hiccupped on a sob, and rubbed her eyes with the ball of her hand. "I thought you'd hate me," she said to Alina, who emphatically shook her head.

"It's my fault you're here. Besides, I've always hated being an only child. Having a twin sounds way more fun." She beamed, suddenly the brighter of the two, and squeezed Caelan's hand. "I'll give you a minute with these weirdos. Find me with the cool people outside."

Hopping off the stool, she gave Kai a curious glance—like she didn't know what to do with him—then scurried from the bar.

"Who's she calling weirdos?" he muttered, miffed that Ama was allegedly more interesting than him.

"Hey," Caelan started, poking his arm. "Can I stay with you guys?"

Kai's heart sank into his gut as he bit back a wince. "Don't you miss your parents?"

"I do," she said, then faltered. "I just...you get me better."

"Friends are supposed to get you better." He gave Caelan a nudge. "It wouldn't be right to hide you from them. I know you've still got some demons, but the one that was getting between you and your family is gone. They deserve a chance."

"And we're not going anywhere," Miya added, pushing off the counter to join them. "If you decide it isn't working, we'll lend you a hand."

"I still want to stay with you," Caelan pressed, now targeting Miya.

"You can't live with us," Kai said, gently clasping her shoulder, "but you can come over whenever you want. Fuck up some unicorns and force me to make you marshmallow puke sandwiches."

At that, Caelan lit up like a summer bonfire. "Really?"

"Sure"—Kai shrugged—"as long as you clean Ripper's shit box." Miya whacked his arm, and he grinned. "Ursula also needs a cat sitter."

"That's *your* job," Miya reminded him with a glare.

"No one said I had to do it alone, Lambchop."

The trepidation melted off Caelan's face. She trusted them—trusted that they meant what they said. "Maybe I can tell my parents I found my long-lost twin," she joked darkly.

"It's kind of true, though." Miya wrapped an arm around Kai's back and leaned into him. Caelan's origins were obscure enough to make the story believable. "Alina's right. You could be sisters if you wanted, regardless of what your parents decide."

"Maybe I'll talk to her about that," Caelan mused aloud, then looked up at Kai. "I think you were right—what you said to me earlier. You find other things to fill the void."

Kai hung his head, hiding a smile. "Hopefully you'll manage faster than I did." He was pretty sure she would.

If Caelan's family had been anything like Alina's, he would've let her monopolize his living room in a heartbeat. But her parents had never given up on her. Even when they were wrong about her affliction, they cared enough to try. They just didn't have the tools to understand what their daughter was going through. Some families were worth abandoning in favor of bonds that were chosen. When Mikhail Zverev died, the shell left behind was handed over to a crotchety old woman named Alice Donovan. She nurtured that husk of a boy, gave him a place to grow new roots and fill the chasm beneath his flimsy skin.

Why did it take him so fucking long to realize? What she'd seeded in him did more to protect him than any of his rage or resentment. No matter how callous the world had made him, he'd been loved by someone who'd chosen him, and in turn, he'd chosen to love back.

62

THE FIRST THING Kai did when he kicked the apartment door shut was carry Miya to the bedroom, her thighs clenched around his waist. The moment her feet touched the ground, her fingers curled around his belt, and she yanked him into a ferocious kiss. Urgency snared them both, and he surrendered to that pull, his hunger matching her own.

His teeth snagged Miya's lips as he shoved her pants away, his hand scraping past her underwear to cup the curve of her pelvic bone. Her gasp warmed his skin, and as her grip closed around his cock, he pushed a finger inside her, steering her back until her legs hit the bed, and he hauled them both onto the mattress.

"So much for the nap," she quipped as he peeled away the rest of their clothes.

He groaned in reply—half protest, half plea. Miya smiled against his lips, basking in his impatience, then pulled back and cradled his face.

"Tell me seriously—are you okay?"

His mouth opened to offer a knee-jerk reassurance, but he stopped, his jaw clamping shut. Was he okay? He'd never really thought about it, absurd as it sounded. So much of his life had been spent in a bullheaded fugue—a stubborn refusal to die. *I'll live* was the only mantra he could muster. But being okay? The possibility never entered his thick skull. Sure, he enjoyed himself—found pleasure where it could be meted out—but that wasn't the same as being okay, was it?

"I don't know," he said truthfully. "I was so pissed today I chewed through a man's neck, snapped his spine with my teeth, and turned his head into a soccer ball."

Miya swallowed, trying vainly to temper her shock. Her fingers slid down his cheeks and traced his jaw. "Do you feel bad about it?"

"No." He shifted his weight to the side. "He needed to die, and I wasn't about to give him the death he wanted. Either way, the cops will never know what happened in that laundromat. An exotic pet loose from its cage? A zookeeper gone berserk?"

Miya nodded slowly, mulling over his admission. "I've seen you hurt people. I've also seen you regret it when it causes more harm than it ends. But this...even I don't feel bad."

"Pyotr got what was coming to him. I'm just...raw." The word tasted sour on his tongue—foreign somehow. It was a different language, one he was acclimating to. He could still see Caelan's face contorted in agony, feel her hopelessness as she begged him to end her life. Caelan, bargaining for death, would haunt him far longer than Pyotr's severed head. She'd rattled him to his core, filled him to the brim with an unshakeable dread that he was looking into a mirror.

And maybe that's all a fetch was—a mirror image, a version of what could've been.

How many times had he plunged headfirst into a fight just to see if it would be his last? How often was the satisfaction of winning tainted by the disappointment that he hadn't lost? For years after Alice died, he'd bargained with death too. "I just wanted to protect her," he said. "Keep her off my path."

"And heal your inner child?" Miya flashed him a knowing smile, then poked him in the ribs. "How's therapy treating you?"

"Well," he feigned, "it made me mad enough to fuck you in a field, but that probably means it's working."

Miya flung a haphazard jab at his stomach, and he caught her wrist and rolled her onto her back, mindful of her injuries. "How does *that* mean it's working?" she sputtered through a giggle.

He leaned in close, his lips gazing hers. "Do you think it's working?"

She pecked the corner of his mouth, her eyes scanning his face. "Yes," she said, the playfulness leaving her. "Yesterday, when you had that nightmare…I honestly didn't think I'd live to see you trust me so much."

"I kept lashing out at you," he murmured, recalling his previous outbursts. "Instead of admitting I was hurt, I snapped my teeth so you wouldn't see how fucked up I was."

"You saved that kid's life," Miya told him. "I'm not sure that would've been possible if you hadn't checked your own wounds. It's hard to empathize with others when you're in pain."

"Maybe I did," he acknowledged, a strange warmth spreading through his middle. The pieces of his life hadn't simply fallen into place. They had to be molded into something workable, so he could fashion them into a reality he actually wanted. Before, all he had was a blank space and a story he told himself to make sense of those disparate fragments. They were jagged, painful to touch.

Yet Kai wasn't finished with the puzzle. That too-comfortable armchair in Hristina Krunić's office would have a dedicated imprint of his ass for months—possibly years—to come.

Miya's fingers raked through his hair, pulling him from his reverie. His eyes drifted to hers, and for the second time that day, he felt a strange reverence for this person who kept choosing him over a world of possibility. And he'd chosen her too, again and again, despite every impulse that drove him to the worst parts of himself.

Desperation crushed him like a fist around his heart. He devoured the space between them, his lips on hers bruising, wild. They were naked in every way, every vulnerability laid bare. Miya's arms wove around him, and her fingernails trailed down his back, reaping a growl from his throat as he pushed her legs open and pressed himself to her center. Her hips rose to meet his as her heart hammered against her ribs, heat blossoming over her skin. Every sharp breath laced with his name was a drug he grew more ravenous for.

Being inside her wasn't just fleeting pleasure. She was a hurricane, uprooting his dark, fucked-up world, shattering the bleak reality he'd painted himself into. Yet being with her was also an equilibrium, the quiet at the center of a storm. And he was helpless against that storm. All he could do was surrender and trust that it wouldn't tear him apart.

A. J. VRANA

"Say it," he whispered against her lips, his fingers tangled in her hair, tugging.

Miya searched his face, her reply catching on a moan. "Say what?"

A momentary waver, a splinter of uncertainty in his chest. His thumb hooked her lip, his mordant gaze steady on hers. "Tell me you love me."

Her murky green eyes seared into him, branding him with a weight he knew he could never cast off—and he didn't want to. He welcomed it, this heaviness that bound him to her, wove them together like roots beneath the earth. Her legs squeezed around his waist, and she pressed her forehead to his, her eyes never leaving him. "I love you," she said, and he felt her heart thud against his chest through every syllable of those abominable words.

This time, at least, they didn't hurt.

Kai swore under his breath, frustration and terror swirling with a bone-deep ache—a yearning he couldn't quell. He fisted the sheets next to her head and dropped his mouth to her ear. Pummeling back his misgivings, he flouted the sheer impossibility of knowing what, exactly, love was supposed to be. Every cell in his body screamed this was it, and if it wasn't, then it didn't fucking matter. It was enough.

With his teeth bared and his heart a barb in his throat, Kai said the words back—uttered them so quietly that even a ghost couldn't hear. They were for her only—perilous, capable of maiming him— but he said them anyway, tasting them on his tongue like he tasted her skin.

Kai gave Miya the blade and let her press it to his heart. He'd always liked sharp and wicked things.

390

ACKNOWLEDGMENTS

All stories are born of passion, but *Wildblood* was forged in a special kind of fire. Anyone who knows me well knows that Kai Donovan holds a unique place in my heart. He's always been something of an ally—a mirror, if you will. We often joke about having imaginary friends as children, but sometimes, the imaginary can tell us more about ourselves than anything out in the real world. That is, after all, the power of fiction. Since writing *The Hollow Gods* in which he first appeared, I knew Kai deserved his own book—to have his story told with boldness that suited his temperament. I don't think I had the tools or the courage to do his story justice when I first embarked on my publishing journey, and I am glad that I told Miya's tale first in *The Chaos Cycle Duology*. Miya and Kai's journeys come from very different parts of me, and I am thrilled to have finally shared them both.

That said, finishing a book and putting it out into the world is hardly a solitary activity despite what writing culture would have us believe. There are so many people to whom this book is indebted. First and foremost, none of this would be possible without my editorial team, all of whom double as wonderful friends: Malorie, Brenton, Laura, and Megan. Each of you are an invaluable pair of trustworthy eyes. With every pass, my work improves because of your effort and your care. Brenton gets an extra shout-out for tolerating me every day, for subjecting himself to my middle-of-the-night rambles, and for being the first person to crack the spine on anything I write. I couldn't ask for a better partner in life and my calling.

Julie—you are irreplaceable where my creative projects are concerned. Thank you for taking hours out of your life to peruse the stars with me. Our conversations have been incredible tools in helping me decide where to focus my attention when exploring my characters' inner worlds. Truly, my fiction would not be the same without all I've learned from you.

Thank you as well to my author friends who have offered both support and mentorship throughout my publishing career, who've endorsed my work and given me opportunities I would have never otherwise had: Katya de Becerra, C.N. Crawford, Clare Edge, Jenny Hickman, Vanessa Rasanen, and many more.

A shout-out goes out to my beta-readers, Gloria and M, who helped me tackle this beast and came into this book without knowing a single thing about these characters or their stories. You've helped me feel a thousand times more confident about my choice to make this novel a stand-alone.

And finally, a special thank you to my Patreon subscribers over at The Spicy Crow. You have all astonished me with your love and support, and I swear, Dear Reader, that this book wouldn't be a fraction as spicy as it is without the two-dozen unrelenting souls who've sustained Kai and Miya's partnership.

ABOUT THE AUTHOR

Photograph by Michelle Davis

A. J. Vrana is a Serbian-Canadian academic and writer from Toronto, Canada. She holds a PhD from the University of Toronto, and her doctoral research examines the supernatural in Japanese and former Yugoslavian literature and its relationship to modern nation-building and historiography. Her published works include the Indie Author Project-winning *Chaos Cycle Duology: The Hollow Gods* (2020) and *The Echoed Realm* (2021), as well as the companion novel *Wildblood* (2024) from Parliament House Press. Her short fiction includes "These Silent Walls" (2020) from *Three Crows Magazine* and "Sapling" (2023) from Clan Destine Press' anthology *This Fresh Hell*.

facebook.com/AJVranaAuthor
x.com/AJVrana
instagram.com/a.j.vrana

ALSO BY A. J. VRANA

The chaos cycle duology:

The Hollow Gods

The Echoed Realm

Stray Feathers: Extras from The Chaos Cycle

These Silent Walls

Sapling